Leave No Trace

MJ White is the pseudonym of bestselling author Miranda Dickinson, author of twelve books, including six *Sunday Times* bestsellers. Her books have been translated into ten languages, selling over a million copies worldwide. A long time lover of crime fiction, the Cora Lael Mysteries is her debut crime series. She is a singer-songwriter, host of weekly Facebook Live show, Fab Night In Chatty Thing.

Also by MJ White

A Cora Lael Mystery

The Secret Voices
The Silent Child
Leave No Trace

MJ WHITE
LEAVE NO TRACE

hera

First published in the United Kingdom in 2023 by

Hera Books
Unit 9 (Canelo), 5th Floor
Cargo Works, 1–2 Hatfields
London SE1 9PG
United Kingdom

A CIP catalogue record for this book is available from the British Library.

Print ISBN 978 1 80436 034 7
Ebook ISBN 978 1 80436 082 8

Look for more great books at www.herabooks.com

Printed and bound in Great Britain by Clays Ltd, Elcograf S.p.A.

1

To my lovely Bob

For listening, supporting and cheerleading

And always believing in me

xx

'Stars, hide your fires;
Let not light see my black and deep desires:
The eye wink at the hand; yet let that be,
Which the eye fears, when it is done, to see.'

Macbeth Act 1, Scene 4
William Shakespeare (1564–1616)

Prologue

(Extract from transcript of *The Missing Son* true crime documentary, a Quaesitor Co. production ©2013 All Rights Reserved)

Interviewer: Your son has been missing for five years. No word, no sign. And then the messages began. One a year, on the anniversary of the date he went missing. Tell me, as Ewan Stokes' mother, how does that feel?

Olwyn Stokes-Norton: It's hard. The messages aren't for my family. They aren't for me. But it's a spark of hope. And that can be cruel, because it constantly reminds me what I've lost. But it's a comfort to know that Ewan isn't forgotten.

Interviewer: Do you believe he's the one sending them?

Olwyn Stokes-Norton: Absolutely.

Interviewer: The messages have been found across Europe, on sheets of white paper, left in prominent places where eagle-eyed watchers have photographed them to share online. How are you so certain your son has written them?

Olwyn Stokes-Norton: It's his handwriting. I would know it anywhere.

Interviewer: After all you've gone through – the indifference of the police, the radio silence for five years, the lack of evidence of where Ewan could be now – do you feel in some way justified that there are people around the world sharing these messages? And talking about him?

Olwyn Stokes-Norton: I'm grateful to everyone for keeping his name alive. As a family, we've been stunned by the response. All these people knowing about Ewan makes me feel we're not alone in our fight to find him. I don't know how to thank everyone for their support.

Interviewer: And what about his rumoured return?

Olwyn Stokes-Norton: [pause] I'm sorry, what?

Interviewer: How do you feel about the Fifteen Year Return? It's been widely shared amongst the Stokesy fan community.

Olwyn Stokes-Norton: [pause] I don't know… What are you talking about?

Interviewer: The community of Stokesy-watchers believe that your son will return home on the fifteenth anniversary of the night he went missing. To exact revenge on those who forced him to run?

Olwyn Stokes-Norton: How do they…? How can you ask me…? I'm sorry, can you stop filming, please? [She tugs at her lapel microphone as the camera quickly pans away.]

THE CLUB

I saw him.

No you didn't.

I'm telling you, man. It was Stokesy.

Okay, where?

Webcam. Suffolk.

Suffolk UK?

Yes.

Couldn't have been him. Last sighting was Paris.

So?

No way would he come home. It wasn't him.

If he's home this is it. The 15-Year Return.

We don't even know he said that. It's all a myth.

Check the date. It has to be him. The Club said we'd get a sign…

It's got out of hand with the Club. This whole thing is messed up.

He said, 'When it's time…'

He didn't write that. Stokesy's gone.

I saw him. It's time. It's finally happening.

Typing… … …

Then we need to warn people. Now.

4

One

CORA

'You're just sore you lost.'

Dr Cora Lael shot her companion a look. DS Rob Minshull was impossible when he won. It was only a Sunday evening quiz in a small Suffolk village pub and it really didn't matter, but the prospect of a week of Minshull's crowing was not something she was willing to endure without a fight.

'If it weren't for you stealing my answers in the music round we would've won,' she returned with a smile.

Minshull clamped a hand to his heart. 'You're accusing me of stealing?'

'I am, officer. Tris saw you telling your team seconds after I told ours, several times. You reckon he was lip-reading, don't you, Tris?'

'You were staring over at our table a lot,' Dr Tris Noakes agreed, his wink proof that he bore no ill will.

'I'm insulted, frankly, Dr Noakes. And Dr Lael.' Minshull's grin was as unapologetic as his humour. 'It just goes to show what happens when psychologists take on coppers. It's all mind games to psych us out of our victory.'

'Don't you listen to him,' DC Dave Wheeler interrupted, elbowing his colleague out of the way. 'He loved every minute, didn't you, Minsh?'

'Yes, Dave,' Minshull conceded, holding open the pub door for his colleagues to pass through. 'Because we *won*…'

It was a perfect summer night out on St Just's Church Street as the party walked away from the pub. Just the right amount of warmth to forgo a jacket, with a gentle, cooling breeze that was a gift after the heat of the packed pub. Cora loved the easy sense of belonging within the group and the other locals spilling out on to the street beside them. So much had happened in St Just that could have made it a place too heavy with ghosts. But everything this group had been through together had only brought them closer. She liked that. Walking beside people she now counted as friends was the greatest reward for all they had endured lately.

'I told you it was a mistake doing two teams rather than one,' PC Steph Lanehan said, her usual dry humour on form tonight. 'Next time we need a combined team to save the post-quiz angst.'

'That's not a bad idea, actually.'

'Admit it, Cora, you love the drama.' Minshull gave Cora's arm a surreptitious nudge as Wheeler stepped back to chat to DC Kate Bennett, who was a few paces behind them.

She shook her head, enjoying the game. 'If I admitted that I'd never hear the end of it.'

'Too right. I never...'

'*Look out!*'

Bennett's yell made the group turn back, just as a blaze of white light blinded them.

'What the...?'

'Get back!'

Suddenly, the street exploded in a shock of sound and movement – a sharp blast of a car horn, squealing brakes, shouts, screams, the ear-splitting screech of metal on metal – too close, too fast, too real...

Someone grabbed Cora's arm and then she was falling, bracing herself for an impact that came with sickening suddenness. She raised her hands over her head and felt knocks and kicks from the heels, elbows and bodies of her colleagues as they landed around her. Above the whirr of stress in her ears and the panicked cries of her friends and the other locals caught in the mêlée, she heard a slam that seemed to shake the ground beneath their tangle of bodies. Somewhere to her left, a woman was sobbing. Cora had no time to think, to process what was happening or prepare for what may yet come, instead focusing on the single source of warmth coming from a hand gripping hers. She held on to it, its presence an anchor as she wrestled her mind back under control.

Around her the noise swelled again, the terrified squeal of an engine and the shouts of more voices. Was that Dave Wheeler?

Lifting her head, she dared to open her eyes – in time to see a heavily damaged white van skidding away down the road, the wing on the driver's side smashed and broken, and Wheeler staggering into the road in its wake.

'I got the reg!' he yelled back, clasping a hand to his lower back as he paused for breath.

'Is everyone okay?' a red-faced man Cora recognised from one of the other quiz teams in The Miller's Arms puffed, jogging over to them.

Moans sounded from the pile of bodies around her as Cora tried to sit up. Everyone had fallen into the darkened doorway of a closed newsagent's shop; the small gap between its two bay-style display windows providing shelter from whatever had narrowly missed them. More people arrived from the pub, helping those involved shakily to their feet. Loud chatter and protestations of disgust merged together, too muddled to make any sense of. Cora leaned her head back against the shop's door, the shock of cold glass a sharp focus to calm her mind.

'Idiot just came out of nowhere,' the red-faced man was saying, helping Kate Bennett to her feet.

'I know…'

'Are you hurt?' Minshull's concerned expression swam into Cora's view.

'I don't think so. You?'

'I think you broke my fall.' His gentle smile didn't mask his shock. 'Sorry.'

Cora risked a smile. Every muscle in her face protested. 'We're quits then.'

He helped her to stand, then reached a hand down to Tris Noakes, who had a large scratch on one side of his brow.

'What the hell was that?' he asked, pulling himself upright.

'Old van drove at you,' the man from the pub answered. 'Right at you, like it was trying to mow you down. Never seen anything like it. Bloody idiot, driving that fast. We should call the police.'

'We are the police,' Bennett grimaced. 'Some of us anyway.'

'I called it in,' Wheeler said, jogging back to them. 'Control have had five other reports of a white van driving like a bastard...' He blanched and raised his hand. 'Forgive my language, girls.'

'No worse than usual, Dave,' Steph Lanehan managed, the moment of humour a balm as all around her shock set in.

'You okay, Minsh?'

Minshull nodded, all trace of his earlier joviality gone. 'We need to locate the car. Are they sending a patrol?'

'Sarge. And there's an all-vehicle alert out on the van's reg. We'll get him.'

'Okay, good.' He turned to Cora. 'Are you okay to get a lift home with Tris? I need to be at the station...'

'No, you bloody well don't,' Tris cut in. 'We need to get everyone back to the pub and wait for your colleagues to arrive. Doctor's orders.'

'He's right, Rob...'

'With respect, Dr Noakes, you aren't that kind of doctor and neither is Cora.'

Tris laid a gentle hand on Minshull's shoulder. 'Until your colleagues get here, consider that I am. You're in shock, mate, same as the rest of us. You aren't getting in a car, let alone driving, until you've been checked by one of my colleagues.'

A chill set itself across Cora's shoulders and she saw Minshull tense as if he felt it, too. 'We need to get inside,' she urged.

Minshull glared back at the damaged bollard on the side of the pavement that had taken the brunt of the impact with the van, the block paving around its base lifted as if it had been pulled up with ease. Shards of rubber, metal and shattered glass surrounded dark skid lines veering from the centre of the road, a large curved piece of wheel arch that had been shorn off the van still rocking by the kerb.

'Fine. But as soon as we're done, we find who did this. And we stop them.'

Two

MINSHULL

Everything ached. Minshull winced as he left his car in South Suffolk Police HQ's car park and made his way inside. He hadn't noticed it last night, adrenaline and fury powering him home from St Just and forcing him to sit up, blankly channel-surfing into the early hours. But this morning the damage from the van's near miss yelled from every muscle.

'You're in early.' DI Joel Anderson frowned, looking up from the kettle in the CID office's tiny kitchen.

'Could say the same for you.' Minshull handed over a large takeaway cup, enjoying his superior's woeful attempt to discard whatever snide comeback he'd been about to unleash before realising one of the cups was for him.

'This is outright bribery,' Anderson growled, his smirk ruining the effect.

'It's also the best coffee in Ipswich. Your choice whether to accept it, Guv.' He edged stiffly across the office to his desk, aware of Anderson's stare hot on his back.

'Reckon I'll take my chances. It would be more of a crime to waste good coffee.' He eyed him from beneath lowered brows. 'I heard about last night.'

Minshull nodded, easing himself into his chair.

'Are you okay?'

'Nothing broken.'

'And the others?'

9

The panic and confusion of last night flashed into Minshull's mind. He'd been quick to grab Cora's hand but hadn't been able to prevent himself landing heavily on her when they fell. Was she in pain this morning, too?

'Paramedics came and checked us all. Minor cuts and bruises, mostly. A woman from one of the other quiz teams sprained her wrist, we think. She went off to hospital; the rest of us didn't need to. It shook everyone up, though. We need to bear that in mind with the team this morning.'

'Are we getting statements?'

'Yes, Guv. The lady who hurt her wrist will be in sometime this afternoon. Cora and her boss Dr Noakes are due in this morning to give theirs. Steph Lanehan did hers first thing when she started her shift. Dave, Kate and I will get ours done by lunchtime.'

'That's good. Have you heard from Cora?'

'I'll see her this morning.' His answer was curter than he'd intended, but discussing Cora Lael with his superior put him on edge. She was his sometime colleague, his friend – and whatever else might be in the wings. If he couldn't define that for himself, there was no way he was ready to explain it to anyone else, least of all Anderson.

Anderson gave a brief nod. 'Understood. Traffic are out looking for the van. I've requested road-cam and CCTV footage from possible routes in and around St Just. We'll find it.'

'Guv.'

Minshull almost said more, pulling the words back before they could fly. But Anderson's wits were quicker than he expected.

'And? Out with it.'

'With what?'

'With whatever it is you were about to say.'

Minshull bristled. Why had his superior chosen this morning to be not only unusually early but also uncharacteristically perceptive? 'It felt deliberate.'

'Deliberate to harm people, or deliberate to target off-duty coppers?'

'I don't know. I mean, we weren't the only ones caught up in it. And it doesn't seem likely that they did it because some of us were police. But as for intent – I thought about it all last night and… I can't shake the feeling that whoever drove that van into us knew exactly what they were doing.'

'They intended to hurt people.'

'Yes.'

'And themselves?'

That was harder to answer. In truth, Minshull had spared little thought for the driver of the van, his anger at the blatant attack on his colleagues and friends blinding him to all else. Had the van driver intended to injure themselves when they drove at the group on the pavement? Or were they wanting to hit and run?

Why would anyone deliberately drive at pedestrians? At that late hour? Were they drunk? Or did they have an agenda?

The possibility troubled Minshull as he watched his team arrive for work. It had only been two months since South Suffolk officers had come under violent attack from a vigilante group. The horror of that had left an indelible mark on everyone. Deliberate attack or not, last night's near miss was a worrying development.

The scratch down DC Dave Wheeler's left cheek looked worse this morning than it had last night. Angry red now, flexing painfully with every word Wheeler spoke. It didn't stop his attempts to lighten the mood, of course, but its presence was a constant mockery of his good nature. DC Kate Bennett appeared to be making the best of it, but Minshull saw her smile fade the moment she turned from the team. When DC Drew Ellis arrived and was regaled with the details by Wheeler, his shock was palpable, the barrage of questions from him that followed proof of his concern.

There was no sign of the final member of the team, but for DC Les Evans this was nothing new. He'd bailed last night at the eleventh hour, an unexpected visit from his sister the reason given for missing the quiz. And it was true to form for him to be tardy in the mornings. Invariably the last to arrive, he rarely made it to the bomb site otherwise known as his desk much before nine a.m. But when he still hadn't appeared by nine thirty, Minshull left his desk and knocked on Anderson's door.

Anderson was on the phone, his voice low as he spoke, but he beckoned Minshull to enter and sit while he continued the conversation.

'And you're sure it wasn't a prank call?' He rolled his eyes at Minshull. 'Yes, of course, Ma'am, we'll start as soon as the team are together...'

Minshull hid a smile. Knowing that Anderson's superior, DCI Sue Taylor, was the unseen caller gave Anderson's grimace all the context needed.

'It is a weird one, I agree. Seems last night was the night for it. Yes, I will. Thanks, Ma'am.' Anderson ended the call and shook his head at Minshull. 'I've heard it all now.'

'Guv?'

'Control received a call at eleven p.m. last night. From Vancouver.'

'Vancouver? In Canada?'

'Choice of two in the world and it isn't the lesser-known one in Washington.' Anderson grinned.

'With random knowledge like that you should be on our team for the next pub quiz, Guv.'

This pleased Anderson, but his smile quickly vanished. 'Expat, living in Vancouver, watching the webcam on Felixstowe Pier while at work, 2:45 p.m. local time, 10:45 p.m. BST.'

'Watching the webcam? Why?'

'It's a thing, apparently. A visit when you can't visit. Became popular during the pandemic, my wife tells me. The point is, our concerned caller witnessed a figure walk into view, hold up a sign to the webcam and disappear a minute later. The sign read: *HELP ME.*'

'Wait a minute – 10:45 p.m.? How did they see anyone on the webcam? It would have been too dark for the camera to pick anything up.'

'There's a spotlight beside the camera that lights up the initial part of South Beach. And the figure was holding a torch above his sign.'

'So the caller thought the person was in trouble?'

Anderson nodded. 'Tech have a screenshot that the caller emailed over but it wasn't good quality, so we've Uniform down there trawling the Felixstowe Pier webcam footage now. We should have a better image in the next hour or so.'

'Any idea of age? Build?'

'The caller reckoned it was a white male, mid-forties, couldn't see hair colour due to the dark hooded sweatshirt the figure was wearing...'

Minshull pulled his notebook from his pocket. 'So, we comb misper files going back – how long?'

'Fifteen years.'

Pen paused mid-loop, Minshull looked up from his notes. 'Sorry?'

'Fifteen years. Specifically, the missing-person report filed on 27th July, 2008. In Kesgrave.'

'I don't understand. Why so specific?'

Anderson placed his hands slowly on the desk as if to anchor himself before replying. 'Because our Canadian caller believes the man to be Ewan Stokes.'

The DI let the name hang in the air between them, keen eyes fixed on his DS. It was instantly familiar yet shrouded in shadow. Why did Minshull know that name? He battled through the fog surrounding it, until the answer arrived.

'Stokesy?'

'The very same.' His superior sat back. 'Ewan Stokes, Suffolk's most famous missing person.'

Of course. Everyone knew that case. In the summer of 2008, Ewan Stokes, an electrician from Kesgrave, disappeared following a floodlit league football match with his amateur team. He was reported missing by his mother and sister, and a police investigation followed.

It had been the mainstay of local news reports for months, the media quickly discarding the facts of the case in favour of fevered speculation that caught the attention of local people. Minshull remembered conversations with his friends about what had really happened to Stokesy. Some believed he'd taken his own life. Some assumed he had run away from something sinister. And a surprising amount of people thought he had stuck a middle finger up to society's expectations and headed off to live the life he wanted.

His case struck a chord with so many of his generation, in an area where unemployment was rising and the housing market was pricing young people out of the villages and towns they had grown up in.

And then, after the investigation was quietly parked, messages began appearing in locations across Europe, one a year on 27th July. A tourist from Suffolk spotted the first, left on a bench in a Paris park. A single sheet of white paper with the message *I'm alive, I'm well, I'm watching*, signed 'Stokesy'. The finder of the message alerted the *Suffolk Herald* and the national press quickly picked it up. What began as a novelty interest story soon gained momentum, with groups of 'Stokesy-watchers' sharing new messages as they were reported. The first online fan collective began on Facebook in 2010, the year after the first message. By 2012, there were several unofficial groups across social media and the first 'official' Stokesy fan page appeared in early 2013.

The news in Suffolk occasionally alluded to the growing interest in the case, keeping Ewan Stokes in the public consciousness. His name became a byword for disappearing – people not showing up for events were jokingly accused of 'doing a Stokesy'. Minshull had heard the phrase on many an occasion. But the case was brought to an international audience when a US true crime documentary featured his story and the mysterious occurrence of the anniversary messages. Fan pages appeared across the world, swelling interest in the unsolved case. A slew of podcasts, magazine articles and radio programmes dedicated to Stokesy elevated what could have been a quietly forgotten missing-person case into a hot topic of speculation and ever wilder theories.

'Did the caller know him?' Minshull asked. It was possible: Suffolk-born people could be found across the world.

Anderson rubbed at his temple with already weary fingers. 'Not personally. But he's a similar age, grew up in Felixstowe and would have seen the news about the investigation when it was active. Turns out he's a bit of a fan.'

'Ah. The true crime thing?'

'Seems it's reared its ugly head again. Look into it for me, would you? If there are armchair detectives across the world spouting their theories again it might throw up information the initial investigation missed.'

'No problem, Guv.' Minshull observed Anderson for a moment. 'Do you think it was him?'

His superior gave a smile-less laugh. 'No idea. But the caller was convinced. Said something about it being close to the fifteenth anniversary – a sign, or something. I guess it's possible it could be him. A body was never found, and there was nothing to suggest suicide. For all we know, Ewan Stokes could have been off on a jolly for fifteen years and decided to come home now. It happens. Rarely, but it does happen.'

'Did you work on the original investigation, Guv?'

'I did a little work on it, but I was involved in other investigations running at the same time. It was your dad's baby.' Anderson's raised hand of apology that accompanied the mention of Minshull's father did little to soothe the kick. Of course South Suffolk Constabulary's most celebrated son would have been involved. It would have been one of his final cases – strange, then, that John Minshull hadn't mentioned it to his sons either during the investigation or in the years since his retirement.

'Right. I can ask Dad what he remembers, if it helps.'

'Hold that in reserve until we've more evidence. But it might be useful.'

Minshull nodded his acceptance, heart heavy. He'd successfully avoided spending any significant time with his father in recent months, regular phone calls with his mother offered instead. But if retired DCI John Minshull knew the Stokesy case well, his input could be invaluable.

Anderson's smile was all solidarity. At least he understood, having worked for Minshull's father years ago.

'Do we inform Ewan Stokes' family?'

'Not yet.' Anderson's sharp reply was softened by his expression. 'We need to ascertain if it's real or a hoax. The family have been through enough. And we haven't exactly served them well thus far. So we wait, until we're certain. If we find more evidence that it's him, we'll talk to them then.'

'Understood.'

'Brief the team, please, as soon as Dr Lael and Dr Noakes' statements have been taken, and we'll start looking into Ewan Stokes. I want to know what information we already have, any rumours circling online, anything to suggest he intended to come home… I realise it's pretty vague now, but once we have a better CCTV image we can move forward.'

'We'll get on to it, Guv.'

'Thanks, Rob. Oh, was there a reason you wanted to see me?'

'Yes – have you heard from Les this morning?'

'Should I have?'

'Well, he isn't here. I thought if he was unwell he might have called in.'

'Wasn't he supposed to be out with you lot last night?'

'He cried off.' Minshull grimaced. 'Unexpected visit from his sister, apparently.'

Anderson raised an eyebrow. 'Families, eh? If he's called in sick I'm yet to hear of it. He doesn't have the day off, does he?'

'Not that I'm aware of.'

'Ah, the joys of working with DC Les Evans,' Anderson groaned. 'Leave it with me.'

Three

CORA

'This is exciting.' Dr Tris Noakes sparkled in the car seat beside Cora as she drove into Ipswich. 'I don't think I've ever been to Police HQ before.'

Cora smiled, keeping her eyes on the road. 'If you like great big grey buildings it'll be a real treat.'

'Any building is a treat for me,' her boss grinned back. 'Plus, it's a whole morning off work, so celebrations all round.'

Working for the perennially sunny director of educational psychology in the local education authority department was an evergreen joy for Cora. He was unlike any other boss she had worked for, able to find the greatest delight in the smallest detail and constantly seeking the good of any situation. Which, in a chronically underfunded department constantly under threat of budget cuts, was a distinct advantage. Cora was relieved to see him back in his usual good spirits this morning. In the aftermath of the incident last night he had fallen unusually silent.

Her arm still ached from where DS Rob Minshull had fallen on it, the pain not helped by a shoulder injury she had received during her first time working with South Suffolk Police over a year ago. She was still on edge, the events of last night replaying as she tried to make sense of everything. Why had the van driven straight at them? Had they been in the wrong place at the wrong time, or had the driver singled them out? Her ears rang with stress, jaw aching from where she had ground her teeth overnight. Despite her colleague's renewed vigour, she'd seen the telltale flick of tension in his jaw. But how were they meant to process something so apparently random?

'Will Rob be taking our witness statements?' Tris asked.

'I'm not sure,' she replied, driving along the lines of parked cars in the car park of South Suffolk Police HQ to find a space. 'He's a witness, too. It might need to be someone who wasn't involved last night.'

'I'm a bit nervous,' Tris confessed as Cora parked. 'It all happened so fast and so much is still a blur. What if my statement comes out in a nonsensical jumble and is no use to anybody?'

Cora twisted in her seat to face him. 'Just say what you remember. Don't try to analyse it. Your response is valid because it happened to you.'

'Thanks, *Dr Lael*.'

'My pleasure, *Dr Noakes*. Shall we go in?'

As they walked into the grey building, Cora noticed Tris was nursing his right leg a little. He'd insisted he was fine when the paramedics examined him last night in The Miller's Arms, but he was clearly in some discomfort today.

DC Dave Wheeler greeted them both like long-lost friends when they entered the CID office, fussing over finding chairs for them and insisting they accept mugs of pale coffee he hastily made. The deep scratch on his cheek he'd incurred last night looked painful, but, like Tris, he insisted it was nothing.

'It could've been a lot worse. I'm just glad I got the reg of the van,' he replied, batting away their concern.

'Any idea who it belongs to?' Tris asked.

'Traffic are on it now. Should have details soon.'

'It's horrific,' DC Drew Ellis said, sitting on the edge of the desk nearest Cora. 'Even if driving at you all was an accident, why was the driver travelling so fast? Nobody bothers speeding down Church Street – even the local racers know it would be suicide with that sharp bend by the Meatcross at the bottom.'

Ellis had changed so much from the first time Cora had worked with him, over a year ago. Gone were the lanky limbs that appeared too long and awkward for the rest of his body; gone, too, the hesitation whenever he spoke, the nervous question mark his voice used to rise to at the end of every sentence. Now a tall, confident man addressed them, his questions considered, his observations pin-sharp. And while the boyish blush still betrayed him, the transformation was remarkable.

'Maybe they weren't local,' DC Kate Bennett said. Cora noticed a distinct tension between her and Drew Ellis – revealed in their averted gazes and the measured space in all their movements around one another, almost as if a reversed magnetic field were constantly pushing them apart. As Bennett skirted her colleague, the notebook she was carrying slid from her hand.

I should tell him...

The sound of Kate Bennett's voice rising from the notebook caught Cora's attention. What was going on there? Cora acknowledged it, and then muted the voice. There were some secrets in the emotional echoes she heard that she didn't need to know.

'Ah, you're both here,' Minshull said, appearing from DI Joel Anderson's office and walking towards them. 'Welcome.'

Cora and Tris stood to greet him. When Minshull had shaken Tris' hand, he reached for Cora's, holding it a moment longer. The warmth transported her back to last night and the simple gesture she'd felt in the mêlée. Had Minshull held her hand then?

'You okay?' he asked, his voice dipping beneath the swell of conversation in the CID office.

'Bit achy,' she admitted. 'You?'

'Same. I don't think stuntman would be a good career move for me any time soon.'

'Will you be taking our statements, Rob?' Tris asked, a dance of nerves present at the edge of his question.

'No. I have to give my own statement this morning, as does Kate. Drew, would you do the honours?'

Ellis smiled. 'Happy to. So, who's first?'

–

The statement process was simple enough, any nerves Cora might have felt calmed instantly by the steady manner of DC Ellis. Her interview was over in ten minutes, and as she passed a very nervous-looking

Tris waiting in the corridor outside the interview room, she gave his shoulder a comforting squeeze.

'Your turn. You'll be fine.'

Tris nodded, uncertainly, as he opened the door.

Back in the CID office every detective was working, their near-silent industry striking in a space so often filled with conversation. But the voices from the wastepaper baskets beneath their desks revealed their frustrations, questions and personal situations.

So tired.

Another thankless task.

How long till lunch?

Don't look at her...

Cora suppressed a grin as she muted each voice in turn. If only they knew...

Minshull looked up and smiled. 'All done?'

'Yes, it was painless. Drew's very good.'

'He is.' Minshull pulled a chair over so that Cora could sit at his desk. 'So how are you really?'

She gave him a wry smile. 'Like I said, a bit achy but fine.'

'I think it's shaken everyone up.'

'It will have done. How are you doing with it all?'

He blew out a sigh. 'Honestly? I don't know. I spent last night trying to figure it out and I have nothing. Why would anyone deliberately drive at a group of people?'

'Could it have been a genuine accident?' Cora suggested, unease taking root in the pit of her stomach. It didn't feel like an accident, but was that because she'd been caught up in it? Was it easier to blame someone's actions than accept it was mechanical error?

'It's possible. I mean, everything's possible until you find the truth. But if it was an accident, why would they leave?'

'They were probably terrified they'd be in trouble. The last thing they would have seen before driving away was a large pile of bodies on the pavement. They couldn't have known we were all okay.'

'Maybe.' Minshull glanced at his working colleagues, lowering his voice. 'I don't suppose you... Did you *hear* anything last night?'

His caution was touching if nothing else. 'It happened too fast. And unless the driver had dropped something at the scene that they'd actually touched I wouldn't have heard their voice.'

Minshull sagged a little. 'Emotional fingerprints, right?'

'Exactly. You wouldn't expect to find any significant physical fingerprint evidence from the debris the car left, so it would be the same for anything emotional. But thanks for asking.'

'You're the expert.' He sent a pointed look at Anderson's closed door. 'You *could be* the expert here...'

Cora shifted a little, trying to ignore the feeling of being cornered. 'I'm thinking about it.'

'Then think *faster*...'

'Dr Lael! Welcome!' Joel Anderson's Caledonian bark boomed into the space as he emerged from his office. 'Here to give your statement?'

'I've just given it.' Cora smiled, rising to accept his handshake. 'I'm waiting for Dr Noakes and then we'll be heading off.'

'A fleeting visit, but still a welcome one. Listen, could I pick your brains while you're here? That's if DS Minshull doesn't mind?'

'Fine by me,' Minshull replied, eyes twinkling at Cora. Of course he'd be relishing this. Since Joel Anderson had formally invited her to join the CID team as an expert consultant two months ago, Minshull hadn't let the subject drop, his insistence that Cora needed the team as much as they needed her a constant feature of their every conversation. He meant well – and Cora was touched by his commitment to the cause – but it was exhausting, too.

There had also been his unguarded confession that he needed her: a brief mention that he'd been careful not to repeat since. It clouded the issue, and she didn't like that. Had it been an impulsive addition to add weight to his argument, or a hint of his feelings towards her, a topic both of them had been carefully skirting for months?

Or did he just want to win?

That possibility seemed the most likely now as Minshull grinned at her.

'Happy to,' she said, casting a withering look at him as she followed Anderson into the office. Minshull could think what he liked: her decision was hers to make, and none of his business.

Four

ANDERSON

DI Joel Anderson was worried. He'd never let on to his team, mind you, but now that he and Dr Cora Lael were safely behind the closed door of his office he could give voice to his concern.

'I was shocked to learn of the incident last night,' he began, because he genuinely was. That any one member of his team should be involved in such a horrific event was abhorrent enough: that it had been so many of them, alongside Dr Lael, was beyond comprehension. 'I hope you are okay?'

'A few bruises and aches, but it could have been worse for us all.'

'Indeed.' He cleared his throat, hands suddenly restless on his desk. 'I need your advice, Cora.'

'Of course.'

She appeared relaxed: that was a good thing considering Anderson was feeling anything but. He turned the monitor of his computer to face her.

'We had an unusual call from a member of the public last night. From Canada, of all places. He was watching the webcam on Felixstowe Pier – virtually visiting Suffolk from his Vancouver office – and he saw a figure walk into shot that he believed to be Ewan Stokes.'

Recognition immediately registered on the doctor's face.

'The missing guy from Kesgrave?'

'The same.'

Cora received this with considered silence.

Anderson knew the thought process she was navigating: he'd steered that course earlier and it still refused to make sense.

'It's got to be, what, fourteen years since he went missing?'

Anderson nodded. 'It'll be fifteen years on the 27th of this month. Which is why this sighting – if it is Ewan Stokes – is particularly significant. We have Uniform over at Felixstowe Pier now going through the footage, so we should have a clearer image soon. But while I was waiting, I did some research online. I knew there had been some internet groups regarding Ewan Stokes, but frankly I was shocked at the extent of interest now.'

He tapped the screen and Cora leaned closer to look. On it was a list of websites, social media profiles and online forums all dedicated to the missing man.

'America, Germany, France, Spain, China, India, Malaysia, Australia… The list goes on. I found this list on a blog post from two months ago, linking to all the current places where messages purportedly left by Stokes have been sighted. He's seen as a folk hero: a maverick who escaped his circumstances, a man who gleefully evades all attempts to capture him.'

'Wow, that's… unusual.'

It was the understatement of the week. Anderson launched the question that had been burning all morning, as he'd found more and more mentions of Ewan Stokes. 'In your professional opinion, why would someone idolise a missing person whose only claim to infamy is their own disappearance? These people don't know him; they've never met him. A good proportion of the commentators on these sites would have been infants when he disappeared. What's special about this case? Why him?'

Cora sat back and considered the question. Anderson guessed it wasn't the one she had anticipated having to answer, his recent invitation to team up with CID still awaiting a reply.

'Well, it's easy.'

Anderson frowned. 'The question?'

'No – the act.'

'I don't follow…'

Cora took a breath, one hand resting lightly on the edge of the desk. 'None of these people know Stokesy. It doesn't matter. It just makes him a blank page they can project anything onto. Their own desires, their frustrations, their prejudices, their rage. The mythical version of Stokesy can be someone who refused to conform, someone who skipped regular society to do his own thing. Or he can be a victim, a cautionary tale of how easily somebody can be forced to disappear from their own life. Any theory can find its proof, any conspiracy its justification, because the real Stokesy isn't there to challenge it.'

'So he's a scapegoat?'

Cora nodded. 'Or a god.'

'Sorry?'

'A graven image. A symbol representing whatever you most aspire to. He isn't a real person saying any of the things his followers claim, but his image can be manipulated in any way they want.'

Anderson considered this. According to DC Peter York, the new night duty CID officer who had fielded the call, the man who had reported the figure in the webcam footage was utterly convinced it was Stokesy — adamant, he'd said.

'It was like he'd seen a rock star,' he'd confirmed when Anderson phoned him earlier. 'He was excited and concerned at the same time.'

Cora's answer gave significant weight to DC York's observation.

A new, troubling question now reared itself. One that Anderson could hardly bring himself to voice.

'Could someone deifying Ewan Stokes in this way pose a danger to others?'

'Hard to say. My best guess would be that they wouldn't. Hero worship like this, especially from people online, is usually contained within a fandom. The conversation with like-minded people is often a mark of belonging. So while the discussions might become heated, the reality is unlikely to be. I would suspect that a majority of users on these fan forums find safety in being online. Real-world existence isn't something they crave.'

This quelled some of Anderson's anxiety, but he knew only too well the potential that 'most of' and 'the majority of' statements could hold. It didn't cover everyone – which meant that, however insignificant, the possibility for concern still existed.

He felt heartened, however, that Cora had answered his question without hesitation or judgement. She hadn't dismissed it out of turn. He needed reliable advisers like that.

'Thank you. I appreciate your opinion.'

'You're welcome.'

'Join our team,' he rushed, his resolution not to mention the invitation this morning gone in a moment. 'Please, Cora. Policing is becoming ever more complex, inextricably linked with mental health issues and problems my predecessors simply didn't have to deal with. Your expertise – and your ability – could be an invaluable advantage for us.'

Her gaze instantly fell from his. A bad sign? Had he said too much? Pushed too hard?

'Forgive my forthrightness. But this is important. With this case alone we may have to lean on your knowledge further, if the situation escalates.'

She looked up, as if considering whether or not to trust him. Anderson didn't blame her reluctance one bit: he had hardly been her biggest supporter in the past.

'I would need to clear it with Dr Noakes.'

Was that a *yes*?

'Of course. Whatever you need. And you will be paid for your time – I hope that goes without saying.' He winced a little at the confidence of his own words. Clearing that hurdle with DCI Taylor would take some negotiation.

'Then yes, Joel. I'm in.'

It was all Anderson could do not to punch the air and yell.

Five

MINSHULL

It looked like Stokesy.

Minshull studied the loop of webcam footage that Tech had sent over, holding up the enhanced still image beside his monitor. Even allowing for the low light and grainy nature of the video, the figure was remarkably similar to the last photo on file for the missing man. A prominent Roman nose, high cheekbones and dark brows, a small mole in the centre of his right cheek – all the markers Minshull would have been looking to match. If it wasn't Ewan Stokes, it was someone who had gone to significant trouble to appear like him.

The likeness, together with the original caller's assertion of his identity, was difficult to argue with. A man bearing a striking resemblance to a man missing for fifteen years, with the dark hood of his sweatshirt pulled up, holding a sign written in thick black letters on a sheet of card that glowed bright white in the beam of the torch he held in his left hand. Two words, centred to draw the eye:

HELP ME

Minshull stared at the image for a moment longer, a plan of action forming in his mind. Then he stood, image in hand.

'Okay, everyone, gather round for a briefing, please.'

He took his place by the empty whiteboard and waited for the team to assemble. Cora and Tris Noakes had left half an hour ago; with no sign of Evans still, and time pressing on, he had no choice but to begin the briefing without him. He wanted to go over to Felixstowe Pier and talk to the security manager there: now they had the footage, he needed to see it for himself. But he couldn't go until the briefing happened and that couldn't wait for Evans to arrive.

'What about Les?' Wheeler asked as he wheeled his desk chair beside his colleagues.

'I'll bring him up to speed when he arrives,' Minshull replied.

'If he arrives,' Ellis muttered.

'He'll be here.'

'Tenner says he won't.'

Minshull saw the shock that Ellis' joke caused. Sweepstakes – particularly of the highly questionable variety – were the firm domain of Les Evans, not the youngest, most conscientious detective on the team. Ellis wasn't a troublemaker. Nobody wanted him to start being one now. Wheeler didn't know whether to laugh or not. Bennett stared at her colleague.

Ellis, however, remained unrepentant. 'What? That's what he'd say if one of us went AWOL.'

Minshull fixed him with a look. 'If you're making Les Evans a role model for your ongoing police career, Drew, we need to talk.' Privately, he couldn't blame the young DC for getting his own back after over a year of incessant mockery from Evans. He would have wanted to do the same. But this couldn't be allowed to develop beyond a sly pop at an absent co-worker. 'You're better than that.'

The deep crimson flush of his DC confirmed a point made.

Minshull turned back to the whiteboard, concealing his involuntary smile. Popping the lid off a blue dry marker, he wrote a name at the top.

EWAN STOKES

Instant recognition reverberated behind his back. He turned to face the team.

'Familiar name?'

'Sarge.'

'Yes, Sarge.'

'Of course, Sarge.'

'What do we know about him?'

Bennett raised her hand but didn't wait for an invitation to speak. 'Kesgrave man, worked as an electrician, disappeared after a football match about fifteen years ago and hasn't been seen or heard from since.'

'Correct. Apart from the last part.'

'Sarge?'

'It turns out Ewan Stokes, commonly known as Stokesy, has been sending messages confirming his existence since 2009. Then, last night, he was reportedly seen in person. In Felixstowe.' He fixed the printed webcam still to the whiteboard and sensed the rumble of scandal pass around his team.

'Where was this taken?'

'By the side of the pier. The webcam fixed there that films South Beach picked him up. And someone watching the webcam in Vancouver called us.'

The team's confusion gave weight to his own. What were the chances that anyone would have been watching the Felixstowe Pier webcam late at night? If it was Ewan Stokes standing with his sign and a torch, had he done so in the hope that someone was watching? Had he tipped off his worldwide fans that an appearance was imminent?

'What time last night, Sarge?'

'Ten forty-five p.m. According to DI Anderson there's a spotlight that illuminates some of the beach. And, as you can see, our man here is carrying a torch to light up the sign he's holding. It reads: *HELP ME.*'

'*HELP ME?*' Bennett read. 'Help him do what? Come home?'

Minshull shrugged. 'It looks that way but let's not rule out other possibilities at this stage. Which are…?'

'He's being held against his will?' Ellis suggested.

'Good, Drew. He could have escaped his captors, found a torch, made a sign…' Minshull laughed along with his team. 'Okay, joking aside, it might have been him reaching out to others.'

Wheeler gave a cough. 'Perhaps someone or something caused his disappearance and he wants to return but needs assistance.'

'Again, another possibility.'

'A sighting for his fans?' Bennett suggested. 'If he's been sending messages over the years, like you said. Wouldn't that be a ready-made audience for his appearance?'

'That's true, and something I would like you to look into, please. Has he ever posted a message like this before? Is it the kind of language used previously or is this different? Assuming Ewan Stokes has dramatically returned to his home county, what might he be seeking help with? We need to establish clear lines of inquiry as soon as possible.'

'Why would he have done it at that time? Why not in the daylight where he could have been seen better?' Ellis asked. 'And what about the person that reported the sighting? Who watches a webcam at night?'

'Homesick Canadians missing Felixstowe, apparently.'

'And they just happened to be watching at the exact moment Stokesy walks into shot?' Ellis asked.

'It does seem too much of a coincidence,' Minshull agreed, proud of his team for their insight. 'Drew, can you check with Control and Pete York to see if our caller left contact details? I think a chat with him would help us understand the chain of events better.'

'Yes, Sarge.'

'Thanks. Now, DI Anderson is looking into the weird celebrity status Ewan Stokes seems to have gained in recent years, but Dave, could you do a bit of research along those lines, please? See what's been written about him in the past six months and, in particular, if there were any rumours of a potential Suffolk sighting this week.'

'No problem, Sarge. You think this could be a publicity stunt?'

Minshull shrugged. 'It's possible. To be honest, everything's possible at this stage. Kate, can you check the original misper report for Ewan Stokes and grab any photos you find so we can put them up here? I know they will be at least fifteen years out of date, but at least we'll be able to do a rough comparison with this latest image. I'm still not completely convinced that he's our webcam man.'

'Webcam Man,' Wheeler chuckled. 'Sounds like a crap superhero to me.'

'Let's hope he's as innocuous as the title suggests,' Minshull returned. 'That's it for now, everyone. Thanks.'

There was a bustle of chatter and noise as the team made their way back to their desks. Minshull accepted the discussions as a key part of the process. With so little to go on yet, any speculation could be useful.

'Ay-ay, look who the cat dragged in,' Wheeler said suddenly, causing the other detectives to turn.

DC Les Evans gave a weak salute from the doorway before shuffling over to his desk.

'Good of you to join us, Les,' Minshull said, irritation bristling.

'Wasn't my fault,' the DC muttered, face flushed indignant red.

'Never is, is it?' Ellis quipped, pushing his luck. Minshull could see the potential for trouble if this new-found cheekiness weren't quickly curbed. He would have to address it sooner rather than later – the team couldn't afford to lose a conscientious DC for the sake of a few cheap comebacks.

'Enough of that, thanks,' he said, pleased to see Ellis immediately comply. 'Everything okay, Les?'

'No, it bloody isn't. My tyres were slashed last night.'

The jovial mood in the office instantly became genuine concern. 'What?'

Les shook his head as if still trying to process the event. 'Ten cars parked in our street, and mine the only one with four tyres slashed. I wouldn't mind but I'd only just replaced them. Had a hell of a job getting anyone out to deal with it this morning, and I didn't want to leave the car because it would just be an easy target for the neighbourhood scrotes to take a pop at.'

'You should have called us.'

'Yeah, I know. Sorry. Ginny said I was daft not to. I just had too much going on to think straight.'

'Ginny?' Bennett asked.

'My sister. She's visiting from Oxford for a couple of weeks. Great introduction to my neck of the woods.'

'Did you get it sorted?' Minshull asked, any residual frustration now channelled into affirmative action.

'Yeah. Best part of five hundred quid to replace them all on an emergency call-out, mind, but it's driveable.'

'Want me to ask SOCOs to check it over?'

Les shook his head. 'No point. I don't reckon they even touched the bodywork. Looks like they used a large knife and just slashed and ran. Bastards.'

'I'm sorry, mate. That's rough. Get yourself a coffee and then come over to my desk. I'll bring you up to speed with the latest news.'

Evans nodded and headed for the kitchen.

Returning to the whiteboard, Minshull attempted to bend his mind around the string of inexplicable recent events. The van driving at them last night, the supposed sighting of Ewan Stokes with his carefully illuminated sign, and the Canadian who just happened to be viewing the webcam at the perfect time, almost five thousand miles away… And now Evans' tyres slashed. Unconnected in every instance, but what a batch of unlikely occurrences to arrive at once!

He was aware of someone in his peripheral vision and turned to see Evans holding two mugs of coffee. His eyes were fixed on the board with its single-entry name in a vast area of blank space.

'Is that one for me?' Minshull prompted, when Evans failed to relinquish the mug.

Evans blinked. 'Yeah, sorry, Sarge.' He handed the mug to Minshull and nodded at the whiteboard. 'That who I think it is?'

'Depends on who you think he is.'

'It's Stokesy, isn't it? Ewan Stokes, the missing man.'

There was something in the way Evans spoke the name, a slight hesitation around his question-that-wasn't-a-question. It caught Minshull's attention.

'Did you know him?'

'Everyone knew him.'

'Did you know him personally?'

Evans didn't look away from the name. 'No. Felt like I did – we all did, right? Bloke you might've seen down the pub. Bloke you might've worked with. Disappearing like that. It was tragic.'

Minshull narrowed his eyes. Why did Evans' reply feel off? 'Well, someone thinks he's back.'

'What?'

'Sarge, the information on the van just came through from Traffic,' Wheeler called across the office.

'Excellent!' Minshull paused to pat Evans on the shoulder. 'Vehicle that nearly mowed us down last night.'

'What?'

'I'll give you all the gory details in a minute.' He smiled. 'Let's just say you picked a hell of a day to be late.'

Ellis and Bennett had joined Wheeler by his screen when Minshull reached the desk, parting to grant him the best view.

'Okay, what do we have?'

'Van is a white 2004 Volkswagen Caddy owned by a Mr Lindsay Carlton. A patrol just contacted his home address but the tenants there told them that he'd emigrated to Australia five years ago. And a DVLA database search confirmed that the van has been under a SORN notification since Mr Carlton left the UK.'

'So was it stolen?'

'Could be. Steph Lanehan and Rilla Davis are on their way over to the registered address to check out the garage where it was kept. We should know soon.'

'Do we have contact details for the owner?'

'Getting them through any minute, Sarge.'

Minshull nodded. 'Okay. I'll try to call him, see what he can tell us about the van. In the meantime, I'm going to head over to Felixstowe and talk to the pier security team. You all know what you're doing now. Let's crack on and find everything we can on Ewan Stokes – real and rumoured.'

As he began to walk back to his desk, Minshull saw Evans staring blankly at his computer screen. He was clearly going to be worse than useless today, but Minshull decided to let him be. The shock of the morning might be better calmed by the familiar surroundings of the CID office, with its banter and ordinariness, than by any intervention from him.

Les Evans didn't get a free pass often. Today would be an exception.

Six

On any other day, being sent to a random lock-up in the depths of the Suffolk countryside would be PC Steph Lanehan's idea of a total waste of time.

But not today.

This one was personal.

And even though the prospect of finding anything there to link the van with the bastard who drove at them was negligible, considering both were still at large, Lanehan intended to comb the site for any piece of evidence. One way or another, they would find the driver. Lanehan would make certain of that.

In the passenger seat of the patrol car, PC Rilla Davis gazed out at the passing countryside and failed to keep her nervous thumbs from twiddling. She'd insisted she was okay when Lanehan had asked first thing, but her hands told a different story. It wasn't surprising, considering she'd endured an unprovoked attack alongside Steph only two months ago. That had been in a remote rural location too: it wasn't difficult to see the connections she might be making.

'It isn't a farm,' Lanehan stated, eyes firmly on the road ahead.

'I know,' Davis returned, irritation dancing with apprehension in her reply.

'I'm just saying, it's a lock-up garage that's part of a row of buildings on the outskirts of a village. I checked it out online and there are a couple of industrial units nearby. One of them's a bodywork garage, other one's a weights gym.'

'Great. So?'

Undeterred, Lanehan pressed the point. 'So, it'll be busy.'

Davis sighed. 'Stop it.'

'Stop what? Briefing you on the job? Kind of my business, Ril.'

Lanehan felt the burn of her colleague's stare but didn't look over. She'd hit a nerve and she knew it. But it was about time they addressed the elephant in the room – or, more accurately, the elephant in the back seat.

Davis, however, was clearly not in the mood for deep and mean-ingfuls today. 'You know what I'm talking about, Steph. I am fine. The counsellor cleared me for working, the Sarge thinks I'm up for it, so I'd appreciate you accepting it, too.'

'Suit yourself.' Lanehan shrugged off her irritation. There was no helping some people.

The police counsellor had cleared Lanehan for duty as well, but it didn't mean the lingering scars from the attack were gone. Every night she battled recurring nightmares of the angry mob, the slam of rocks and bottles, the scent of her own blood as she lay in the mud. Every morning she watched her own hands shaking as she made coffee and took her pills. Police work was the only work she'd ever known – she lived for the job. But the attack had soured that. And last night's near collision had brought it all back.

Even her partner Fred had noticed – and he never usually noticed anything unless it was on a plate for him to eat or running around a pitch kicking a ball. He'd started making sure he was up when she was getting ready for a shift, despite him being tired from working nights as a security guard. A strong coffee ready for her, an extra-long hug at the door. Daft beggar. She appreciated the gestures, knowing it was his version of in-depth heart-to-hearts. It was just as well: she'd never find the words to express what was going on in her head.

Maybe driving the patrol car on too little sleep and too much caffeine wasn't the best idea today, but Lanehan was damned if she'd let on to anyone. Head down, press on through the shit. That's what she'd always done. Today was no exception.

All the same, she worried for Davis. The young PC was barely six months out of training, wet behind the ears and nowhere near prepared for the daily rigours of a beat officer's day. She'd been a firebrand when she'd first joined, but that was gone. Of course, she'd learn to assimilate it, like everyone did. Box it away, deal with it later. But she wasn't there yet.

The row of lock-up garages was in surprisingly good condition, considering their location. Lanehan had seen similar buildings on the periphery of Suffolk villages before, like those on the edge of the Parkhall Estate in her home village of St Just, and they were nearly always rusting, graffiti-covered targets for local youths bored out of their skulls with village life. While these buildings bore some signs of age, they were clearly cared for.

Leaving the patrol car, Lanehan walked along the line of square buildings with identical, red-painted steel doors. Davis trailed in her wake, saying nothing. They reached number 6, the last but one lock-up, and stopped. Both donned plastic gloves in silence.

The padlock was in place. The door paint bore no signs of tampering. At the concrete edge where the fabric of the building met the steel door, no telltale scratches or damage were visible. Crouching down, Lanehan scanned the surface of the door for dents where someone might have kicked it, and looked at the ground for any scuffs or disturbances where the sun-bleached grass met the structure.

Nothing.

No damage, no sign of forced entry, no footprints.

Had they picked the lock? She straightened and carefully inspected the brass padlock. It shone like new in the late-morning sunshine. Beside it the keyhole for the door lock appeared equally unharmed. No scratches where a pick might have slipped. Nothing to suggest it had been tampered with.

'I thought you said they nicked the van,' Davis said, behind her.

'That's what Minsh reckoned. But unless they stole the keys to this place I can't see how that's possible.'

A low rumble from the road made Lanehan turn. A dusty pickup truck was bumping over the uneven ground towards the line of garages. The driver swung the vehicle in a wide arc, reversing it towards number 3. The ratchet grate of the handbrake sounded, quickly followed by the protesting squeak of the driver's-side door as it opened, revealing a middle-aged man in an equally dusty dark green boiler suit.

'Everythin' all right, officers?' he boomed, jogging across the hard-standing towards them.

'Know anything about the owner of number 6?' Lanehan asked.

The man scratched at the close-shaved hair on the crown of his head. 'Bit of a weird one, that. Fella that owns it went to Australia a few years back. I'm here most days and normally don't see a soul. But every now and again I do a late shift and sometimes I've seen someone opening it up. I chatted to some of the other lads and a few of 'em have spotted him, too.'

'What did he look like?'

'Ooh, now you're askin'. Youngish, medium height, pretty regular build? I mean, I say it's a bloke, but all the times I've seen 'im it's been dark and he was wearin' one of them baggy hoodie things. My daughter's sixteen and she wears one of those, so, you know, could be *eether-either.*'

'Is there any CCTV on the site?' Davis asked.

The man nodded and pointed to a camera mounted on a telegraph pole. 'Chap who owns the estate put them up last year. We had kids tryin' to break in and one of your lot suggested we should get some cameras.'

'What's the landowner's name?'

'Ian Hobson. He owns all of this site and the next two farms. Couldn't do much with this strip of land so he put these garages up and those units over there. We all own our lock-ups but we have a maintenance agreement with his company. I've got his number if you want it?'

'That would be great,' Lanehan said, grateful to the cheery-faced arrival for their first real lead. 'Thank you, Mr…?'

'Noble.' The man beamed. 'Jonny Noble, at your service.'

'I'm PC Steph Lanehan and this is my colleague, PC Rilla Davis,' Lanehan replied, liking him immediately. 'When was the last time you saw someone here, Mr Noble?'

'Gotta be – what – two weeks ago? I only caught sight of 'em when I was drivin' off. Must've been in the garage, I s'pose.'

'Were they carrying anything? Or could you see any vehicle in the garage?'

'Chap had a bag, I think. Holdall-type thing? Like you'd take to the gym if you were bothered enough to go.' He gave a deep chuckle. 'Probably tools for fixin' that old van in there.'

Lanehan and Davis exchanged glances. 'You've seen the van, sir?'

Jonny Noble nodded. 'Once or twice. Right beaten-up heap of junk it is. How that thing's still on the road is beyond me.'

'What colour is it?'

'White, although it's so bashed up and dirty you'd hardly know.'

Lanehan smiled. 'If we needed you to make a statement about this, would you be willing to come to the station in Ipswich?'

Noble flushed. 'Happy to. Not sure how much help I can be, mind.'

'It'll be a great help,' Lanehan assured him. 'If you give PC Davis your number and Mr Hobson's number, we'll be in touch.'

She walked back to number 6, checking the door and lock again. Who else had a key if the owner was on the other side of the world? She pulled her radio to her lips. 'PC Lanehan to Control, over.'

'Go ahead, over.'

'We're at the garages just off Church Road in Playford. No sign of forced entry or damage. Over.'

'Received. Shall I patch you through to CID, over?'

'Please.' She waited for the call to connect, watching her colleague chatting to Mr Noble, enjoying the reappearance of Davis' smile after so long. Maybe Jonny Noble could prove to be their angel in disguise.

'Steph, what've you got?'

'No sign of a break-in, Sarge. But we just met Mr Noble, one of the other lock-up owners, and he says he's sometimes seen someone going in there. They obviously have a key.'

'Could he give a description?'

'Bit vague – medium height, average build, usually wearing a hoodie. But he did tell us he'd seen the white van in the lock-up and that it's old and in a bit of a state.'

37

'Brilliant, Steph. Any CCTV?'

'Several on-site, one specifically aimed at the lock-ups. We're just getting the estate owner's number from Mr Noble.'

The surprise in Minshull's laugh was welcome. 'He sounds like a godsend. Any chance we can second him into Uniform?'

'I reckon he'd like that.'

'Did he see anyone near the garage last night?'

'No, Sarge. Two weeks ago was the last sighting.'

'Ah, okay. Great work, though. Can you call the estate owner and get hold of that CCTV footage, please?'

'Will do, Sarge.'

'Cheers, Steph. You doing okay?'

She wasn't prepared for that question. Disguising the squeak in her voice with a cough, she replied, 'I'll live. Takes more than a bastard joyrider to stop me.' She wished her feelings matched her words.

'Even still, take care, yeah? Let me know what you find.'

Ending the call, Lanehan turned to her colleague, who was waving to Mr Noble as he headed back to unload his truck. 'Right, Ril, come on. Bit more of a goose chase for us this morning.'

'Hoo-bloody-ray,' Davis muttered, her smile vanishing as they returned to the car.

Seven

MINSHULL

Felixstowe's promenade was bright and breezy today, a perfect summer seaside view. Wisps of pristine white clouds skipped across the summer-blue sky and the breeze blowing off the sea was wonderfully cool against the midday heat. If he hadn't been there on official business, Minshull might have been tempted to settle on the beach for a while, or maybe even take a dip.

But he had a job to do.

With one last wistful glance in the direction of the sea, he walked on to the boardwalk of the pier, raising a hand in greeting to the uniformed officer waiting for him by the entrance.

'Nice day for it, Sir.' PC Mitch Owens grinned.

'Shame we're working, eh?' Minshull smiled back. 'Good to see you, Mitch. How's the family?'

'Growing,' Owens chuckled. 'But that tends to happen fast with two sets of twins.'

'I'll bet. So, there's CCTV footage of our friend?'

'There is, Sir. The pier's security have their own camera set up alongside the webcam, so it caught the fella, too, from a slightly different angle. I've got them both ready for you to view. And the security manager is waiting to meet you in there.' Owens grimaced. 'Right bundle of joy he is, an' all.'

'Lovely.' Minshull watched a small group of people milling around the edge of the promenade, close to the pier. Day trippers, most likely. The coach tours of the Suffolk coast were already in full swing: by next month coastal towns like Felixstowe would be packed with them. 'Right, shall we?'

Owens wasn't joking about the security manager. He stood in the corner of the cramped CCTV suite like a disgruntled shadow, shoulders hunched and folded arms welded tight across his chest. Minshull kept his smile hidden as he sat beside Owens, watching the CCTV on one screen and the original webcam view on another.

'There,' Owens said, pausing the footage on both.

The figure walked calmly into shot, the light from his torch momentarily flashing the picture to white as he wrestled the sign into place. And then he stood still, eyes trained directly at the webcam, torch illuminating the sign written on what appeared to be a large sheet of white cardboard. The only hint of movement was the occasional fluctuation of the torch beam and the pinprick beats of moths drawn to the spotlight beside the cameras. And then, the torchlight extinguished, the figure walking calmly off-screen.

'How long does he stand there?' Minshull asked.

'Two minutes,' Owen confirmed, consulting the timestamp notes he'd made in his notebook. 'Exactly.'

'That's very specific. So was there someone else there, telling him when to leave?'

'Possibly. Or he could've set an alarm on his phone in his pocket? The webcam has no sound so we don't know.'

'Does it matter?' a gruff voice enquired from the corner of the room.

'Everything matters, sir,' Minshull replied flatly, not taking his eyes off the adjacent screens.

His reply was met with an overblown sigh. Minshull didn't rise to it. So the security manager was going to be one of *those*, was he?

'Not my bloody idea to have that webcam here,' the man muttered, unbidden, directed at the room itself rather than the two police officers sitting beside the screens. 'Tourist board bollocks, foisted on me for no extra money. Like I haven't enough to do already. Like we're not already stretched to capacity. And now this.'

'We appreciate your co-operation, sir,' Owens replied, the flicker of a smile tugging at one corner of his mouth.

'How long have you had the webcam here?' Minshull asked.

'Five years. Chap from the tourist board comes to check it when he can be arsed.' He sniffed. 'Which is pretty much never.'

'Where exactly would this guy have had to stand to face the webcam?'

'Just on the beach. But he must have done it before.'

Minshull turned in his seat. 'How do you mean?'

'To get the angle right. A little bit to the left or the right and he wouldn't have been in shot. Look at him: dead centre. Close enough to get the sign in, so the light caught it. No way he just wandered into shot. That's been planned.'

Minshull looked back at the screen. Until now he'd assumed this stunt was a one-man event, as spontaneous as it appeared. But to get the precise location, the perfect timing, preparation would have been essential. Either Ewan Stokes or someone working with him had to have visited the site prior to the stunt. Which meant they were looking for someone trying out angles with the webcam. It would be a laborious task to identify them, but a valuable lead if they caught them on camera. 'Could we get the recordings from the last week from your CCTV, please?'

The security manager groaned. 'You're welcome to them. But with respect, officer, I'm not trawling through them.'

'I wouldn't dream of asking, sir,' Minshull replied, his sardonic tone thankfully lost on the sullen manager. 'My team will be more than happy to do the job.'

Les Evans wouldn't. But maybe hours of inspecting CCTV tapes would bring the DC back to his usual grumpy self. His odd air in the CID office was unnerving everyone. This job would hopefully level his mood.

'I'll put them on a flash drive,' the manager said, opening the door. 'If you'd like to follow me?'

Minshull and Owens left the room, squinting in the bright sunlight as they emerged from the security cabin.

'Can you wait for the drive?' Minshull asked his colleague. 'I need to get back.'

'No problem.' Owens smirked. 'Might get a candyfloss and play some slots while I'm waitin'.'

'Perks of the job, eh?'

'There have to be some sometime, Sir.'

Minshull grinned back and offered his hand to the security manager. 'PC Owens will have the flash drive from you. Thanks for your help, Mr...?'

'Rainsford. Jim Rainsford.' His handshake was brisk, the grip painful. 'So what are your lot going to do about *them*?'

'Them?' Minshull followed the direction of Rainsford's nod to the pier's entrance. Where the handful of day trippers had been before, a small crowd now gathered. All male, most of them carrying rucksacks with cameras hung around their necks. They could be mistaken for birdwatchers, or possibly ramblers out for a seaside hike.

'Creepy bastards. I've tried moving them on but they just keep coming back. Bringing more with them.'

'Creepy in what way?'

'They were hanging round when I opened the gates this morning at seven a.m. Taking photos. Muttering among themselves. They'll put off paying customers if they stay there.'

As he said this, a young couple quickly changed direction from the pier entrance to give the group a wide berth.

'Did they say why they were here?'

'Didn't say anything. Bunch of weirdos. I wouldn't be surprised if they're off their faces on something.'

'Leave them to me, sir,' Minshull replied, a thought forming. 'Mitch, bring that flash drive up to CID when you get back, okay?'

'No problem.' Owens smiled.

Leaving his uniformed colleague and the still-glowering security manager beside the security cabin, Minshull walked towards the group. They eyed him cautiously as he approached, several of them shuffling closer together as if to create a barrier.

'Afternoon, gentlemen,' Minshull called, reaching them. 'Enjoying the view?'

Several muttered responses failed to make any coherent reply.

'So what brings you to the pier today?'

'Who wants to know?' asked a tall man wearing a khaki beanie and camo jacket.

Minshull retrieved his warrant card from the inside pocket of his jacket and instantly the group fell silent. 'Detective Sergeant Rob Minshull. And you are?'

'Here on a day trip.'

They were eyeing him now. Minshull glanced up at the clouds being blown across the blue overhead. 'Lovely day to be by the sea.'

The group made no reply, their eyes still trained on him.

'Are you planning to visit the pier?'

'This side of it,' another voice replied, quickly shushed by those around him.

'Why?'

The tall man rolled his eyes as if Minshull had just debated the location of the sky. 'Because *he* was here.'

'Who?'

'Stokesy.'

How did they even know that? To Minshull's knowledge the only people aware of last night's webcam activity were the Canadian caller, his CID and unformed colleagues and the surly security manager of the pier. Keeping his expression steady, he pushed for more.

'Stokesy? You mean Ewan Stokes? He went missing years ago, and not from this pier.'

'He was here. Last night. That webcam caught him,' the man replied, pointing to the side of the pier where both the webcam and CCTV cameras were. 'And that's why your lot are hanging around, right? Trying to catch him. But he won't be caught.'

There was something about the man's attitude that made Minshull uneasy. His eyes were glassy, a fixed tension in his smile. *Creepy*, Jim Rainsford had said. He wasn't lying.

'Did you see it? On the webcam?'

'One of the forum guys did. He posted the screenshot on the sightings thread.'

'Which forum?'

'StokesyFans. Don't you know anything?'

'So you're all members?'

Gazes were dropped, feet shuffled. Only the group's apparently elected spokesman retained eye contact. 'We just wanted to see it.'

'Well, he isn't here now,' Minshull replied, carefully choosing his words. 'And the security guy on the pier is concerned that you're blocking the entrance. So maybe take this on the beach?'

'It's a free country. We can stand here if we want to.'

The group seemed to huddle closer around him as he said it, a hesitant cordon gaining strength from each other.

'Of course you can, sir. I'm just trying to stop any trouble.'

For a moment, the man didn't reply, staring defiantly back. Minshull held his ground and waited. Sure enough, the disquieting silence stretched sufficiently to unseat the ringleader.

'The beach might be better,' someone muttered in the group.

'I need coffee anyway,' mumbled another.

Minshull saw the resolve flicker in the tall man's expression. 'Fine. But we have every right to be here.'

'As long as you don't get in the way of the pier visitors you can stand where you like.' Chancing his arm, Minshull pulled a handful of business cards from his pocket. 'I would be really interested to talk to any of you about the forum. If anyone would like to give me a call.'

The group shrank back from the fan of cards he offered them as if scared their fingers might get burned should they accept one. The tall man took one with another roll of his eyes.

'I won't call,' he said, as he and the others turned to go.

Minshull watched them leave, spikes of snapped retort from the group sounding above the sounds of the beach and pier.

Very odd.

Shaking his head, he pulled out his mobile and made a call.

Anderson answered on the fourth ring. 'Rob, what do you have?'

'There's CCTV in addition to the webcam, Guv. Security manager reckoned the stunt was planned in advance, so Mitch Owens is fetching the recording files for the last seven days. He'll be with you in the next hour or so.'

'You think Webcam man had help?'

'It's looking that way. If it was planned before then, someone must have tried out the webcam shot, either in daylight or at night. It'll be a trawl to find them but I reckon we might get footage.'

'Excellent. A job for Les, no doubt?' Anderson's amusement buzzed down the line. Where Minshull had given Les leeway so far, he knew his superior was feeling less than charitable.

'Thought it might give him something nice to moan about. I'm on my way back in.'

'Ah – before you do…' The pause was worrying. Joel Anderson's pauses invariably meant some unappealing request was imminent. Minshull braced himself. 'Dave and I have been going through the files of the original investigation. They're a total mess. I hate to ask, Rob, but I need you to speak to your father.'

Of course.

The moment retired DCI John Minshull had been identified as the detective in charge of the investigation, Minshull had known this request was coming. It didn't make it any easier that Anderson understood the gravity of what he was asking.

'How much of a mess?'

'Incomplete files, abandoned leads, bad decisions. There's blessed little information on suspects, theories, lines of inquiry followed. From what we've seen so far, I can't tell what your father was doing. It seems he just dropped the case when it didn't bear fruit. And then, six months after Ewan Stokes vanished, his sister Marilyn changed her statement to say that their mother, Olwyn Stokes, had been at the football match that night as well, and not, as she'd first claimed, away visiting friends. According to Marilyn, both she and her mother witnessed a pretty savage fight between Ewan and his former girlfriend.'

'Was it followed up?'

Anderson's long exhale was little comfort. 'Not at all, according to what I've read. It was parked. No further records of interaction with the family, no further reports of investigation.'

'I'll ask him to come in,' Minshull stated, already dreading the phone call.

'No. I'm sorry, Rob. I need you to go and talk to him. Right now.'

45

'What?' It was out before he could think better. Scrambling to regain his composure, he rushed, 'I – I mean, of course, Guv. If you think that's best.'

'It is. We need to know what we're dealing with here and it's best not to forewarn John. Knowing your father, he'd take any advantage to prepare his answers. We can't afford to give him the opportunity.'

'Of course. I understand.'

When the call ended, Minshull stared at the blank screen of his phone, his whole body tense.

It was inevitable, of course. And long overdue. But confronting his father would take every ounce of resolve Minshull had. He needed time to ready himself, to rehearse the lines and cover his bases, but there was no time. Like so much of their relationship over the years, he found himself ambushed by circumstance, thrust into a fight he was ill-prepared for.

There was no backing away this time.

Accepting his lot, Minshull headed for his car.

Eight

CORA

The online Stokesy fandom was so much larger than Cora had anticipated. Sitting in the cramped office she shared with her colleagues, she scrolled through page after page of search engine results on her laptop, taking screenshots of each one for further research.

It was her lunch break and she was alone, her two fellow educational psychologists out with clients and Tris mired in an interdepartmental meeting regarding a new raft of budget cuts. She had intended to go outside, taking advantage of the warm, breezy day, but the unexpected fruitfulness of her search had rooted her to her chair.

From what she could make out, the fandom was roughly split three ways: fans of true crime programmes and shows who cited the Ewan Stokes case as one of the most intriguing; casual observers who shared their own theories about the reasons Stokesy had disappeared and watched for so-called 'Stokesy sightings'; and the diehard fans, those most active in the online forums, who held him up as both a hero and proof of the heartlessness of society. It was this final group which drew Cora's attention, largely because they shared the most developed sense of a 'Stokesy world': where every detail, no matter how insignificant, could be spun into justification of their own world views.

As a psychologist, it was fascinating: noting the personality types connected to this group and the specific language terms they used to communicate within it. There were frequent mentions of the 'inner circle' and something called 'the Club', although her searches for more information on this term had so far drawn a blank. Whatever the relevance of it, those in the most extreme category clearly considered themselves greater than mere fans of Ewan Stokes. They were the faithful, his most trusted men-at-arms, upholders of his memory who loyally awaited his return.

One thing connected all of the most avid fans: their absolute belief that Stokesy would return. It was almost messianic in fervour.

'Thinking of joining an online forum?'

Cora looked up to see a weary, smiling Tris Noakes.

'Just looking,' she replied, watching her boss as he flopped down into the nearest chair. 'How did it go?'

He blew out a long sigh. 'The usual bollocks. I don't know how the council is still functioning, with all the hoops they expect us to jump through. Every meeting is a direct copy of the last, with nothing achieved but blood pressures raised and department heads like me condemned to lose sleep until the next one.' He rubbed the back of his neck and grinned at her. 'You know, my predecessor here always kept a bottle of Whyte & Mackay in the bottom drawer of his desk. Now I know why.'

'If you helped yourself to whisky from your desk drawer every time this job stressed you out you'd be asleep in minutes.' Cora smiled. Tris' low tolerance for spirits was a well-known fact in the department office.

'Ah, but think of the blessed sleep I could enjoy...' He grinned back, peering over at Cora's laptop. 'So, what is that stuff?'

'It's something DI Anderson mentioned to me. An online fandom that's grown around an unsolved missing-person case in Suffolk.' She turned her screen to face Tris. 'Do you remember Ewan Stokes?'

Her colleague's face lit up. 'Stokesy? Everyone remembers him. Is that what you're looking at?'

Cora nodded. 'It's unlike anything else I've seen before. Like they've stolen his image and just invented a whole narrative around it.'

'It's intense. I did a study on the phenomenon a few years ago, actually.'

'Really?'

'It was Stokesy's case that set me off on the search. My older brother Ciaran knew him well – they were in the same football team. I saw

48

the impact his disappearance had on Ciaran and my friends, even years later. Then I heard about the re-emergence of interest in the case after it was covered by a true crime documentary, and when I started to look into his virtual fandom, it sparked the whole study. Fascinating stuff.'

'What can you tell me about it? I keep finding references to an inner circle group called "the Club", but beyond mentions of the name I can't find anything else.'

'I'm not surprised,' Tris said with a wry smile. 'They're very much a closed shop. I had a brush with them, quite by chance, late on in my study. I'd been asking some questions in the main Stokesy forum and they didn't like it.'

'Questions about what?'

Tris let out a long sigh. 'There's a theory many of the most avid members of the forum ascribe to. I traced it back to a mention about a year before the true crime documentary aired. They call it the "Fifteen Year Return". You see it in mentions using the hashtag "15". Apparently, the theory proposes that Stokesy is waiting for the fifteenth anniversary of his disappearance to come back to Suffolk.'

'Why do they think that?'

'Well, this is what I was trying to establish. It seems widely accepted and yet I couldn't find any supporting evidence for the claim. Not in any of the supposed yearly messages from him, not in any of the reports that followed in the wake of the true crime documentary. His fans believe he's returning to take revenge on those he holds responsible for making him run.'

Cora stared back. 'Wow. So a messianic-style return?'

'Exactly. There's a list — several lists, in fact — of likely revenge targets. It's passed between users, often with more names being added. His ex, a former boss, one of the other players on the football team who played in the match on the night he went missing, the coach of the team, several other names that come and go. It's all conjecture: there's no evidence beyond the mentions on the forum. And, as I discovered, the members aren't too happy to discuss why these lists exist.'

'What happened?'

'I was warned off. Private messages telling me to back off or there would be consequences.' He laughed at Cora's surprise. 'Implausible as that sounds. I thought it was playground stuff to begin with – bully boys putting a new kid in his place, you know – but it quickly took a turn. They said they'd track my IP address, leak personal details online, contact my employers, the whole shebang.'

Cora couldn't believe what she was hearing. 'Threats from an online fan club? Who does that?'

Her colleague's smile faded. 'They're no fan club. The last message I received had a photo of my house attached.'

'That's insane. Did you report it?'

'I should have. But back then I don't think police took online threats seriously. They know better now, of course.' He glanced at her screen. 'You're not approaching them, are you?'

'No, just looking.' She smiled at his concern. 'Arm's-length information gathering only.'

'Be very careful, okay? They look like a bunch of sad losers idolising a missing man, but some people connected to the fandom take it deadly seriously.'

Cora held up her hands. 'I'm not looking to talk to any of them.' She offered Tris a smile. 'It's just some background stuff for Joel Anderson.'

'Ah, the new moonlighting gig.' Tris grinned. 'I'm kidding. I think it's great, by the way, in case I hadn't already said.'

He had said this, several times in Anderson's office when Cora called him in to discuss the DI's offer and pretty much constantly on their way back to work. Having Tris onside was a definite perk of Cora's job. She had never worked with anyone so unabashed in their support of her.

'Let's just say I'm not in any doubt of it. Thank you.'

'My pleasure. You've made such a difference to this department – it's the least I could do in return.'

Cora smiled and turned back to the online forum on her screen. 'I don't suppose you kept any of the research you did on the Stokesy fans, did you?'

Tris raised an eyebrow. 'Seriously? You're asking the man who can't even bear to throw till receipts away if he binned important research materials? I'll dig out the files for you.'

'You're a star, thank you.'

Hauling himself out of the chair, Tris headed for his office. At the door, he looked back.

'Don't interact with anyone on there, okay? Not until you've seen the files.'

'I won't,' Cora promised, her eyes drawn to a single new entry that had just appeared in the forum thread:

SIGHTING UPDATE: Felixstowe Pier, Suffolk, UK.

Coppers already on the scene, asking about him.

It must be real if they're investigating.

He's back. It's happening.

#Stokesy15

Nine

ANDERSON

Minshull would loathe him for it, but talking to his father was necessary.

Even still, Anderson had hated asking. The old bastard had been bad enough to work for: he couldn't imagine the hell of having DCI John Minshull as a father.

Reading the fifteen-year-old documents in the original case files for Ewan Stokes was like travelling back in time. Anderson pictured his sour-faced, sharp-tongued former boss holding court in the office he now called his own, barking orders at everyone, making every interaction a battle. DCI John Minshull, South Suffolk Constabulary's famous son, the legend of whose tenure still hung around Police HQ like a stubborn odour.

John Minshull had insisted on staying within the CID offices, despite his senior position, sticking his oar into every aspect of everyday investigations. Not for him the comfortable office at a distance from operations, as favoured by the current DCI, Sue Taylor. Paperwork wasn't John Minshull's style. Interference and intimidation were.

The memory of the former incumbent of his office wedged behind the desk made Anderson get up and pace the space instead, the movement a silent signal to the ghost of his former superior officer that he was nothing like him and never would be. Rob Minshull would never be like his father, either. He didn't even look like the old sod – an added blessing. They didn't always see eye to eye, but Rob Minshull was driven by a fierce sense of justice and fairness. Anderson held a deep respect for that. The fire in Rob burned for the benefit of everyone else, never himself. That must stick in his father's throat the most.

'Everything okay, Guv?' Wheeler asked, arriving in the doorway with fresh mugs of coffee. Or Wheeler's interpretation of coffee, at least.

'Tell me what you think of this,' Anderson replied, handing over a stapled bundle of sheets.

'Maisie Ingram,' Wheeler read. 'Why does that name sound familiar?'

'Former girlfriend of Ewan Stokes. She appeared with Stokes' mother and sister at the initial press conference appealing for inform-ation. She was reportedly the last person to see him on the night he disappeared. According to her statement she had argued with Stokes alone in the car park following the football match, and he had driven away.' He pointed to the top sheet of the set Wheeler now held. 'But then, six months later, Ewan Stokes' sister Marilyn changed her statement to say she had seen her brother fighting with Ms Ingram and heard Maisie say she wished him dead.'

Wheeler flipped the page and did a double take at the revised statement. 'And the mother corroborated the story? But she wasn't at the football match, was she?'

'That's where it gets muddled. In the sister's first statement the mother wasn't listed as being among the group that attended the match. In Mrs Stokes' initial statement she said she'd been visiting a friend on the night her son vanished. Then, within weeks of the sister changing her statement – saying now that her mother was in the party – the mother follows suit.'

'So what changed? And why was it never investigated?' Wheeler's confusion mirrored Anderson's own. He acknowledged a sense of satisfaction in this: another spit in the eye for retired DCI John Minshull. 'There's nothing here to suggest anyone even asked the question.'

'Your guess is as good as mine. Other witness statements I've seen say Ms Ingram and Ewan Stokes had a fractious, volatile relationship.

One friend of Ms Ingram cited an argument that turned physical as the reason for her ending the relationship. If that was the case, did the mother and sister change their statements to protect Ewan Stokes, or punish Ms Ingram for leaving him?'

'Or did they have something to hide? Was Ms Ingram a useful distraction to deflect attention from them?'

Anderson considered this. 'It's a possibility. Everything's a possibility at this stage.'

Wheeler's eyes narrowed. 'You've asked Minsh to talk to his dad, haven't you?'

Chastened by the tone of the question, Anderson faced his colleague. 'I had no choice. John Minshull wouldn't deign to come in, and we couldn't wait for him to lead us a merry dance anyway.' He thought for a moment. 'Has Maisie Ingram's name come up in any of the online stuff the team have been looking at?'

'Better ask Ellis, Guv. He's been trawling the online fan sites. Don't envy him that task. Right bunch of weirdos, they are. Never seen anything like it. Grown men getting gooey-eyed about someone they've never even met. It isn't normal.'

'Call Drew in, would you?'

Wheeler ducked out and moments later returned with a stony-faced Ellis in tow.

'Drew, have you come across any conversation regarding Maisie Ingram, Mr Stokes' former girlfriend?'

Ellis rubbed the back of his neck. 'Plenty. Nasty stuff, a lot of it. Some of them think she was to blame for him leaving. They reckon that's why Stokesy's family turned against her.'

Anderson and Wheeler exchanged glances. 'How do they know that?'

'According to them it was in that true crime documentary that set the fan thing off. The mother and the sister said the girlfriend was the reason Stokes left. Seems the story got embellished over the years so all the blame got shifted on to her, poor woman. She spurned him, they say: she pushed him away. Some even think she tricked him into running away just to get rid of him. I reckon it's a load of rubbish, but that lot don't seem concerned with whether something's true or not. I mean, he's supposedly been sending messages every year on the anniversary of him going missing, but the way some of them talk about Maisie Ingram you'd think they suspected her of his murder.'

The assertion sat uneasily with Anderson.

'Does Ms Ingram still live in the area?' he asked Wheeler.

'I found a last known address and phone number we can try,' he replied.

'Do that, please,' Anderson replied. 'I think it's important we talk to her, as the last person to see Ewan Stokes. If she's still at that address, I'll ask Rob and Kate to go and see her. And I think we need to talk to Stokes' mother, too.'

'Yes, Guv.' Ellis headed back into the main CID office, leaving Wheeler standing beside Anderson.

'Dave, can you work with Drew to pull together any mentions of Ms Ingram or her family? It might help us to understand the background of the investigation better. From the case notes we have, it isn't clear at all.'

'Will do.' Wheeler nodded.

'And we need to watch that documentary, too. There may be obvious leads in it missed by the original investigation.'

'Drew's on the case. He's tracking down a copy for us.'

Anderson acknowledged this with a thumbs up. 'Good.'

Wheeler looked down at the piles of investigation files littering Anderson's office floor. 'You know, Guv, I've been trying to remember what was said in the office about it at the time, but I can't remember working much on the case. Can you?'

Anderson had attempted to do the same, until he'd checked the dates of the original investigation. 'That's because we were out on another job.'

'Were we?' Wheeler frowned.

Anderson walked across to his desk and pulled out an old desk diary, opening it to the week of Ewan Stokes' disappearance. 'Remember the Salt brothers case?'

He watched Wheeler's confusion suddenly give way to recognition. 'Now there's a blast from the past.'

'Old John Minshull had us working with a team from Norfolk trying to bust that smuggling ring up in Lowestoft. Most of the time the Ewan Stokes investigation was happening me and you were knee-deep in seaweed doing night stake-outs on the beach.'

'And stinkin' of fish! Bloody hell, I'd forgotten that. What a shout. John Minshull really hated us, didn't he?'

'Aye, he did.'

'Blimmin' Nora, Joel. Fifteen years ago. Me and you, the trouble-some upstarts of CID. Kids, we were.'

'Tell me about it. Although you'd not long got divorced. I remember you kept telling me you preferred hugging piles of old herring to waiting for her to make up her mind.'

'You're right! I meant it, too. That was before I met Sana and realised what a real woman was like,' Wheeler chuckled. 'I swear old Johnny Minshull chucked us out to Lowestoft on purpose just so he could get his sticky fingers on the case.'

'I wouldn't put it past him.'

'He wasn't even meant to be still in the CID office with us lot. But he just couldn't let go, could he?'

'Old bastard was never good at standing back. I thought the only way we'd ever get him out of this office was in a body bag when he'd breathed his last.'

Wheeler looked around the small office; Anderson followed his line of sight. The space was so different now from the way it had been in John Minshull's day. 'I bet you had to do a deep cleanse when you moved in here.'

'Full-blown exorcism, mate. Burning bundles of sage, chants, spells…'

Wheeler's laugh boomed into the office then ebbed away. 'And Minsh is facing all that right now.'

The heaviness returned to Anderson's stomach. 'It's necessary,' he repeated, wishing it wasn't.

Ten

MINSHULL

The Minshull family house was bathed in hopeful sunlight when Minshull arrived, far removed from how he felt. This place represented struggle and frustration, small bright moments of hope interspersed through it all, largely due to the calming influence of his mother and sister.

His sister Ellie wouldn't be here today, released from her appointed peacemaker responsibilities during the week as she worked as a teacher and cared for her own family. The sole remaining guardian of common sense in the family met him at the front door, his mother's smiles little comfort for what had to follow.

'Go easy on your dad,' she warned, the steel edge to her words impossible to miss. 'He can't unmake those mistakes.'

Minshull squared up to his mother, hating that once again he was forced to be on the opposing side to her by virtue of his father. 'He needs to answer for them. A family have lost their son…'

'Fifteen years ago.'

'Mum, I know what you're trying to do. You can't smooth this over. I need answers and he *will* give them to me.'

Fran Minshull's sigh fell like a dead weight on Minshull's shoulders as he passed her in the hall.

Retired DCI John Minshull sat where he always did these days, enthroned in an assisted mobility armchair, his skin and body and clothing as beige as the walls and furnishings around him. For a man who had prized power above all else during his career it was a sad, empty kingdom to preside over now. In gentler moments, Minshull could muster a little sympathy for his father's reduced situation. But not today. Today, he saw the architect of a failed investigation, a man who had preferred to sweep the evidence away rather than admit his operation had been flawed; a grifter who valued his own reputation and fame above the needs of a panicked family.

And John Minshull knew it.

From his curt word of welcome to the easy way his gaze passed from his son to the ever-burning gas fire in the hearth, every action screamed his objection.

'Seeing your old man on a school day? Must be my lucky day.'

Minshull ignored the jibe, centring his breath as he sat on the armchair opposite. 'I'm guessing you've heard the news?'

'Do you even have to ask?'

'We have good reason to believe the person captured on Felixstowe Pier's CCTV on Sunday night is Ewan Stokes.'

'The long game, then.'

Minshull frowned. 'Excuse me?'

John Minshull gave a hollow laugh. 'Suspected it from the beginning.'

'Suspected what?'

'The family. The *grieving mother*. The prodigal son returns. They had that script written from the start.' He turned to look at his son, disappointment large in his stare. 'And you fell for it. I might have guessed.'

So that was how it was going to be, was it? Minshull forced breath into his lungs, steadied his core, prepared to fight. 'I've fallen for nothing. The original investigation…'

'…was sound. Better than they all deserved.'

'…was littered with inconsistencies, hasty decisions, failures…'

'You won't say that word in my house!'

'*Failures*, Dad. You did the base minimum. And when results didn't materialise and press scrutiny grew, you dropped that family like a hot rock.'

'How dare you!'

It was wrong: everything about this exchange was wrong. Minshull had anticipated a little leeway before his father slammed the doors, some level of discussion before it descended into all-out war. His father was glowering, the muscles in his jaw and neck set like stone. Any moment now, the coughing would begin: John Minshull's favoured tactic to end potentially damaging arguments. But Minshull was ready for it this time.

It had been a long time coming.

John Minshull had wormed his way out of responsibility too often, had used his son's own better nature to silence him. Not today.

'I need to know everything you did in the original investigation. Who you suspected, who you interviewed, what leads you followed.'

'The case notes are there for you to read. I assume you know how to do that?'

'I want to hear it from you.'

His father gave a snort of disgust, launching into an impressive coughing fit to silence his son.

Minshull waited, head held high. He didn't flinch when the living room door flew open and his mother hurried in with a glass of water. He didn't accede to her warning stare. When the coughing ceased, he continued, his voice coolly controlled.

'You owe that family an explanation. You owe *me* your co-operation. Because we wouldn't be here if those mistakes hadn't been made, Dad. And I think you are acutely aware of that.'

John Minshull stared back, mouth slightly agape. Clearly, he hadn't expected such resistance from his son. But he wasn't done yet.

'I won't accept that tone, Robert. From you or anybody.'

'Robbie, maybe this conversation is one for another time,' Fran Minshull urged, ever the no man's land between these two seasoned battlers.

'I need answers now,' Minshull pressed. 'It can't wait.'

'It can take a break while you help me make coffee,' his mother insisted. 'You two need a time out.'

On any other day, Minshull would have agreed. Even now, as he prepared to refuse, the age-old fear of disappointing his mother reared up in his gut. His father was already waiting for it to happen, banking on the strength of his son's conscience to drag him back into line.

Not this time.

'It can't wait, Mum. I'm sorry. Dad needs to answer my questions and I need to get back to the investigation.' Hating the hurt he saw in her eyes, he turned back to his father. 'Why did you close the case?'

'There were no leads. No evidence. All hearsay. He fell out with his girlfriend, got a bit lairy and flounced off. My officers had better uses of their time than to be out looking for someone who clearly didn't want to be found.'

'And when Marilyn Stokes changed her story, six months later?'

'A desperate attempt to drag us back. I saw through it immediately.'

'Saw through it? You didn't even give it the time of day!'

'They were lying, Robert. That woman...'

'The distraught mother or grieving sister?'

'Both of them. But the mother was worse. She was a chancer. Something not right about the woman. That "concerned mother" act of hers was just that. An act. I didn't buy it then and I wouldn't buy it now. She played us for as long as we let her, then went running off to those bastard film-makers to drag us all through the mud.'

So that was what this was really about. John Minshull's precious reputation attacked after the fact, criticism he no longer had the authority to bury.

'I'm not concerned about that,' Minshull lied, resisting the urge to suggest that if his father had done his job correctly in the first place the documentary might never have happened. 'I want to know which avenues you pursued. What theories you formed.'

John Minshull groaned. 'All of which will be in the files.' He eyeballed his son. 'You're the one who insists on doing it all by the book: this should be right up your street.'

'I need answers now!' Minshull exploded.

'*Enough!*'

Both Minshull and his father stared at Fran Minshull, who had sprung to her slippered feet. She rarely shouted. But when she did, you listened.

'John, you will tell your son what he needs to know. If that missing man is coming back and promising revenge, the police have to be one step ahead of him. And Robbie, once you have your answers, I think it's best you leave. You both need time to calm down.'

Minshull sat back, his father bowing his head.

'There were rumours of an altercation Stokes had with the other striker on the team, but when we questioned the lad he denied it. Stokes' sister initially claimed she was the only other family member present; that is until she apparently remembered her own mother being there, six months later. Something shifty about her, too. We interviewed the girlfriend, ex-girlfriend, whatever she was – she confirmed she'd seen him after the match, but when Stokes tried to confront her she'd told him to leave her alone and he'd driven away. Unlike the mother and sister, who claimed the girlfriend had fought with Stokes and wished him dead. The girlfriend's sister told us Stokes was a thug who'd knocked the girl around. But none of his family or friends mentioned that, so I dismissed it.'

Of course, Minshull thought, gritting his teeth. According to his father, any altercation between lovers must automatically be the woman's fault and most likely a figment of her imagination. He glanced at his mother to see if she betrayed any response, but her expression remained set like granite.

'What about the other players on the football team?'

'None of them knew anything. I got the impression he was tolerated rather than liked.'

'And the manager?'

'Said he hadn't seen Stokes after the game ended.'

'Did he say anything about Ewan Stokes as a team player? How he got on with the rest of the team, or any worries he'd expressed to his coach?'

'None that I can recall.'

'Then who was your chief suspect?'

'Nobody. It was a dead-end case from the start. Clearly, the lad just wanted to leave, so he did. We were never going to find him, despite what those idiots in the press thought.'

'But you did try to find him?'

'Of course we did!' John Minshull snorted, his bony hands gripping the arms of his chair. 'What do you take us for? We did ground searches, checked ports and airports, circulated details with neighbouring forces. Covered the well-known suicide spots. What more could we have done?'

Minshull's stomach balled with tension. It was infuriating, but the investigation had covered all bases. Apart from one.

'Why didn't you investigate Marilyn Stokes' altered statement?'

'I told you: she was clearly out for attention. Just like her mother.'

'They were desperate to find him!' Minshull retorted. He shouldn't have been surprised to discover his father's prejudiced judgement, yet it hit him as hard as a physical slap. 'Scared that the police were closing ranks against the family, preparing to bin the case.'

'Exactly! And what better way to keep us on a wild goose chase than to suddenly discover new evidence?'

'Did you double-check with any of the people originally interviewed about that night?'

'Are you questioning the integrity of my investigation?'

'*Did* you?'

They were both on the edges of their seats again, John Minshull's ragged breathing louder than the vociferous mantel clock that underpinned every exchange in this room with its harsh, insistent beat. He made to fight back, then dropped his stare.

'No.'

The word hung defiantly between them in the stifling heat of the room. John Minshull slumped a little.

'They weren't credible. My team needed to focus on results and we had bigger fish to fry.'

'Results.' Minshull shook his head, the fury in his voice replaced by calm, cold disgust.

'Robbie, I think it might be best if...' Fran Minshull began, but her son was already on his feet.

'Don't worry, I'm going.' He shot his father one last, unflinching stare. 'You failed them, Dad. You failed that family. I won't make the same mistake.'

Denying John Minshull any chance to reply, he walked out.

THE CLUB

@424gav The coppers were there. We saw them.

@flamestr You went to the pier?

@424gav Bunch of us did. And a copper came up asking about Stokesy.

@flamestr What did you tell him?

@424gav Told him to mind his own business :)

@flamestr Yeah right.

@424gav Nah, he just moved us on because the security bloke on the pier was whining. Gave me his card, asked us to talk to him about Stokesy.

@flamestr Name of the copper?

@424gav DS Rob Minshull. Ipswich CID.

@flamestr Legit?

@424gav 100%. We saw his card.

@flamestr Wasn't there a copper called Minshull when Stokesy went missing? They named him in The Missing Son.

@424gav Don't know. Probably. Will check.

@flamestr Did you tell him anything?

@424gav I'm not dumb.

@flamestr That's not what your missus says :D :D

@424gav Stokesy's got the jump on them. They're playing catch-up.

@flamestr All the same keep an eye out. Especially this Minshull. If it's a family thing he might be out to get him. #Stokesy15 is happening. We can't let anyone stop him.

Eleven

MINSHULL

It didn't hit him until he was driving back to South Suffolk Police HQ. When it did, Minshull had no choice but to pause his journey.

His head felt light and dizzy, a clench of tension at the centre of his chest constricting his breath. A familiar old panic gripped him, beads of cold sweat pooling where his palms held the steering wheel. He had to get his breath, wrestle back control. It wasn't safe to drive until he did.

He pulled off the main road into a lay-by beside a popular beauty spot. A small mobile food wagon served the best breakfasts here, and beyond that a path meandered through lush woodland to emerge beside the river. He'd come here many times over the years – to think, to get away from the constant pace of his job, to breathe.

A few weeks ago, he'd brought Cora here, too.

The memory of their conversation on the riverbank that day made him reach for his phone. Leaning his head back against the seat rest he closed his eyes as he waited for the call to connect.

'Detective Minshull! This is a pleasant surprise.' The playfulness of her tone danced against his ear.

'Hey, Cora.' She'd hear it as immediately as he did: the breathless pain, the heavy grate of his words. It was too late to think better of this.

'What's happened? Are you okay?'

'I…' He kicked himself for faltering. 'I just visited my dad. On official business.'

'Is he in trouble?'

A humourless laugh escaped Minshull's chest, a stab against the crush of panic still resident there. As if John Minshull would ever answer for his misdemeanours, many though there were. He wouldn't know accountability if his livelihood depended upon it.

'Rob?'

'He ran the initial investigation into Ewan Stokes. He bodged the whole thing. Joel Anderson sent me to talk to him...' He forced a breath into his tight lungs. 'We didn't talk.'

There was a long pause from Cora, so long that Minshull wondered if his words had embarrassed her. Then her question came: velvet-sheathed, diamond-edged. 'How bad was it?'

'Bad.' The word left him on a deep exhale. 'I don't know, Cora. He won't ever accept that he's wrong. He stuffed up the investigation, he destroyed that family's trust in the police, and then he has the gall to suggest that the family deserved it.'

'What?'

'I should have kept a cool head, refused to rise to his bullshit. But I lost it. I just... *lost it.*'

'You were in a stressful situation. Probably with little warning or time to prepare, right?'

It helped that she understood that. Minshull suspected she understood so much more of the situation than she was letting him see. 'I had no time. Apart from most of my life.'

'Maybe it was time to say it.'

'It didn't feel like that. My mum didn't see it that way.'

'Ah.' She paused again. 'You haven't let her down by expressing how you feel.'

Minshull watched the people in the snack van queue and said nothing. He swallowed down the emotion, willing it away.

'You had to ask the questions. His response was at fault, not your confrontation.'

'Maybe.'

'It's so hard. But you had a job to do and you did it.'

Her words were kind and some solace lay in their warmth, but he had embarrassed himself enough. Straightening his spine, he forced power into his body. 'Have you found anything new on the fan forums?'

Cora didn't appear surprised by the sudden swing of topic. Minshull knew she wouldn't be. 'I've been tracking some conversations surrounding the forum members' theories of why Stokesy went missing. The sighting seems to have dredged it all up again.'

'And?'

'There's so much vile stuff directed at his ex-girlfriend, Maisie. A lot of it misogynistic, using her as an example to support their own prejudices against women. But what concerns me are the brags about what certain members would like to do to punish her. And what they hope Stokesy will do in his supposed Fifteen Year Return revenge attacks.'

'You think they're making credible threats?'

'I told Joel I thought it was unlikely. But that was before I saw the actual interactions on the fan forum. It's enabling violence, growing a culture where that kind of threatening language becomes a trading currency. It would be too easy for someone fed a diet of that to take it as licence to act in real life.'

'Bloody hell. Do they think Stokes is violent enough to carry out real-life attacks?'

'Their version of him is. It doesn't matter what the real Ewan Stokes is like: the idol they've built in his likeness can be anything they decide.'

This was new, uncertain territory and Minshull didn't like not understanding the terrain. 'I need to talk to Stokes' mother. There were things Dad said that...' He killed the end of the sentence, regrouped. 'She knows her son, better than any of his so-called fans. It's time we talked to her. She's been let down and ignored enough.'

'I can't imagine that's going to be easy.'

Minshull smiled despite the weight bearing down on his shoulders. 'It's the day for it, it seems. Better to do it all in one go.'

Cora laughed. 'Good attitude.'

'Thanks, Dr Lael.'

'My pleasure. You can talk to me about anything, any time. You know that?'

Minshull hated that he'd brought his problems to her door. But the relief he felt with her response outweighed the loss of control. 'Thank you, for listening. It... helped.'

When the call ended, Minshull rolled the knots from his shoulders. He gave a last longing look at the start of the woodland path, the coolness of the tree shade calling to him. Then he found Anderson's number and dialled.

'Rob. How did it go?'

'He's not going to help us, Guv.'

'Ah. I thought as much.'

'I want to go and see Olwyn Stokes. We need to show her a better intention this time.'

'Agreed. I'll make the call. Head back here and then take Bennett with you when we get the go-ahead. Two-person jobs for the rest of today, eh?'

God bless Anderson and his bumbling attempts at compassion. Theirs wasn't the easiest of relationships, but at least Anderson was trying. And Minshull wasn't about to argue. It would be better with Bennett there.

It was time to show Olwyn Stokes that she could rely on them. And that together they could uncover the truth about her son.

Twelve

MINSHULL

Waiting by the front door of the moderately sized detached house, Minshull rehearsed his opening gambit, doing his best to hide his nerves from Bennett. He had no reason to be nervous: he hadn't been involved in the original investigation. Hadn't even been in the police at the time of Ewan Stokes' disappearance.

But his father *had*.

Would Olwyn Stokes make the connection? How many other Minshulls were there in South Suffolk Police? There could be many – it wasn't an uncommon surname in this part of the world. Except Minshull knew no other fellow coppers in South Suffolk Police shared his last name.

She was a chancer. Something not right about the woman.

His father's condemnatory words muscled uninvited into his mind. How dare he say that about a worry-stricken mother of a missing son? Those two sentences summed up John Minshull's attitude perfectly. She hadn't been of use to him, more like: the case remaining unsolved an irritating mark on the *great man*'s career. He had dropped her the instant her case attracted unwelcome scrutiny of the DCI's effectiveness. Some judge of character he proved to be!

Maybe it was time to say it.

Cora's words returned to bolster his resolve, as potent now as they had been when he'd called her. Confronting John Minshull with his litany of past mistakes was necessary – and long overdue, both for him and the woman he hoped wouldn't slam the door in his face. Olwyn Stokes had agreed to Anderson's request for a visit, but that was no guarantee she would welcome Minshull and Bennett into her home.

The shadow of an approaching figure smoked the patterned front door glass like the dark approach of an impending storm. When the latch was lifted, the woman revealed was shrouded in dark shades and sadness: jet-black dyed hair worn short at the sides and voluminously spiky on top, a fitted smoke-grey dress and a long black cardigan draped over her angular shoulders. Her pale face and heavily shadowed eyes glared out at Minshull and Bennett, her thin burgundy-red lips forced into a single, grim line.

'Mrs Stokes? I'm...'

'I know who you are,' she said, her reply severing the end of his words like a diamond-sharp blade. 'And I'm Mrs Stokes-*Norton*, thank you.'

Already on the back foot, Minshull scrambled to make his apologies. 'I'm sorry. May we come in?'

She didn't answer, her back inclining towards the open door instead. The thinnest of invitations. Resisting the urge to glance at Bennett, Minshull stepped into the house.

It was comfortably furnished, warm and filled with the kind of quiet order Minshull's mum kept at the family home. But when Minshull and Bennett sat on the striped linen sofa, the room felt starkly empty. A dimming of the light, despite summer sunshine bathing the living room from the large windows. The expectation of a heartbeat here where there was none.

She's lost her son, he reminded himself, shrugging off the discomfort. Something was missing here: a life that should have remained vital and present. How did the families of the long-term missing deal with the stubbornly empty space where their loved one should be? Ewan Stokes could be dead or alive, the messages sent by anyone to maintain the myth about him. Could you mourn, not knowing whether a death had occurred?

And what of the current developments? All of this Minshull planned to ask Olwyn Stokes-Norton. Whether he would get that far into the conversation before being shown the door was another question. Judging by her guarded body language and conscience-piercing stare, that was far from certain.

'Thank you for agreeing to see us,' Minshull began, careful to maintain eye contact. 'I appreciate how difficult it must be.'

A slight rise of her eyebrow. Nothing more.

Minshull pressed on. 'I understand you've seen the CCTV footage from Felixstowe Pier?'

'I'm aware of it.' When Minshull waited to reply, Olwyn relented a little. 'Your superior emailed me the clip.'

It was a tiny opening that could snap shut at any moment. Minshull picked his words cautiously. 'I have to ask – in your opinion, was that Ewan?'

She didn't reply immediately, as he'd thought she might. Either to affirm her belief it was, or vehemently deny it wasn't. Instead, she kept her eyes trained on him as she took a long, unhurried breath. Minshull wondered if journalists had attempted to reach her since the sighting was circulated on the fan forums: if she was already weary of the question.

'It's difficult to tell,' she said at last, nothing in her body language betraying her feelings about this. 'He has the height and appearance of Ewan, but it's been fifteen years since I last saw him. I don't know what he looks like now.'

'Of course,' Minshull replied, aware of Bennett fidgeting self-consciously beside him. 'Forgive me, these questions may seem unfeeling and direct, but I have to ask them.'

'That's your job.' Her tone was hollow. If Minshull thought he could detect an unseen weight attached to her reply, he dismissed it quickly. Olwyn had every right to be angry with the police.

'Has he attempted to contact you?'

'No.'

'Or anyone in your family? Your daughter, perhaps?'

'My daughter wants no part of this.'

The reply was whip-fast, her expression instantly stony. What was going on there? 'I see,' Minshull replied, winded. 'May I ask why?'

Olwyn's eyes narrowed. 'The years haven't been kind to my daughter. Marilyn found it… taxing. On her mental health. She has her reasons for stepping back.'

'And you support them?'

'I'm her mother.'

Pushing his luck, Minshull tried a different route. 'If there are more sightings, if they prove to be your son, a time may come where I need to speak to everyone in the family. It's possible that other family members may have had some contact. His sister, perhaps, or his biological father.'

'His father is dead. Died twenty-five years ago, long after he'd left me. Ewan wouldn't want to have anything to do with him even if he were alive.'

'His sister, then?'

'I told you, DS Minshull, leave my daughter out of this.'

'With respect, Mrs Stokes-Norton, your daughter changed her statement. She's part of this whether she wants to be or not.'

'She was protecting me, okay?'

Minshull was aware that Bennett was staring, as was he. 'Protecting you?'

Olwyn Stokes-Norton gave a shuddering sigh. 'It was my fault – I was so distraught when Ewan went missing, and in the first few days I didn't handle things well. I'm not ashamed to admit that I fell to pieces. I think Marilyn wanted to shield me from all the questions, all the accusations swirling in the papers. I discovered what she'd done after she'd made her first statement: I couldn't contradict her with mine. So I said I was with a friend that night. Which I had been, prior to the match. But I was there. And as time went on, and the police increasingly lost interest, I persuaded Marilyn to tell the truth. For Ewan's sake. I thought it would make a difference.' She gave a hollow laugh. 'More fool me.'

'But Ewan could have been in contact with Marilyn. Could she be shielding you now?'

'She's not capable of… She isn't *well*, Detective Sergeant. And are you implying my son might have chosen to leave me out of his communications?'

'No, I—'

'He was my world, DS Minshull. My reason for living. I was always the one Ewan ran to first. *First*, do you understand?' Tears welled in her eyes, visible pain evident now.

'My sincere apologies.' He was losing ground, and fast. Something needed to change. 'Our initial investigation failed you, Mrs Stokes-Norton. That's what I came here to say.' He ignored the stiffening of Bennett beside him, forcing his focus to remain on the woman they had come to see. 'I believe things were missed that could have helped us locate Ewan sooner. That you weren't believed when Marilyn altered her statement. I won't make the same mistake. If you work with me – if you agree to trust me – I will do everything in my power to rectify those mistakes.'

It was a hell of a gambit, but Minshull followed his gut. Anderson would kick him all the way from the Stokes-Norton residence to Police HQ if he knew the admission Minshull had just made. Ignoring the twisting of his nerves during the marked silence that followed, he held Olwyn's stare. Had her frown softened? Or had he just played into the potentially litigious hands of a very publicly wronged woman?

If it failed, he would have no other course to pursue. He would lose any hope of the family's co-operation and potentially damage the reopened investigation in its earliest days.

And as for explaining this to the rest of the team and Anderson…

'I want him home.'

The fire was gone from her, the weight of loss evident once again. 'Of course.'

'That's all I've ever wanted.' Her sigh shuddered as it left her. 'Ewan liked to play tough but he was fragile inside. I'm the only one who truly understood that. He was a good boy, deep down. I can't bear to think what must have happened to drive him away from us – and keep him away all these years. If he is coming back – if that really is my son – I just want him home.'

That 'concerned mother' act of hers is just that. An act. I didn't buy it then and I wouldn't buy it now…

Minshull mentally kicked his father's opinion to the dusty recesses of his mind. John Minshull had failed this woman badly and then had the audacity to blame her for his actions. But he was no longer the one steering the search for Ewan Stokes. John Minshull's opinion meant nothing here.

'I won't promise to bring Ewan home,' he said. 'I can't do that. But I will do everything in my power to find him. You have my word.'

Olwyn Stokes-Norton observed him for an elongated moment. 'Then I'll help in any way I can.'

Bennett was silent in the car on the slow drive back from Felixstowe to Ipswich. Minshull resisted the urge to press her for conversation: he knew the reason for her silence. It was only when the suburbs of Ipswich came into view that she spoke.

'I think you made a mistake, Sarge.'

There it was.

Minshull kept his eyes on the road. 'Why?'

'Admitting the police let her down. *Failed* her, you said. That's litigious.'

'I know.'

'Do you? With respect, Sarge, that was a bad move. She has every reason to blame police for how the investigation was conducted: you just handed her ammunition to open fire on us.'

She was right – he hadn't intended to say those words. But fury still raged within him following the exchange with his father. He knew it would fuel his actions moving forward, regardless of how wise this course would be. 'We need her onside. She is the only person who can say for certain if the webcam guy is her son.'

'Her daughter could tell us,' Bennett countered.

'Marilyn Stokes wants nothing to do with the case.'

'So her mother said. But if we could find a way to talk to her...'

'Kate, I understand your concern, but you have to trust me.'

'I do,' Bennett replied, but it was a small, mumbled answer that offered little comfort.

'But?' He was irritated now, his hands taut on the steering wheel.

'Just be careful, Sarge. That's all.'

She didn't elaborate and he didn't ask her to. A loaded silence hung between them for the rest of their journey back to CID.

Thirteen

ELLIS

'We approached South Suffolk Constabulary for a comment but they declined...'

'Bollocks, did you,' Ellis mumbled, biscuit crumbs tumbling from his mouth as he noted the claim. His notebook was already two pages full of notes he'd taken while watching *The Missing Son*, the true crime documentary allegedly responsible for propelling Stokesy and his unsolved case to a global audience. Tech had managed to track down a copy of the full documentary, rather than the edited videos, widely shared on YouTube, which had been all Ellis could find. Searches for the original documentary makers had so far proved fruitless, but the complete film they had produced made for eye-opening viewing.

'Criticism of the police investigation was widespread, with many in the media calling for an inquiry into systemic failures that led to the new statement from Marilyn Stokes being disregarded and the case shelved. I asked Marilyn how that made her feel.

"They just didn't listen to us. I think they'd already made up their minds."

"About dropping the case?"

"About everything. About our family. About me. The DCI in charge couldn't get us out of his office fast enough. I never felt like he trusted us. I mean, he was supposed to be helping us find Ewan. Nobody should be made to feel like they made us feel."

"And how did you feel?"

"Betrayed. Abandoned. I don't think we'll ever recover..."'

Ellis bit down on his criticism as he reached for another biscuit. What he'd wanted to say in response to the clearly targeted questioning would have made him no better than the original investigators. But had they really been openly disrespected, as Stokesy's mother and sister were claiming here? Or was it inflated rhetoric to reignite interest in a cold case?

'Oi! Leave some biscuits for the rest of us,' Wheeler called from the tiny kitchen area in the corner of the CID office. 'I only brought those in this morning. Chocolate biscuits are a treat, not a commodity.'

'Sorry.' Ellis grinned, mouth full.

Wheeler's good-natured eye-roll was the softest rebuke. He strolled over to Ellis' desk. 'How's it looking?'

Ellis patted his notes. 'Plenty of food for thought. Happily bashing our lot, though.'

'No surprise there. Wouldn't make good telly if they said we were competent and did everything we could. Doesn't fit the narrative, does it?'

'I can see why people got obsessed with this doc, though. They spin it like Stokesy is this huge victim. A bit of a lad who didn't deserve to be made to run.'

Wheeler squinted at the screen. Sooner or later he would have to accept that he needed glasses, as all his colleagues knew, but today was not that day.

'Do they mark out any suspects?'

'Not really.' Ellis flicked back a page in his notes, running his finger down the feint-ruled lines and hasty scrawl until he found what he wanted. 'They hint at there being trouble with a few of the other players on the football team – some banter that got out of hand. His mum says he was unhappy at work, that he had a couple of run-ins with his boss. Then there's the insistence from Marilyn that she heard Maisie Ingram wish Stokesy dead. But they don't go into that, or even mention if they approached Ms Ingram for comment. It's just dropped like a grenade and then they move on.'

'Clickbait TV, in't it?' Wheeler offered. 'Everything's a sound bite: dropping little nuggets here and there like a crumb trail, slapping some ominous music under it all so you believe there's a conspiracy. But nothing concrete so they can't be sued. Clever, if you think about it.'

Ellis frowned at the screen, paused on Marilyn Stokes' pained expression. 'Exploitative, more like. Look at her face – she doesn't want to be there.'

'Exploitative for sure, but she's on camera giving her story. She must have agreed to that. Maybe the memory of it is making the interview uncomfortable.'

'I'm not sure.' Where the other interviewees in the documentary all seemed at home during their vox pops, Marilyn looked scared. Could she have known more about why her brother ran than she was letting on here? 'If we could talk to her, I reckon we'd find stuff Minsh's dad missed.'

'You'll have a job.' Wheeler smirked, pinching a chocolate biscuit from the packet Ellis held. 'Nobody knows where she is. I tried tracking her down, but the address we have on file isn't hers. Journalists haven't found her, either, judging by the archive reports I found. Seems this is her only appearance.'

'Her mum would know,' Ellis countered, snatching the packet out of reach as Wheeler went in for a second helping. 'She could be telling Minsh and Kate where to find her right now.'

'She could be. But I doubt it. Look at Marilyn's eyes: terrified. If her mother has any sense she'll keep her daughter safe.'

Ellis turned his attention back to the screen as Wheeler returned to his workstation. He checked the timestamps he'd logged and scrolled back to an earlier section of the documentary.

The film-maker was doing a piece to camera, standing in a wide, empty playing field.

'This is where Ewan Stokes was last seen alive. An hour after the football game that had seen him score the winning goal in extra time, somewhere around where I'm standing, which would have been the sideline of the match. Initial statements revealed an argument with his girlfriend of two years, Maisie Ingram. It was no secret that the couple had had problems and had temporarily split, but in recent weeks Ewan Stokes had said he believed they were close to reconciliation.

The heated exchange was witnessed by several of his friends. Most dismissed it as yet another row in a long line of lovers' tiffs. However, in the changed statement Ewan's sister Marilyn made, six months after her brother disappeared, a darker story emerged...'

The picture cut to a slow pan of the football field, a bottle-green filter applied to the shot, a low minor-key drone underpinning the scene. Over the visuals came the voice of Marilyn Stokes.

"'It wasn't their usual fighting. Maisie was yelling at Ewan, slapping and punching him. He was trying to calm her down. I'd never seen her so angry. It was like she was possessed. Ewan managed to grab her hands and that's when I heard her say it – *I wish you were dead!*..."

"Was it just something said to shock your brother away?"

"No. It scared me. Because in that moment I believed Maisie was capable of anything."

"Even murder?"

"Even that.'"

The playing field shot began to merge with a blurred photo of Maisie Ingram posing on a beach with Ewan Stokes, their arms entwined, their bodies close, grinning for the camera. The sinister juxtaposition of the happy image and his sister's words achieved everything the documentary makers had intended.

It presented Maisie Ingram as a potential killer.

Pausing the video, Ellis flicked his computer screen to an open window of StokesyFans, showing a recent speculative thread aimed at the young woman.

Maisie Ingram started this. Stokesy's going to finish it.

Finish her, more like.

One for the List. Justice for our boy. #Stokesy15

Ellis shuddered.

'How goes it?' Anderson had stealth-entered the main CID office once again, his sudden appearance making Ellis start.

'It's no wonder this rubbish is being spouted on StokesyFans,' Ellis said, turning his monitor so Anderson could see the screen.

His superior's instant reaction spoke volumes. '*The Missing Son* documentary totally threw Maisie under the bus. His fans think she's responsible. That she threatened to kill him and that's why he ran.'

'Then we need to talk to her immediately.' Anderson turned to Wheeler. 'Dave, any joy on contact details for Maisie Ingram?'

'She's still living at the address we have on file,' Wheeler replied. 'St Ives Close, Kesgrave.'

Behind him, Evans looked up from his desk.

'Right. I'll call Rob and Kate and ask them to head there when they are done with Olwyn Stokes.'

Wheeler frowned. 'Really, Guv? Drew and I could go...'

'Not this time. We need continuity. I'll make the call.'

As he swept back into his office, Ellis and Wheeler exchanged grimaces. Evans ducked his head and returned to work.

Fourteen

MINSHULL

Minshull's head ached. His mind protested at the relentless onslaught today had brought. But Cora's concern over forum discussions about Maisie Ingram, coupled with his father's easy dismissal of the 'girl-friend, ex-girlfriend, whatever', who may well have been subject to violent attacks from Stokes, strengthened his resolve. This was about putting right John Minshull's wrongs – and finding the truth that had evaded them for so long.

He had to admit he was surprised that Maisie was still at the same address, given the vitriol directed at her online and the negative focus *The Missing Son* thrust upon her. If it had been him, he would have put as much distance between himself and the area as he could.

Maybe Maisie Ingram was made of sterner stuff.

But what were the chances of anyone still being at the same address fifteen years on *and* having the same mobile number? Minshull couldn't fathom it. He had moved three times during that period and had several changes of mobile number. Even his father, stubbornly stuck in the family home for the past forty years, had changed his phone number at least three times.

When they met, he would ask her.

The drive out to the small town of Kesgrave, east of Ipswich, was a pleasant one this afternoon, warm July sunshine flooding the passing fields and the road ahead of the pool car as Minshull drove. In the passenger seat, Bennett scrolled through a potted history of the Stokesy case, compiled and sent to her by Ellis.

'Man, the family pulled a fast one on the girlfriend,' she said, frowning at her phone. 'Why change their statement six months after Stokesy had gone missing?'

'Maybe they fell out with her. Maybe they blamed her for him leaving.'

'Or maybe they thought new evidence would keep police investigating when the trail had gone cold?'

Minshull glanced at his colleague, wishing his father's theory wasn't reverberating in his mind. 'I don't think we can discount that, either.'

'I don't understand why their new evidence was never investigated.'

'It should have been.'

'I guess the bods in charge decided it was a lost cause,' Bennett said, her mouth quickly clamping shut.

Too late: Minshull felt the kick. *The bods in charge* – or one *bod* in particular...

He was still seething over the casual manner with which John Minshull had defended his decision. It was wrong: it went against every point of good practice. A decent SIO would have made sure any new information was gone into. But John Minshull was anything but decent. Cutting corners, dismissing evidence when it suited him: that was his *modus operandi*. It was entirely conceivable that he'd decided the Stokesy investigation was a non-starter and shelved it to make his department look good. Open-ended cases didn't make your team look efficient. Picking and choosing cases with the potential for fast results did – and where fast results meant improvising with the truth, John Minshull was only too happy to make it happen.

His hands gripped the steering wheel.

He'd fought hard at work to distance himself from the towering legacy of his father. Until now he thought he'd done well to avoid any comparisons. But this was going to bring it right back to the fore, wasn't it? Being reminded of his father's unswerving belief that Rob was John Minshull reincarnate – a second generation sent to continue the first's work. Being lectured, judged and found wanting. Cast back into the shadow he'd battled so hard to avoid...

'I'm sure the bods in charge did exactly that,' he replied flatly.

'Sarge, I didn't mean…'

'Don't worry about it. You made a good point.'

He heard Bennett swear under her breath, the rustle of her suit jacket as she twisted in her seat to face him. 'You're not him, Minsh. You're worth a hundred of him.'

Stunned, Minshull stared at the road ahead.

'Sorry, Sarge. I think I've been spending too much time with Dave Wheeler. He reckons we should be more honest with each other in the team. So, for what it's worth, that's what I think.'

Minshull steered the car to a halt beside a modest bungalow set back from the road with a long stretch of well-cared-for lawn in front. Killing the engine, he looked at Bennett.

'Appreciate that, thanks.'

She offered him the briefest pink-cheeked smile before turning her attention to Maisie Ingram's home. 'Oh. Looks like Ms Ingram is planning to move after all.'

Minshull followed her pointing finger to a very new-looking For Sale sign rising from the low garden wall that separated the lawn from the pavement. In this at least, their timing had proved fortuitous. They might have easily been too late to find her here if she had sold her house.

They left the pool car and walked up the neat gravel path to the bungalow's front porch. Minshull rang the bell, the sharp yapping of a small dog sounding in reply. After a while the barking receded and the shadow of an approaching figure filled the opaque glass. A click of a chain and the scrape of two bolts sliding back followed, before the door opened to reveal a stern-faced young woman wearing cut-off jeans and an old, faded bottle-green sweatshirt over a white vest, its hem ripped and torn. Her dark hair was pulled back into a ponytail almost as severe as her expression.

'Ms Ingram?' Minshull enquired, the image not quite fitting the photo from the case notes that Ellis had sent. He should have been better prepared for this. For all of it. Fifteen years could change much about a person, as he'd witnessed with Olwyn Stokes – now Stokes-Norton – who looked markedly different from the image the media had splashed across their headlines when Ewan Stokes disappeared. 'I'm Detective Sergeant Rob Minshull and this is Detective Constable Kate Bennett. I believe Detective Inspector Anderson told you to expect us?'

The woman stared at them impassively. 'You want my sister. Come in.'

Boxes filled every available space, stacked up on the pale grey carpet in the hall, crowding the small kitchen visible at the end of it and shouldering every wall in the bright living room the stern-faced sister led them into. Marooned in a packed-cardboard-and-parcel-tape sea across the room's expanse was a small denim-blue sofa where a woman perched, watching them.

She was a negative image of her sister, ash-blonde ponytail and olive skin, peppermint-green shirt over a storm-grey T-shirt and dark cargo shorts beneath. Like her sister, she didn't smile, but hers was an expression pinched by pain, eyes hollowed by lack of sleep.

As Minshull and Bennett edged between the towers of boxes, Maisie Ingram stood.

'I thought you'd come, sooner or later.'

'Thanks for seeing us, Ms Ingram,' Minshull began, his opening gambit cut short when Maisie Ingram's sister shoved a pair of dining chairs at him and Bennett. 'Uh, thanks.'

'Sit,' she commanded, glancing at her sister. 'And listen to her this time.'

'This time?'

'Tabs, give it a rest,' Maisie admonished, earning the scowl of her sister. 'They're here now.'

'Ten years too late,' the dark-haired Ingram shot back, holding up her hands as she marched out of the room.

Maisie gave a long, slow blink. Everything about her was weary, resigned, as if even the act of existing required more energy than she possessed. Her movements were sighs, her expression pain. Minshull instantly understood her sister's protectiveness. He felt as if too strong a breath from him and Bennett could bruise this fragile woman.

'Sorry. Tabitha means well.'

'Good to have someone looking out for you,' Bennett said – and Minshull wondered if she too sensed Maisie Ingram's fragility.

'Sometimes.'

Minshull gave a smile. 'Apologies for interrupting your day, I can see you're both busy. We won't trouble you for long. We just have a few questions...'

'I know why you're here,' Maisie cut across Minshull, her abruptness a slap to his face. 'So please don't pretend this is routine, or a fact-finding mission.'

'I wasn't...'

'He's been seen, hasn't he? In Suffolk.'

Of course she would know by now. Ellis had told Minshull it was all over the forums. Even still, he'd harboured vain hopes that she might have been spared the news. Given what Cora had told him about comments from Stokesy's fans about Maisie, he'd hoped she hadn't seen her name appearing on the forums again. 'We don't know for certain. There's been a report that we're investigating.'

'I know – for certain.'

Beside him, Bennett tensed.

Minshull picked his words with care, thrown by the sharpness of her tone. 'Ms Ingram, has Ewan Stokes contacted you?'

Maisie gave a bitter laugh, her pale eyes rising to the bare light bulb in the ceiling. 'No. But his minions have.'

'You've been contacted by users of the fan forum? Recently?'

'Recently? You mean every day since that documentary aired?'

'Forgive me, I don't understand...'

'Do you know what the last ten years have been like for me, DS Minshull? Since that documentary came out? Emails, direct messages, comments on my social media. Letters posted through the door and phone calls at all hours. Shit pushed through my letter box. Damage to my car. Every time that documentary was shown or the anniversary rolled around. Every time some bastard thought they saw a message from him and posted it online. It's endless, DS Minshull. Relentless. And it's getting worse.'

What could Minshull say to that? Bennett's shock was palpable beside him.

'Did you report this?'

Bennett's question was received with weary disdain. 'Of course I did. Every time, for years. But the police never did anything about it. They stopped taking details. They told me it was just a few cranks and it would pass. The last few times I didn't even get a call back.'

'I'm so sorry...' Bennett mumbled.

'When were you first made aware about the Felixstowe Pier sighting?' Minshull asked, careful to keep his tone respectful. The shocking behaviour of his own force towards Maisie was a bitter pill, made worse by the certain knowledge that his father was most likely instrumental in some of the buck-passing.

'I started getting messages online from midnight. *He's coming for you. Now you'll pay.* They blame me. They cite the statement Ewan's sister changed as proof. And that documentary did the same. The film-makers never contacted me. I'm guessing they weren't interested in my side of the story. So his supporters have drawn their own conclusions from what they've seen on TV.'

'Were any of the messages signed?'

'No. They never are.'

'And where do these messages appear?'

'On my private Facebook page. On comments I've made on friends' posts that were supposed to be friends-and-family restricted. I've tried to keep my online identity protected, changing my profile name and account details often, only telling close friends and family. But Ewan's trolls find me every time. Tabby thinks I shouldn't be on any social sites, but why should I be unable to chat to friends there? I've done nothing wrong.'

Minshull looked at the boxes piled high in the space, the sense of imminent departure making sudden, awful sense. 'Is this why you're moving?'

'What do you think?'

'Sorry. Stupid question. But why stay here for so long?'

The woman gave a long sigh. 'At first I hung on because I was determined they wouldn't hound me out of my home. But then our dad was diagnosed with Alzheimer's and I wanted to stay close to him and Mum. They live two streets away, in Penzance Road, and it meant Mum could call me any time if Dad decided to wander off… But he died, two months ago. Mum's gone to live with my aunt in Woodbridge. So those bastards online have finally got me to leave this place.'

'I'm sorry for your loss.' Reeling, Minshull forced his mind back to the notes he'd made before leaving the CID office. 'Ms Ingram, I want to understand what happened fifteen years ago from your perspective. I'm sorry to ask you to go over it again, but I want to make sure nothing is missed this time.'

'Isn't it all in the case files?' She didn't quite meet Minshull's eye.

Minshull hated asking. Given what the woman had endured already in the name of Ewan Stokes the question was little more than an insult. How cruel was it to subject her to more?

'Apparently not,' he said. 'So I want to start from the beginning. Leave nothing unchecked.'

'That's very noble of you.' It didn't sound like a compliment. 'The last time I saw Ewan Stokes was at that football match. It was his team playing, in the amateur floodlit league. He played for the Felixstowe team because he thought they had better prospects than the local team here in Kesgrave.'

Did that explain why the latest so-called sighting had been at Felixstowe Pier? Was it intended as a reference to his last known location prior to his disappearance?

'Who was with you?'

'A group of friends. Girlfriends and wives of the players, mostly. Some hangers-on from the local pub, but I didn't have much to do with them. Ewan's sister Marilyn was there, pretty drunk, and her friend Bella, who was more interested in trying to pull one of the team than talking to any of us.'

'And Marilyn Stokes' mother?'

Maisie's expression became flint. 'Olwyn was never there. Whatever she later decided to claim.'

'You're certain of that?'

'She wasn't in our group. I never saw her at the football field. Marilyn made no reference to her, which made sense, given how much beer she'd had that night. Olwyn didn't approve of drinking. There's no way Marilyn would have been necking it like she was if her mother had been there.'

'What happened after the game?'

Minshull watched Maisie's fingers close around a ring on the middle finger of her right hand, twisting and pulling against it as if it anchored her. 'Ewan came over and started bugging me. The team had won with his last-minute goal and he was full of himself. He wanted to come back here, pick things up again with us.'

'And what did you say?'

'I told him to get lost. We'd broken up a month before – a friend helped me move Ewan's crap out of my house and change the locks – but he didn't seem to get the message that we were over. I didn't wish him dead, like they said on that documentary. Like his minions believe. He thought me going to the match was proof I wanted him back. I didn't. I was there for my best friend, Jules. She'd been dumped by her boyfriend who was on the team and wanted to do the whole *looking good to make him jealous* thing.'

Minshull dropped his gaze to his notebook. 'Do you have any idea why Mrs Stokes and her daughter changed their statements?'

Maisie considered the question for a moment before replying. 'I think they wanted it to be considered as new evidence. The police said they were going to call off the investigation and I guess Olwyn and Marilyn were desperate to stop that happening. But I also think I was an easy target. Ewan had told them before he left that I was making his life hell: that's what they said in that documentary that started all of this shit.'

'You were making his life hell?' The statement was wildly dramatic considering what Maisie had said. A broken heart was horrible, but did it warrant that kind of language? 'By saying you didn't want to get back together?'

'*He* made *my* life hell,' she replied, her words pushed through gritted teeth. 'Until I found the guts to leave him. He controlled me for two years – with his words and occasionally his fists. It was only when we broke up that I found the confidence to stand up to him. Ewan just couldn't cope with his power being taken away.'

'Did you ever wonder if him going missing was a ploy to get you back?' Minshull asked, not certain if it was a wise question to ask.

'In the beginning. He'd threaten to hurt himself when I tried to leave him before. But when they didn't find a body, I just thought he'd gone somewhere else to start again.'

'Was he close to his mum and sister?' Bennett asked.

'That's the crazy thing: they fought all the time. Ewan regularly talked about moving away from them while we were together. He wanted to move to Scotland and insisted he wouldn't tell his family where he'd gone. They were polar opposites, and would row at the slightest thing.'

'So they tried to change the narrative after he disappeared?'

Maisie observed Bennett as if presented with a possibility she hadn't considered before. 'Because they could, I guess. Ewan wasn't there to contradict them.' She shook her head. 'And then all of the idiots online did the same. None of them really knew the man Ewan was. But in their messages it's like they're speaking for him. Like he's a martyred saint. And they believe it, too.'

'Were there any messages prior to the latest sighting?' Minshull asked, a thought occurring. 'Have you noticed any rise in communications in recent weeks?'

'Try the last four months.' Her bluntness cut the air around her. 'It's the moment they've all been waiting for. The fifteenth anniversary.'

The mention of this caught Minshull's attention. Ellis had mentioned it, as had Anderson and Cora.

'Those losers think he's coming back.' The dark-haired sister was back in the room and now stood protectively between Maisie and the detectives.

'The Fifteen Year Return?'

Tabitha nodded. 'The lie they're all invested in. It's the legend they've concocted in their sick little minds. Ewan Stokes is coming back on the fifteenth anniversary of the day he disappeared, to have his revenge on the people who made him run. On Maisie…' Fury cracked her voice. 'She was supposed to be getting on with her life. She'd dumped him, weeks before he left. For good reason, too…'

'Tabs. Enough.'

'*You've* had enough. They've ruined your life.' Undeterred, Tabitha Ingram pressed on. 'There are others who should be worried about Ewan Stokes coming back. People with something real to hide. Not my sister.'

'Which people?'

Tabitha snorted. 'Like I'd tell you.'

Sensing doors slamming all around him, Minshull changed tack. 'Do you have any of the messages you received that we could see?'

Ignoring her sister's exasperation, Maisie stood and opened a large cardboard box on top of the stack next to the sofa. She pulled out a heavy box file and dropped it at Minshull's feet.

'Thank you,' he began, but stopped when five identical files were added to the pile.

'That isn't all of them,' she stated. 'But I'm guessing they'll keep you busy enough for now.'

Iron-heavy, the realisation slammed Minshull. These weren't pranks by cruel strangers: this was an all-out offensive. 'Can we borrow these?'

'Have them. I'm not taking them with me when I move.'

'Thank you.' He laid a hand on the top file and looked up at Maisie. 'We'll find the people responsible.'

'No offence, but I've heard that before.'

'Where will you go?' Bennett's question made Minshull stare at her. Her compassion was commendable, but was it wise to ask now, in light of what they'd learned?

'Far from here. Out of Suffolk for good. They won't find me. I'm closing all my online accounts, changing my name and ditching anyone who might feed those vultures information.'

'If you need protection,' Minshull cut in, 'we can arrange that.'

'I needed protection ten years ago. And every year since. I have nothing to hide, DS Minshull, but there are too many people who believe I do.' A frown creased her brow. 'Minshull – I've heard that name before. Another detective, right at the start of this. He tried to imply I'd pushed Ewan away, that him leaving was a lovers' tiff blown out of proportion. And then he stopped taking our calls.'

Minshull cursed his genes for the hundredth time that day. 'He no longer works for CID. I do. And I'm going to make sure you are safe, Ms Ingram.'

'Don't promise that.' Maisie shook her head. 'What makes you think you're any different to the rest of them?'

'Because I am,' Minshull replied, fire burning in his belly.

And because I am not my father.

Fifteen

CORA

A new client was not what Cora needed this week. Already her case-load was fit to burst, but with the educational psychology department stretched far past its limits, her most recent case newly signed off and all of her colleagues handling at least five cases each, she could hardly refuse.

'Reece Bickland, aged six,' Tris Noakes had informed her during their afternoon briefing. 'A total sweetheart, by all accounts. He had some time being homeschooled following a case of bullying at his former primary school. Now he has a new school but is struggling to attend due to anxiety.'

'Poor little one,' Cora said, flipping over the notes in the boy's file and finding a photo of a bright-eyed, smiling youngster with the kind of hair that never quite lay flat no matter how much brushing it received. Reece reminded her of her own brother, Charlie, now settled in Australia and about to start a family of his own. Charlie was forever being told to smarten himself up when in reality the mess was part of his character. 'What's the arrangement at the moment?'

'He's receiving work from the school online and has started attending some morning sessions with his mum. A little progress has been made already and he is aware of the issues. But I think we need to get to the root cause of the anxiety. I don't think it's all linked to the bullying, but he's very much resolved not to talk about what else could be making him feel anxious.'

The address on the child's notes led Cora to the winding Ferry Road that skirted the coast out of Felixstowe towards the River Deben estuary. The house was a recently extended Sixties concrete construction overlooking Felixstowe Ferry Golf Club, not far from the famous domed monument of Martello Tower, where sentry rows of brightly painted beach huts were the only things that stood between the greens and the sea.

The area was less than a mile from Cora's apartment, but it might as well have been another country. Here the most expensive houses commanded the view, their driveways populated by carefully parked sports cars and top-of-the-range four-by-fours. The houses nestled closely together along the road were designed to be admired, each making the most luxurious use of its plot for the ultimate definition of kerb appeal.

At the edges of the golf course itself many of the original properties had been given eco-conscious upgrades: flat roofs artfully lined with grass, full-length windows and bifold doors opening to wide balconies, each with a perfect view of the greens and the sea beyond.

Cora smiled as she parked her car on the brushed Yorkstone chipping drive of the house nearest the sea. Tris Noakes would think he'd died and gone to architect-design heaven if he saw this.

Memories of another striking house further up the coast suddenly invaded her thoughts, stealing her good mood. Only two months ago, and nothing like this building, but the memory was still barbed. Pushing it away, she fixed her smile back in place. This wasn't that place: this was Reece Bickland's home.

The front door opened as she reached it, revealing a smiling, blonde-haired young woman with her arm around a shy little boy who was clinging to the long linen folds of her sea-blue dress.

'You must be Dr Lael,' she said, extending her hand. 'I'm Alex Bickland and this is Reece.'

'Lovely to meet you,' Cora replied, directing her words at the young boy staring uncertainly up at her. 'I'm Cora.'

'Do you like fish?' Reece asked, his brow furrowing.

Cora caught his mother's smile and offered one of her own. 'You know, I do.'

'We have a tank!' he announced, reaching for Cora's hand. 'Come and see!'

Cora was pulled into the house and up a stone staircase to a wide first-floor living space, past a sleek kitchen and dining area towards a set of large, comfortable moss-green sofas arranged around a rainbow-hued rug, to an impressive blue glass and steel fish tank at the far end. One side of the space was floor-to-ceiling windows and bifold doors opening out to a concrete balcony, offering a wonderful, panoramic view of the golf course and the sparkling sea beyond.

Toys, books and papers covered the rug and one of the generous armchairs, this space far from the show-home-sparse interior Cora had expected. From each one rose the chatter of a happy family home – giggles from the stuffed toys, a man's voice praising his son from the folded newspapers, Alex's laughter and Reece's delighted daydreams from the stack of books.

That's the best one yet!

Look, Dad! Look at me!

I want to fly in this rocket.

This is so good…

Cora would usually mute these object voices as soon as she arrived, but they were so filled with joy and laughter that she let them speak for a while. It made such a change from the voices she generally encountered in the homes of her young charges. As she listened to Reece namechecking all of the many-coloured fish in the tank, Cora let the happy voices play as a soundtrack to the scene. It was only when she reluctantly turned down their volume in her mind that a set of whispered voices of dissent emerged from a stack of papers and notebooks on the breakfast bar at the far end of the room.

There has to be more than this.

Why aren't they talking to me?

Cora sent her focus around the phrases – spoken in multiple versions of a man's voice – her ability seeking out the surrounding air. She had heard emotional echoes from objects since she was sixteen but had only begun to investigate the potential for that ability in recent years. Now she was able to not only hear the unspoken voices but also build a three-dimensional picture in her mind of where they'd originated at the moment their owner thought them, together with a physical sense of the emotion the voices contained.

There were no more words to be discovered in this space, but a pool of tension at odds with the rest of the room's calm atmosphere briefly knotted at her neck. What was happening here? And could it be influencing the anxiety Reece Bickland was experiencing?

Intrigued, she stored the idea away, muting the voices and turning her attention back to her new charge. His mother had joined them now and was encouraging her son to tell Cora more about his beloved fish.

'The orange and white one is George,' Reece informed her. 'He wants to be a superhero but he can't wear a cape underwater. And the little blue one is Norrie. She's a secret scientist and she does experiments in the glowy castle over there at night when the other fishes are sleeping.'

Cora smiled as he continued. He certainly seemed at ease in his own surroundings, and even the potentially unsettling event of a new person coming into his safe space didn't appear to challenge that.

Eventually, Alex Bickland coaxed Reece away from the tank and they moved to the sofas. Reece busied himself with his felt pens and paper on the rug while Alex poured fresh coffee from a cafetière into two cups on the low wood coffee table. Cora fetched her notebook from her bag.

'Thanks so much for coming to see us,' Alex said, her tone deliberately light so as not to concern her son.

'My pleasure. I'm your caseworker now until we find a solution that works for everyone.'

'I hope you can. We've been working with Reece's new school and they've been brilliant, but they can't always spare extra staff to help when we go for sessions and I can't attend every day. Obviously, we need to sort the issue so that he can enjoy school.'

Cora smiled. 'That's what I'm here for. What was his attitude to school like before the issue began?'

'He loved it. He's always been a sponge for new information and he learned so much. His reading age is eighteen months beyond the expected level for a six-year-old and he has excellent written skills, too. His English and maths work are fine. He loved spending time with other children – being an only child I was very keen for him to have friends and learn how to socialise. The kids who caused this problem stole all of that from him.'

'Was the matter dealt with at his previous school?'

Alex's expression darkened. 'They considered it was. But we made the decision to move, partly to bring Reece to more calming surroundings and partly because we felt the damage done to his self-esteem in our previous town was irreparable. My husband's job currently means we could move anywhere commutable to London, and as he's from this area originally we felt the Suffolk coast was a perfect choice.'

Cora made notes and smiled at the young boy happily drawing beside her. 'Have you noticed any anxiety around any other aspect of his day-to-day life?'

'Not really.' Alex paused to watch Reece for a moment. 'Although he's nervous when he hears a phone ring.'

'Any particular phone?'

'Any phone in the house. Our mobiles, the home phone, even if he hears a phone ringing on TV.'

'And how does this anxiety present itself?'

'He gets upset. Wants a hug, sometimes there are tears. We've tried playing a game where he calls his dad's phone from mine while we're all in the same room and that helped a little. But it's when it rings unexpectedly that he reacts badly.'

'When he isn't in control of it?' Cora asked.

Alex nodded.

'Did any of the issues at his previous school happen during phone calls?' Cora was careful not to mention the words 'bullying' or 'bully' in order to keep the conversation as gentle as possible around Reece.

'No. Could it be something he's latched his anxiety on to? I've read some articles suggesting kids can do that.'

'It's possible. Sometimes if children have experienced problems with other kids or adults, they can attach their anxiety to an object, a sound – something unrelated that helps them have a focus away from the person causing the issue. It can be a coping method. Projecting fear on to something that can't actually make the situation worse.'

This appeared to reassure Alex, her shoulders dropping a little. 'The strange thing is that for the first term Reece was absolutely fine at his new school. Loved it, made a ton of new friends, couldn't wait to get there every morning. But then, overnight, it changed. That's what I don't understand. If he'd been scared of his new surroundings or fearful of starting over right from the beginning it would have made more sense.'

'Did anything in his life alter around that time?'

'No. We'd settled into a good routine. He loved the house and his new room. He was sleeping well for the first time in months. And then everything changed...' She stared at her hands, emotion stealing her words.

'I understand.' Cora rested her hand on the sofa cushion between them. 'I'm here now, and we're going to make this better.'

When Alex Bickland looked up her eyes glistened with tears. In the relaxed and happy surroundings of her home they were cruel reminders of the crisis threatening the family.

Why would an otherwise contented six-year-old take such violent objection to a place he'd enjoyed before? The notes Tris had passed Cora from the teaching staff at the primary school in Felixstowe documented a thorough investigation that had been carried out, seeking out any adverse factors that may have sparked Reece's reaction. They had found nothing.

Beyond the challenge of lessening a child's distress – always Cora's first priority – a puzzle lay. It called to her and she couldn't resist its invitation.

Aware that Reece was now observing them, she steered the conversation towards safer ground, laying out her plan for working with the family. This was just an initial meeting: from their next session tomorrow morning she would begin to build a framework around the boy to gain his trust and start to peel away the layers of the problem, establishing coping strategies in their place.

'We won't rush anything,' she assured Alex as Reece handed her his toys one by one, a brightly coloured pile of plastic and plush growing on her lap. 'Reece will set the pace; we'll follow.'

A distant door slam made Reece's head snap upright.

'Dad!' he announced, dropping the handful of Lego he held and racing to the stairs.

'Careful,' his mother called after him. 'No running on the stairs, remember?'

'Yes, *Mu-u-um*,' he called back as he disappeared through the open door, his tone heavy with the kind of exasperation only a six-year-old can muster.

Alex smiled and shook her head. 'You know he'll be running.'

'Oh, that's a given,' Cora laughed. She liked this family, this home. And even the dissenting echoes she'd sensed in one corner of this light-filled room couldn't shake her resolve to help them. She was learning in this job that some cases got under your skin, made you care far beyond your professional remit. This family were going to be one of those.

The deep notes of a man's voice rose up the stairs, peppered with the high chatter and shrieks of his son. Cora looked over the back of the sofa to see a tall man entering the room, dangling Reece by his ankles. He stopped when he saw Cora and Alex, carefully righting his boy with an apologetic smile.

'Hey – hi, sorry. Bit of a tradition with us at home time.'

'Stair dangle!' Reece yelled, butting against the man's legs.

'No,' he chorused with his wife. 'Sorry, kid. Your mum says no.'

Alex gave Cora a wry smile. 'Mum says *no* every day, but it hasn't stopped you yet. Chris, this is Dr Lael.'

'Of course. Forgive me for being late – traffic on Ferry Road was insane. Temporary lights again.' He dropped his leather rucksack beside the breakfast bar.

It's impossible, a voice snapped as the bag hit the floor. The same voice Cora had heard from the pile of papers above where his bag now lay...

Muting it immediately, Cora steadied her smile as Chris strode across the room towards her. What was impossible? Was it aimed at her work with his son or something else entirely?

Chris Bickland carried a laid-back air that didn't quite fit him. It rested awkwardly on his shoulders like a badly tailored jacket. His

99

easy smile and unashamed eye contact didn't do enough to remove the contradiction. He was dressed in an open-necked shirt and grey trousers as if he'd come from an office, but he had the stance and salt-mussed hair of a surfer. Cora sensed a man whose personal and professional personas were unhappy bedfellows. There was no question of his love for his wife and son, however. As his son pulled at his arm, Chris bent down to deliver an unhurried kiss on Alex's lips, smiling at Cora when he straightened again.

'Lael… This might be a weird question, but was your dad Bill Lael? Councillor over in St Just?'

The mention of her father stole the wind from Cora's sails. It always did, his loss still raw after so many years. But in the unfamiliar setting of this house it was magnified.

'He was. Did you know him?'

'Everyone knew your dad. You're Cora, aren't you?' When Cora hesitated to respond, he slapped a hand to his chest. 'Reception – Mrs Griffiths' class – St Bart's Primary? Everyone called me Christopher back then. Christopher Michelson?'

A distant memory of a sandy-haired boy with shoelaces forever untied edged into Cora's mind. 'Yes, I remember you! You always had the best pencil cases.'

He laughed. 'I did – bonus of having a grandma who owned a newsagent's. Man, small world, eh? And now you're a doctor?'

'Doctor of psychology. And you're a Bickland?'

'I am.' Chris chuckled and moved to sit on the furthest sofa in the group, Reece jumping onto his lap for another hug. 'I took my stepdad's name when my mum left him. He raised me from the age of twelve. That's why I didn't go to secondary school with you all. We moved to Bournemouth and then Brighton.'

'I see. Well, good to meet you *again*.' Cora remembered the papers and notebooks on the breakfast bar. 'Do you work from home?'

'Mostly, at the moment. I had meetings in London today, hence the smart stuff.' He waved a hand at his shirt and trousers. 'I'm a journalist, writing for *The Sentinel* among others.'

Cora tensed. National paper *The Sentinel* had been less than complimentary about her new colleagues in South Suffolk CID in the past, and she had seen the hurt and anger the newspaper coverage had caused Minshull, Anderson and the team. Had Chris written any of those stories?

'What do you write?' she asked, careful to keep any note of caution out of her question.

'Features, mostly. Not news desk stuff these days. Glad to be out of that viper den, to be honest with you. I tried it for a few years when I started out but it wasn't me. So I moved to Features and found my niche.'

'My dad likes words,' Reece stated. '*Lots* of words.'

Chris raised his hand. 'He's right. Self-confessed fan.' He turned his attention to his son. 'You've been having a good time with Dr Lael?'

The boy gave a non-committal shrug. 'Sort of. Mum was talking a lot.'

Alex laughed. 'Sorry. Next time you can have Cora all to yourself.'

'And play Lego?' he asked, eyes hopeful.

'Whatever you like,' Cora replied. Aware of the natural break in the conversation she shouldered her bag and stood. 'I should let you all enjoy your afternoon. Reece, lovely to meet you and I'll see you tomorrow, okay?'

'Okay,' the boy replied, heading towards the pile of toys on the rug.

'I'll see you out,' Chris said, already accompanying Cora across the room without waiting for her reply.

Cora passed the disgruntled voices of the bag and papers as she made her way out.

By the front door, Chris paused, his hand on the handle, his easy smile suddenly absent.

'So what's the prognosis?'

Surprised by the change, Cora stumbled over her reply. 'I don't… That's not how this works.'

'He's well, though?' He lowered his voice to a hurried whisper. 'In his mind?'

It was an odd question to ask, although once spoken it made sense. Did Chris Bickland have something to fear from the potential for mental ill health?

'Are you concerned he isn't?' she replied, deliberate in her deflection back to him.

His head dropped. 'My mum… She left my brother and me with our stepdad because she… *struggled*.'

A weight of history hung on that single word. Cora waited until Chris dared to raise his eyes from the shining green slate floor.

'I had no sense of that kind of issue,' she replied, every word smooth-edged.

He released a shot of breath halfway between a laugh and a sigh. 'Thank you. I don't know how I'd cope if… Do you have any idea what might be causing this?'

'It's too early to say. But I think there is a cause, possibly even a single event that triggered Reece's anxiety. If we can discover what that is, we can build strategies to combat the effects and address the assumptions that are making him link how he feels with attending school. It will take time, though. There aren't any quick fixes. We have to build something that lasts a lifetime.'

'I can wait,' Chris said, his smile still noticeably absent. 'I'm used to that.'

Sixteen

MINSHULL

Vancouver was washed in warm early-morning sunlight. Minshull could see the gilded windows of skyscrapers beyond the glass of the smartly dressed Canadian's office. Behind Minshull, stubborn South Suffolk rain pelted the windows, making the scene on his laptop screen appear like a golden dream he was being afforded a glimpse of.

How had they ever conducted international investigations without Zoom? Video-conferencing had transformed police work in recent years. Not everyone was a fan, of course, but it was a necessary evil. Today, seeing the sunny image on screen while the fury of the county's rain clouds stole the afternoon light from the CID office windows, it was positively pleasant.

It was a blessed relief after the highly charged exchanges with his father, Olwyn and Maisie yesterday. The morning had passed with steady, methodical schedule, work still ongoing to process the original investigation files, while the CCTV recordings sent from Felixstowe Pier were painstakingly pored over for evidence of likely accomplices prior to Ewan Stokes' appearance. No more sightings had been reported for now. But Minshull guessed that wouldn't remain the case for long.

Miles O'Donnell had the easy-going nature Minshull had expected from the tone of his email reply earlier to arrange the meeting, reflected in his relaxed pose in his office chair and his casual work attire. Having that view probably helped, too. Minshull estimated him to be in his early forties, with close-cropped dark hair just beginning to silver at the temples and hooded pale blue eyes. He worked as a senior architect for a leading city firm, and from what Minshull could see had a very comfortable office.

'Thanks for talking to me today,' Minshull said. 'And apologies for the early hour.'

'I try to get here early,' Miles replied, the slightest hint of a Suffolk lilt playing at the edges of his Canadian accent. 'Six thirty most mornings. Eight a.m. is practically lunchtime for me.'

Minshull smiled. 'I see. I won't keep you long. I just wanted to go over what you saw in a little more detail.'

'Sure. Ask away.'

'Thank you.' He consulted the list he had made earlier as he'd waited for the right time in Canada to call the eyewitness. 'So, do you often check the Felixstowe Pier webcam?'

Miles gave a self-conscious chuckle. 'Pretty often, I'm embarrassed to say. It's a pastime of sorts. Started in the pandemic and just kind of stuck. I miss Suffolk, though it's years since I was last there. Sometimes it's only when you can't go to a place that the longing starts, you know?'

'Is it just the pier webcam you visit?'

'No. Places I remember – Felixstowe, Aldeburgh, Lowestoft. Webcams are everywhere, it seems.'

'Even at night?'

The smile in the sunny city office flickered for just a moment. 'Hazard of the time difference. The pier cam is better than most because of the spotlight beside it. Seeing just a portion of the beach is better than nothing.'

Was it? It seemed a bit of a stretch as an explanation, but Minshull parked the thought for later. The chance of O'Donnell choosing to watch the webcam at the precise moment Ewan Stokes walked into shot was a hell of a coincidence. He would get to that soon; for now he needed to keep the conversation light, encourage the Canadian to keep talking and hope that he would reveal more.

'Can you talk me through exactly what you saw, please?'

'No problem. I logged on just after a meeting with my team. I had some downtime before my next appointment, so I went to the SuffolkView website.'

'Suffolk view?' Minshull asked, noting it down.

'Yeah, written as one word, capital S, capital V. It has webcams from across the county, most of them on the coast but a couple in towns, too. I have it saved on my work browser for emergencies.' He laughed. 'Missing-my-home-county emergencies, that is.'

'Even at night?'

'Night-time UK is daytime Canada.' That flicker again.

'Indeed. So, you went to SuffolkView. Did you look at any other webcams before the one on Felixstowe Pier?'

O'Donnell blinked. 'Nope. Straight to the pier.' When Minshull left a deliberate pause, the Canadian filled it. 'Always the first place I head when I come home.'

'When was the last time you came back?'

A frown. 'Well, I… I haven't been back for a few years. No, I mean, I always look at the pier first on the website. It's *like* coming home, you know?'

Was his smile a little tighter than earlier?

'And how long were you watching, would you say, before you saw the person with the sign?'

'Before I saw Stokesy? Uh, I dunno… Maybe five minutes?'

'And did you see much happening on the beach during that time?'

'I mean, it was pretty quiet. But you get dog walkers, that kind of thing.'

Dog walkers? At 10:45 p.m.? Minshull kept his smile carefully on display. This was a fact Evans could verify. As soon as this interview ended, Minshull would ask. Keen to keep O'Donnell talking, he asked, 'How many dog walkers did you see? Or just dogs?'

'I can't remember. But I did see some.'

Minshull gave a slow nod. On the screen, Miles O'Donnell seemed to pale.

'So, there were some late-night dog walkers and then the figure stepped into shot?'

'That's right.'

'Can you tell me what the figure was wearing?'

'Dark clothing. Black hooded sweater, jeans maybe? I couldn't see below the sign.'

'Was his hood up or down?'

'Up. But I could clearly see his face. It was Stokesy.'

'You seem very certain.'

'I am. I know it was him.'

Minshull made a show of taking notes, although his pen never touched the page. From under his brows he glanced at the man on-screen. He definitely looked uncomfortable now. Why?

'Have you seen him before?'

'Everyone knows what he looks like.'

'From what? The photo issued when he went missing?'

'Yeah.'

'The fifteen-year-old photo of Ewan Stokes?'

'He hasn't changed.'

Who could say they hadn't changed in fifteen years? Especially given the image he'd seen was at night on a grainy webcam picture. 'Have you seen Ewan Stokes before? Not in a photo. On a webcam, or in an image that might have been shared online?'

'I – I don't understand the question…'

His hackles were up now, but Minshull didn't want to risk spooking him into silence. Even Olwyn Stokes-Norton hadn't conclusively confirmed the figure on the webcam was her son. Right now the only positive identification of the figure on the Felixstowe webcam was by Miles O'Donnell. His testimony was key.

'Forgive me, sir, I just want to establish how certain you are that you saw Ewan Stokes on the webcam.'

'One hundred per cent.'

'Okay. What did Mr Stokes do when he stepped into view?'

O'Donnell appeared to relax a little, his gaze drifting to the right, which Minshull's mother termed the recollection pose. 'He was holding a sign and in one hand he had a small torch balanced between his fingers and the edge of the sign.'

'A small torch?' Minshull asked, looking at the still from the webcam. The area around his left hand was cast into shadow by the bright beam of light coming from the torch. 'Could you see how small?'

'It was hard to see, but I caught a glint of light on it at one point. I think it was one of those super-powerful LED torches – the kind with the metal body?'

'Ah, right.' It would have had to be something powerful to cast the beam visible in the webcam still. Minshull had a similar one on a key ring that he kept on a hook just inside the door of the cupboard in his apartment where the fuse box lived. For a little torch it had an impressive beam. 'And what did the sign say?'

'*HELP ME.*'

'And that concerned you?'

O'Donnell stared directly from the screen. 'Of course it did.'

'Have you seen a sign like that before?' Minshull asked, picking his way back towards the question he really wanted to ask.

'Not on the webcam.'

'At any time before? Have you seen a *HELP ME* sign held like that before?'

A frown again. 'Forgive me, I don't know what you're asking.'

Subtlety was no longer an option. Minshull offered a smile before making his move. 'Have you seen Ewan Stokes on a webcam before?' When the Canadian didn't reply, he pressed on. 'I'm aware Mr Stokes has become an unlikely celebrity of late and that there have been reported messages from him over the past few years, but no actual sightings prior to this. You knew who he was immediately. Can I ask why you are so certain that's who you saw?'

Miles O'Donnell gawped at the screen. Minshull held his expression and his nerve.

'I'm intrigued,' O'Donnell admitted at last, his gaze falling away. 'I've seen *The Missing Son* and it made me want to know more.'

A hunch proved, Minshull pressed on. 'Have you visited any of the online forums?'

'A few.'

'How often, would you say?'

'I check in maybe once or twice a week. I've made friends there.'

Minshull took time to note this down, carefully constructing his next question. 'In those forums, did you see any forewarning of the Felixstowe Pier webcam appearance?'

'No.'

No hesitation. *Damn it.* Minshull regrouped and tried again. 'The fifteenth anniversary of Mr Stokes going missing is next week. Did you see any suggestion that he may be heading back to Suffolk?'

'No.'

'Any mention of the Fifteen Year Return? Any theories shared? Or clues to where he might reappear?'

'Everybody knows he's coming back,' O'Donnell snapped, the sudden change in him startling. 'It's all anyone talks about in the forums. I know the fifteenth anniversary is soon. But I didn't know I would see him that night. That was a total fluke, a coincidence. All I can tell you is that the moment I saw him I knew it was Stokesy.'

It wasn't the answer Minshull wanted, but it opened a door to another line of inquiry. Any information he could gain now was better than none. 'If it was Ewan Stokes, why do you think he's returned, after so many years away?'

O'Donnell leaned closer to the screen, a strangely defiant smile aimed directly at the camera and Minshull beyond. 'To get his revenge.'

Minshull's stomach twisted. The transformation in the previously laid-back and calm Canadian was profound. He recalled some of the language and rhetoric Ellis had reported finding on the Stokesy-Fans forum, the chilling predictions and threatening misogyny that appeared apparently at will. 'Revenge on who?'

'Everyone who made him run. The friends that screwed him over. The family who lied. The bitch who broke his heart.'

Minshull baulked at the reference to Maisie Ingram, having heard of such abuse from her perspective. Was O'Donnell one of her anonymous aggressors?

'If you know this, why did you call us? Wouldn't his return be something you'd celebrate?'

O'Donnell's fervour dipped a little. 'I thought you should be aware. Because when Stokesy returns, he's bringing hell with him. And his enemies better be ready.'

'Who are his enemies, Mr O'Donnell?'

'They know. And they should be afraid.'

'How involved are you in this?' Minshull watched his question register with the changeling in the well-appointed Canadian architecture office. The sudden rise of the eyebrows, the reddening of the cheeks.

'I'm thousands of miles away,' he replied, a dangerous edge framing his words. 'What could I do?'

'Did you have prior warning of the appearance?'

'Not at all.'

'Forgive me, Mr O'Donnell, but I find that hard to believe. You're telling me you just happened to watch a webcam, thousands of miles away, at the exact time Ewan Stokes appeared?'

O'Donnell shrugged, a smirk still in place. 'Guess I got lucky.' He made a show of lifting the cuff of his shirtsleeve to check the large watch on his wrist. 'And that's our time done, I'm afraid.'

'I will have more questions,' Minshull managed, before O'Donnell's screen vanished. 'Shit.'

'Everything okay, Guv?' Bennett asked, placing a fresh mug of coffee on his desk. Minshull appreciated the gesture: he knew she was concerned about him, even if neither of them quite knew how to address the subject.

'Our Canadian caller just went full Dr Jekyll and Mr Hyde over Zoom,' he breathed.

'Par for the course with this case,' Bennett replied, offering a cautious smile.

Minshull didn't return it. 'He may have been bluffing, but the commitment to Stokes is scary. If he can flip like that, thousands of miles from Suffolk, what might a fan living here be prepared to do?'

'Threaten Maisie Ingram?'

'And worse.' Minshull ran his hand across the back of his neck, the stress knots there refusing to yield. 'If they mobilise, if the Fifteen Year stuff becomes a call to arms… there's no telling what might happen.'

'Sarge,' Wheeler called from his desk. 'I just had a call from Steph Lanehan. The van's been taken from the lock-up.'

Minshull and Bennett turned. 'How long ago?'

'Our friend Mr Noble is there now. He just returned to the site. The lock-up door's open and the van's gone.'

'Call her back. Ask her to stay with Mr Noble. Can you head over there to check it out?'

'Will do,' Wheeler replied, racing into action.

Minshull left his desk and hurried to Anderson's office. Peering around the open door, he raised a hand at his superior. 'Guv, development. The van's on the move.'

Anderson stood. 'Right.' He snatched up the receiver of his desk phone and dialled Control. 'Lena, it's DI Anderson. I need an all-vehicle alert put out on a white 2004 Volkswagen Caddy van with damage to its front right wing...'

Seventeen

WHEELER

By the time Wheeler arrived at the Playford site, the sky was beginning to darken. The relentless rain had banked thick grey clouds overhead, so the soon-approaching early-evening dusk was amplified as the remaining daylight began to fade.

PC Steph Lanehan was deep in conversation with a middle-aged man next to the empty lock-up, a thick set of tyre marks in the muddy ground leading away from them towards Church Road. Wheeler crouched beside the tracks just as Lanehan looked up.

'He went thataway,' she observed drily.

'So I can see. Looks the about the right size for Caddy tyres.' He straightened and nodded at Mr Noble. 'Appreciate you calling us, sir.'

'Least I could do. Sorry I can't tell you where he went.'

'What time did you return here?' Wheeler asked.

'...'bout half an hour ago, forty minutes tops.'

'And was the van here when you arrived today?'

Jonny Noble shook his head. 'Not out, no. But the door was shut, padlock on, and those tracks weren't there.'

'How long were you away?'

'Only an hour. Just did one quick job this afternoon. Supposed to be my day off, but I had a mission of mercy for a mate of mine.' He pulled at his earlobe with dirt-stained fingers. 'Although my missus weren't too merciful about it.'

Wheeler smiled back. Lanehan's description of the man had been spot on when she'd mentioned him in the pub last night. Wheeler had popped in for a swift pint after work and had met Steph and her husband Fred at the bar. 'Proper ray of sunshine, he was,' Lanehan had said. 'Old-school bloke, you know? Like I remember my uncles being. We could do with more of his sort around here – honest, salt of the earth, happy to help.'

'Do you need me to hang around? Only I ought to be gettin' home.'

'We'll take it from here, Mr Noble,' Wheeler smiled, registering the mix of relief and disappointment from the man. 'Thank you so much for your help.'

'Is he in trouble?' Noble asked.

'We need to talk to him about an accident at the weekend.'

'Bad, was it?'

Wheeler opted for the safest reply. 'He can help us with our inquiries.'

'I see. No idea how you'll find him out here. Like a rabbit warren with all these country roads.'

'Our patrols are keeping an eye out.'

'Right. Good, then. I'll… er…' He took a step back, thumbing over his shoulder at his waiting pickup truck.

'Thanks, Mr Noble.' Lanehan raised her hand to wave.

'You're welcome, PC Lanehan. Always happy to help.'

Lanehan smiled as the dirt-covered pickup rumbled away. 'God love him.'

'He's a good chap,' Wheeler agreed. 'Shame he didn't see the van leave, though.' He followed the tracks back towards Church Road, Steph walking alongside him as he did so. Where the site met the road there was a lip of raised edging stone marking the boundary. Bending down, Wheeler noticed two distinct deposits of mud, squared by tyre treads, caught at the edge, blades of grass protruding from one of them. They looked fresh. Beyond the stones two thick mounds of mud arched onto the tarmac of Church Road, moving in the opposite direction from Jonny Noble's departure.

'Reckon the van made those?' Lanehan asked.

Wheeler looked back towards the lock-ups. 'Not sure. They don't look big enough to have come from Mr Noble's truck. And look – you can see the pickup's tyre tracks arcing back clear of these ones.'

Steph made a radio call. 'PC Lanehan at the Church Road lock-ups in Playford, over.'

'Go ahead,' the reply crackled back.

'It looks like the van headed left from here, heading towards Playford village. Over.'

'Received. We'll relay it to the other patrols. You happy to hang fire, over?'

'Affirmative. I have DC Wheeler attending, over.'

'Received. Await further instructions, please.'

Steph ended the call and grinned at Wheeler. 'So much for an early finish tonight.'

'Story of my life,' Wheeler returned. 'I've got some Mars bars in the car if I can tempt you?'

'Be rude to refuse. Got a flask in mine. Fancy a cuppa?'

It wasn't how Wheeler had envisioned spending the later hours of his shift today, but he had long since accepted the job's ability to change plans at will. 'Sounds like a plan to me, Lanny. Your car or mine?'

'Definitely my car. It doesn't reek of moss and sweat like that pool car your lot all share. Besides, Oz Synett gave mine a valet yesterday. Still smells fresh as a daisy inside.'

Decision made, Wheeler headed to the CID pool car to fetch chocolate bars while Steph returned to the patrol vehicle to make tea. Just as he opened the door, a screech of tyres nearby snapped his head upright, in time to see the damaged front wing of a white van reversing at speed from the site.

Wheeler yelled to Steph, who was already starting her car, then jumped into the pool car, slamming it into reverse and taking off after the van.

'DC Wheeler in pursuit of a white van from Playford lock-ups,' he barked into his radio, 'heading north on Church Road away from the village towards Bealings Road...'

Ahead the tail lights of the white van were in view, glaring bright red as it reached the road junction. Wheeler slammed his foot on the brake as the van swung hard right, its back wheels skidding wildly out on the rain-greased road.

Checking for traffic, Wheeler followed, glancing in his rear-view mirror to see the blue lights of Steph's patrol car swing out behind. 'Subject has turned east on Bealings Road heading towards…' He struggled to picture the map of criss-crossing lanes that edged the wide fields on either side of the road, while flooring the accelerator and gripping the steering wheel. '…Great Bealings and Little Bealings…'

The road narrowed ahead, trees crowding either side, a motorist in the opposite direction thankfully pulling into a passing place to allow Wheeler and Lanehan's cars to pass. Beyond that would be a fork in the road: the left side becoming Boot Street, the right Holly Lane. Which one the van driver chose depended upon which of the twin villages they were aiming for. Over the radio he could hear the barks and clicks of other conversations, Steph's voice rising between them.

They were almost at the junction now. The van slowed a little, then continued forward.

'Vehicle proceeding on Boot Street towards Great Bealings,' Wheeler confirmed, accelerating hard. The blues and twos of Steph's car were right behind him now, both vehicles closing in on the speeding white van.

It had been some time since Dave Wheeler had driven in pursuit, and it showed. Stress screamed in his ears, his heart feeling as if it might burst from him. He clung to the steering wheel, mind racing ahead to decipher potential places where the van could be cornered or coaxed to the kerb. There was one place further up ahead where the road would widen just enough to allow him to overtake. If he could make it there…

Suddenly, the van's brake lights fired red and, with a scream of rubber against road, it began to turn. Shocked, Wheeler stamped on his brake, but the van had swerved 360 degrees now and was driving straight for him. Wheeler grabbed the steering wheel and flung it as hard left as he could.

There was a sickening crack as the van caught the pool car's wing mirror, slamming it flat against the driver's-side window. As the van passed within millimetres, Wheeler caught sight of a white driver shrouded in a black hoodie and the fleeting ghost of a figure gesturing beside them in the passenger seat. And then it was gone, just as the patrol car butted the rear of the pool car, sending a sickening judder through his body.

It was over in a heartbeat, but getting out of the car seemed to take Wheeler an unworldly amount of time. Steph was emerging from her vehicle as Wheeler wrestled his way out onto the road. The woodland on either side of the road was eerily quiet, with just the distant roar of a speeding engine ebbing away along Holly Lane.

'Are you hurt?' he puffed, meeting his colleague halfway between the two cars.

'Seat belt punched me in the chest, but at least I managed to miss you,' she replied, nodding at the crumpled pool car bumper and the smashed plastic of the patrol car's left front headlight. 'Mostly.'

'There's a comfort.' It hurt to smile, but Wheeler did it anyway. 'Let's head up Holly Lane, see if he's stopped somewhere. He might have slowed if he thinks we aren't behind him. You okay to drive?'

'I radioed it in. There's a patrol car about two miles up there. If we're lucky they'll nab him. Control said to stand down.'

'Shit!' Wheeler spat through gritted teeth, slamming his palm against the boot of the damaged pool car. 'Bloody bastard van driver!'

'Hey, we'll get him, Dave,' Lanehan offered, resting a warm hand on his shoulder. 'Just not right now and not us. Bloody impressive bit of pursuit there, though, Detective Constable. Didn't reckon you still had it in you.'

It was kindly meant, and he accepted the compliment. But being so close to apprehending the vehicle that had caused them such trouble was a kick that would take time to get over. Pulling his phone from his jacket, he called Minshull.

'We lost him, Sarge. I'm sorry.'

THE CLUB

Watcher89 NEW SIGHTING: petrol station, outskirts of Felix-stowe, 17th July, 11pm. It's definitely him. Check the CCTV photo below. 'HELP ME' written on a white sign again. If you know you know.

#Stokesy15

COMMENTS

davep221 Is that him? It looks like him but do we know for sure?

stokesyyfan Look at the photo! He's back!

grumpyg1t Where did you get this @Watcher89? Do we know it's legit?

Watcher89 Came in from one of ours. It's legit.

Me54c How far is that from The Bitch house? Do we tell her?

davep221 @Me54c No. Back off.

Me54c @davep221 Calm down Princess. Stokesy wants help. U chicken?

davep221 @Me54c He doesn't want your kind of help.

Me54c @davep221 Talked to him did you? You know nothing.

davep221 @Me54c I know coward shits like you don't care about him.

Me54c @davep221 You still here? Don't know what your problem is mate. You know the score. OK to have a bit of sport with the prey before the kill. That's what Stokesy wants.

davep221 @Me54c What do you care about Stokesy? You're just a sicko.

Me54c @davep221 She ain't going to shag you mate. Might shag me tho.

– Watcher89 closed comments on this thread –

Eighteen

BENNETT

The two loops of grainy camera footage played side by side as the CID team gathered around Minshull's desk. On Wheeler's laptop beside Minshull's computer ran the now familiar webcam footage from Felixstowe Pier. On Minshull's monitor, the new, marginally clearer image from the BP petrol station on the outskirts of Felixstowe. In both, at a certain moment, a hooded figure stepped into view. He held a sign and balanced a small torch in his left hand – in the well-lit garage forecourt video this was more for effect than illumination. The messages were identical: *HELP ME.*

'What do we think?' Minshull directed his question over his shoulder at his gathered colleagues, not taking his eyes off the twin screens.

'Looks like him,' Ellis said. 'What do you reckon, Les?'

Evans, who had been remarkably subdued since the incident with his car's tyres, gave a groan of boredom. 'It's a bloke in a hoodie holding a sign. It could be anyone.'

'The garage CCTV is clearer,' Wheeler said. 'I mean, that looks like our man.'

'It's fifteen years since anyone took a photo of him. He could look like Jabba the Hutt now, for all we know.'

Bennett remained unconvinced. Sure, both so-called sightings had a figure in a black hoodie holding a sign, but it wasn't possible to really make out the face. It was a rare occasion she agreed with Les Evans, but on this point he was right. It could be anyone. And the deluded idiots on the forum would happily lap it up because of the stupid fifteen-year anniversary thing. She imagined that if all you ever talked about in a closed online community was some mythical, messianic return for the best part of ten years, you'd probably believe anything that remotely fitted the bill.

It was a prank: it had to be.

Why wait fifteen years to return home and construct an online following where any number of nutters could appropriate your name for their own cause? And why play to the crowd? Wouldn't you be horrified that this army of weirdos had stolen your image to further their own prejudices?

'I don't get it,' she said, causing her colleagues to look at her. 'If he's doing this as some kind of call to action, how does he think people are going to see CCTV footage?'

'Well, we're seeing it,' Wheeler countered. 'If it found its way here you can bet it's gone to the online forums.'

He had a point, but so much of what they were learning about the strange online cult that had constructed itself around Ewan Stokes seemed fantastical. Why would anyone pledge allegiance to a person they had never met, who possessed no claim to celebrity status beyond his own disappearance fifteen years ago?

'Okay, but how are they going to *help him* if he isn't communicating with them beyond these camera stunts? What kind of help does he need? How is anyone supposed to understand a two-word message with no further explanation or link to find out more?'

Minshull grimaced. 'Unfortunately, Mr Stokes hasn't deigned to let his fans in on that information yet. Until he does, all we can do is guess.' His stare travelled from Bennett to Drew Ellis standing uncomfortably close beside her. 'Kate, Drew, go over to the garage, would you? I spoke to the owner, Mr Kavish Rai, first thing and he's expecting us. Find out what he knows and if he has any connection to Ewan Stokes. I feel like these sightings are being planned by someone and we need to work out the significance of the locations being chosen. Until we do, we're going to remain on the back foot.'

'Okay, Sarge,' Bennett replied, shuffling awkwardly past Ellis to grab her bag and pool car keys from her desk. As she passed him she heard a frustrated shot of breath from her colleague. Irritated, she left the CID office, not waiting for Ellis. He had long enough legs to catch up when he was ready.

Striding along the corridor, she chided herself for letting the strange air between them get to her. She should have worked out how to ignore it by now. The physical scars from the ambush they'd been caught up in two months ago were almost healed – so shouldn't everything else damaged that day be? Whatever had changed in the darkened shell of the river warehouse as they'd waited for rescue stubbornly refused to yield to explanation or their efforts to move past it. Its shadow-like uncertainty remained as a permanent wedge between them. Bennett wouldn't address it first and neither would Ellis.

It didn't help that her divorce was proceeding at last. Or that Dave Wheeler was her unlikely guide through the soul-sapping intricacies of marital law, all kept secret from her colleagues in CID. With so much else in her life in free fall, she needed work to be solid, unmovable and as predictable as possible.

There was little chance of that while the awkwardness remained.

'All right, Speedy Gonzales,' Ellis puffed, pulling level with her. 'You okay?'

'I'm fine,' she shot back, softening her snap with a smile. 'Just frustrated by all this, you know?'

'Yeah, I get it. Minsh seems convinced it's some orchestrated campaign but I can't see it. Feels like someone just taking the piss.'

They pushed open the double doors that led to the stairwell and headed down to the car park. Near the rear gate was the bank of pool cars. Three, where there were usually four – the car Wheeler had chased the white van with yesterday afternoon out at the body shop having the damage repaired. Wheeler had been upset about it this morning and Bennett understood why. To be so close to catching the van that had so far eluded them must have been a real kick in the guts.

Bennett had made sure she selected the keys for the newest vehicle, which meant little beyond its number plate. It was nominally cleaner than the others but the crucial difference was that its air con still worked. Oz Synett, the station mechanic who had been at South Suffolk Police HQ longer than anyone could remember, kept promising to refill the bottles on all the pool cars but so far had found more pressing matters to attend to.

'I got my priorities,' he'd insisted last week, when Ellis had complained. 'And trust me, if you have to choose between functionin' brakes and air con you're not likely to be that worried about stayin' cool, are you?'

Bennett drove as she usually did when she was out on a shout with Ellis. Concentrating on the road ahead was preferable to riding in the passenger seat with too much time to think. All the same, she made some surreptitious checks on her colleague as they drove to the outskirts of Felixstowe. Apart from their shared frustrations with the case, he appeared in good spirits. He was a good DC and a kind co-worker; whatever else they may disagree upon, she had to protect that.

The petrol station was a small one, with only four pumps in its forecourt. A single row of cars for sale graced one side of the lot, with a two-space car park on the other. Bennett parked the car in one of the spaces and as they headed into the mini-market, she noticed a young man washing the row of vehicles in the car sales section. He looked bored to tears.

Bennett and Ellis waited while a gruff-looking driver paid for his fuel, before moving to the counter. Behind the Perspex window sat a man Bennett placed around his early fifties. Kavish Rai observed them with a nod and indicated to the door at the side of the counter. Moments later, he emerged: a tall, commanding figure with an impeccably maintained beard and an unnerving skill for eye contact.

'I take it you're from the police,' he observed.

'Yes, Mr Rai. I'm DC Kate Bennett and this is my colleague, DC Drew Ellis.'

Handshakes were exchanged, the garage owner carefully observing Bennett and Ellis.

'I appreciate you coming so quickly.'

'No problem at all, sir. I understand you had an unlikely star of your CCTV last night?'

'We did.' Kavish Rai shook his head. 'I don't know what he was doing here or what he wanted to prove. At first I thought it was local kids mucking around – you get that a lot these days. But then I learned it was the missing man. The one people think is coming back.'

Stokesy's legend had beaten them to it once again, it seemed. Was there nobody in Suffolk unaware of Ewan Stokes?

'Did you recognise Mr Stokes from the CCTV?' Bennett asked.

Rai laughed. 'Not me. My son Jas is the fan.' He nodded across the forecourt to the bored young man slapping a soap-covered sponge on the windscreen of a Renault Clio that had seen better days. 'Jas told me who our visitor was. He was annoyed when I was unimpressed.'

'What time did he appear on your CCTV?' Bennett asked.

'Eleven p.m. We'd closed the mart and were doing night pay only. Ordinarily, we close at ten, but it pays to stay open later in the summer.'

'Are your later opening hours common knowledge, sir?' Ellis asked, before Bennett had a chance to speak.

'I should hope so,' Rai chuckled. 'We do enough advertising locally.'

'Have you had any other dealings with Ewan Stokes in the past?' Bennett asked, remembering the stated belief of the Stokesy superfans that the missing man was returning to settle old scores.

'Not that I'm aware of.'

'Did you see him arrive last night?'

Rai considered the question. 'Not directly. I did see a white van park up where your car is parked now. It hung around for a while and nobody got out. I was expecting them to use the cash machine or ask for something from the mart but they just sat there. I kept my eye on them: we've had trouble before at night when it's quiet. A van can mean a bunch of people coming to ambush you.'

'Did you see the man with the sign get out of it?' Ellis asked, glancing at Bennett.

'No. But as it was the only vehicle on the forecourt I assume that's where he came from. We're too far out of town for anyone to walk to reach us, especially late at night.'

Bennett checked her notebook. 'So at some point he walked onto the forecourt and held up the sign. Did he know where the CCTV cameras were?'

'I was in the stockroom, but Jas saw him. He said he thought the guy was looking at the pump numbers, which was strange because he was on foot with no vehicle at the pumps.'

'And he recognised the man as Ewan Stokes?'

Rai nodded. 'He tried to speak to the man but by the time Jas had unlocked the door, he'd gone.'

'And the van you mentioned?'

The garage owner turned his stare on Bennett. 'It had gone, too.'

Bennett let her gaze stray across the forecourt to the young man cleaning cars, a plan forming. 'We need to see the full footage, if that's okay, Mr Rai?'

'Of course. My nephew is in the stockroom – let me get him to cover the till and I'll show you.'

'Thanks.' Bennett smiled, waiting until he had disappeared into the side room before turning to Ellis. 'Right, keep Mr Rai talking until I come back, okay?'

Ellis frowned. 'Where are you going?'

'I think that kid knows something beyond recognising Ewan Stokes. But if we talk to him with his dad there he may not admit it. Just keep Mr Rai busy and follow my lead, okay?' She pulled her mobile from her pocket, looked up and offered the returning garage owner her brightest smile.

'If you'd like to follow me.'

'I just have to return a call from my Sarge. Drew, would you go with Mr Rai and start looking through the footage, please?'

'Sure.' Eyes narrowing, Ellis fixed a smile of his own in place. 'Sarge bugging you again?'

Ignoring the edge in his question, Bennett exacted a sigh. 'You know what he's like. Stickler for details.' She grinned at him before heading for the door.

Outside the heat of the day was already beginning to build. Once the sun burned off the light cloud cover it would be very warm indeed.

Perfect weather for lounging on a beach; not so wonderful for being stuck in a cramped pool car or an airless CID office. Still, at least Bennett had grabbed the single vehicle with functioning air con. She congratulated herself for this as she walked across the forecourt, phone pressed to her ear for effect.

Jas Rai didn't notice her approach, nodding his head to whatever music his earbuds were delivering. Bennett watched him rinse one windscreen and pick up the bucket and sponge to move to the next, before he looked up with a start. Easing an earbud from one ear, he stared at her.

'You interested in the Fiesta?'

'Not today, thanks.' She held out her warrant card. 'Detective Constable Kate Bennett. Mind if I ask you a few questions?'

Jas frowned. 'My dad's expecting you. He's inside.'

'I just met him,' Bennett answered, keeping her tone light. 'My colleague is going through the CCTV with him now. I wanted to talk to you.'

'Me? Why?'

'Your dad tells me you recognised Ewan Stokes straight away?'

'Yeah. Dad didn't know who he was but I did.' He seemed to relax a little. 'I couldn't believe it.'

'How certain are you that it was him? I've seen the picture your dad sent to us – he's wearing a black hoodie and it's dark outside despite the forecourt lights. Easy to make a mistake?'

'Nah, no mistake there. It was Stokesy, one hundred per cent.'

'Okay.' Bennett nodded. Question was, how did Jas Rai know Ewan Stokes so well that he'd immediately recognise him in person? He couldn't be much more than nineteen or twenty: how did someone who would have been a primary school kid fifteen years ago know about the missing man? Understandable that the name would be familiar – it had pretty much passed into recent folklore in Suffolk and most people in the county would have heard of Ewan Stokes. But recognising a name was very different from identifying the person on sight, fifteen years after the last official photograph.

'Any idea why he chose your family's garage to do this?'

'No, but it's cool he did.' Jas beamed. 'Dad's been wanting more business for months. We've had four visits already this morning from fans wanting their photos where Stokesy last appeared.'

'His fans have been turning up?' Bennett glanced at the CCTV camera where the man purporting to be Ewan Stokes had stood to make his point. 'But how had they seen the CCTV footage? Your dad only reported it this morning.'

The young man's smile faded. 'Well. Word travels.'

Her hunch proven, Bennett faced him. 'Or someone who saw the footage last night shared it somewhere Stokesy's fans might see it?'

The hand holding the sponge dropped to Jas Rai's side, a stream of water and soapsuds puddling around the toe of his white sneakers. 'Am I in trouble?'

'Tell me what happened.'

He dropped the sponge into the bucket, wiping his hands on the back of his jeans. 'I posted it in the StokesyFans forum.'

'When?'

'About half an hour after it happened.'

'How did you edit the footage?'

'Dad asked me to download the section with Stokesy so we could send it to you lot this morning. I copied the file, sent it to my phone and uploaded it to the forum while Dad was serving someone.' His nervous eyes sought out Bennett. 'I saw the webcam stuff from Sunday night. People losing their shit over it, travelling to Felixstowe to be in the place Stokesy stood. I wanted some of that.'

Bennett said nothing, her expression steady.

Jas kicked the soap bubbles at his feet. 'I know what you're thinking, and you're wrong. It wasn't for me, okay? This place has been dying a death for years. Do you know how hard my dad works to keep us afloat? I just thought if the Stokesy forum lot came here it might help turn this month around.'

'And have his fans spent any money yet?' Bennett asked.

Jas rolled his eyes. 'I told them to on the post. Said they could get a photo here if they spent a fiver. Dad thinks his prayers have been answered.'

Bennett made a deliberately bad attempt to hide her smile. At least the kid's motives were commendable even if the person he'd chosen to eulogise was questionable. 'If you get any repeat visits from Mr Stokes or anyone looking like him, you'll tell us first, right?'

'Yeah.' He risked a shy smile. 'Thanks.'

'My pleasure.'

'They're okay, though, the Stokesy fans. Like a family. They just want him home.'

'How long have you been using the forum?'

Jas rested the dripping sponge on the windscreen of the car beside him. 'About two years. One of my mates told me about it. I dunno, I just liked the banter on there. And the idea he's out there, doing his own thing.'

Bennett decided to push for more, considering the young man appeared happy to discuss it. 'So, how does it work? Are there moderators, anyone in charge?'

'It's like a normal forum. There are some users who check the chat, make sure nobody's being a dick. I mean, there are some nutters on there, but I avoid that stuff.'

'Do you know who those users are?'

Jas sniffed. 'Nobody really knows. Everyone's posting under handles, aren't they? But there's a few that seem to be senior.'

'Did any of the senior members repost your post?'

'Watcher89.' He beamed, as if this were an honour. 'They're one of the top bods.'

'Bet you were chuffed when that happened.'

'Yeah, man. Watcher89's like royalty or something.' His smile faded. 'You aren't going to tell anyone I said that, are you?'

'I'm just interested,' Bennett replied, deflecting. 'What do the people on StokesyFans think is making him come back now?'

'The fifteenth, isn't it? It's always been about that.'

'The fifteenth anniversary of him disappearing?'

'Yeah.'

'Why is that so important?'

'Honestly? I don't know. There's a lot of stuff you just accept in the forums because people say it all the time.'

'What are they making of these appearances?'

'People are going nuts over them! It's like waiting for your birthday that's days away,' Jas replied, with all the frustrated excitement of a child. 'They're saying he's getting closer to Kesgrave to show he's coming back for what's his.'

Bennett crafted her next question with utmost care. A wrong step now could stop the flow of information coming from the young man. 'What do you think he'll do to take back what he considers his?'

Jas picked up the sponge and slapped it against the car window, soapsuds leaving an arched trail as he began to wash it. 'I don't know. But if I'd done something to make Stokesy run, I'd be packing my bags right now.'

—

'You're quiet,' Ellis said as they drove back towards Ipswich. 'Where did you disappear to? And don't give me that *calling Minsh* crap.'

'I spoke to the kid. He posted the CCTV footage on a Stokesy forum last night.'

'What?'

'He said he did it to get some business for his dad, and I believed him. But when he started talking about the fan forums…' She braced her hands against the steering wheel as a shiver of distaste traversed her shoulders. 'It gave me the creeps.'

'The whole thing is twisted. I can't believe the things I've seen discussed on the site.'

'I got one of the organisers' handles.'

'How did you do that?'

'The kid started talking when he thought I was interested. He mentioned a "Watcher89" – apparently getting reposted by them is akin to a celebrity mentioning you.'

'Bloody hell, Kate, you don't hang about.'

She gave a wry smile. 'You underestimate my abilities, DC Ellis.' Instantly, her nerves reared up. Joking felt too risky, given the strangeness still between them. 'I'm concerned, though. The kid was a casual user of the site, but he was utterly convinced Ewan Stokes is coming back for revenge. If he's repeating it and not seeing any problem with what he's saying, what are those more invested in the rhetoric thinking?'

'I've seen that,' Ellis agreed. 'There's an edge to what they're discussing. Like they're a pack of hyenas waiting to watch a kill.'

'They think he's going to kill someone?'

'It's almost like they're hoping that will happen. The language used, the rhetoric repeated, it's legitimised hate against people they don't know. Threatening, nasty. They're projecting the anger and injustice they feel about those who've wronged them on to the people they see as having wronged Ewan Stokes.'

'Like Maisie Ingram.'

'Exactly. Did you see the files Minsh brought in? Actual, physical threats. And that's before all of this anniversary crap had kicked in.'

Coming to a halt behind a row of stationary traffic, Bennett looked at Ellis. 'I think there are others, Drew. I'm concerned that these fans and the person claiming to be Ewan Stokes are way ahead of us.'

Ellis observed her, his stillness unnerving. 'We need to find a way into the heart of those groups. Not the casual fans, but whoever is pushing this agenda. Find Watcher89, work out how involved they are. Ewan Stokes may well be the guy in the videos, but others have to be helping him.'

Of course he got it. Bennett reprimanded herself once again for underestimating him. Whatever else was out of kilter between them since the attack, her reliance upon his instinct remained. 'I think you're right. No way is he doing this alone. So how do we do this?'

'We get back to the office and we formulate a plan. If we work together we can find a way to reach the kingmakers.' Uncertainty flickered for a moment in his expression. 'Can we work together?'

'Of course.'

'That's not what I meant.'

A car horn blared behind them, summoning Bennett's attention back to the road. Aware of the question heavy in the air between them, she accelerated into the gap in the traffic that had opened up ahead.

Nineteen

CORA

'Come *on*!' Reece Bickland demanded from the doorstep as Cora locked her car and walked towards his house. 'I've been waiting a *hundred hours*.'

Beside the boy, his father offered an apologetic smile. 'Reece may have been a little excited about your visit today.'

'That's good to hear,' Cora replied, reaching them. 'I don't always get lovely welcomes like that when I arrive.'

Reece hefted a sigh and held his hand out to Cora. 'The Lego is ready.'

As he pulled on her hand, his father caught the file about to topple from Cora's arms.

'Allow me,' he said, tucking it under his arm. 'I'll take your bag for you, too, if you like?'

Already being dragged to the bottom step of the staircase, Cora handed Chris the leather rucksack and her jacket, which he took just as she was yanked up the stairs to the first floor.

The coffee table, rug and wooden floor around it appeared to have been hit by a large explosion of rainbow-hued bricks. As Cora passed the breakfast bar where before she'd heard Chris Bickland's dissenting voice from his belongings, it was empty of both. Instead, the happy object voices of the Bickland family flooded the space like the morning light. All the same, Cora sensed words not being said, tensions carefully concealed.

'Alex will be here in a while. She just had to pop out,' Chris said, standing beside the central sofa as Cora sat down. 'I'm on Reece Service this morning.'

'Butler!' Reece called, giggling when his father exacted an over-dramatic eye-roll. This was clearly a well-loved game.

'Yes, sir, of course, sir,' he replied. 'What can I get for sir?'

'Milk, please, Mister Butler.' His son grinned. 'And crisps for Cora.'

Cora laughed with surprise. 'It's a bit early for crisps for me,' she replied. 'Hold that thought, okay?'

She looked at Chris Bickland, who was watching his boy with unbridled pride. But Cora sensed something else – something shadowy and dark – hidden far beneath the layers of love. She remembered the conversation they'd had at the end of her first visit yesterday, that sudden change, the hint of deep pain fuelling his worst fears. Is that what this was?

'How about coffee?' he asked, the moment gone as quickly as it had arrived. 'Or tea?'

'Coffee, please. If that's okay with Reece?'

'Coffee is like bins and burning,' he pronounced. 'But I'll let you have some instead of crisps.'

'Perfect, thank you. Now, what are we building?'

She kicked off her shoes and knelt on the rug beside the delighted boy. As the multicoloured towers grew across the coffee table, Cora was aware of Chris watching from the kitchen.

She was used to parental angst. In her job she encountered more than most, always called into a familial situation because of an issue too big for the parents to handle alone. Usually, she was made welcome – a blessed relief for weary families who had sometimes battled for months to receive help. Very occasionally, her arrival was seen to be another level of interference: her presence with their child enforced by others and therefore something to be endured.

She liked this family already. Talking to Tris Noakes yesterday after-noon, she had mentioned the closeness of Chris and Alex with Reece, the calm after the horror of the bullying at his former school and the bewilderment they had that Reece's anxiety should be triggered now by a seemingly happy home.

'Projecting?' Tris had asked, as Cora had expected.

'Possibly. I think there may be another factor.'

'Bullying at his new school?'

'No. Something closer to home.'

'But you said the home was a contented one?'

'It is. Most of the object voices I hear there are happy and relaxed.'

Of course, Tris spotted the omission immediately. Cora liked that he did. Having a self-confessed fan of her ability was a rare gift after so many years of suspicion and being made to feel an outsider because of it. 'What have you heard?'

Cora considered it again now, in this room where twenty-four hours previously the single voice of disquiet had refused to be silenced. She wasn't certain what the words meant, but their tone had spoken volumes. The air around them had felt stifling, as if they were packed within a space far too small to contain them. Even the memory of the words as she described them to Tris had made Cora experience a feeling of constriction in her throat.

It had been frustration, for sure. But its cause remained stubbornly uncertain. What was Chris Bickland dealing with? And was it connected to his son?

'Look, Cora!' Reece was wiggling a long tower of blocks with a wider set at the base. 'It's a Space Explorer 3000!'

'That's so good,' she replied, pushing the questions away. They could wait for another time. 'What is its mission today?'

The boy beamed, his game affirmed. 'There's an alien signal coming from the Gamma Quadrant. Nobody's heard it before so they're going to investigate.'

'Wow, that's an exciting mission! Who's in the Space Explorer crew?'

'Captain Thunder – he's the boss. Doctor O'Tay – she's the medic but also the one who can speak all the alien languages. Then there's Gatcha the robot pilot, and ZimZim the shapeshifter alien who can go invisible when they reach the alien planet so they can investigate with nobody seeing them.'

Cora smiled. 'Who's your favourite?'

Reece observed her for a moment. 'ZimZim.'

'What do you like about them?'

'They can hide when they want to. But they keep everyone safe.'

'Is that important?'

The boy nodded, suddenly shy. Cora felt the air close around them. 'What does ZimZim keep the crew safe from?'

Blue eyes mooned up at her, a lip bitten. Then, a whisper: 'It's a secret.'

'Are we all having a good time?' Chris Bickland's voice split the moment. Reece returned his attention to his spaceship. Cora forced a smile.

'Reece was telling me about the space mission,' she replied.

'Ah.' Chris handed her a mug of coffee. 'His favourite game. We watched some old episodes of *Star Trek* a couple of months ago and he's been obsessed ever since.' He settled himself on the sofa, watching his son.

Cora felt an easing in the atmosphere, the earlier constriction gone. But now she had a way in. Like all of her cases she would bide her time until she could use it again. But it was what she had learned to look for. Tris called these moments 'keys'.

'There's one for every person in every situation. Sometimes it can take months to find, so you keep hunting until you do. All the children we see have an intrinsic need to share the root cause of the issue affecting them, but it's hidden deep behind layers of fear, of shame sometimes, or a need for control. As soon as you discover the keys, it's your way to bypass all of those things.'

Reece's 'secret' could just be part of his game. Cora could so easily have missed it had it not been for the distinct change in his demeanour and the atmosphere around him. From now on she would be watching.

'I'm just going to have a chat with your dad, is that okay?' she asked him.

'Okay, but if the space crew need you, you have to come straight back.'

'Just say the word.' Cora smiled, lifting herself from the rug to sit on the sofa.

'Going well?' Chris asked, low to pass beneath his son's happy chatter.

'Very well. Thanks for the coffee – spaceship building is thirsty work.'

'Has he said anything?' It was an interesting question. Was it a general inquiry or was he testing the waters, knowing more than he should?

Cora shook her head as she sipped her coffee. 'It's very early. Hang in there.'

'Yeah. Sorry.' He rubbed the back of his neck. 'It's just this situation, you know? When he's like this most of the time the school stuff doesn't seem to fit.'

'I know. Anxiety is a strange beast sometimes. It affects people in many different ways, and children even more so.' The man beside her looked so lost, so bewildered. Cora's heart went out to him. 'If it helps, focus on the positives. The anxiety isn't consuming his world: it's in one clearly defined area. That makes the chances of us tackling it far easier. We have a way forward, and if we can deal with the issue now it won't spread to other areas.'

Chris stared back. 'That does help, thank you. With my family's history, you know, I worry. I've worried for myself for years and the thought that Reece might…' The end of his sentence was stolen by emotion.

Cora averted her eyes to the view of the sea beyond the wide windows. As she did, the shrill sound of a mobile ringtone sounded. Chris swore under his breath as he wrestled his phone to silent, but it was too late.

The toy brick spaceship fell to the floor and shattered, a scream exploding from the pieces.

Make it stop!

Cora braced against the slap of fear Reece Bickland's secret voice brought, as a loud wail erupted from the boy's mouth.

'*Nooo!*'

'Reece, buddy, it's okay. It was just Daddy's phone…' Chris held up the mobile but dropped it to the sofa when he saw the wide-eyed terror staring back at him.

Not now, the phone growled as it hit the cushion.

'Don't answer!' the boy yelled, now on his feet beside his father.

'I'm not. I won't. I'm sorry, matey. Calm down.'

But his son wasn't listening. Tears streaming down his angry red face, he flew at Chris and started to push him away from the phone. 'Get away from it!'

'I turned it off! I won't answer!' Chris looked helplessly at Cora. 'This is what happens.'

Shaken, Cora remembered her training and moved to Reece's side, her hand gently resting on his shoulder. 'Reece, you need some breath. Take a deep breath for me…' She ducked as the boy's hand punched out at her face, keeping her voice calm and steady. 'I know you're scared. It's okay. Look at me, Reece. Look at me…'

He was shaking, unblinking terror claiming his expression, but slowly his face turned to hers.

'That's great, thank you. Now take a deep breath…' She made an exaggerated inhale, eyes locked with his. His breath shuddered as he tried to follow. 'Good, now blow it all out at me.' When he hesitated, she pressed on. 'Go on, as big a blow as you can do.'

She nodded her encouragement as Reece began to blow out, slowly at first and then all at once, a loud sob following on its tail.

'Great. Now, let's do it again. Even bigger this time.'

She held her nerve as the young boy gradually calmed down, his shocked father watching dumbly on. When the worst was over, Reece climbed onto his dad's lap and curled up small against his chest.

'Why were you scared, bud?' Chris asked, raising his eyes to the ceiling in frustration when his son's head shook in vehement refusal.

'We don't have to talk about it now,' Cora said quickly, not wanting his impatience to break the spell. 'You did so well, Reece. I'm proud of you.'

A distant door slammed, causing Chris to turn his head. Moments later, Alex Bickland hurried into the room.

'I heard him crying from the drive. What happened?'

'My phone,' Chris said, coaxing Reece into Alex's arms as she crouched beside the sofa. 'I forgot to turn the damn thing off…'

'Silent, always silent in the house,' Alex hissed between her teeth, cradling her son close and stroking his hair.

'I know, but I was waiting for an alert. The story…'

'I don't care about *the story*. I care about our *son*.' She pointedly turned from her husband to offer Cora a strained smile. 'I'm sorry. We're *trying* to limit Reece's exposure to ringing phones while we work out the cause.'

'It's a good thing I was able to see it,' Cora replied, careful not to let the shock still reverberating within her sneak into her reply. 'We won't discuss this any more today, but perhaps I can call you later?'

'That would help, thank you.'

Driving away from the Bicklands' house, Cora pieced together the events she had witnessed: Chris Bickland's frustration, Reece's startling change from contented soul to terrified child, the rumble of discontent and words not spoken from Alex. Clearly, the family had more to deal with than was visible at first.

What could Reece be projecting on to the sound of a ringing phone? It wasn't unusual to find children focusing their fear on an otherwise innocuous object, place or sound, but Cora hadn't seen a reaction as strong as the six-year-old's before.

He had calmed considerably in the thirty minutes after the event, but remained close by his mother, bruised by the experience of earlier. After a pointed comment, Chris had gone to his office on the ground floor of the house – only then had Alex relaxed. But as her son resumed his spaceship building, her eyes rested warily on his every move.

The puzzle remained with Cora as she drove back through her home town on her journey to Ipswich. Seeing her favourite bakery ahead, she decided to grab lunch to take back for Tris, who was once again wading through bureaucratic red tape in yet another meeting and was unlikely to have had a chance to eat. As she pulled into a parking space by the bakery's sunshine-yellow frontage, her mobile buzzed.

Killing the engine, she pulled her phone from her bag and read the alert that had just flashed on-screen.

StokesyFans.com Alert

NEW SIGHTING

Rai's Garage, outskirts of Felixstowe, Suffolk, UK.

Stokesy is going home!

#Stokesy15

Twenty

ANDERSON

So much for keeping a lid on the investigation.

Anderson bowed his head as the gaggle of journalists swarmed around the steps of South Suffolk Police HQ.

'DI Anderson! Any comment to make on Ewan Stokes coming back?'

'Are South Suffolk on the back foot again?'

'Are the rumours true? Does he want revenge?'

'No comment,' Anderson muttered, shouldering them out of his way.

Why had he chosen this lunchtime to treat himself to a decent coffee and sandwich from his favourite Ipswich deli? He should have stayed in the sweltering, airless pit of his office with the depressingly healthy packed lunch Ros had insisted he bring to work.

He should definitely have given in to temptation with those *maritozzi* cream buns the deli had on special. Today was a day for cream and high fat to combat the pressure of an investigation now made the business of the media, and nothing in the station canteen could hope to deliver those like the delicacies he'd foregone. He could have turned around and travelled back to rectify the mistake, but that was impossible now this tide of hacks was here.

Bastard journalists.

And even more bastard for keeping him from much-needed treats.

'Friends of yours, Guv?' Pauline, the usually gruff-faced desk sergeant, smirked as he bustled into reception.

'They're no friends of mine,' he returned, clutching his takeout coffee cup and precious baguette to himself as he swiped his card on the door entry.

'I'll tell them you don't want to play, then, shall I?' Pauline called in his wake.

It was probably for the best that he was out of Pauline's earshot when he launched his reply.

In the CID office the news had already broken. A news report was playing on the small television screen as Minshull watched, hands punched onto hips. Anderson could guess his expression even with the DS's back turned. Around him, the team peered around computer screens, Ellis and Evans watching from the kitchen area.

'When did they go with the story?' Anderson asked, not even bothering to announce his arrival.

'It's just gone live on the lunchtime news,' Minshull replied. 'There was a small item on the Sky News website, but stupidly I thought that's all there would be. Nothing from the other news agencies yet, though.'

'Oh, they all know. Most of them are blockading the front steps.'

Minshull turned, his expression too weary this early in the day. 'Who?'

'The usual suspects. *Daily Call*, *The Epoch*, *Daily Signal*. No sign of *The Sentinel* yet but they'll be biting our heels with the rest of them soon enough.'

'Let me guess: *Failed case comes back to haunt South Suffolk CID?*'

Anderson snorted. 'You clearly have a career in gutter journalism if the DS gig doesn't work out.'

'Lucky me.' Minshull's half-smile was a sign of solidarity.

'I see our friend's getting his fifteen minutes of fame,' Ellis said, collecting mugs from his colleagues' desks for the coffee round.

The delighted garage owner was being interviewed, his grinning son proud by his side. *BREAKING: Missing man appears on petrol station CCTV* ran the rolling news banner across the bottom of the screen.

'Fair play to him, I say,' Wheeler said. 'I hope he charged the journos to film on his premises.'

Bennett gave a small smile before returning to her work.

Anderson thought of the Italian cream bun he could have been eating. At least someone appeared to be pleased by the breaking news story. It stuck in his throat to see the glee with which the story was being reported, knowing only too well what was bound to follow: scaremongering, slander of the police and whipping the story wildly out of proportion.

'Any news on our white van?' he asked.

'Traffic are still looking, Guv,' Ellis said. 'I checked with them an hour ago.'

'How can it just disappear? No sign of it back at the lock-up?'

'Steph Lanehan went over this morning. Her friend there said it's not been back since.'

'Laughable, that's what it is. One bloody van and the whole of South Suffolk's combined investigative might can't find it,' Anderson snorted, noticing too late the effect this had on Wheeler. 'You did what you could, Dave.'

'Not enough to stop him, Guv.'

'DCI Taylor called, too,' Ellis said, his apologetic smile little comfort. 'She wants an update.'

'I'll bet she does,' Anderson muttered, holding up a hand when he saw the uniform grins of his team. 'And you didn't hear that, okay?'

Great. Sue Taylor on the warpath, journalists laying siege to Police HQ and a white van and missing man giving them the runaround. And today had seemed like it might be a quiet one when it began.

It didn't help that the summer temperatures had soared today after the stubborn rain of yesterday, the beginning of a promised heatwave. True to form, what little air con the CID office possessed had already admitted defeat: apologetic ancient fans positioned around the room were doing little more than moving heat around. Today was not a day to be doing battle with an investigation that had no concrete leads.

Anderson wanted an advantage, a step ahead, but Ewan Stokes – or whoever was pushing the story of his apocryphal return – currently held all the cards. He hadn't broken the law, from what they could tell. A webcam appearance and a CCTV shot were nuisances but not illegal. And the worldwide cult of idiots idolising their version of the missing man were little more than furious keyboard warriors stirring up trouble. Nothing linked. No doors opened. And pretty soon the gathered gannets of the media would work this out.

All the *maritozzi* in the deli couldn't make this better.

'Right, can we gather for a briefing?' Minshull asked, his expression a perfect mirror for Anderson's mood.

The movement of detectives and their chairs to face Minshull and the whiteboard could hardly be described as a rush. Nobody could blame them: the oppressive heat in the office coupled with the stubbornness of the investigation was enough to make anyone drag their heels.

Evans was the last to join the gathered group, his muted conversation and distinct lack of jokes noticeable. Anderson watched him slouch across, head bowed. It took a great deal to pierce the distinctly thick skin of CID's most questionable DC, but it appeared that he'd taken the damage to his car on Sunday night particularly to heart. While it was never pleasant to experience, Anderson wondered why it had taken something so seemingly trivial to tip the scales. He wouldn't challenge him yet, however. With everyone in the team battling heat, frustration and now unwelcome media interest, a little introspection was understandable. If it continued, though, Anderson would have a word.

Minshull offered his team a weary smile.

'Right. Where are we?'

'Kavish Rai's son Jas confirmed that he uploaded the CCTV footage to the StokesyFans forum last night, about half an hour after it happened,' Bennett answered.

'Is he a fan?'

'More like a kind opportunist.' When Minshull frowned, Bennett explained. 'He did it to drum up business for his dad. Quite sweet, really.'

Minshull shook his head. 'Nothing would surprise me about this case. Okay, if he knows about the forums, he could be a useful person to visit if we need to know about the command structures and who might be running them.'

'Mr Rai's son mentioned a Watcher89. A senior member on the forums,' Bennett said. 'I did a search for their posts and they're the ones breaking these stories and corroborating them. Might not be actual command, but they seem to know what's going on more than the regular forum members.'

'Good. Keep digging on that.' Anderson nodded.

'I've been looking at StokesyFans, Sarge,' Ellis said. 'The forum is registered to a Richard Beech. I did a business search in the area and found that he's a web developer over in St Just. I've called the number listed for his business but haven't had a reply yet.'

'Interesting. Keep trying, please. Let me know if you speak to him and if you do, arrange a meeting.'

'Yes, Sarge.'

'Is that the main forum?' Anderson asked.

'One of them, Guv. I've looked at those listed – about twenty that I've found so far – and from what I can tell there are three main forums: StokesyFans, FindEwan and one called SuffolkMystery, which was originally set up to cover all kinds of unsolved cases in the county but for the last couple of years has exclusively focused on Ewan Stokes.'

'These people are *insane.*' Anderson welcomed the weary smiles of his team. This was not the weather for standing on ceremony. Today they were all in the same sweaty, airless place and they were better united.

Minshull stared at the whiteboard, the few spartan pieces of information pinned there frustratingly unconnected. Taking his red board pen he drew a box in the top right-hand corner.

'So, judging by what we've learned from Maisie Ingram and the speculation on the main Ewan Stokes fan sites, we'll work on the theory that he is returning for the fifteenth anniversary of his disappearance. That is the 27th of July. Today is the 18th, giving us nine days.' He wrote a large number nine in the box. 'We have to assume the countdown has begun and that if this is a campaign linked to the belief that he's coming back, there could well be more sightings between today and the anniversary date. Especially now that the press are involved.'

'You think he'll court the papers?' Wheeler asked.

Minshull shrugged. 'Who's to know, Dave? But if I wanted to gain maximum exposure for my cause, I would be milking the media for every scrap of attention.'

Anderson considered the number in the box. Nine days. Written down, it didn't look a lot. Nine days to solve a mystery fifteen years in the making. Nine days to find the link.

'There is your countdown,' he told the team, pointing at the white-board. 'We have nothing, but we keep pushing, keep knocking, until something shifts. There *is* a solution. Someone is behind this, planning it to happen exactly as it's playing out We have nine days to find them.'

Twenty-One

MINSHULL

According to speculation on the Ewan Stokes fan forums, more sightings were imminent. Minshull suspected it was more a case of overactive imaginations than genuine tip-offs, but it still warranted notice if not action. Of course, the savvier members of the press had now latched on to the forums' existence and were gleefully grabbing any new theory to feed their readers, no matter how insane and unfounded it appeared to be.

EWAN STOKES: HOMECOMING OR REVENGE?

STOKESY: FORMER BOSS IN HIDING

RETURN OF MISSING MAN: A LOVER'S REVENGE?

'Bollocks, the lot of it,' Wheeler scoffed, nodding at the latest updates on *The Sentinel* website. 'And saying "a source close to the missing man" doesn't make it legit. They've just been trawling the forums, same as we have.'

'At least they've managed to reach some conclusions,' Minshull muttered, three hours of fruitless wading through the delusions of so-called superfans sapping his energy faster than the oppressive heat. 'Why do I feel we're missing something?'

'*They're* missing something, more like.' Wheeler gave Minshull's shoulder a reassuring pat. 'Most of it isn't real, so there's no evidence to find. Trailing a bunch of, frankly, odd bods for information is only ever going to make you relieved you aren't one of them.'

Minshull looked up at his friend. 'So if this is all fabricated, who is pushing it? And why? I get that the fifteenth anniversary looks like a significant milestone, but it doesn't mean anything beyond a date. Why has he waited fifteen years? What's he been doing since he disappeared? How has he been living, eating, moving about, all of it under the radar of police in every country he's supposed to have visited?'

Wheeler flopped down on the chair beside Minshull's desk. 'Beggared if I know, Sarge. He wasn't a millionaire when he went missing, was he?'

'Not according to the information the first investigation gathered. He was an electrician doing cash-in-handers on building sites. He couldn't even afford his rent after Maisie Ingram threw him out.'

'See, that's another mystery: the travel thing. I went back through his so-called "anniversary messages" – they're right across Europe. There have been international alerts out on this man in every country: how has he evaded them? Someone has to be helping him. There's an agenda here beyond a miraculous return from the dead. He needs internet access, the means to set up and maintain these forums, money to make it all happen. If he's been supporting himself with no need for a bank account, passport, any legal documents and managing to build a huge online community at the same time as travelling freely across Europe, he must have had help.'

Wheeler tapped the edge of the desk with his biro. 'So we need to find out who his closest friends were. Who he trusted. Who missed him when he left. We know Ms Ingram stepped away from him just before he went missing: so who stayed?'

'Yes!' Minshull would have hugged Dave Wheeler had it not been for the sweat currently soaking his shirt. 'Brilliant. Right, can you and Les do a search through the witness statements, please? See which names come up.'

Wheeler reluctantly vacated his seat. 'On it.'

Who missed him… Minshull found Olwyn Stokes-Norton's number. If the CCTV story was across the papers she would have seen it by now.

The call rang out several times, Minshull tapping his pen on his notepad as he willed her to answer. On the final ring, she did.

'Hello?'

'Hi, Mrs Stokes-Norton, it's DS Minshull.'

'I've seen it.' Her statement was flat.

'Do you think it's Ewan?'

There was a pause. Then, 'I wasn't sure before. But that's my son.'

'You're certain?'

'Yes. I don't understand why he hasn't contacted me, or what he's doing with these appearances. I just want him home.'

Who missed him... Minshull was chastened by her words. He'd spent all morning scoffing at the folly of those on the forums, but this was what really mattered: a mother, denied answers or the right to grieve for fifteen years, finally getting a glimpse of the son she had never stopped searching for. And yet, denied access still. 'My team and I are doing everything we can to find him.'

'What if those people on the forum find him first? Or he sees what they're expecting him to do? I have no idea what Ewan's mental state is after all this time. If he's seeking validation from those monsters...' Minshull heard a stifled sob, followed by a cough. 'It's not the first time.'

'Sorry? Not the first time for what?'

'Before he went missing. There were people he was hanging around with, people with questionable motives. Egging him on to do stupid things, take idiotic risks. I tried to get him away from them.'

'Did you tell the investigators this when he disappeared?'

'I may have. I can't remember. I was worried he'd get into trouble, be blamed for things in his absence that he couldn't counter.'

'Who were these friends?'

'I don't know their names. Their reputation preceded them. Into drink and drugs, forever starting fights. Just local layabouts, but I worried for Ewan. He wanted friends; he liked being popular. That's why I pushed him to join the football team in Kesgrave, why I was delighted when he signed with the Felixstowe team. I thought it would be a better influence, keep him away from the others. But fifteen years away and all this questionable interest from people who don't know him — I can't say what effect that will have had.'

'We're going to find him,' Minshull reaffirmed, even if right now it seemed unwise to say it. 'In the meantime, if you can remember any names of the group you mentioned, it would really help us.'

'I'll try.'

'Thank you.'

'Find him, DS Minshull. Please.'

Ending the call, he walked over to Anderson's office. When his knock was answered by a gruff invitation to enter, he stepped inside.

Anderson looked up from paperwork spread over his desk. 'Please tell me you have good news?'

'I just spoke to Olwyn. She's confirmed the figure on the Rai's Garage CCTV as her son.'

'Bloody hell.'

'I know. She's concerned he may be influenced by the wild speculation over his return.'

Anderson frowned. 'In what way?'

'She reckoned Stokes was impressionable, easily led. Was hanging round with a bad crowd prior to his disappearance. She couldn't recall names.'

His superior rolled his eyes. 'Of course.'

'If what she says is true, could Stokes be manufacturing the Fifteen Year Return in response to the fan theory?'

'Being led by them?'

Minshull shrugged. 'If he's believing all the folk hero rubbish, he might be playing to the crowd. And what worries me is that the rhetoric on the forums is becoming more violent the more evidence they see that he's back in Suffolk.'

'So they're setting an agenda they expect him to follow and he'll do it because of the affirmation?' Anderson ran a hand through his hair. 'This gets crazier by the minute.'

'I think we need to find who's directing these appearances, Guv. I don't think he's working alone: and if someone helping him has a violent agenda…' He didn't need to finish, Anderson already under-standing.

'We need to talk to the owner of the website. And identify this Watcher89 person. Find anyone mentioned in the original notes as a friend or acquaintance.'

'Guv.'

'Also, any word back from the owner of the Caddy van? Two collisions now, and apparently someone has the keys to the lock-up, even if the van isn't there.'

'I emailed Lindsay Carlton again this morning. I've heard nothing back.'

Anderson gave a long groan. 'What is it with people? If my vehicle had been used in two RTCs and was now being driven heaven knows where, I'd want to know.'

'Me too. I'll keep trying.'

'Sarge.'

Ellis was in the doorway, looking as if he was about to sprint away, his phone pressed to his ear.

'Yes, Drew?'

'Reported intruder at a house in Felixstowe. Caught on a doorbell camera twice before, and he's still there.'

'What?' Minshull was across Anderson's office in four strides. 'When?'

'Just. Steph Lanehan and Rilla Davis are on their way. Control have sent me the address.'

'Great, let's go,' Minshull said, following Ellis back into the main office and grabbing a set of pool car keys. 'Want to come, Drew?'

'Sarge… Yes, Sarge…' The DC struggled to pack away his surprise. 'DS Minshull and DC Drew Ellis attending,' he spluttered into the phone as he ended the call.

Minshull's heart was hammering by the time he got behind the wheel. The dash from CID to the car park was fast, fuelled by adren-aline but a battle against the heat. The pool car had been parked in direct sun for hours, the plastic coating of the steering wheel searing into his skin as he steered out of the car park.

'What do we know?' he asked Ellis as they sped through Ipswich.

'Control just sent the details. A Mr Damien East called it in just after three p.m. His wife is at home and saw the intruder standing on the doorstep first at nine a.m., again at around 12:20 p.m. and then she called her husband in panic because the intruder had returned. She's locked all the doors and is hiding in the house, but according to Mr East the man on the doorstep is still there.'

'Did the man knock on the door?'

'No. Just stood there. Mrs East could see him through the glass.'

Minshull frowned at the road ahead, opting to take a side road shortcut to avoid the building traffic. 'Has he posted anything? Damaged anything?'

'No, Sarge. He's just standing there.'

'Are we in contact with Mrs East?'

'No, just her husband. He said he doesn't want anyone ringing her in case the intruder is alerted.'

Minshull wound down the windows in an attempt to expel some of the stifling heat in the car. 'And he's been there before?'

Ellis nodded. 'This morning and again at lunchtime. Mr East said they have doorbell camera footage of it all.'

'Is the intruder anyone he recognises?'

'I don't know. I think only his missus has seen the guy – Mr East was calling us because she's on her own in the house and he isn't there.'

'Control to DS Minshull…' The radio barked into the hot car.

Ellis responded. 'DC Ellis speaking, go ahead.'

'Officers in pursuit of intruder. Urgent assistance required.'

Ellis glanced at Minshull, who accelerated. 'Understood, we're attending. ETA – er – what we looking at, Sarge?'

'Not bloody fast enough,' Minshull cursed, flooring the accelerator.

Twenty-Two

LANEHAN

Today was not a day for an on-foot pursuit.

PC Steph Lanehan swore as the hooded figure kicked speed into his escape, widening the gap between them.

Little scrote!

She'd surprised him when she had approached, and at first it appeared he would be compliant. Some hopes of that. Usually in this job you had a pretty good sense of who would stay and who would run. Standing on the doorstep with his white cardboard sign, Steph would have laid odds on him being the former.

Maybe all that crap with the van chase and collision yesterday had addled her brain. Or she was losing her touch.

'Police! Stop!' she yelled, as if that would make a difference. The bloke in the black hoodie knew she was police: that was why he was running.

She followed him as he turned sharply to run down a side alley passing between the streets of the Felixstowe housing estate. It was the kind of layout Lanehan was familiar with, having been brought up on a similar estate as a kid. But this leafy suburb of the town was a world away from the Parkhall Estate in St Just, the faded and forgotten estate of her childhood.

'Suspect has gone down the alleyway on Western Avenue. I'm in pursuit,' she yelled into her radio as she chased after him.

PC Rilla Davis had dashed off in the opposite direction, and Lanehan hoped it was to take advantage of her own local knowledge. Davis, still a rookie recruit, hailed from Felixstowe. A college grad who decided policing was preferable to the law degree her parents were hoping for. Did she miss the cosier side of the law? Lanehan had thought her perfect copper material when she'd first joined. But now?

The hooded figure grabbed a garden fence, attempting to climb, but the cardboard sign he was still inexplicably holding hampered his progress. There was a moment of indecision as he appeared to be choosing between the fence and the sign. That was the advantage Lanehan needed. She pushed forward, gaining on the preoccupied man.

Just steps away now. She reached out...

Smack!

The punch came from nowhere, connecting with her jaw with a sickening crack. The force caused Lanehan to lose balance, tumbling to the unforgiving tarmac of the alley path. Seeing stars, she shut her eyes and fought against her flailing body to push herself upright. The thud of footsteps ahead confirmed her worst fears.

Bastard!

That did it. Bad enough the little shit had made her run on the hottest day of the year, but adding a punch into the mix? Nobody did that and got away. She'd seen it all during her police career – verbal abuse, sudden violence, spitting, threats – but a punch to the face was a new, unwelcome addition in recent years. In the past it was more shoving and kicks, fists only caught in the face when flailing arms were resisting arrest. She'd seen her male colleagues cop a punch countless times, but lately everyone was fair game.

Fred wouldn't be happy. She could already feel the glowering bruise forming on her chin – it would be impossible to hide when she got home. Besides, he knew. He'd known for years, but since the attack she and Davis had been subjected to, her husband had started to voice his concerns.

'It isn't that you're too old, girl,' he'd insisted last night, during their latest row. She'd made the mistake of telling him about the van chase and the damage done when her car had hit Wheeler's. Steph hated arguing with him, but she wasn't backing down for anyone, even Fred. 'I know you can handle yourself. You'll likely be kickin'' butt when most of us are dribbling in our care homes. It's that lot out there I worry about. They don't care who you are. They'll attack you because you're the enemy. And they don't just use their fists any more.'

He was entitled to be worried, of course. It was nice to have someone to worry about her; many of her longest-serving colleagues didn't any more, their marriages a casualty of the constant demands of the job. But that didn't mean she had to agree with him. She'd always been a copper: it was as much a part of her as her blood and bones. What else would she do?

She loved Fred. But Fred was wrong. And so was the pesky sod who thought one punch would floor her.

Despite her protesting limbs, she forced her body on, cursing the man, the heat and everything else as she ran.

When I catch up with you…

He slowed at the end of the alley where the path opened out into a cul-de-sac, head whipping left and right to gauge the best route. Either way there was only one way out unless he turned and ran back at Lanehan. He opted for the left side…

…then suddenly slumped to the floor, yelling obscenities as he fell.

When Lanehan reached the end of the alley, she saw why.

Jamming the man's hands behind his back, her whole weight trained on pinning him down, was Davis.

'You took your time,' she smirked, as Lanehan joined her, both officers bracing themselves against the furious, squirming man beneath them, while Davis cuffed his hands.

'Might have guessed you'd know the shortcut.' Lanehan grimaced under the strain as she reached for her radio. 'PC Lanehan to Control. Suspect apprehended at the top of Barons Close.'

'Received, Steph. Hang tight, DS Minshull and DC Ellis will be with you in five minutes.'

'Received, thank you.' She pressed down harder on the hooded man who tried to jerk his way free. 'Stay where you are, sir. My colleagues are keen to have a word with you.'

'Get off me, bitches,' the man spat, eliciting rolled eyes from Davis.

'Lovely language, sir. Is that what you use on the people you freakily doorstep with your little sign?' Steph glanced down at the cardboard rectangle still clutched in his hands, his knuckles now as white as the surface of it. The cardboard was scratched but the message unmistakeable:

HELP ME

Was this the hooded figure from the pier webcam and the CCTV at Rai's Garage? Had apprehending Ewan Stokes really been so easy?

'I'm not meeting anyone, bitch!'

'But they're all so excited to meet you, sir. Might even ask for your autograph. Apparently, you're a bit famous. Have to think of your fans, don't you?'

'You can't do this! I've done nothing wrong!'

'Is that so? Let's see… well, there was the creepy standing on a doorstep thing you've done three times today and, what else? Oh yes.' She leaned closer to his ear so he definitely wouldn't miss what she wanted to say. 'There's assaulting a police officer and resisting arrest. Two *very wrong* things, in my opinion.'

'You're not arresting me!'

'Actually, you'll find she is,' Davis said, holding his arms fast while Steph read him his rights. As she did so, the sound of running feet heralded the arrival of Minshull and Ellis, red-faced and out of breath, their eyes wide when they saw the man and the sign beneath Lanehan and Davis.

'Bloody hell, you got him!' Ellis exclaimed, as he joined the officers on the ground to keep the hooded man still, shock stealing any attempt at professional calm he may have wanted to make.

'Don't sound so surprised,' Davis retorted. 'Took two PCs to do your work for you, did it, Detective? Sounds about right to me.'

'You've given us one hell of a runaround, sir. And you have a lot of questions to answer. Hell of a return, mate…' Minshull bent down beside the man and pulled back the hood obscuring his features.

When the face was revealed, silence stole their thunder.

It wasn't Ewan Stokes.

Twenty-Three

ELLIS

It was quite possible Minshull was about to spontaneously combust.

Ellis eyed his superior as he visibly reeled from the news. They had been so certain on the race over to Felixstowe that this was the break the investigation had been praying for. Hearing that Lanehan and Davis were in pursuit had only raised their expectations. The black hooded sweatshirt, the sign, the silent standing – it all pointed to Ewan Stokes. But while the uniform of the silent intruder fit, his face didn't. Neither was he as silent as the man he'd clearly hoped to convince Mrs East he was. Right now, Ellis was learning a whole new vocabulary when he thought he'd heard everything in this job.

Minshull caught Ellis watching him and the smile the DC sent back did nothing to appease the DS's frown. Then he crouched down beside the Stokesy pretender, his voice a deep growl.

'Shut *up*.'

'You aren't arresting me for anything! My solicitor's going to string you bastards up! He's going to…'

'You impersonated a person of interest in a deliberate attempt to fool your intended victim. You assaulted my colleague. You resisted arrest. I think your solicitor will have more than enough to occupy him, don't you?'

The man on the ground said nothing.

Minshull nodded at his colleagues. 'Let's get this gentleman to his feet. Drew, come this side of me.'

Ellis did as he was told, arms outstretched ready to grab the intruder's arm.

'On my count... one... two... three...'

The walk back to Tarn Hows Close where the CID pool car was parked next to the patrol car was longer than Ellis remembered, the added complication of a foul-mouthed, struggling man at the centre of the four officers hampering their onward progress. Finally, after acquiring several interesting bruises Ellis was certain would spark conversation at the gym, the cars came into view and the man was bundled ungracefully into the back of the patrol car.

'Good work, everyone,' Minshull said, slamming the patrol car door. 'I've called Support to assist us but they're stuck on a job in Ipswich. Drew, can you hop in the car with our friend, please?'

'No problem, Sarge.'

The sound of a fast-approaching vehicle made the group turn as a dark blue four-by-four screeched to a halt on the drive of the Easts' house.

'I'm going to hang back here. I want to talk to Mrs East, and this looks like it could be her husband. Good timing.' Minshull grinned at Ellis. 'See if you can get our Stokesy wannabe chatting on the journey back, will you? I want to know what his connection to Ewan Stokes is and why he chose this location. Who is he? A fan? A copycat looking for his five minutes of fame? Does he know Ewan Stokes personally?'

Ellis didn't fancy his chances of getting anything coherent out of the furious suspect beyond more brand-new expletives, but he accepted anyway.

'Did you get him?' the man from the four-by-four panted, hurrying over to them.

'We did, sir.' Minshull offered his hand. 'Detective Sergeant Rob Minshull, and these are my colleagues who apprehended your visitor.'

'Is Nat okay?'

'Nat?'

'Natalie – my wife. She's been terrified.'

'I'm just going to see her, sir,' Minshull replied. 'Perhaps I can accompany you? There are some questions I need to ask you both.'

'Of course... yes, er... We should go...' East stumbled to reply, wringing his hands as he looked between his home and the detective.

Ellis caught Minshull's expression as he followed the husband to the house. He might have put the husband's stilted reply down to the surge of adrenaline and fear he must no doubt be feeling, but Ellis knew the Sarge better than to accept that. Something else was at work and, if DS Minshull had noticed, it wouldn't stay hidden much longer.

'Interesting character,' Lanehan observed, beside him.

'Minsh thinks so.'

Lanehan laughed. 'If Minsh is on his case that poor sod'll have more to worry about than finishing a sentence.' She pulled the patrol car keys from her pocket. 'Right, Drew-boy, you ready for the back seat rollercoaster ride back?' The left half of her chin was already blueing and her smile was tentative on that side, but she didn't appear rattled by it. The poor Stokesy pretender had picked the wrong copper to mess with today. Lanehan was clearly enjoying her victory.

He smiled back. 'Bring it on.'

As predicted, the first ten minutes of the car journey consisted of wounded silence, punctured by furious obscenities. Lanehan and Davis maintained a chirpy conversation in the front seats, the act specifically designed to make a point. In the back seat beside the still-unnamed Stokesy impersonator, Ellis watched the passing countryside and bided his time. The interior of the car was sweltering – no hint of air con in this vehicle, of course. Ellis could feel a steady trickle of sweat moving down his spine, his shirt damp wherever it made contact with his skin. Even his feet were sweating, an uncomfortably warm, swampy sensation inside his polished work shoes. To take his mind off it, he pictured the long shower he could enjoy after his shift today and the beer already chilling in his fridge. He loved his job, but some days the thought of home at the end of them was the dangling carrot needed to endure the hours at work.

'Are you going to tell us your name, sir?' he asked again, more to take his mind off the heat than because he expected a reply. 'Seems a bit rude when you know all of ours.'

The man harrumphed and glared out of his window.

'Fair enough. You're entitled to keep it to yourself.' He caught Lanehan's grin in the rear-view mirror. 'It's just a bit strange, considering you say you're innocent. If it was me, I'd want people to know my name. Especially if, as you said, my solicitor was about to make mincemeat out of us police officers for wrongful arrest. I mean, if you're sure you've done nothing wrong, why wouldn't you want us to know?'

'I don't have to say anything.'

Except you just did, mate, Ellis congratulated himself. 'Of course.'

There was a pause as the man considered the situation. Ellis turned his head slowly back to the view passing his window. It was a game, feigning disinterest in order to invite a reply. He remembered his mum telling him how best to deal with the cat on the farm he grew up on, which had famously hated him from the moment he was born.

'You're trying too hard, Drew. Cats don't like folks that make it too easy. They're not like dogs that crave your attention. They want to make it their decision to give you the time of day. So ignore her. Walk away. Act like you're not bothered and she'll be all over you.'

In truth, Ellis never expected it to work on humans but during the few years of policing already under his belt he had found this approach to be surprisingly effective. Farm knowledge, it turned out, went a long way in police life.

And sure enough, the tactic won yet another tricky cat over.

'Rick Beech,' the man mumbled.

'There now, isn't that better?' Davis asked from the front seat.

'I'm not talking to you.'

'Charming, that is, isn't it, Steph?'

'She's very nice to talk to, you know, Mr Beech. Much nicer than me.'

Ellis hid his smile. He was aware how quickly this opened door could slam. 'Where are you from, Mr Beech?'

'Felixstowe.'

'Whereabouts?'

'Dellwood Avenue. Near the cricket club.'

'Nice bit of town,' Davis commented.

'So not far to come, then?' Ellis asked. 'With your sign.'

Beech said nothing.

It was time to push his luck before the man clammed up completely. 'Okay, why choose that house for your Stokesy appearance?'

'Why not?'

'So you just chose a random house, hoping it would have a doorbell camera to capture you pretending to be Ewan Stokes?'

'No.'

'So what, then?' Ellis gave a sigh not altogether for effect. It was too hot to be playing this game. 'I'm trying to understand the logic, Mr Beech, but honestly I can't work it out. Do you know the owner of the house? Or his missus?'

'Everyone knows him.'

'Local celebrity, is he?'

Rick Beech glared at him. 'You work it out. I'm saying nothing till I see my solicitor.'

Ah well, it was worth a try. All the same, Ellis kicked himself for giving way so easily. He'd had Beech's attention – he should have capitalised on it while he had the chance.

'Suit yourself, sir.' He let his gaze travel back to the window. But this time the itch of irritation got the better of him. 'It's just that if you say everyone knows Mr East, I'm presuming Ewan Stokes knew him. That's if what you were doing was following a Stokesy forum theory. Why would Stokesy turn up on Damien East's doorstep, just before the fifteenth anniversary? Was he a mate?'

Beech gave a derisory snort.

'Were you trying to scare him? You aren't Ewan Stokes, but you wanted him to think you were. Why? What are you to him?'

'I'm a portent, mate,' Beech suddenly hissed.

'A what?'

Beech rolled his eyes as if Ellis should have already known this. 'They were both in the floodlit league football team. Stokesy should have been star striker but that bastard talked the manager out of it. Then tried to beat the living crap out of Stokesy when he challenged him on it. If Stokesy's coming back for anyone, that piece of shit is first on the list.'

Twenty-Four

MINSHULL

'I don't know why he chose this place. He has no business here.'

Minshull caught the briefest look between Damien East and his wife. Natalie East quickly averted her eyes but the damp tissue in her hands twisted tighter.

'And you say he first stood there earlier this morning?'

Natalie nodded. 'At nine a.m. I have the video from the doorbell cam.' She reached for a sleek laptop on the sofa arm and fidgeted as she opened it and selected the footage. When she gave it to Minshull, her hands were shaking.

Sure enough, there was the hooded intruder they had just apprehended, standing motionless on the doorstep, cardboard sign held across his chest – an identical pose to that of the silent man captured by the pier webcam and the CCTV at Rai's Garage. Had the man they'd just arrested been responsible for all the Stokesy appearances? If so, why was Stokes' own mother convinced by them? Was this incident nothing more than a blatant ruse to grab the attention of his worldwide following, or was something more sinister at play?

Minshull leaned closer to the screen, scrutinising the paused video for similarities and differences with the footage he had previously viewed. Without a side-by-side comparison it was impossible to say for certain. If it were an elaborate hoax, the man now in custody would have to explain why. If it were proved he had wasted police time with his publicity stunt, Minshull and Anderson would push hard with the Crown Prosecution Service to have everything thrown at him. Even if on paper wasting their time was all he had done up until today.

Did he intend this to be a stunt?

Minshull stared again at the hooded figure on the screen.

Knowing the terror the so-called followers of Ewan Stokes had wreaked on Maisie Ingram and her family, perhaps the revelation that the real Stokesy wasn't heading back for his predicted revenge would be welcomed by those that knew him. That said, explaining it to Olwyn Stokes-Norton would be tough, considering she now believed her son to be back in Suffolk. But what did it mean for the ongoing abuse? And if Stokesy didn't return as his faithful hoped, where might their anger and disappointment lead? Would they even believe the news or assume it to be yet another conspiracy to silence the missing man?

He hoped Ellis could encourage some answers from the counterfeit Stokesy, but given the man's resistance to arrest – and the current state of Steph Lanehan's chin – he didn't expect much success. It was most likely the arrested man would *no comment* his way through an interview, while some puffed-up solicitor called the shots.

'How did you know he was on the doorstep?' he asked, looking up in time to see Damien East mouth something to his wife. Both quickly averted their eyes. Minshull let it pass without comment.

'When he first appeared at nine a.m., I was looking for something in the cupboard under the stairs and I saw his outline through the front door. I thought he might ring the bell, but when he didn't, I opened the door.'

'What happened?'

'Nothing. He just stood there, staring straight at me.'

Minshull tapped the laptop screen. 'Holding that sign?'

'Yes.'

'Did you speak to him at all?'

'Yes.' Natalie East took a shuddering breath. 'I asked him what he wanted, but he didn't say anything. I told him to leave and he walked away. Then at lunchtime he appeared again.'

'What happened?'

Her eyes dipped to the writing shreds of tissue in her hands. 'He just stood there again, but this time he started smiling, looking me up and down like a creep. Like he was about to attack me. I got scared so I slammed the door in his face and yelled that I was calling the police.'

'But you didn't call us then?'

'No. I – I should have.' A pointed glance at her husband. 'I called Damien first. He said to lock the doors and call him again if the man didn't go away.'

Her voice shook with emotion but something else lay beneath it. Anger, perhaps? Why wouldn't a concerned husband tell his terrified wife to call the police in that situation?

'And where were you, sir?'

'In my office. I have a small graphic design business and our offices are in a converted farm complex in Evernam.'

'Close enough to get back, though?'

'Yes – but… I couldn't get away. Nat understood that.'

Did she? Minshull let the husband's reply hang in the air for just a moment as he observed the couple. When their involuntary body twitches registered the awkward pause, he continued. 'Did you see the man leave?'

Natalie East shook her head. 'I was hiding in the kitchen. But I heard a vehicle pulling away about ten minutes later.'

'What kind of vehicle?' It was a strange choice of word. Minshull decided to pursue it.

The woman gave a nervous double blink. 'A – a car, I assume. I didn't see it, just heard it. I mean, it might not even have been his. I was just so scared that everything sounded threatening.'

That was odd. Steph Lanehan said the man was on the doorstep and ran off on foot. No mention of a car. Surely if he'd had access to a vehicle it would have made far more sense as a means of escape than running away. And there were no other cars visible when Minshull and Ellis had arrived. Noting it down, Minshull pressed on. 'Did it sound like a large car or a small car?'

'I don't know. It sounded loud but I was hiding in the kitchen, terrified. Everything sounded loud.'

'I see. Forgive me, Mrs East, I know these questions may come across as insensitive or repetitive, but it's to give me the clearest picture of what you experienced. Small details often tell us so much more.'

She nodded. Her husband seemed to have shrunk a little on the sofa.

'Did you recognise the man?'

'He was wearing a hood.'

'Of course. But in this image his face is still quite visible. I just wondered if you might have seen him before?'

'Not here. I haven't seen him here before today.'

'But you might have seen him somewhere else?'

Natalie bit her lip. 'I mean, he looked like someone I knew a long time ago.'

'Who was that?'

She realised her mistake immediately, the remains of the tissue abandoned in her lap. 'Well… he looked like Ewan Stokes.'

'Honey…'

'No, Damien, the detective asked me a question. He looked like Ewan Stokes. Like the image of him from that webcam that's all over Facebook and Twitter.'

'Did you know Mr Stokes before?'

'Everyone did. Everyone knew of him. You didn't grow up around here and not know who he was.'

Damien East was no longer looking at his wife, his furious frown directed straight at the tops of his knees.

'Did you know him personally?'

'I didn't… But he dated the sister of a friend of mine.'

Minshull held her stare. 'Who was that?'

'Tabby Ingram. Ewan went out with her sister Maisie for a few years.'

Minshull took his time to write this down, the sudden turn of the conversation presenting possibilities, connecting lines that had so far eluded the investigation. 'Do you have any idea why someone fitting the description of Ewan Stokes chose to visit you today?'

Natalie East took another breath, then shook her head. 'No. No, I don't.'

'Mr East?'

'I believe my wife has answered the question.'

'She has. I'm asking you.'

'Whoever this person is just wants to cause trouble. I don't think he planned our doorstep any more than he planned the webcam or appearing at that garage. If he has a reason to choose our home for his stupid publicity stunt, it's a mystery to me.'

He was lying, of that Minshull was convinced. But any good grace Minshull might have been afforded was quickly disappearing. He had one, maybe two questions, he guessed, before the squirming couple showed him the door. He consulted his notebook, buying time, working and reworking potential next questions.

Just as he made his choice, his mobile buzzed.

Masking his relief, he pulled his phone from his pocket. 'Forgive me, I just need to take this.'

He stood up and moved into the bright hallway, noting the door to the understairs cupboard was still ajar as he passed through into the kitchen. On a smart wooden central island in the middle of the sleek kitchen lay a large carving knife. Its presence there seemed at odds with its ultra-tidy surroundings. Had Natalie East grabbed it to protect herself?

'Drew, what do you have?' he asked, keeping his voice low.

'He started talking. Most of it bollocks, to be honest, but he reckons Damien East was on the football team with Stokesy and they had a huge bust-up just before he went missing.'

'So what were his reasons for imitating Ewan Stokes here?'

'He reckoned Damien East stole Stokesy's place in the football team, then beat him up when Stokes confronted him. He said it's common knowledge in the fan community that Mr East is one of Stokesy's intended revenge targets.'

Minshull frowned at the knife on the kitchen island. If Damien East was aware of this, could it be why his wife had armed herself? 'So it was an attempt at intimidation?'

'Looks like it, Sarge. He called himself a "portent". Big word for an idiot.'

'Indeed. Do you have a name yet?'

'Rick Beech. He lives on Dellwood Avenue.'

'Well done for getting that out of him. Did he say if he knew the couple here?'

'No. I reckon he's just a fan who got carried away. Hang on, Sarge, I've got to go – the Guv wants me.'

Thus outranked, Minshull allowed himself a small chuckle, despite the questions filling his mind. 'Best hurry, then. You don't want to keep him waiting.'

Ending the call, he walked back to the living room, noting the sudden silence that greeted his return. He resumed his seat, eyes trained on the couple, whose expressions betrayed so much more than either of them intended.

'Sorry about that. So, is there anything else about the incidents today you'd like to tell me?'

Stony-faced, the Easts shook their heads.

'Right, then. Just one more question, Mr East. Exactly what did you argue with Ewan Stokes about shortly before he went missing?'

The Easts paled as one.

THE CLUB

davep221 Stokesy seen at Damien East's place, Tarn Hows Close, Felixstowe.

grumpyg1t Who told you that?

davep221 Posted on the Felixstowe local page an hour ago.

grumpyg1t Link?

davep221 Hang on…

davep221 *Typing…*

davep221 *Typing…*

davep221 fel1xstowe-link.co/is-this-stokesy.html There's a photo, too. From the back. He was on the doorstep!

grumpyg1t That could be anyone. Does Watcher89 know?

Me54c They got Stokesy!

grumpyg1t Who?

Me54c Police!

davep221 @Me54c Sod off. Shit-stirring as always. Don't you have a life?

Me54c @davep221 Better than yours, saddo.

grumpyg1t @Me54c @davep221 Not this again. Why don't the two of you get a room?

Me54c Didn't you see what I said? They got Stokesy! Bundled him into a cop car and drove off!

grumpyg1t Proof?

Me54c One of ours on Tarn Hows Close. Photo here is blurry but you can see it's him.

davep221 Black hoodie. Could be anyone.

grumpyg1t Look at that photo on the Felixstowe forum. Black hoodie and sign.

davep221 We need Watcher89's take. Anyone heard from them?

Me54c Last time I saw Watcher89 was 7am on main forum.

davep221 Any way we can get a message to them?

grumpyg1t I know someone in The Circle.

Me54c Bollocks you do.

grumpyg1t @Me54c Think what you like sunshine. Do you want my help or not?

Me54c @grumpyg1t Knock yourself out.

davep221 Tell them to confirm or deny ASAP. We need to know for sure. If Stokesy's been taken in then we need to do The List for him.

Me54c @davep221 You and whose army?

davep221 @Me54c Plenty of us, mate. We have The List and we're local. If Stokesy needs his work completing, we're ready.

Me54c Except the Ingram bitch. We all know you don't have the stomach for that.

davep221 @Me54c Whatever. There's more on The List than her and you bloody know it.

davep221 @grumpyg1t Say the word and we'll start.

grumpyg1t @davep221 Good to know. Hang fire but get everyone on standby.

grumpyg1t @Me54c Get those photos circulated everywhere OK?

Me54c On it.

[Conversation ends.]

Twenty-Five

ANDERSON

'A fight over a football match?' Anderson looked incredulously at Minshull and Ellis as they stood in the corridor leading to the custody suite.

'That's what Rick Beech reckons.'

'We'll ask him when we get in there. What did Damien East say?'

'Not much.' Minshull scuffed the corridor carpet with the toe of his nut-brown shoes. 'He was scared, Guv, no doubt about that. And he'd lied through his teeth to me before Drew called and told me what Beech had said. His wife, too. She'd got a carving knife out in the kitchen.'

'What?'

'Bit extreme for an argument fifteen years ago,' Ellis observed. 'Although if she was on her own and scared by the bloke on her doorstep maybe she wanted to protect herself.'

Minshull conceded the point. 'True. But I still think East knows more than he's saying.'

Anderson leaned against the corridor wall. Could this investigation get any odder? 'Why do I feel like we're chasing our tails here?'

'Maybe because we are?' Minshull offered a rueful smile. 'Do you want to sit in on the Beech interview?'

'Yes – if you don't mind, Drew?'

Ellis appeared surprised he'd even been consulted. 'Fine by me, Guv. I'm going to go and check the forums again, see if there was any mention of the doorstep thing before it happened.'

'Good idea,' Minshull nodded. 'And see if anyone's cottoned on yet that it wasn't Ewan Stokes. We need to monitor this closely. If Beech confesses to it being him all along we need to prepare for the fallout. The fans are expecting a showdown: if it ends here they may well decide to create their own.'

'Keyboard warriors laying siege? What are they going to do, type furiously at us?' Anderson scoffed.

Minshull appeared unmoved. 'Keyboard warriors who have physically and emotionally terrorised an innocent woman for ten years, you mean? I think we absolutely should expect them to be capable of actual violence, Guv.'

Anderson was stunned by his reply, lifting his hands in concession. 'Understood. Do what you think is best, Rob. Drew, could you also keep an eye on Les for me, please? Check he's okay?'

'You think he isn't, Guv?'

'I'm not sure. He still isn't over what happened to his car. But I think there may be more there. Of all of us he was the only one who refused counselling after the vigilante attacks a couple of months ago. I'm concerned it might be affecting his work.'

'Of course, Guv.' Ellis nodded at Anderson and Minshull and headed for the stairs.

Anderson watched him leave, then turned to Minshull. 'Do you think it's a hoax?'

'Search me. Right now I'd believe anything is possible.'

'And you really think those online idiots are a threat?'

'I do. Whatever we find out in there is going to change this. What worries me is that confirmation of a hoax won't make it go away. It might make it a hundred times worse.'

Anderson felt his humour leave. 'Let's hope Mr Beech talks, then.'

—

Twenty minutes later, Rick Beech and his flint-faced solicitor took their seats opposite Minshull and Anderson in Interview Room 3. The cramped room was as airless as always but today an extra fug of scent added to the oppressive atmosphere. Had the last occupants brought food in with them? It smelled suspiciously of cheese and onion crisps. Anderson's stomach grumbled, reminding him again of the unfinished lunch now going stale on his desk. The unwanted press attention, the fake Ewan Stokes and seemingly everything else today had conspired to keep Anderson's much-needed meal from him.

He eyeballed the arrested man. This had better be good for making him forego food…

The solicitor introduced himself as Clive Logan. He wasn't a brief Anderson had seen before, but he appeared to recognise Minshull. Whether or not that was a good thing remained to be seen.

'My client has asked me to read out a prepared statement,' he began, beads of sweat glistening across his long top lip.

Anderson's mood darkened further.

'"I wish to make it known that my actions this morning were a light-hearted tribute to Ewan Stokes, and not intended to cause concern or harm to any person or persons. I had no intent to cause criminal damage, nor trespass illegally on anyone's property. I was acting on my own, in conjunction with nobody else, and accept that my attempt at humour was poorly conceived and executed. I accept full responsibility for my actions today at 3, Tarn Hows Close, Felixstowe. As instructed by my legal representative I will not be making further comment at this time." It's signed by Mr Beech, as you can see.'

He pushed a decidedly damp-edged copy across the interview desk, the imprint of his sweaty hands clearly visible. This delivered, he relaxed back as if his job was complete.

Anderson accepted the paper and passed it to Minshull, never once taking his eyes off the sweating solicitor.

'For the recording, Mr Beech's legal representative, Mr Clive Logan, has just passed the signed statement from his client to Detective Sergeant Rob Minshull.' Anderson finally released Logan from his stare and eyeballed Rick Beech instead. He didn't appear to be as confident as his solicitor that the statement was enough to warrant the end of the interview. He was correct.

'Thank you, Mr Logan. I just have a couple of extra questions not covered by your statement.' Anderson watched the slump of the solicitor's shoulders with no small amount of satisfaction.

Minshull opened his file and laid out three black-and-white stills side by side. Anderson tapped each with his finger as he spoke.

'Felixstowe Pier webcam, Sunday 16th July, 10:45 p.m. Rai's Garage petrol station CCTV, Monday 17th July, eleven p.m. And today, Tuesday 18th July, three times. This photo is from doorbell camera footage taken at 9:02 a.m.'

Beech and his solicitor stared back.

'In all these images you'll notice a single figure, presenting as male, holding a white cardboard sign upon which is written a single phrase: *HELP ME.*' Anderson paused as Minshull pulled a long, clear plastic evidence bag from behind his chair. The sign Rick Beech had reportedly been so unwilling to relinquish during his dash from police and subsequent arrest. 'This sign, Mr Beech, that you were apprehended holding at 3:45 p.m. today.'

He saw Beech's eyes flick to the sign and quickly away.

It was enough.

'Is this you?' Anderson asked, his tone as light as he could manage. He swivelled the printed camera stills around to face Beech and his frowning solicitor. 'Here. Here. And here?'

'I think my client has already answered your question, Detective Inspector.'

'*One* of them. One location.' Anderson tapped the doorbell cam still. 'This one.'

'So that is beyond doubt.'

What kind of law did he specialise in? Stating the bleeding obvious? Aware he had far more ire available to launch today than the solicitor warranted, Anderson reeled himself in. 'I am not disputing that. What I am asking is if your client is *also* the person in these two images. He is dressed identically. He is carrying an identical sign. He is standing in an identical manner. I'm sure you can understand our assertion that he is, in fact, the same person in all three instances.'

Beech cleared his throat. His solicitor held up a hand.

Anderson stared at them both.

As if sensing the storm gathering above their heads in the too-hot interview room, Minshull cut in. 'Mr Beech, we need to know this because there is currently widespread speculation that the man in two of these images is Ewan Stokes, a person of interest to us who went missing fifteen years ago. With his significant online following and the current level of interest in his perceived return, we are concerned for the safety not only of Mr Stokes but also the individuals he is believed to be returning for revenge upon. Not to mention his family, who are distraught and want him home. You can help us. It's clear you are aware of Mr Stokes and of these previous sightings since Sunday. Are all of these you?'

'I remind my client that he has already supplied a written statement and does not have to answer any further questions,' Logan interjected.

'You don't have to say anything.' Minshull kept his eyes trained on Rick Beech, who had begun to look extremely uncomfortable. 'It's your prerogative. I'm asking for your help, Mr Beech. If the other images are you, we need to know now. It isn't just the memory of Ewan Stokes at stake here. His family are desperate for news. And people with other agendas are invested. People who don't care about Mr Stokes. People looking for an excuse to cause trouble. The only person who can put the record straight on this is you.'

Anderson watched his DS at work, marvelling again at how unlike his father he was. John Minshull wouldn't give two hoots about further complications: one arrest would be all he cared about.

Not his son.

Beech squirmed a little.

Minshull pressed on.

'I need to understand why Damien East was a person of interest for you. I know Ewan Stokes quarrelled with him shortly before his disappearance. I believe it was concerning his place in the football team. Is that correct?'

Beech didn't reply.

'The reason I need to know is that if Mr East could potentially have been responsible for Mr Stokes going missing, he is a person of interest for us. We want to find Mr Stokes, as we promised we would do fifteen years ago. But without knowing the full facts that led to his disappearance, it's impossible to know what might be keeping him from coming home. If he's scared, if he thinks trouble may be waiting for him...' He spread his hands out, inviting Beech to complete the sentence in his mind.

Anderson knew exactly what Minshull was doing, and it was brilliant.

'Here's what I think, Mr Beech: I think you care a lot about Ewan Stokes. I think you want him home. So much so that you would attempt to point the finger at one of the people you feel did him wrong. I don't for a second think you meant Mr East harm; I think you intended to give him warning that the truth was known. Am I right?'

'My client has already...'

'Yeah,' Beech said, so quietly that his blustering solicitor almost missed it.

Anderson clamped his teeth together to contain his delight.

'Mr Beech?'

'Damien East beat him up when Stokesy confronted him about being sidelined as star striker. He's not the butter-wouldn't-melt innocent he wants you to think he is. Check your records: on the day Stokesy went missing his face was covered in bruises. That bastard wasn't content with stealing his place on the team; he wanted to hurt him, too.'

'And you think Stokesy's been biding his time for revenge?'

Beech nodded.

'Do you believe he's back in Felixstowe?' Minshull asked carefully.

'I know he is.' Beech reached across the interview desk and placed his right hand on the first and second images of Stokesy. 'Because that's him.' He glanced at his disgruntled, note-taking solicitor, before placing his left hand on the third image from the doorbell cam. 'And that's me.'

Minshull nodded at Anderson.

'Thank you, Mr Beech. Answer me this, if you will, just so I understand: why did you try to look like Mr Stokes today?'

Rick Beech shrugged. 'Banquo's ghost, innit?'

'Pardon me?'

'East needed to know what's coming for him. Reckon he knows now.'

Anderson leaned a little closer. 'And who else deserves a visitation?'

Beech ignored the glare of his solicitor. 'I can only say what I've seen on the forums.'

'Of course. And that is…?'

'Three more people. One of them is Maisie Ingram. The others… It's not my place to speculate. But you'll find the names on the forums if you look hard enough.'

Minshull didn't react, his calm observation of Beech continuing. 'The forum is hosted on a server you own, correct?'

The killer piece of information. Anderson resisted the urge to smile.

Beech hadn't anticipated that. His goggle-eyed silence was a gift. 'I don't…'

'You own the SuffolkView website, and StokesyFans is run as an extension from that server.'

'I – I may have helped in the early days.'

'Define *helped*.'

Beech shook his head, staring at his hands on the interview room desk. 'The original forum was kicked off its hosting service. I was doing web development at the time and I was asked to help.'

'Who by?'

'A friend had been posting on the site in its original home and they responded to a call on the forum for help with relocation.'

'Do they pay for this?'

Beech shook his head. 'I offer webspace for a few charity groups, so it's theirs on that basis.'

Anderson cut in. 'Is StokesyFans a charity?'

'No. But I earn enough from other work to do it. I believe in Stokesy and what he wants to do. It's my contribution to the cause.'

Anderson scoffed. *The cause.* It made it sound like a political movement, not a bunch of saddos following a myth.

'Who runs the site?'

'I can't tell you.'

Anderson eyeballed the solicitor. 'Can't?'

'I believe my client has...'

'Your client has just admitted that he owns the server upon which a forum of interest to police is hosted.' He turned his stare back to Beech. 'I need names. Contact details. You presumably have access to those for legal reasons?'

'We have an agreement...'

'You and *who* else?'

'I don't know their names!' Beech yelled.

'Excuse me?'

Red-faced from his sudden outburst, Beech lifted his eyes to meet Anderson's stare. 'I'm sorry. It was part of the agreement. I could get access to the top tier of management in exchange for hosting the site.'

'So you can start by telling us who else is in the top tier of management.' Anderson was fast losing patience. He could feel the prickle of tension from Minshull beside him.

'There are no names. Just handles. And you couldn't identify them from that.'

'So were you instructed to pull this stunt?' Minshull asked.

'I acted alone.'

'Forgive me, Mr Beech, but I don't believe that any more than you do. Was it an attempt to up the ante? To present an escalating series of events to support Mr Stokes' longed-for return?'

Beech lifted his chin. 'People are watching now. The papers are all over it. We haven't had publicity for this case since *The Missing Son* dropped. I wanted to give them something to talk about.'

'And scare the living hell out of Damien East?'

'He should be scared. They all should be.'

'Who's *all*? I need names.'

'His ex. There will be others.'

'Who?' Anderson demanded, sick of this blatant deflection.

'People on the team. The coach. The guy he worked for at the building site who sacked him for no reason.'

'They're targets?'

'They've been mentioned. Not by me. Or any of the top tier. But I've seen them listed on the forum.'

Minshull folded his hands slowly on the top of his notes. 'Have you been instructed to threaten these people?'

'No.'

'Have you been assisting Ewan Stokes in his appearances?'

'No.'

'And today's stunt?'

'I acted alone.'

'I don't believe you, Mr Beech.'

'It's the truth.'

'We need names.'

'I can't. It's not possible.'

'Then close the forum.' Anderson glanced at Minshull.

'I can't do that!'

'Why not? Your server, your business implicated if anything illegal happens.' Minshull's eyes narrowed. 'Anything *else* illegal.'

'You don't understand. People rely on the forum. There's a community there, lots of people who find they belong.'

'By sharing threats and discussing violence?'

'By caring about someone the world has forgotten. If the forum closes, what happens to them? What do you think disenfranchised people will do if they have nowhere else to go?'

Anderson couldn't believe what he was hearing. 'Your little supportive community has been responsible for encouraging attacks on Maisie Ingram for ten years. And today, for encouraging an act of intimidation against Damien East. It's hardly a philanthropic endeavour.'

'I can't close it,' Beech repeated, and for the first time Anderson glimpsed the fear hidden behind the statement. 'Any attack on Ms Ingram was not encouraged by the forum. Not by me. But I'll hold my hands up to this. It was my action, my mistake. I wanted to give the papers something to talk about, that's all. It wasn't my intention to harm anyone.'

It was a relief to leave the interview room thirty minutes later, but Anderson remained irritated. Rick Beech had admitted impersonation, resisting arrest and assaulting a police officer. Maybe they could pin more on him, but it was unlikely. Anderson's bets were on a first-time fine and community service. He had co-operated to an extent – the revelation of names on Ewan Stokes' supposed revenge list took them further than their own investigations had so far achieved. And now they knew he had access to the upper echelons of the forum they could press him to help them get inside. But his point-blank refusal to name anyone involved in the forum's management was a kick in the teeth.

What was he so scared of? Or whom?

And it didn't answer the most important question: where was Ewan Stokes now? And who was his next target?

Twenty-Six

BENNETT

'Okay, we know Maisie Ingram has been named as a target. And Rick Beech mentioned the football coach. What's his name and can we contact him? The owner of the building site that gave Stokes his marching orders, too. Who was that? Can we speak to him as well?'

'The football coach is Ted Patrick,' Anderson said, consulting the notes he'd made from the original case files. 'Not at the address we had for him but someone has to know where he is now.'

'If he's still coaching he might be working for a sports organisation in the county,' Bennett suggested. 'I can check.'

'Okay, Kate, good,' Minshull replied.

'How about other members of his family?' Wheeler asked. 'His sister? Stepdad? Biological dad? They could be the other names on his revenge list.'

'Biological dad died twenty-five years ago. He'd been estranged from the family for several years prior to that. Stepdad is a good call, but from what Stokes' mother told me he'd been a model father for her kids.' Minshull frowned. 'You think Stokes had a grievance against his family?'

'Possibly. What if Maisie Ingram was right and he wanted to get away from them? What if he felt trapped at home?'

Bennett jumped in. 'That might explain their insistence on keeping the case open – and why they changed their story to say that his mother had been there on the night he disappeared.'

'Because they wanted to shift focus from them?' Anderson asked.

Bennett shrugged at the DI. 'Who's going to question a mother and daughter worried out of their minds about their missing loved one? Could be a great cover.'

'I don't see it,' Evans said. It was such a surprise to hear his voice after almost two full days of unusual silence that the entire team turned to look.

'Why?' Even Anderson's question was careful, as if not wanting to break whatever spell had caused his colleague to speak.

Evans looked past everyone to the old headshot of Ewan Stokes pinned to the whiteboard. 'Whatever the issues with his family, he must have seen how hard they fought to keep the investigation open. Assuming he has been at large all this time and watching the progress of his case.'

'Would that make a difference to him?'

Evans gave a nonchalant shrug. 'I don't know. I never met the guy.'

Minshull considered his reply. 'I'm in contact with Stokes' mother, Olwyn. She told me Marilyn had lied about Olwyn not being at the football match initially because she was protecting her. Then, when the case appeared to be falling from favour, Olwyn persuaded Marilyn to tell the truth.'

'Can we talk to Marilyn?' Anderson asked.

'Olwyn said she isn't well. I took that to mean she had mental health issues. She's refused to pass on details.'

'Could she be protecting her daughter?' Ellis had his hand raised, the only member of the team who ever did.

'She is protecting her. But not because she's in contact with her brother.'

'Must be tough for them,' Wheeler observed. 'Not surprising it's affected the woman given what the family has gone through. Where does the daughter live now?'

'She moved house, not long after the documentary came out,' Bennett replied, checking her notes. 'I did a search for her but she seems to have dropped off the radar. I'm guessing we weren't her favourite people after our predecessors declined to reopen the invest-igation.'

As soon as she'd said it, Bennett wished the words back. Everyone in the room knew which *predecessor* had made that call. If Minshull felt the stab of it, he didn't show it. But it couldn't be easy, cleaning up a historic mess his father had made. How personally was Rob Minshull taking this investigation?

'I'm guessing the documentary didn't help things,' Anderson hurried, pushing words into the awkward silence.

'I think we park the Marilyn Stokes idea,' Minshull replied, careful to maintain eye contact with his team. 'But we need to find and contact other names on the so-called revenge list. If there's a suggestion they could be at risk – however unlikely – it's our duty to protect them. Keep searching the forums please, Kate.'

Bennett nodded.

'Thanks. Drew, would you hop on this with Kate, please? I have a feeling it's likely to become a bigger task once more names are uncovered.'

'Sarge.' Bennett and Ellis answered together, looking at each other and sharing a smile at their synchronicity. It felt good to sense lightness return between them, even if Bennett knew she was more than capable of doing the task alone. She caught Minshull's expression and guessed his motive. He'd been trying to push them to work with each other for the last two months since the attack they'd endured together. As a tactic it was about as subtle as a sledgehammer, but today Bennett didn't mind. There was too much to unsettle the CID team with this case: anything that lessened the atmosphere in the office was welcome.

'Thanks, both. One last bit of news is that I've finally secured a Zoom interview with Lindsay Carlton, the owner of the white van.'

A small cheer rippled around the team. Any movement on the van was worth celebrating. The events of Sunday night and the failed pursuit Wheeler and Lanehan had made on Monday were still reverberating through the team. With the van – and driver – still stubbornly at large, everyone was hoping for a break in the stalemate.

'Finally,' Anderson remarked. 'So what bloody awful time do you have to do that, Rob?'

Minshull winced. 'I'm coming into the office for just before six a.m. tomorrow.'

'Ouch.'

'Indeed. But I'm hoping he can give us something we're missing.'

'Pete York'll be in, though,' Wheeler offered. 'He brings his fancy espresso-pressy thing in with him while he covers the night shift. I'll ask him to bring in extra coffee to keep you awake.'

Minshull laughed. 'Appreciate that, Dave. Okay, thanks, everyone. Let's keep going.'

The office filled with the rumble of conversation as the team moved chairs back to their desks. It was good to hear it back after the subdued strangeness of the last few days. Ellis brought his chair to Bennett's desk without discussion – a move she was glad of. There was more room here than squeezed between Ellis and Wheeler on the other side of the office. And having her own space made Bennett feel happier. Small things like this had become important in the turmoil of her life. When everything else was shaking, you clung to immovable things.

She didn't want to think about the depressing pile of paperwork building up on the coffee table of her rented home – solicitors' letters marking the pointless back-and-forth bickering of their clients. Why Russ wanted to make the process so difficult was beyond her. He was the one who had left; the one who had begun a family with another woman; the one who had sold their home without consultation. He clearly wanted out of their marriage. So why obstruct its end at every turn? Was he punishing her for his own stupid decisions? The only mistake she had ever made in their marriage was to trust Russ Bennett. That mistake, it transpired, was going to cost her dearly in every respect.

'Are you okay with… *this*?' Ellis asked, not yet sitting on the chair he'd placed beside hers.

'Sit down.' She smiled, shaking her head at him.

At least there was this. One previously immovable feature of her work life that, following an inexplicable wobble, was beginning to steady once more.

Ellis settled himself, his ever-present notebook primed for action. 'Right then. Which bunch of idiots shall we start with?'

'StokesyFans?'

'Might as well.' He watched as Bennett found the forum and logged in with the fake profile the team had created in order to access every discussion. 'So who are we looking for first?'

Bennett consulted her notes. 'Well, we already know the threats against Maisie because she documented them. So, Ted Patrick, the coach? Or should we try to find the boss of the building site?'

Ellis bowed his head a little, his voice little more than a whisper. 'I think we find Marilyn Stokes.'

Bennett stared back. 'You heard what Minsh said – she doesn't want to be involved.'

'So her mum said. But what if she has something to hide? And what if there are discussions on here about her, and why she changed her story? It was in the documentary, and everything else in *The Missing Son* has been subject to conspiracy theories. So why not her?'

'Drew, Minsh said to leave it.'

'And I don't think you want to do that any more than I do.' His smile was annoyingly knowing, especially considering he was right. 'Come on, we can at least look while we're searching for the other stuff. If we come across something useful, Minsh won't be angry.'

Bennett glanced over her shoulder. The rest of the team were occupied by their work. Nobody was looking up apart from her. She shouldn't do it. But Ellis had a point.

'Okay, fine. But if Minsh or the boss get wind of it, we shut it down, understood?'

Delighted, Ellis held up his hands. 'Understood.' He offered a self-conscious smile before looking back at the screen. 'Is there any way we can search topics on here beyond basic terms? I tried putting in names and hashtags but didn't have any joy.'

'I don't think there's an advanced search function – it's too basic a set-up for that.' Bennett scrolled down some of the forum posts listed. 'I wonder if there's a code.'

Ellis frowned. 'A code?'

'Abbreviations commonly used in posts. Bit like Mumsnet.'

'What are you doing browsing Mumsnet?' Ellis laughed. 'Something you want to tell me?'

It hit like a boulder, but Bennett steadied her smile. 'Why, Drew? You volunteering for godfather duties?'

He reddened. 'No.'

'Then shut up, yeah? Anyway, stop worrying. I had to search that site last year when someone started making threats in a local group. They use a common set of abbreviated terms in the chats, to save time typing, I guess, but also it's like an accepted club thing. LO for little one – meaning child. OH for other half, meaning partner. DS1, DS2, et cetera, for darling son number whatever it is. DD for darling daughter. Have you seen any abbreviations like that when you've been reading posts here?'

'I don't think so.' He stared at the screen, pen tapping against his notebook. 'Hang on...'

Bennett sat back as Ellis reached across her to type *SM* into the search box. When the search found no mention of the term, he cleared the box and tried *M&S*.

'Going shopping, are you?' Bennett joked, a little surprised by the proximity of him to her.

'Mother and sister,' he replied, with an eye-roll.

'And SM?'

'Stokesy's mum.' He groaned when the screen revealed no results found.

'Whatever you do, don't type SS into the search box for Marilyn Stokes. Knowing the idiots on this site you're likely to run into far-right waters.'

'Good point.' He drummed his fingers where his hand rested on the desk beside the keyboard, arm still stretched across Bennett. 'What, then?'

An idea occurred to Bennett. Reaching carefully around Ellis' arm, she typed *OS MS* into the search. Instantly, the screen filled with results.

'Jackpot!' Ellis exclaimed, trading celebratory grins with Bennett until both remembered the strange position they were now in. Ellis gave a self-conscious chuckle and carefully withdrew his arm.

Bennett turned her face to the screen, flushed with the unexpected success of her hunch. Scrolling quickly, she found several references to

OS, Olwyn Stokes, and *MS*, Marilyn Stokes. Most referred to quotes from their appearance in the true crime documentary. But one caught her eye.

'Wait – look at this.'

Ellis leaned closer. 'An address?'

Bennett shook her head. 'No – a sighting.'

'When?'

'Four months ago.' She read the contents of the forum post. '"MS spotted in Alderton Stores, Alderton, posting parcel."'

'Alderton? That's over the river from Felixstowe, isn't it? Near Bawdsey?'

'Yeah. Short hop by ferry, but half an hour or more by car. So she moved across the river. Near enough to get to Felixstowe but far enough away not to be noticed.'

'Genius. So we search for residents named Stokes in Alderton.'

'And widen the search if nothing turns up there. My guess is if they're using the post office they must be pretty local or work nearby?'

Ellis grinned at Bennett. 'Nice one.'

Bennett grinned back. 'Back atcha.' She watched his eyes stray to the screen, his mouth drop open. 'What?'

'Look!'

A large banner had appeared across the top of the search results.

STOKESY: NEW PHOTO!

'Sarge!' Ellis called as Bennett moved the mouse to click on the banner.

'What've you got?' Minshull appeared beside them as the image opened.

As one, they stared at the screen.

'Is that…?' Minshull began.

'Rai's Garage,' Ellis said.

'Another one?'

'No, Sarge, look…' Ellis pointed at the caption across the bottom of the slightly grainy photo. *New photo from Monday night!* 'It's the one from before.'

'But a different angle,' Bennett finished.

The photo revealed the hooded figure from the back, holding his sign towards the CCTV camera.

'Where is that taken from?' Minshull breathed.

Bennett did her best to recall the layout of Rai's Garage from her visit with Ellis there that morning. 'There's a jet wash bay at the rear of the garage, between the shop and the used car lot. I think it's taken from there facing out towards the pumps and the main road beyond.'

'By someone else,' Ellis said.

The team, now gathered around Bennett's desk, took this in.

Surprise lifted Minshull's features. 'He wasn't there alone. Somebody is helping him.'

'Could it have been taken by the garage owner's son?' Wheeler asked, ever the voice of caution.

'No – wrong angle,' Bennett replied, her pulse beginning to rise. 'Jas told me he was in the shop with his dad and ran out to talk to Stokesy, who had gone by the time he got outside. He couldn't have taken that photo and neither could his father.'

'Right.' Minshull rubbed his hands together. 'This changes things. He isn't working alone. He has help – support. Which means this isn't one person's agenda any more. We're looking at an orchestrated campaign.'

'But who would be helping him, Sarge?' Wheeler asked. 'And why?'

Minshull glanced at his team. 'That's what we've got to find out.'

EARLY EVENING NEWS

'The search for a Suffolk man missing for fifteen years has today taken another twist. After two alleged sightings of Ewan Stokes, now forty-five years old, a series of three reported sightings today have been revealed as a hoax. Our reporter, Ben McAra, is in Felixstowe this evening. Ben.'

'Thanks, Elodie. Confusion here this evening in Felixstowe as the latest in a bizarre string of so-called appearances of a missing man is proved fake. Ewan Stokes, known across the world as Stokesy, was believed to have appeared on the doorstep of the house behind me, here in Tarn Hows Close.

'According to an eyewitness, a man dressed in a black hoodie and jeans, carrying a sign identical to that seen in earlier sightings this week, stood on the doorstep at number 3 on three occasions today. The third time, police were alerted and officers apprehended the man.

'But any hope Stokesy's many online followers may have had of this being the missing man were quickly dashed. It was a hoax. South Suffolk Police have confirmed that a forty-seven-year-old local man was arrested earlier today for resisting arrest and assaulting a police officer. As investigations are ongoing, his name hasn't yet been released.

'This throws into question all of the reported sightings across the town since the first on Sunday night. Police have this evening refused to comment further on whether the man in custody is responsible for the other appearances. Is Stokesy back in Felixstowe? Or is this an elaborate ruse? Until confirmation comes either way – or the hooded man with the *HELP ME* sign is spotted again – we just don't know. Ben McAra, *Early Evening News*, Felixstowe.'

Twenty-Seven

CORA

The news bulletin ended and Cora switched channels to something calmer. The Ewan Stokes case had been uppermost in her mind since Anderson had formally brought her into the investigation, but the 'fake Stokesy' story revealed much about the expectations, prejudices and beliefs of the forum users. She'd seen the announcement on the StokesyFans site and watched the fan reactions appear in real time. There were theories ranging from possible names of the pretender to wild accusations of a staged event to dissuade Stokesy's true fans from believing he was back.

> It was @Liam4Town. Anyone seen him here since Monday? Proves it!
>
> More like @jeff0076. Kind of stunt he'd pull for attention...
>
> Police are worried now we're turning up at the locations. They probably staged this one to pretend it's all a hoax...
>
> I reckon Stokesy sent a body double for a laugh...
>
> They're rattled. They don't want us to be right...

Was it a stunt? A Stokesy fan getting carried away? And if this had been proved not to be Ewan Stokes, did that mean all the so-called sightings this week had also been fake?

The psychology of the Stokesy faithful was fascinating to see in action. But the potential for harm was strong, too. Already, angry voices of dissent were citing police, Maisie Ingram and even members of the Stokes family as collaborators intent on stopping Ewan Stokes in his mythical mission. The level of belief was concerning, especially the growing number of calls for retaliation and attacks on anyone who stood in their hero's way.

Cora was unsettled by the tide of vitriol on the forum. If a fan of Ewan Stokes could so easily impersonate him to intimidate someone the site that users had deemed to be on his alleged 'revenge list', what else might they be capable of?

Something else worried her, too. The brief slip Chris Bickland had made that morning about waiting for an alert on a story and the pointed remark Alex Bickland had countered it with. At the time it had seemed like nothing, but what if the alert Chris had been waiting for was the story of the Stokesy sightings that *The Sentinel*, his employer, had broken just two hours later? Was that a coincidence? Or was Chris more involved in news desk stories than he'd claimed? If he was, and faced the pressures that inevitably came with that kind of work, could that be a factor in Reece's anxiety? Children were always the first to pick up on changes in stress levels in their families – could this have unsettled the child?

Cora had begun to note down her concerns, both with the Stokesy fan forums and with the Bickland family. With no hard evidence on either score, she resolved to keep watching and record anything she observed. It helped to have it all on paper – even if, right now, both issues presented a tangle of incomplete, inconclusive information. They were puzzles she wanted to solve.

Her mobile buzzed on the arm of the sofa, pulling her attention back into the living room of her apartment. She smiled when she saw the caller ID.

'DS Minshull, good evening.'

His laugh was warm down the line. 'I'm at home. You can dispense with titles, *Dr* Lael.'

'Okay, then. Hi, Rob.'

'Hello, Cora. How was your day?'

Cora looked across the living room to the *Early Evening News* still playing on her television. 'Better than yours, by the look of it.'

'Yeah, we're stars of the national news again.'

'Any idea how they got hold of the story?'

'Same way the rest of us did, I suppose. Someone on the Stokesy forums, most likely. And as for the latest story, maybe someone who lives nearby. It's not every day you get a patrol car, a CID car and a live police chase in your neighbourhood.'

'The forums are full of it tonight,' Cora said, glancing back at her laptop screen.

'You're looking at them now?'

'I wanted to see how the latest development was influencing the rhetoric.'

'And?'

'Most of it's still bluster. But there is a small undercurrent of forum users that concerns me. There's a definite sense of intent in the way they're talking.'

'You think they'd act for real?'

'I don't know.' Tension formed a ball in Cora's stomach. 'It's a possibility you shouldn't rule out. Some of them are assuming it's their responsibility to act for Stokesy if he's unable to.'

'That's what I was afraid of. Today's hoax hasn't helped.'

'Who was he?' Cora asked before realising what her question implied. 'Sorry – I know you can't tell me that.'

'You're part of the team now,' Minshull corrected her. 'It's important you're up to date.'

'Is that why you called?'

'Well, I – partly. Maybe.'

Cora laughed at Minshull's groan. 'So that's a no, then?'

'It isn't why I called. But you should be briefed on latest developments, so this serves two purposes.'

'I see. So who was the fake Ewan Stokes?'

'Local guy, works as a web developer. A massive Stokesy fan, of course. And the owner of the server that hosts StokesyFans.'

'Wow. Is he in charge of the forum?'

'He claims he isn't, but he reckons he offered them the use of his server in exchange for being allowed into the inner circle.'

'Do you believe him?'

Minshull's sigh was heavy on the line. 'Honestly, I don't know what to believe. What I do know is that he was willing to go to stupid lengths to boost the Stokesy return myth.'

'What happened?'

'He chose that house because the man who lives there was on the football team with Ewan Stokes. They fought just before he disappeared. Stokesy fan wisdom has it that the row was partly responsible for Stokes going missing.'

'So he's a potential on the list?'

'Allegedly.' He sounded tired, every sentence requiring effort. 'This case... Every time I think we have a lead, there's another complication. It feels like somebody's playing a game with us only we don't know the rules yet.'

'I know what you mean,' Cora replied. 'So what's happened to the guy pretending to be Stokesy?'

'He's been charged but released on bond. CPS didn't consider him a threat beyond being a dickhead. But if he knows who the inner circle are, he could be our way in. I'm not ruling out the possibility of pressing him for more.'

'That's something.' Cora picked her next words carefully. 'So why did you call?'

'I wanted to check you were okay. When we spoke last it was all about me... Thank you for that, by the way.'

'Like I said, you can always talk to me.'

'I know. That means a lot. But – uh – I haven't asked how you are. Sunday night shook everyone up – me included. I don't think any of us have had time to deal with it yet. I wanted to make sure you're all right.'

'Thank you. I'm getting there.' Cora stood and walked to her window, looking out across the still-bright sky and blue-grey waves breaking on North Beach. 'I've been keeping busy, too. It helps, sometimes.'

'I get that.'

Cora had debated whether or not to tell Minshull about Chris Bickland. But the unexpected phone call was as good an opportunity as she might get.

'Listen, I wanted to talk to you about someone I'm working with. He's the father of a little boy I'm currently helping with school-related anxiety.'

'Oh?'

Cora watched a small speedboat bounce across the waves, out from the shore, a shock of bright white against the blue-grey sea. 'He's a journalist. He tells me that he works in Features but this morning when I was at his house he said he was watching his phone waiting for an alert from work. He mentioned 'the story' but didn't elaborate. He said it by mistake and his wife shut him down before he said anything else. But he works for *The Sentinel*.'

Minshull was quiet on the line.

Cora continued. 'That was at ten a.m. And at noon…'

'…*The Sentinel* broke the story,' Minshull finished. 'You think he's part of it?'

'I don't know. But I think he might have known it was coming.'

'Is he aware you consult for us?'

'No. I haven't told anyone that, aside from Tris. I have no reason to in my work. I just thought you should know.'

'Thanks, Cora. I appreciate it. Would you let me know if he says anything else? I know it's probably unlikely, but keep your ear to the ground for me? It feels like we're constantly playing catch-up with this right now. Anything that gives us an advantage would really help.'

'I will. Are *you* okay?' She could hear the weariness in his voice and knew he was unlikely to have talked with anyone else about how he felt. It was still strange territory between them, this half-friendship, half-undefined air.

Minshull took some time to reply. 'I think so. I want some answers and then I'll feel better.'

'And Sunday night?'

'I'm still angry.'

'Angry is good sometimes.'

'Yeah. I'll remind you of that when it isn't.'

Cora watched her reflected smile dancing across the ocean beyond her window. 'I'm going to keep asking, you know.'

'I'm counting on it. Look, I'd better go. I have to be in the office unreasonably early for a video call to Australia tomorrow.'

'I don't envy you that.'

'I don't envy me, either. Good to talk to you, Cora.'

'You, too.'

She ended the call and looked over towards her kitchen, contemplating what to make for dinner. Resolving to check the fridge, she began to walk across her apartment when a notification chime from the laptop summoned her back.

On the open StokesyFans forum page, a brand-new banner had appeared:

> ** MODERATOR UPDATE **
>
> Many members have expressed concern with today's events.
>
> Inner Circle wishes to make it known that no harm was done and the Plan continues. Stokesy is well and watching. He thanks you for your support. Nothing has changed. Keep alert. #Stokesy15

Twenty-Eight

MINSHULL

The CID office just before six a.m. was a very different beast to its usual daytime guise. The silent computers, the empty desks, the clicks and ticks of the building usually masked by constant conversation and activity. Only DC Pete York, the detective covering the night shift, broke the stillness with his quiet working. He looked up as Minshull entered, a wide grin to welcome his bleary-eyed colleague.

'Morning, Minsh.'

'Pete. Been a busy one?'

'Quiet as. I half expected an army of wannabe Ewan Stokeses to lay siege to the county but so far no sign.'

'Maybe they don't do overnighters.' Minshull smiled, dropping his bag by his desk and turning on his computer. 'I don't blame them.'

'You and me both.' York nodded, rising from his chair and cracking the vertebrae in his lower back. 'Now, Davey Wheeler told me you would be in need of some magic beans this morning.' He pulled a crumpled brown paper bag from the rucksack beside his desk and wiggled it at Minshull.

'God bless Dave,' Minshull replied. 'He said you had an AeroPress.'

'I have indeed.' York produced an impressive-looking gadget and headed for the kitchen. 'How strong would you like it?'

Minshull thanked his stars for such excellent company. York was a total joy after the swift departure of his predecessor, DC Bruce Ovenden, who had been anything but a welcome sight in the early-morning office. 'Strong as possible, please.'

'Right y'are. I'll make this and then I'll be off.'

Ten minutes later, quite possibly the best morning coffee he'd ever had in hand and video call in progress, Minshull selected Lindsay Carlton's name from the waiting room list and waited for the connection to be made.

The man who appeared on the screen looked tired, deep shadows beneath his eyes and cheekbones despite the golden Aussie tan of his skin. His sandy-red hair hung in curtains around his face and his pale eyes peered through them. He was dressed in a short-sleeved shirt and tie and the room behind him appeared to be an empty hotel room.

'Mr Carlton, hello.'

'Hi, DS Minshull. Apologies this has taken a while to arrange.'

'Not a problem, sir. Thank you for meeting with me.'

Carlton nodded.

Minshull straightened the notes beside his keyboard and began. 'As I said in my email, I have some questions regarding your van.'

'Have you found it yet?'

'Not yet, sir, no. We do unfortunately know that whoever had access to it removed it after one of our patrols attempted to intercept them. It hasn't been returned to the lock-up. I was wondering if anyone you know might have taken it? If you've issued anyone else with a set of keys? One of your tenants, maybe? Or your lettings agent?'

Carlton didn't reply. There was a slight delay on the call and the picture quality wasn't the best, so Minshull waited a moment before prompting him. 'Sir? I'm not sure if you heard my question. I—'

'I heard it.' His tired eyes blinked at Minshull. 'You're certain it's gone?'

'Unfortunately, sir, that seems to be the case. We really need to track it down. It sustained damage both in the original collision on Sunday night and while attempting to evade my colleagues on Monday afternoon. If you think it might have been stolen…'

'There is another key.' His gaze dropped. 'And if it's been used then, no, it hasn't been stolen.'

What was that supposed to mean? Minshull pressed on. 'Who has the other key, Mr Carlton?'

'You have to understand, when I got offered this job my visa progressed faster than I was expecting. I didn't have time to sell the lock-up and as the van was SORN-declared I didn't think anyone would want it. So I just locked the van in the garage and left. The other key... the other person with the key... We weren't exactly on speaking terms when I left, so...'

He was stalling for time, eyes darting anywhere but the image of Minshull that filled his computer screen.

'Who was the other keyholder?'

Carlton rubbed his cheek. A sign of nerves? 'A friend I haven't seen for a long time. To be honest, I'd forgotten he still had it. But then I saw the news and...' He took a deep, shuddering breath. 'I bought the lock-up with him, you see. The van, too. Another reason I couldn't easily sell them. We started a market stall years ago. Ran it for seven months but it never brought in the turnover we were expecting. The lock-up was meant to be a stockroom as well as a garage. That didn't last. And then we fell out, so...'

'Mr Carlton, I need a name.'

'Yes. Sorry.' Carlton gave a cough. 'I bought the van and lock-up with Ewan Stokes.'

The revelation slammed against Minshull. The white van that had driven at them – and that had tried to run Wheeler and Lanehan off the road – was co-owned by Ewan Stokes: the only other keyholder for the lock-up. The only person who could have been driving the van. Unless...

'Are you certain he didn't give the key to anyone else?'

Carlton shook his head. 'I can't say for certain, but there's no way he would have known I'd SORN-declared it. We fell out and then he disappeared about four months later. I haven't seen him for fifteen years. As far I knew he wasn't ever coming back.'

Still reeling, Minshull pressed on. 'But you knew him well. Well enough to start a business with him, buy property... Do you think he's back?'

'I don't know. Before he left there was a lot of stuff he was doing that wasn't good. All that business with his missus – taking it bad when she dumped him and threatening the friends who helped her leave. And there was other stuff, too. Dodgy cash-in-handers he was doing, being suddenly flush for cash when he claimed to be on the breadline. It was why we fell out: I called him out on the company he was keeping, the brags he was making about the gangster lifestyle he thought he was getting into. He was a git, no doubt about it. To be honest when he went missing it was a relief.'

'Were you interviewed by police when he left?' Minshull asked, already guessing what the answer might be.

'No. We hadn't spoken for four months so I wasn't someone they thought was a close enough friend. It all came to a head with us when the stall ended. He kept on about new contacts he had, questionable gear we could shift – I wasn't into that. It was always my intention to buy him out of the lock-up but then he disappeared so it didn't happen.'

'Hang on, you said you bought the lock-up and van with him. Why wasn't he listed as part-owner?'

Carlton looked uncomfortable. 'He paid me cash for his half. Said he didn't want to be on the paperwork.'

'And you agreed?'

'I shouldn't have, but I was too focused on the stall and this huge profit we thought we were going to make.'

Minshull stared at his list, none of the remaining questions now being useful. 'You said he was doing dodgy work. Any idea what that was?'

A firm shake of the head. 'He wouldn't tell me. Frankly, I didn't want to know. There was some bloke his mum knew who'd set him up with some building site jobs. But I think he'd met someone else through that and started doing stuff for cash. I don't know what it was.'

'Okay. Thank you. Just one more thing: you said he threatened friends who had helped Maisie Ingram leave him. Do you know who they were?'

'Sorry. I only knew Maisie from when they were together. He knocked her around, I think, reading between the lines. Not the saint he was made out to be.'

'Were other people aware of this?' Minshull asked.

'Oh, sure. But you know what it's like, people don't like to say anything in case it makes it worse for the girl.' He rubbed his cheek again. 'I half wondered if someone had bumped him off, you know, when he disappeared? He wasn't happy about her leaving him. I don't think he'd ever have stopped trying to get her back.'

'If he really is coming back, do you think she's in danger?'

Carlton stared directly into the camera. 'Yes. That bastard is capable of anything, even waiting fifteen years to get his own way. I think she should be scared. And her friends, too.'

—

Half an hour after the video call ended, Minshull was still in his seat, the list of questions on his notepad now obscured by heavy black-ink doodles that covered the page as he mulled over the news. If Ewan Stokes was driving the van, why had he chosen them as targets? What possible motive could there have been for doing it? And had he driven to St Just after his webcam appearance at Felixstowe Pier? There was enough time to make the journey, but why make it in the first place? How could he have known Minshull, Cora and the others would be walking out of the pub at that time?

Or was it a random act, aimed at getting everyone's attention? Minshull dismissed this immediately: had it not been for Lindsay Carlton's confession this morning nobody would ever have made the connection. Plus, the incident on Sunday night hadn't been reported in the news: so far the media reports on Ewan Stokes had made no mention of a white van.

But Kavish Rai had mentioned a white van parked beside his garage shortly before the figure and sign appeared on his forecourt. Was that the same van? He hadn't mentioned any damage – which there would have been had it been the same vehicle. Could it have been parked so that the damaged driver's-side front wing wasn't visible from the garage shop?

None of it made any sense. None of it linked to anything else. No clear motive, no co-ordinated plan and no clear targets.

What was the truth here?

'Did the coffee help?'

Minshull looked up to see the cheerful face of Dave Wheeler as he walked into the CID office. 'It was incredible stuff.'

'I keep saying to Pete he should start a coffee shop when he retires next year. We'd all be in there every day.' His smile faded a little. 'You okay?'

'I don't know.'

'Everything all right, though? Call went through okay?'

'Yeah, it was fine. But get ready for this: Ewan Stokes was driving the van.'

Wheeler's eyes grew wide. 'On Sunday night?'

Minshull nodded. 'And during your chase on Monday. Or he gave someone else the keys. But he's the only person who had access to that lock-up and the van besides Lindsay Carlton, who's in Australia.'

Wheeler sat heavily on the chair beside Minshull's desk. 'Bloody hell. No, that can't be right. Can it?'

'I don't know. Kavish Rai said there was a white van parked beside his garage shortly before the Stokesy figure walked up to his CCTV camera. If it was the one that almost hit us, it would have had damage to its front wing – I mean, we all saw that.'

'Depends which way he parked it, I guess.'

'Exactly. Which means, however unlikely it seems, it could have been the same van.'

'When the van passed me I saw the driver. Only fleetingly. But he had a black hoodie on. And I'm pretty sure there was someone in the passenger seat.'

'Could it have been Stokes?'

'If he had a key and got into that lock-up – and Mr Noble said he'd seen someone in a dark hoodie going into the lock-up before.'

'Shit, Dave.'

'I know, Minsh.' Wheeler raised his eyebrows. 'This bloody investigation.'

'Shame Les hasn't called a sweepstake on this one. He'd have made a killing.'

Wheeler grimaced. 'For once I wish he had. I don't like him being so quiet. It's unnatural for Les.'

'True.' Minshull rubbed his burning eyes.

'Well, how do you fancy yet another bit of random information?' Wheeler grinned and pulled his mobile phone from the pocket on the strap of his cross-body rucksack. 'Check out what I found.' He selected an app on his mobile screen and handed it to Minshull. 'Just play that.'

It was a video from a local TV news report, showing a group of men in tracksuits running and stretching in a park.

'What's this?'

Wheeler folded his arms. 'Keep watching.'

'This morning the team were out early, warming up for what promises to be a crucial match. Head coach Ted Patrick has his eyes firmly set on promotion...'

The report cut to a bald-headed, gruff-faced man in a large padded jacket.

'"The lads have worked hard this season and their commitment has paid off. If we win on Sunday, we make top tier of the floodlit league. That means sponsorship and the chance of our own ground. I believe this team can go all the way..."'

The shot changed to one of a young man with dark hair, running and kicking a ball, calling to his teammates.

'New team recruit Ewan Stokes is quickly becoming a star of Felixstowe Fishers. Scorer of four goals in the last three matches, he is confident of their chances on Sunday evening...'

'No way,' Minshull breathed.

'It gets better,' Wheeler replied.

The next shot made Minshull catch his breath. The man from the photo pinned to the whiteboard, in a head-and-shoulders close-up.

'"Yeah, I'm proud of what we've achieved. We've come from the bottom half to dominate the league. We know what we want. No one can stop us getting it..."'

Minshull paused the video, Ewan Stokes' expression frozen into a snarl. 'Where did you find this?'

'I was looking this morning while I had my breakfast,' Wheeler replied. 'Thought I'd google the football team name, see if there were any lists of his teammates. That came up on the fifth page of results.'

Minshull observed the man on the screen. 'He doesn't look like someone who would run away.'

'My thoughts exactly. But I could see him planning to get what he wants. Look at that determination, Minsh: you can't fake that.'

Minshull looked at his colleague. 'Do you think he's planned all this? Or is it someone else manufacturing it to make us think he's back?'

'Beggared if I know,' Wheeler replied, rubbing the back of his neck. 'But him having access to the van when nobody else did… It changes things, doesn't it?'

The sharp trill of Minshull's desk phone made them both start, Wheeler taking his mobile back as Minshull answered the call. 'DS Minshull?'

'Thank God you're in. It's Damien East. I've had a delivery. It's… horrific.'

'What's happened, Mr East?'

'It was left on our doorstep. Natalie found it when she was bringing the milk in. She's beside herself.'

'What's been left?'

'You need to see for yourself.'

'Okay, have you moved it?'

'No. It's just… *there*…'

'Right. I'm on my way. Go inside and lock the door. I'll be with you shortly.'

As Minshull ended the call, Anderson strode in. 'Morning, all.'

'Guv, Damien East just called. Someone has left something on his doorstep. He wouldn't tell me what, but he sounded scared. I'm heading over now.'

'Yes, of course. Dave, why don't you go, too? And take evidence bags. Call me the moment you get there – if you need assistance I can send it.'

'Thanks, Guv.'

Anderson gave a wry grin. 'And there was me hoping it might be a quiet start this morning.'

'No fear of that.' Wheeler grimaced, following Minshull out of the door.

Twenty-Nine

WHEELER

The football shirt lay where Natalie East had found it, spread across the doorstep of the Easts' home. It was a Felixstowe Fishers shirt, the familiar blue and white waves across the chest and a gold bishop's mitre in the centre of the design, similar to the motif on the Felixstowe Town Council coat of arms. But where the football team badge should have been was now an ugly scar, the material ripped and frayed where the badge had been wrenched off. Staining the shirt around the ragged hole was a deep red substance that looked like blood.

'Right over the heart,' Wheeler murmured beside Minshull as they crouched to observe it.

'Some message,' Minshull replied, noting a smattering of black dots in a horizontal line on the lower third of the shirt. 'What do you reckon those are?'

'Looks like ink to me.' Wheeler looked up at Damien East, cowering in the doorway. 'Have you turned this over?'

'No. I didn't want to touch it.'

'I reckon there's something on the back, Sarge.'

Minshull straightened up. 'Right. We need to get some photos first of where it is. Do you have the camera?'

Wheeler jogged to the car to fetch it, offering East a reassuring smile as he handed the camera to Minshull who began to photograph the shirt in situ.

'Won't take a minute,' he promised, pulling on a pair of blue surgical gloves.

'It's him again, isn't it?'

'Who?'

'The bastard pretending to be Ewan Stokes.'

'We don't know that, sir. But we will look into it.'

'I'm on a list, aren't I? On those bloody fan forums. My brother found stuff on there last night, repeating what that bloody reporter said when he named our house, telling people where to find us. It won't stop now, will it?'

Wheeler saw real fear staring back at him. 'We'll do everything we can to find who's responsible.'

'Okay,' Minshull said, handing the camera to Wheeler and putting on his own gloves. 'Ready?'

'Sarge.'

They crouched down again beside the doorstep and carefully flipped over the shirt. As they laid it back out, Damien East swore loudly, his hand quickly slapping over his mouth.

Across the lower section of the shirt, beneath a large number seven in gold fabric, a message had been written in thick black permanent ink:

EVERYTHING YOU CARE ABOUT

'Do you recognise this, Mr East?' Wheeler asked the visibly shaken man on the doorstep.

East nodded, eyes wide with shock over his hand-clamped mouth.

'Is it your shirt? Number seven – the striker, isn't it?'

Damien East pulled his hand away, his face taut with fear. 'It's what he thought was his.'

Minshull looked up. 'When you argued?'

'Yeah. He wanted to be striker. Said Ted Patrick had promised him the gig after he'd scored the goals leading to the final match.'

'And had he?'

'If he had, he'd promised me, too. Stokes was good, but he was a loose cannon. All the lads on the team knew it. Yeah, he scored goals, but he got more red cards. He'd kick off in training if anyone got in his way. And he knocked his missus around, too, when he got home.'

'He was violent?'

'Everyone knew it, his family included, whatever they said afterwards.' East let out a snort. 'He was a thug who could score a goal. But he was off his head, man.'

Wheeler recalled the accusations levelled against Damien East that he'd read on StokesyFans. They didn't paint him much better than his description of Ewan Stokes. 'The word on the fan forums is that you attacked Ewan Stokes, sir.' He held his hands up when he saw East's scowl. 'I'm just saying what I've read. What's the truth there?'

East slumped against the door frame. 'They got that right. But only because he wouldn't shut up about it. We were in the pub after training, the week before the big match. We'd had a few, things got heated... You know the rest.' He stared at the shirt. 'But *that*... That's no hoax.'

'How can you tell? Surely anyone could have found out the striker position in the team was number seven?'

'Not the number.' Fear was back in his expression, pulling at every muscle. 'The message. That's what he said to me, before he left. The last thing he said to me. *I'm going to destroy everything you care about.*'

Wheeler glanced at Minshull. 'Could anyone else have overheard that, Mr East? Anyone in the pub?'

East shook his head. 'It didn't happen in the pub. We went out, past the car park to a side alley. That's where I hit him. There was nobody else there.'

Minshull took this in. Wheeler looked from his colleague to the terrified man on the doorstep.

'What about your coach – Ted Patrick? Was he there?'

'No, he'd gone not long after the first round. His missus wanted him sober and you didn't cross Ursula Patrick for anything.'

'And where does Mr Patrick live now?'

'He's still in the area, as far as I know. He coaches under-elevens and under-sixteens.'

'Where?'

'I don't know exactly. But he does it for one of those coaching academies. Deben River, I think.'

'We need to talk to him, hear his side of the story. See if he's had any attempts at contact from Ewan Stokes over the last fifteen years.'

East stared at the detectives. 'Keep him safe, please. Ted's a good man. Saved many of us from getting into trouble. Saved me.'

'We'll do our best, sir.' Wheeler noted the new information down and hoped this would be a spark of hope in the darkness of everything else.

East's gaze dropped to the shirt. 'What are you going to do with that?'

'We'll take it with us, see what we can get from it,' Minshull said, as Wheeler photographed the back of the shirt. 'How is your wife?'

'She doesn't want to stay here.'

'Understandably.' Minshull nodded. 'Is there somewhere else you could go for a while? Family you could stay with? Friends?'

'You think we're in danger?'

'I think you're currently an open target. Mostly for any idiots wanting to make a point. But maybe, for your own peace of mind, it would be best to put some distance between you and your house for a few days.'

East shrank back a little. 'Nat's mum lives in Cambridge. I'm due some time off. My works manager and team can handle things while I'm away.'

'I think that might be best, sir.'

'Till the 27th has passed, yeah? The anniversary.' He let out a long sigh. 'You know, I never asked for any of this. I was trying to stop him being a dick, ruining the match for everyone. That's why I faked the injury on the field that night.'

Wheeler and Minshull stared back.

'You faked an injury in the match?'

East hung his head. 'I'm not proud of it. But Stokes was on the subs bench, yelling shit at everyone, kicking off. He was putting the lads off their game. So when I got tackled, I milked it. Said my hamstring had gone, got helped off the pitch. Stokesy went on, scored the hat-trick – we got the result and he calmed down. At least, I thought he did.'

'Did you tell the police this?' Minshull asked.

'No,' East replied. 'I said I was injured so I didn't see him after the game, which was the truth. They didn't need to know the rest.'

–

'What d'you reckon to that?' Wheeler asked, as they drove back to Ipswich.

'I think the initial investigation cocked up by not asking the right people the right questions. If they knew Stokes was violent, that should have changed the discourse. I don't understand why it didn't.'

'Maybe because only Maisie Ingram claimed he was violent?'

'And Dad wouldn't want to hear that.'

Wheeler felt the punch of Minshull's words as if they were his own. 'We know now. And we have a lead on Ted Patrick. If he knew what Stokes could be like, he can help set the record straight.'

Minshull almost managed a smile. 'True. It's more than we had before.'

'So, what's the plan with the shirt?'

'Forensics. But I want Cora to see it first.'

A slow smile spread across Wheeler's face as he kept his eyes on the road. 'See what she can hear from it?'

'Exactly. And if she does hear any voices attached to the shirt, we'll play her that video you found. If it's the same voice, we'll know who we're dealing with.'

Thirty

CORA

'...And Dave Bear is in charge.'

Reece Bickland moved the small golden-furred teddy bear to the front of a classroom of toys he'd laid out on the rug.

'Is Dave Bear the teacher?' Cora asked, catching Chris Bickland watching them from the group of sofas.

Reece gave her a withering look. 'No. He's security.'

'Ah, I see. Is that an important job?'

'The most important. He watches out for trouble. That's why he has this.' He picked up a small plastic sword from a Playmobil set. In the bear's paw it looked more like a flick knife.

Cora noted it without comment. She'd encouraged the game to get Reece talking about his school experience. Reports from his teacher suggested that he had initially loved his new classroom and seemed very at home there, until he suddenly changed his mind. Cora was working on the theory that a school-based experience was responsible for the change.

She'd begun by asking Reece what his classroom at school was like. She had expected an immediate refusal, or to sense the fear she'd witnessed during her last visit. But Reece appeared encouraged by it and had taken great delight in recreating the layout of his classroom using his toys on the rainbow-coloured rug. As he placed the toys, his subconscious voice attached to each one remained as happy and conversational as his vocalised chatter.

'This is Chloe. She wears glasses.'

She let me try them on and everything went wobbly.

'And Eden sits here.'

She played Pokémon with me at playtime.

'Niall and Jacob are here.'

Niall says my name like 'Reeth'. I like it.

'So which one is your teacher?'

Reece considered the mound of toys he'd piled beneath the coffee table, finally selecting a girl pirate figure and placing her at the head of the class, facing the grouped toys he had laid out.

'This one.'

My teacher. My new one. She's sad I'm not there.

Was Reece aware of the concern of his teacher? Or was he projecting something his parents had said in an attempt to chivvy him out of his fear?

'What's your teacher's name?'

'Miss Kennet.'

'Is Miss Kennet nice?'

Reece looked up at Cora, a mere hint of a line between his dark brows. 'I like her.'

Cora smiled back. 'She likes you, too.'

'That's what Mum says.'

'It must be true, then.'

Reece glanced at his father, who quickly busied himself with a sheaf of papers in his hand. He wasn't reading them any more than Cora was playing schools. It was all about observing Reece. Did the child sense what was going on? Cora couldn't tell. But the happy chatter – and contented inner voice – betrayed no sense of the fear she had seen in him yesterday.

So if it wasn't confrontation in the classroom, or some aspect of the class experience, what was causing the boy's visceral fear about going to school?

'What do you like about being in class 2C?'

Reece was rearranging the groups of seated toys. 'Topic. Guided reading. Sometimes maths.'

'Sometimes? What kind of maths do you like best?'

'Adding. Number lines. Multiplying.'

'Times tables,' Chris prompted.

'Only old people call it that,' his son retorted, dropping a Pikachu figure in the centre of the toys.

You think you know, but you don't.

Cora felt the sudden change of tone of the object voice at the centre of her chest. A retort. A rebuke. She hadn't heard that from Reece when his mother was present. It wasn't fear like before, but the force with which the words appeared was fuelled by strong emotion.

'That's it: I must be officially old if my six-year-old says it,' Chris said. His tone was light but had an edge, too. Frustration? Concern? It felt older than that, somehow, as if a dusty, faded emotion lined his words.

'Oh, wow, what's this?' Alex Bickland smiled, hurrying into the room past her husband to kneel beside her son.

'School.' Reece gave an overdramatic wince as his mother stroked his hair, leaning into it at the end. Clearly these two were close. Cora didn't get the same sense when Reece was alone with his father. But that was often the case with children who would favour one parent over the other, especially where they spent a disproportionate amount of time with one.

Alex glanced at Cora. 'School?'

'Reece is telling me where everyone sits in his class,' Cora replied, watching Alex's relief register.

'Is Dave Bear Mr Chandard?' Alex asked, adding, 'The head teacher,' to Cora.

'No, Mum. Dave Bear is *security*.'

'Oh.' Alex's smile fell for just a moment, reinstated quickly when Reece looked up from Dave Bear's patrol across the front of the class. 'He looks like he's doing a good job.'

'He is.' As Reece sat Dave Bear down, his voice whispered loud into the room.

Keeping us safe. All of us.

'I need the loo, Mum.'

'Okay, that's fine.'

Reece stared at Alex. 'Come with me.'

'You don't need me to come with you.'

'I do this time. You can talk to me outside the door.'

The sigh his mum tried to mask as she stood carried the weight of months on its exhale. 'Forgive us. Chris, why don't you make Cora a drink?'

Her husband jumped up as if he'd been kicked, rolling up the papers and shoving them into the back pocket of his jeans. 'Sure. Come to the kitchen?'

Knees stiff from kneeling on the rug, Cora gratefully accepted. She observed Reece's laid-out toy classroom for a moment longer before joining Chris in the kitchen.

'That was clever, what you were doing,' he said, fetching two mugs from a sleek frosted-glass cupboard above the workspace. 'I haven't heard Reece talk about school like that since the problem started.'

'I want to know where the boundaries are,' Cora replied. 'If we can reinforce the positives Reece feels about school, we can start to balance out the areas he struggles with.'

'And what do you think? Initial thoughts, sorry. I realise this isn't going to be solvable overnight.'

Cora understood his impatience, but the sharp edge to his words made her uncomfortable. 'He clearly likes his classmates, so no hint of conflict there. And he's at ease with his teacher, too. The security bear is interesting. Do they have any visible security at the school?'

'It's a primary school, not a high-security prison.' Chris paused, coffee jug in one hand and mug in the other. 'Sorry. That worried me, actually.'

'I can understand why. It might be a personality he's giving his anxiety. A protective image to calm his worries. I'll ask him more as we go on, but it's an encouraging development, trust me.'

'How is a security guard in a child's classroom encouraging?'

Cora sensed the scared child within the parent. 'He's presented a persona for us to refer to. Dave Bear is doing an important job for Reece. So if we want to find out more, we reference the bear. Reece has given his emotion a name. That's a good thing. Children often find an object that's focused on a big emotion is easier to understand than the feelings alone.'

'So his fear is in the school?'

'It was today.'

'How is that an answer?'

'Trust me, it's a process.' Cora accepted the mug of coffee Chris held out, noting the ripples appearing in the surface of the dark liquid as Reece's father's hand shook. 'One conversation at a time.'

'Of course, sorry.' Chris leaned against the granite worktop, shaking his head. 'Ever feel like life is conspiring against you? This thing with Reece – I want to be totally present for him, but at the same time work is really kicking off.'

Cora sipped her coffee, remembering her promise to Minshull to note any comment Chris Bickland made about his job. Sure enough, her silence encouraged more from the journalist.

'I'm guessing you've seen the news. About the missing man?'

'What news?'

'Ewan Stokes. Stokesy. He's been spotted back in Felixstowe. Fifteen years he's been missing and then, days away from the fifteenth anniversary, boom! He's back.'

'I saw something about it on the news,' Cora replied, her pulse quickening.

'It's everywhere right now, so it's hard to miss.' Chris nodded. 'The paper I work for broke the story.'

'Your story?' Cora asked.

Chris laughed. 'Yeah, in a manner of speaking. I've been research-ing the strange fan forums dedicated to Stokesy for five years. There's been a significant shift since the first sighting and I sensed something was happening. But because I was busy here – I mean, with working from home – I missed the tip-off. I'd tasked one of my junior reporters with keeping an eye on the forums and she spotted it. If I'd been watching...' He shook away the rest of the thought. 'Anyway, the thing is that my editor was pretty pissed that I'd missed it. She's given me a week to file the whole investigative piece and unmask Stokesy, or at least identify those operating the main forum.'

'Is that possible?' Realising she'd spoken out of turn, Cora back-tracked. 'I mean, if he's just appearing now. How would you find him?'

Chris poured the last of the coffee from the coffee jug into his mug. 'There are clues. Key forum users who always seem to know more than the rest, the first ones to confirm or deny any new information. I've got close once or twice, but they've so far eluded me.'

'The leaders of the forum?'

'Yeah. It's not like any forum you've ever been on. I mean in construction it's pretty crude. Very old-school design, all lineal discussion threads, no bells and whistles. But it means there's a definite command structure that's easy to monitor. If I could just get in with one of the leaders, gain their trust...'

Cora nodded, willing him to continue.

'I've followed it for five years. I can see how it works, who manipulates the discussions, who moderates when users get carried away. That's what makes the scoop so frustrating to miss. The tip-off wasn't even hidden: I mean, someone posted a damn photo. If I'd been watching that could've given me an advantage.'

'I see. I can imagine that was tough to accept.'

'It was. It is. But it isn't my only iron in the fire. I've also been investigating the original investigation by South Suffolk Police, which was, in a word, incompetent.'

'In what way?' She shouldn't have asked, her natural protectiveness for Minshull and the team forcing the question out. But it was too late to take it back.

'Leads not followed. Rumours not investigated. And then the whole thing dropped seven months later. His family painted him as a saint but – I'm not sure he was.'

'Why?'

'I've talked to people who knew him. He wasn't a pleasant person. Quick-tempered, out for himself, happy to use his fists first. There was some suggestion that he'd had dodgy work dealings, although I found little evidence to support that. But could that be why he disappeared? And where has he been all this time? How has he stayed under the radar for almost fifteen years? Those kinds of questions are catnip to me.'

'Do you think someone is helping him?'

'I'm certain of it. The fan sites, the yearly messages – it's always felt orchestrated somehow. And now things are happening, it's even more obvious. Stokesy isn't acting alone. Someone's setting the narrative.'

'Why would anyone do that?'

Chris gave a long shrug. 'I don't know. Maybe it's in their interests to keep the legend alive. Maybe the triumphant return serves their purpose. Anyway, whatever they're doing is coming to a head. And I have a week to out them.' He gave Cora a brief smile. 'Sorry. You probably didn't want to know all that.'

'It's interesting,' Cora replied, her mind alive with the new inform-ation. She needed to talk to Minshull as soon as possible. Even if most of what Chris had told her was wild speculation, some of it might help the team. 'It helps me to know what other pressures might be affecting Reece's home life. If he senses that you or Alex are particularly stressed, it might contribute to his own anxiety.'

'That's what I've been afraid of. I've tried to keep it from him, but every development with the Stokesy story is another indicator that I don't have enough to find him or the people helping him. Five years of work could go – like *that*...' He tossed a teaspoon from the kitchen worktop to land with a jarring clatter into the Belfast sink.

And then he will have won – his voice echoed from where the spoon had dropped.

–

Cora only drove a short distance from the Bicklands' house to a small car park overlooking the shingle spit leading to a row of brightly painted beach huts. Parking her car, she wound down both front windows and sat back in her seat, breathing in the warm, salt-scented air. What did Chris Bickland know about the original investigation – the case led by Minshull's dad? What did he know that the police didn't? And was his theory about Ewan Stokes correct? Was he violent? Involved in questionable work that may have necessitated his disap-pearance? And was someone calling the shots on events now?

Minshull needed to know.

Cora found her mobile in her bag and dialled his number. Immediately, the call cancelled, followed by a call notification from Minshull.

'Hey Rob, I was just calling you.'

'Great minds, eh? We have something that we need you to look at for us. Can you come in?'

'What is it?'

'A development,' Minshull replied. 'Could be a big one. I need you here, as soon as you can.'

Cora was already pulling her seat belt back across her body. 'I'm on my way.'

Thirty-One

CORA

She made good time. Minshull greeted her at the door to CID and seemed relieved she was there. Cora understood a little of his trepidation: this would be the first real test of her ability since officially joining the team.

The detectives' eyes were on her as she accompanied Minshull to his desk, their expressions a world away from the first time Cora had entered the CID office over a year ago. Cora smiled at Wheeler, Ellis and Bennett as they welcomed her. Evans remained at his desk, his head down. He was yet to be convinced, of course: the last of them to accept her ability. Cora heard the grumblings of dissent from the overflowing rubbish in the bin beneath his desk and mentally muted it immediately. She didn't need to hear that today.

'Ah, Dr Lael, you're here.' Anderson beamed, walking in from his office. 'Thanks for coming in so quickly.'

'My pleasure, DI Anderson. What do you want me to see?'

'This.' Anderson indicated a large clear plastic evidence bag lying on Minshull's desk. 'It was left on the doorstep of a former teammate of Ewan Stokes. There was an attempt at recreating a so-called Stokesy sighting yesterday at his home.'

Cora nodded. 'The hoax? I saw the messages about it on the forum.'

She saw surprise register with Anderson.

'Indeed,' he replied. 'The football shirt appeared this morning. It would be easy to dismiss this as another Ewan Stokes follower's idea of limelight stealing. It may well yet be.'

'But there are a few details that make us believe it could be a legitimate threat,' Minshull insisted. 'The badge ripped from the chest at the front, what looks to be a bloodstain around the scar and, specific-ally, the message written underneath the number seven on the back.' He carefully turned the bag over to reveal the inked message:

EVERYTHING YOU CARE ABOUT

'That was the threat Ewan Stokes allegedly threw at Damien East after they engaged in a physical fight over East being given the striker's position for the final game. According to him, those words were delivered in a side alley with no witnesses. The fight itself has never been discussed openly on the forums, as far as we know. It hasn't been referenced in the ongoing speculation, either, only that Damien East was given the position on the team that Ewan Stokes believed was his.'

'Is this blood?' Cora asked, the sight of it twisting her nerves.

'We can't say for certain,' Wheeler said. 'Not until Forensics can test it.'

'It's what it represents, rather than what it might actually be,' Anderson added. 'It's intended as a threat. A very specific threat, using a phrase only Mr East would recognise.'

Cora moved slowly around the desk, peering at the plastic-sheathed shirt from every angle she could. It was important to gain as accurate a map of the object in her mind as she could before the evidence bag was opened. Once the rush of voice and emotion was unleashed, Cora would have to navigate through it – blindly at first as she gained control of the sound. Instinctively feeling her way around the sections of the object now, before the bag was open, would help her navigate the initial onslaught.

As she did this she was acutely aware of Minshull watching her. There was no judgement here today where at the beginning there had been. Now fully convinced of her skills, he had fought hard for her to be on the team and was doing his best to understand the mechanics of her ability. That meant a great deal.

'When you're ready, Cora, I'll open the bag,' he said, his voice soft and his smile respectful. 'Obviously don't touch the shirt – I know you know that already.'

'Good to be reminded,' she answered, amusement dancing in her reply.

Minshull turned his focus to the evidence bag. 'I'll hold it open for as long as you need me to, okay?'

Cora nodded. 'Okay.'

Minshull looked over at Anderson, who nodded back. Slowly, he pulled apart the ziplock device sealing the two sides of the bag together.

Out the voice rushed, a hissed curse delivered through gritted teeth close to the fabric, as if the voice's owner were leaning over it. What it lacked in volume it made up for in almost tangible power. A male voice, mid-tone in range, the words formed with a Suffolk accent.

We know what we want. No one can stop us getting it…

Everything you care about…

Cruel intent fizzed through every word, its meaning inescapable. Each word scrawled on the shirt was spoken in angry stabs, hate staining each one as the ink stained the fabric. It was shocking and close, as if the voice's owner were snarling over her shoulder as she allowed the voice to play at its natural volume.

Knowing the team were watching her silent reaction to voices only audible to her, Cora placed her voice over the secret voice, speaking in time with it, matching the tone and delivery. It was a new approach she'd been working on, a way of interpreting the object voices in real time.

Eventually, Cora opened her eyes and nodded at Minshull. He closed the bag in one swift motion and she bowed her head as the voice was silenced.

She was aware of collective breaths held around the CID office. Only Evans, at the back of the group, appeared unconcerned by it all.

Anderson rubbed his chin. 'Could you hear anything else? Any other voices or sounds? Any echoes to suggest the location?'

Cora smiled. 'It's almost as if you've seen this before, DI Anderson.'

A ripple of nervous laughter traversed the group.

'I may have, but you surprise me every time.'

'Then I'm doing my job correctly,' she replied, a smile edged with effort spreading. 'Okay. In addition to what I just did with repeating the object voices for you all to hear, I've been working on expanding the sound that I hear attached to the objects. So at a basic level, the object retains emotional fingerprints alongside physical ones; I hear these as actual spoken voices. But in recent months I've begun to train that ability to view this sound as a three-dimensional landscape around the object. I listen for how the air changes around each voice – whether it is restricted or free enough to create an echo. It helps me to map out the location the object was in as well as the vocal identity of the person who touched it. So, in this case, the person or persons who damaged the shirt, wrote the words on the back and delivered it.'

'Could there be several people involved?' Wheeler asked.

'Yes, that's completely possible. Say, for example, if one person damaged the shirt, another wrote the message and a third person delivered it. But with this one, I only heard one voice.'

Cora caught glances passing between Minshull and his team.

'Clear enough to recognise it again?'

'Yes.'

Ellis brought over a tablet with the archive video report loaded and ready to play. 'Do you have it set in your mind?'

'I do.' Cora's eyes narrowed. 'Why?'

'Okay, let's try something here. I want you to listen to the video on Drew's tablet, but don't watch it. Then tell me if any of it sounds familiar.'

Ellis pressed play and the team waited in silence as the video played again. Cora felt their eyes on her as the voices of what sounded like an old news report filtered into the CID office. A reporter, a coach, the reporter... and then there, right at the end, the voice she'd just heard from the damaged shirt. It was unmistakeable, even at a normal volume.

The CID team waited.

Cora looked slowly around her new colleagues and let her gaze fall back to the bloodied, defaced football shirt in its clear plastic shroud.

'Yes,' she said, firmly. 'The voice I heard was Ewan Stokes.'

Thirty-Two

CORA

Minshull's gaze held hers. 'How certain are you?'

Cora didn't even have to consider his question. The words from the news report danced with the hate-filled words embedded into the fabric of the football shirt, merging and melding as one.

We know what we want. No one can stop us getting it…

Everything you care about…

Cora could sense some time stretching between the bright-eyed footballer and the vengeful vandal, a scratching of the edges of tone, as if time and anger had frayed the very strands of sound, pulled and stretched and torn like the damaged fabric surrounding the place where the football shirt's badge had been ripped away. But the rise and fall of the words, the sound trapped between tongue, teeth and roof of mouth was identical.

Ewan Stokes had carved his intention into the shirt and left it on Damien East's doorstep. It was more than a warning: it was a threat that bore all the anger and hate necessary to carry it out.

'As certain as it's possible to be. It's the same voice: older, attached to the shirt, but unmistakeably him. Ewan Stokes wrote those words with every intention of carrying them out.'

The moment she said this, a feeling of purpose filled the CID office, as around her every detective sprang into action.

Cora watched Minshull briskly delegate new tasks for everyone based on a theory proved. How different a scene this was to her first visit to CID over a year ago. Even Les Evans was joining in now, which was greeted by a definite sense of relief from everyone in the room.

Encouraged that her input had paid off, but still experiencing the after-effects of hearing Stokesy's voice, Cora moved away a little from them to sit slowly down on Dave Wheeler's chair. She needed a moment to regain her breath, to steady her thoughts again.

'We need to go back and find anything on Ewan Stokes, from press interviews to newspaper reports, especially any comments from people who knew him,' Minshull said, bright determination returned to his voice at last.

'Sarge, we've found Ted Patrick, the football coach,' Ellis said, the news rippling through the team. 'Mr East was right about the coaching company. Deben River Football Coaching. They gave me Mr Patrick's number and I spoke to him about an hour ago. He's going to come in just after five p.m.'

'Brilliant, Drew! We'll ask him about the issues Damien East mentioned. See if his recollections tally. I think we have to work on the theory that some key voices were likely missed in the original investigation.'

Minshull's grimace gave everyone permission to share his frustration – and put DCI John Minshull well and truly in the frame. Cora thought that a brave move – proof of how much Minshull trusted his team.

'So check everything, from the day Ewan Stokes disappeared to when police shelved the investigation, when the documentary aired, anything between then and now. And those of us old enough to remember the original news stories fifteen years ago, think back. Can you recall anything said at the time – even conversations with friends or family? Could any of us have known him, or known of him?'

'I remember it happening,' Bennett said, 'but only vaguely. It was one of those things people talked about and you noticed it because it was in your neck of the woods, but I didn't know him.'

'We were here then but working on that other job, weren't we, Guv?' Wheeler asked, turning to Anderson.

'Aye, up to our noses in stinking fish,' Anderson chuckled.

Minshull laughed. 'Sounds like a dream.'

'Ah, the good old days when policing gave you gems like that.' Anderson smiled. 'You young upstarts don't know what you missed out on.'

'What about you, Les?' Ellis asked.

'I never had my nose in fish,' he replied. 'I was still in uniform when it happened, studying for my exam to get in here.'

'No, with the Stokesy thing. Didn't you live in Kesgrave for a bit?'

Evans rolled his eyes – and Cora wondered how often he'd been asked this over the past few days. 'Yes, but I didn't know him.'

'You must've seen him around,' Bennett countered.

'No, actually, Kate. We moved in different circles. I'd heard of him, but I don't remember ever talking to him.'

Cora sensed the mood in the room dip suddenly.

'How different were your circles?' Anderson asked. 'Kesgrave is hardly the biggest place.'

'With respect, Guv, that's like me expecting you to know everything that goes on in your home town.'

'Motherwell's a sight bigger than Kesgrave...'

'I didn't know him, okay?' Evans' sudden shout cut the conversation dead. 'I saw him on the news reports, same as everyone else. Except Ellis, who was ten.'

'I saw it, too,' Ellis returned, his tone defensive.

Cora caught Minshull's eye. Being a confirmed part of the CID team dynamic was a new experience, and one she loved immediately. Before, all had been carefully observed seriousness and control when she was there. She had always felt rivalries, frustrations and mockery hastily stowed away in her presence, for fear of her seeing how it really was. Seeing everything on show now was the best welcome gift she could have asked for. No longer an outsider: she was right in the thick of it.

She was going to love it here.

'Okay, well, assuming that everyone at least *saw* the news reports,' Minshull cut in, 'make a note of everything you remember. There could well be details we've missed. In the meantime, let's start to compile a list of potential targets, working on the theory that Ewan

Stokes is returning to have his rumoured revenge. Who are our leading names? Who might we have missed? Which names are being bandied about on the forums?'

'Lots of talk of there being three other names on his supposed hit list,' Wheeler said. 'We know Maisie Ingram is one.'

'That poor woman,' Anderson said. 'She should have had our protection.'

'Yes, she should,' Minshull bit back.

'Should we warn Ms Ingram, now we are working on the theory that this is Ewan Stokes?' Bennett asked. 'She should know.'

Minshull nodded, his expression grave. 'Good point. If we can hope to reverse some of the damage done to her she has to be first in the loop on all developments. Thanks, everyone. Let's get back to it.'

Cora stood as the team returned to their workstations, moving to the side as Dave Wheeler resumed his seat. As she did so, she passed the messy desk of Les Evans, the corner of her bag catching the edge of a pile of papers, sending the top sheets fluttering down to the threadbare office carpet.

If he hurts Maisie I'll kill him.

Cora stopped dead, the hissed threat in Les Evans' voice hitting her like a physical slap. She looked down at the three sheets of paper resting against her shoe. Had she imagined it?

'Sorry,' she rushed, reeling from the voice.

'Ah, welcome to the team,' Wheeler chirped, his bright words clashing hard against the threats now repeating in triplicate at her feet. 'Knocking stuff off The Desk of Les is a rite of passage in this office.'

'Shouldn't give me so much damn paperwork, then, should you?' Evans barked without looking up from his screen.

I'll kill him…

I'll kill the bastard…

If he hurts Maisie…

'Shall we go and grab a coffee?' Minshull said, the closeness of his voice startling Cora.

'What?'

'Let's head to the canteen. Grab a coffee before you have to get back.' A small frown line formed along his brow. 'Good idea?'

'Yes – sorry – great idea.' Cora stuffed away her concern, glancing at Evans as Minshull caught her elbow and steered her between the desks towards the door.

'Thanks, Cora,' Anderson said, raising his hand. 'Great to have you on the team.'

The gathered detectives followed suit, only Evans notably abstaining from the agreement.

Les Evans, who moments before had angrily denied any knowledge of Stokesy or the circumstances leading to his disappearance.

As Cora left the CID office, the DC's true thoughts were still growling up from the dropped papers strewn around the legs of his desk.

If he hurts Maisie…

…I'll kill him.

Thirty-Three

MINSHULL

Something was wrong.

Minshull pressed on with his contented chatter, more to fill the noticeable gaps where he'd expected Cora's replies to be than because he had anything important to say. He could hear nerves in his own voice; feel his smile becoming tighter as he forced it to stay in place.

He thought a coffee together before the demands of their respective afternoons pulled them apart again was a good idea. Now, he wasn't so sure. Had he offended her? He'd been so keen for her to join the team, so adamant that she was needed here – but had he made her a performing monkey for his own credit?

'Sorry, I'm gabbling,' he apologised, halting the torrent of meaningless chatter to allow Cora a moment to speak.

'You're not,' she replied, a ghost of a smile fleetingly present.

'Are you okay?'

She lifted her pale eyes to look at him. 'I don't know.'

Minshull kicked himself. Why hadn't he asked when he'd first noticed her quietness? 'Was that too much – in there? Did you need more time? Should we have done it in Joel's office, away from the team? It was very full on. I didn't think...'

'Rob,' she cut across his flow of apology. 'It wasn't that.'

'It wasn't?'

'No. I came to do my job and I did it.'

'You did. You were amazing – what you heard changes everything.'

'Thank you.'

'But there's something else?'

Her gaze dropped to the apologetic brown liquid masquerading as coffee in her mug. 'I'm not sure.'

What did that mean? 'Have I offended you?'

'No.' Exasperation edged the word. 'You have to stop thinking I'm taking offence if I'm quiet, Rob. I need space to process what I hear. I don't need to vocalise every thought, every emotion. Sometimes, I just need to work it out first.'

'Right. Sorry.' He watched her drinking her coffee, slow and methodical, wondering what was going on in her mind. Her reaction could just have been to the experience of hearing Ewan Stokes' physical voice so close after his emotional echo attached to the shirt. But he'd seen Cora deal with far worse and she'd never responded like this. When the silence became uncomfortable, he broke it. 'Did you hear something else?'

Her eyes met his, her mouth held in a firm line.

'You did, didn't you? Talk to me, please. What did you hear?'

'I don't know yet...'

'Cora...'

'How well do you know Les Evans?'

The question came from left field, Minshull reeling for a moment as he processed it. 'Les?'

'I know he isn't my greatest fan. But of all the CID team I know him the least.'

Was she concerned Les Evans was judging her? It was such an unlikely concern that Minshull almost laughed aloud. 'Les is just *Les*. He's exactly what he says on the tin.'

'But what do you know about him?'

Why did it matter? 'I know he's a git most of the time but he cares about the job, deep down below the layers of grumbling and dodgy attitude.'

'I think you need to ask him about Maisie Ingram.'

'What?'

He expected her to relent, to claim it was a joke. But nothing about her body language or expression suggested this was likely.

'Ask him about Maisie.'

'You heard what he said. He knew of Ewan Stokes – probably Maisie, too – but he didn't know them personally.'

She was shaking her head now, fingers gripping the handle of her mug. 'You need to ask him again. Alone. Away from the others.'

'Okay, I will.'

She stared at him as if still uncertain.

'I will. I promise.'

'Thanks. And don't take his first answer, please. It will be a lie.'

How could she know that? Unless… 'What did you hear from him?'

'I'm still working it out. But I'm convinced he knows her.'

–

Cora's words bit at Minshull's heels as the afternoon wore on. Why would she suggest Evans was lying? Was the history between Cora and Les clouding her judgement? Or perhaps his vehement denials of knowing Ewan Stokes had worried her. To someone unfamiliar with the rise and fall of banter within the team, could it have looked like an unnecessary pile-on of accusations on the DC? There was so much about life in CID that Cora had yet to experience. In time, she would most likely accept things, as Minshull and his team had done.

But he'd seen that adamance in her before. It had scared him…

'Any sign of Mr Patrick?' Minshull asked Ellis, replacing one frustration in his already overcrowded mind with another. A glance at the clock above the evidence board confirmed it to be almost ten to six.

'Not yet, Sarge.'

'Have you tried calling him?'

'I have. All calls straight to voicemail. I called his home number and spoke to his wife. She reckons he will have forgotten to charge his phone – he's infamous for it, apparently. I've left a message to say we're leaving at six thirty and asking him to call me in the morning to rearrange.'

'Right.' Minshull's gaze strayed across to Evans as Ellis and Bennett resumed their work.

He left his desk and walked past his colleagues who were working with renewed vigour, the confirmation Cora's ability had given them fuelling their resolve.

'Les,' he murmured beside his colleague, drawing level with the preposterously untidy desk. 'A word?'

He didn't wait for a reply, walking quietly out of the CID office into the corridor beyond.

'Sarge?' Evans asked behind him.

'Walk with me,' Minshull said, without turning. He led Evans down to the far end of the corridor, to one of the unoccupied meeting rooms. 'In here.'

Evans said nothing as he followed Minshull inside, the door closing with a gentle thud, sealing them in with stale air and unanswered questions.

'This won't take long,' Minshull said, already seeing his colleague bristling with defiance. 'You're not in trouble. I just wanted to talk away from the rest of the team.'

'Well, that's a comfort.'

Minshull let it pass. 'Did you know Ewan Stokes?'

'This, again?'

'It's not a hard question, Les.'

'No, it's bloody easy to answer. *No*, I didn't know him.'

'Think, please. It's important.'

Evans flushed. 'So I see. Are you calling me a liar?'

'No.'

'Sounds like it to me.' His eyes narrowed. 'Someone's said something, haven't they?'

Minshull stood his ground. 'I'm asking you. As a colleague. Your reply in there – your attitude now – it's not you. You laugh this stuff off usually. You tell us to sod off and leave you alone. Then the next minute you give as good as you get to Dave, or Drew, or Kate. What's changed?'

'For the love of… Nothing's changed, Minsh, okay? Nothing. Apart from the fact that it appears you all think I'm lying.'

'Oh, come on, Les. I'm not accusing you of that.'

'Aren't you? You've asked me the same question three times today and you still aren't satisfied with the answer.'

'Then how about Maisie Ingram?'

Evans punched his hands into his pockets. 'What about her?'

'Do you know her?'

'I can't believe you're even asking me.'

'It isn't a trick question.'

'It bloody is. No, I don't know her.'

'Did you know her then?'

'I said *no!*'

'I have to ask. You lived in Kesgrave, streets away from the house Ewan Stokes shared with Maisie Ingram. It's a small, tight-knit community. People will have talked. You must have heard something?'

'You can state those facts all you like. None of them changes my answer.'

This was getting Minshull nowhere fast. He pulled back. 'I'm concerned, Les. You haven't been yourself this week…'

'Yeah, well, having your car vandalised tends to murder your sense of humour.'

'Are you scared?'

Evans stared back. 'Excuse me?'

Cora had been so certain. He had to ask, but now the question was out in the open, Minshull could see how ridiculous it was. Evans wasn't scared of anything – except hard work and paying for a round. 'Finding your car attacked like that. It must have been horrific.'

'It was.' The tiniest break in his voice belied the truth, making Minshull feel worse for questioning him. 'It still is. But I'm not scared, Sarge. I'm bloody angry, but it takes more than a tyre bill to scare me.'

It was pointless to continue. Grasping for an exit strategy, Minshull changed tack again. 'I know we don't always see eye to eye, but please, if there's anything concerning you, or you just find elements of this case difficult, talk to me. We can discuss whatever you like. The others don't need to know.'

Evans observed him for what felt like an age. 'I would *like* to be *believed.*'

227

That was it: the slammed door. Minshull acceded. 'Fine. Let's go back.'

At his desk once more, Minshull dismissed the niggle that remained. Cora had misread the situation. He would call her later, assure her that he'd spoken to Evans in private and was satisfied he knew nothing.

Whatever Cora thought about Evans and Maisie Ingram, she was mistaken.

Thirty-Four

MINSHULL

'Rob, can we talk?'

Anderson's stealthy arrival at Minshull's desk caught him by surprise, as it always did. How such a broad, tall individual could traverse the CID office so silently remained a skill nobody on the team could fathom.

'Of course, Guv.'

Anderson glanced to his right, taking in the rest of the detectives already busy at their desks. Everyone had arrived early this morning, unbidden. Minshull guessed that none of his colleagues had enjoyed much sleep last night, the adrenaline of yesterday's breakthrough still pumping. 'Best do this in my office.'

Minshull hastened after his superior, closing the door to Anderson's office without being asked. 'What's up?'

'Traffic just called in a job. Crashed car on Back Lane, Falkenham, one fatality. SOCOs are already there but they've requested CID in attendance. Are you and Dave good to go?'

It was the last thing Minshull needed this morning, keen as he was to crack on with the increasingly long list of tasks he had yet to tackle. But all of the team were similarly employed: after the frustrations and dead ends of this week, he couldn't foist this responsibility upon them.

'No problem, Guv.'

–

'Bloody *hell*.'

Minshull had nothing to add to Wheeler's summation of the scene before them. A blue car – or what remained of it – crumpled to half its length against a tall oak tree. A wide, angry crack snaked up the tree trunk from the stricken vehicle's ripped roof, a vertical scar of impact that made Minshull wince just looking at it.

SOCOs were already at work, measuring the furiously swerving tyre marks marring the tarmac of the country road, photographing the wreckage and laying markers across the scene. They worked in that quiet, unhurried way of theirs, what little conversation they shared communicated mostly in gestures and solemn nods. It was comforting, Minshull thought, in the midst of such horror. A reverent calm after the clamour.

Leaving the CID pool car just outside the cordon on the already closed stretch of road, Minshull and Wheeler approached the crash site, showing their warrant cards to the stoic-faced PC guarding the entrance and heading towards their colleagues.

Brian Hinds, senior SOCO, gave them a grimace of welcome as he looked up from his clipboard. 'A pleasure, as always.'

'Good to see you, Brian,' Minshull replied. 'What do we have?'

'One white male deceased, approximately fifty to sixty years old. We're waiting for the duty pathologist and a fire service cutting crew so we can get the poor sod out.'

'Any idea how long he's been here?' Wheeler was already scribbling notes.

'Difficult to say exactly, but overnight at least. We'll know more when we remove the body. Judging by the condition of the car and its location, I'd say death was pretty much instantaneous. That kind of impact, the speed he looks like he was doing when he came off the road: not much chance of surviving that.'

Minshull looked back at the tyre skids streaking away from the car. 'Accident?'

'You'd think. But I found something interesting.' He motioned for the detectives to follow as he walked towards the car. Crouching down by the rear wheel on the driver's side, he pointed at the bodywork. 'See this damage? It wouldn't have been caused by the collision with the tree.'

Minshull and Wheeler leaned in to look at the significant dent and scraping above the wheel arch. Deep within the crumpled metal, white streaks of paint were clearly visible.

'He was hit?'

Hinds nodded. 'Side on. With some considerable force.'

Wheeler peered closer. 'Could it be damage from a previous incident?'

'Possibly. But I reckon it's recent. There are no signs of rust or age around these marks, see? If it happened even a few days ago you'd expect to see some flaking of the paint, some fading of the scratches. These look new to me.'

Minshull frowned at the evidence. 'So you think another vehicle was involved?'

'Like I said, we won't know until we get the car in for investigation.' Hinds stood up slowly, his hand pressed to his lower back for support. 'But if you ask me, I reckon our chap was *helped* off the road.'

'Sarge!'

A shout from the front of the crashed vehicle summoned Minshull over. Letting what Brian Hinds had said sink in, he jogged across. A SOCO held out an evidence bag in her blue-gloved hand.

'We found this in the footwell. Looks like an ID.'

Within the clear plastic bag lay a bloodied lanyard, the card clipped to it bearing a photograph under the title *Deben River Football Coaching*. Beneath the photo was a name that sent every other question skittering from Minshull's mind.

TED PATRICK

'What've we got?' Wheeler asked, arriving at Minshull's side.

'We need to issue a Fast Action on this. Inform DI Anderson. And better call Drew Ellis, too,' Minshull replied, anger already balling inside. 'Tell him it looks like we've found his missing football coach.'

BREAKFAST NEWS REPORT

'I'm standing not far from the scene of what appears to be a horrific crash. Police have closed the whole of Back Road in Falkenham, following the discovery of the damaged car. Although we've had no formal statement, we believe the car was not unoccupied when it was discovered. A small tent has been erected: we've seen specialised scene of crime officers working around the scene, and a fire service cutting crew were on the site when we arrived. It's as yet unclear how many people might have been in the car, but we're expecting confirmation of at least one fatality.

'It's a horrible prospect: from what I've managed to ascertain from other onlookers, the car was discovered here in the early hours of the morning and had likely been here all night. The chances of anyone surviving such a devastating crash, given the likely length of time they might have waited to be found, are slim at best.

'This is a developing situation and likely to be several hours before an official statement is released. We will of course be waiting. Elodie, back to you in the studio…'

Thirty-Five

MINSHULL

Ursula Patrick was sitting on the sofa, tiny and frail between the towering figures of her grave-faced twin sons, Adam and Roan, who flanked her on either side. They clasped her hands to theirs, as if she might topple to the floor without their support.

Conversations like these never became any easier. Minshull counted his blessings that he had encountered a remarkably small number compared with those dealt with by his colleagues in other forces. His brothers made several a month in their respective positions, both Joe in West Midlands Police and Ben in Devon and Cornwall Police and he knew from their conversations how much they dreaded them. But for Minshull the relative rarity of such visits made each one harder to bear. Other colleagues spoke of a certain amount of professional detachment that formed over years of repeating this task, as if the body somehow grew numb due to the frequency and necessity of it. Minshull doubted he would ever *not* feel the gravity and horror of such occasions. How could you look into the face of the suddenly bereaved and not feel their pain?

'Mrs Patrick, I am so sorry to bring you this news,' he said, meaning every word, hating the way her frame bore the blows. 'It appears your husband's car was involved in an accident, sometime yesterday evening. His vehicle came off the road, at some speed, and hit a tree.'

A sob sounded from one of the sons, his free hand flying to his mouth. Minshull saw Ursula Patrick's fingers tighten around his other hand.

'Is he – are you certain it's him?' the other twin asked, eyes hollow.

'As certain as we can be. We found his coaching ID in the car. The photograph on it…' He broke off, the recognition from Ted Patrick's family enough to cease his words.

'Did he suffer?'

Minshull's heart went to the woman, her question defiant despite her visible shock and pain. 'No, Mrs Patrick. We don't believe that he did.'

He'd asked the same question of Brian Hinds at the scene this morning, grimly aware that he would require the answer for this visit.

'Speed he was doing, impact on the body, I doubt it,' Brian had replied with a sympathetic shake of his head. 'Split second before impact, maybe? But it would have been pretty instantaneous.'

He didn't comment on the minutes prior to the crash, nor his theory that Ted Patrick's car was forced off the road. He didn't need to: Minshull was already mulling over potential lines of inquiry. When the report came back from the investigations team, he might have to address the subject with the family then. He didn't relish the prospect.

'Will you need us to do an identification?' the twin on his mother's right asked.

Another question Minshull dreaded. 'I'm afraid so.'

'Even though it was his car, his ID?'

'I'm sorry, but yes.'

Paling further, the young man nodded.

'When?' Ursula Patrick's question was carved out of grief.

'Soon. We'll let you know when it needs to happen.'

'I'll do it.'

'Mum, no. It should be me and Adam.'

'Roan, he is my husband, I should…' Her voice cracked and both sons hurried to comfort her.

'There's time to decide that,' Minshull assured them. 'Don't worry about it now.' He looked over to the PC who was standing at a respectful distance in the doorway of the living room. At his invitation she entered. 'This is my colleague, PC Flora Watkins. She will be your family liaison officer, so she's going to stay here with you while the investigation is carried out.'

'Hello.' PC Watkins gave a warm, reassuring smile as she clasped hands with Ursula and her two sons in turn. 'I'm a FLO in both name and occupation.' Her gentle remark coaxed the ghost of a smile from the family group.

'Anything you need to know, Flora can help,' Minshull added. 'She can answer any questions and help with whatever you need. She also makes a mean cuppa.'

'He's right, I do.' PC Watkins smiled again.

Sensing the moment had come for him to entrust the family to his colleague's care, Minshull stood. As one, Ted Patrick's loved ones followed suit.

'When there are any developments, I'll let you know. I'm so very sorry for your loss.' He began to walk out.

'Who else was on the road?' Adam Patrick asked, suddenly.

Surprised, Minshull turned. 'Sorry?'

'Adam…' his mother warned.

'No, Mum, DS Minshull needs to know.'

'Ad – leave it, man,' Roan Patrick rushed.

'You heard what he said, Roan. The lights…'

Minshull's pulse throbbed at his neck. 'What lights?'

Roan and Ursula looked distraught. Adam held his ground. 'Dad reckoned someone was following him. He's been saying it for a few weeks: lights following his car when he was driving home from football practice, vehicles parking up at the end of the road when he got home.'

'Did he say what the vehicles looked like?'

'No,' Roan said. 'It was always too dark to make them out. He reckoned it was around the size of his car, though. Not a truck or a transit van.'

'Ted had been under a great deal of stress lately,' Ursula said, her voice weary. 'He thought he saw a lot of things. People in the garden, strangers he didn't recognise at the edge of the playing fields. Phone calls he answered where nobody replied. He thought someone was stalking him. The doctor prescribed antidepressants for a while but I don't think he took them.' Roan put an arm around her shoulder and she slumped against him. 'It's been such a worry – and now this...'

Had someone been stalking the football coach?

And could they have driven Ted Patrick to his death?

Minshull battled to steady his voice, his mind in a hundred places at once. 'Could you make a list with PC Watkins of everything you remember him saying?'

'You think someone did this to him?' Adam asked, emotion choking his question.

'I don't know. But anything you can remember could prove useful to our investigation.'

He hated leaving the family with the possibility, knowing that it would be the only thing on their minds as he walked away from the Patrick family home. He hated not having answers: not being able to bring the bereaved family the peace they needed.

But Adam Patrick's revelation had turned Minshull's plans on their head. Someone had driven Ted Patrick off the road in Falkenham, on the day he was due to talk to police about Ewan Stokes. They had possibly been stalking him for some time beforehand.

Why?

THE CLUB

BREAKING: FOOTBALL COACH TED PATRICK'S CAR IN TREE COLLISION.

All over local news in Suffolk today. Ted Patrick's car came off the road sometime yesterday and hit a tree. No confirmation yet, but judging by news pics little chance he survived. Accident? :) :)

COMMENTS

debenboi3981 They got him!

nasher_01 One less on the list. #goodriddance

scoutr103 That's what happens if you leave our man on the bench.

jenghiss8 Buhbye bastard. Hope it wasn't quick.

– Moderator has closed comments on this post –

Thirty-Six

ANDERSON

The team gathered in the centre of the CID office in subdued silence. The buzz of conversation was gone: heads were bowed, shoulders rounded against the ache of investigation. As Minshull prepared to address them, Anderson arrived.

'Apologies,' he mumbled, his voice gruff. 'I just spoke to Dr Amara. She'll be commencing the post-mortem shortly.'

'Okay thanks, Guv. Okay, so this is where we are. We believe the body found in the car on Back Lane, Falkenham, was involved in a fatal road collision sometime yesterday late afternoon. The car belongs to Ted Patrick, football coach, who was due to visit us after his last coaching session of the day. SOCOs found his football coaching ID in the footwell of the car and from an initial view it looks likely to be him. There will be a formal identification, but until then we work on the hypothesis that it's our man. Judging by witness statements we've pulled together, the last time anyone saw him was around 4:35 p.m., after the coaching session on the recreation ground in nearby Kirton. He was on his way home when his car left the road, colliding with a tree. We're yet to hear from the accident investigators but from the damage to Mr Patrick's car, it appears he may not have been alone on the road when the collision occurred.'

He pointed to an enlarged photo of the back right wing of the car, the streaks of white paint clearly visible in the considerable dent. 'I spoke to the chief SOCO, Brian Hinds, at the crash site and he reckoned this was significant. Until we receive confirmation we won't know for certain, but I think this damage suggests his car was hit from behind.'

'Deliberate, Sarge?' Bennett asked.

'We can't rule that out. At the very least we're looking for a hit-and-run. At worst, someone wanted him off the road.'

'Could it have been a warning shot that went wrong?'

'It's possible, Drew. We're ruling nothing out. Added to this, Mr Patrick's family said he'd been concerned he was being stalked. Figures in the garden late at night, strange cars parked at the entrance to the training grounds he worked at, that kind of thing. Obviously, we need to check this. So Dave and Les, can you track down any CCTV we can find in the areas around Mr Patrick's home and the football grounds where he worked?'

'Sarge.'

'Thanks. Drew, see if we can find any doorbell cam footage from the immediate area, too. And talk to Mr Patrick's coaching assistants – Mr Patrick's sons have sent over a list. See if they noticed any unusual activity, and if Mr Patrick mentioned his concerns to them at all.'

Ellis nodded as he made notes in his ever-present notebook.

'Kate, was Ted Patrick interviewed for the *Missing Son* documentary?'

Bennett checked her list. 'No. The only footage of him was the news report Dave found about the team.'

'Any joy tracking down our elusive film-makers?'

'Not yet, Sarge. The production company they released it through went bump a few years ago. So far I've only been able to find the new distributor, and they bought it as a rights package from the receivers handling the assets of the production company. They aren't online, they don't appear to be making films at all.' Seeing Minshull's expression, Bennett raised her hand. 'I'll carry on looking.'

Minshull glanced at Anderson. 'Anything to add, Guv?'

'I don't think so. As soon as we hear back from the post-mortem we can get the formal identification done. I'll update you when that happens. Good work, everyone.'

'Guv.'

The team dispersed to their desks, leaving Minshull and Anderson standing by the whiteboard.

'What do you think?' Anderson asked, staring at the frustratingly separate scraps across the board.

Minshull gave a hollow laugh. 'At this point? No idea.'

'Liar.'

Why had Anderson chosen now to become aware of how Minshull's brain worked? He glanced across to see his superior's wry grin. 'If we take it as an isolated incident, it could just be an unfortunate accident.'

'And if we don't?'

'Ted Patrick has been mentioned on the fan forum as a potential target. Several times. There's a theory he had something to do with Stokes' disappearance, although the original investigation only ascertained that Ted hadn't seen Ewan after the match.'

'Could someone not want him to talk to us?'

'I don't see how they could've known he was coming here. I think he just forgot: didn't charge his phone, like his wife suggested, and missed Drew's call about rescheduling. His wife said he'd been under a great deal of stress lately. It stands to reason that he could have forgotten he was visiting us.'

'Was he followed home?'

Entertaining that possibility meant opening a whole new line of inquiry. Any number of people might have borne a grudge against the football coach. But there was no escaping it, not given what Ursula Patrick and her sons had told him about Ted's concerns. 'It could be unrelated to Ewan Stokes. We need to explore that.'

'Or?'

Was it possible he had become a target for the Stokesy fandom? It seemed fantastical, but nothing that had happened in recent days made sense. 'We've had so many seemingly unrelated incidents. The threats to Maisie Ingram, the false intruder at Damien East's home, the van that drove at us in St Just – and now this? I think they're linked. I think someone has an agenda and they are tying it into the Fifteen Year Return myth.'

'Fandom gone too far?'

'Or someone manipulating it to look like that.'

'Threats are one thing. But attempted murder?'

Minshull shoved his hands in his pockets and looked back at the photos and notes traversing the evidence board. 'We're nearing the anniversary. Each event has been more significant than the last. It's escalating: it has to. The fandom demands it.'

'What if it was Ewan Stokes?'

'Guv?'

Anderson held up both hands. 'I know it sounds insane. But we know he has access to a vehicle. From Cora's evidence we know he planted the football shirt at Damien East's home, too.'

'The damage to Ted Patrick's car…' Minshull's voice drifted, horror painting his features.

'What about it?'

'Brian Hinds pointed it out to me. The flecks of paint deep in the point of collision looked white…'

'Stokes drove him off the road?'

'Or someone with access to the van did.'

'Attempted murder.' Anderson went cold. 'Is he capable?'

'I think we have to consider it. We can't rule it out. But that's the problem: right now we can't rule anything out.'

'Check the forums. Ask Cora to keep an eye out, too. If this is supposed to play into the Fifteen Year Return theory you can be sure they'll be talking about it.'

'Guv.'

'We'll get there, Rob. Heaven knows how, but we will.'

As Minshull slunk back to his desk, Anderson felt everything within him sink.

Thirty-Seven

BENNETT

...The family of Ewan Stokes, including his mother and sister who fought so hard for so long for the missing-person investigation to be kept open, have yet to comment officially. But a friend close to the family told The Sentinel that they are in contact with the police and are therefore unlikely to make a formal statement unless Ewan Stokes is found. They wish, understandably perhaps, to have privacy on this matter...

'I'll bet they do,' Bennett scoffed, as Ellis finished reading the report on *The Sentinel*'s website.

'That's if any of it is even true. "A friend close to the family" is usually just "some bod in the newsroom", I reckon.'

Bennett returned to the electoral roll lists for Alderton and the surrounding area. 'I don't get it. The sighting on the forum was certain it was Marilyn Stokes. So why isn't she listed on any of these?'

'Maybe she doesn't vote,' Ellis suggested. 'What about council tax records?'

'Did them this morning. Nothing.' Bennett let out a long sigh and threw the lists down on her desk. 'I don't know. Maybe she was just visiting friends in Alderton and posted a parcel there. We're going to have to go countywide, aren't we?'

'I don't get why she doesn't want to be part of this new investigation. From what she said in *The Missing Son*, it sounded like she had been the one pushing to keep the investigation going. Why then and not now?'

'Maybe she got sick of fighting.' Bennett stifled a yawn. Insomnia was an unwelcome bedfellow this week and her lack of sleep was weighing heavily. It didn't help that despite reading endless lists of names today she was no closer to achieving her aim. Ellis had already caught her drooping over the lists a few times. He was sweet enough not to mention it to anyone else, but that didn't make Bennett feel any better. 'It can't be easy yelling at closed doors for fifteen years.'

'True.' Ellis clicked his pen three times in succession, as he often did when he was thinking. 'I did find one thing.'

'What?'

'It might be nothing...'

'Or it might be what we've spent hours already searching for. If you've found anything it's worth telling me.'

'I know. It's just that I think *this* thing is better if I show you.'

Bennett groaned. She had no energy for games today. 'Why don't you tell me first and I'll tell you if I think I should see it.'

'I could do that...' He wore the annoying smile of someone who knew full well he had killer information. 'But why not make it more fun?'

'Drew, I don't have time for this.'

'Okay, okay.' He held up his hands, the irritating smirk still in place. 'I have an idea. But you're going to hate it. You're going to say no and tell me to sod off.'

Bennett despaired. 'How do you work that out?'

'Educated guess.' He wheeled his chair closer to hers, giving a quick glance to check their colleagues weren't watching. 'Have a drink with me. Tonight.'

Bennett stared back. Whatever she had thought he might suggest, this wasn't it. 'What?'

He lowered his voice, head bowed a little beside hers, eyes fixed on her from beneath his brows. 'I know a great little pub, out in the sticks.'

'What? I really don't think...'

Ellis produced his phone and held it so that Bennett could see the screen. It was a website for a pub. 'A great little pub. In *Alderton*...'

It took a moment for the location to sink in, before the enormity of the task at hand crashed back in. 'So there's a pub there. If we can't find Marilyn in the council tax lists or electoral roll, she's hardly likely to just rock up in the local pub, is she?'

That annoying grin Ellis wore still didn't shift. 'You'd think.' He swiped across to bring up a gallery on the pub's website, expanding one of the photos with this thumb and forefinger as Bennett watched the movement, unable to look away. 'But what if she was contracted to work there?'

Bennett's breath caught. Behind the bar was a woman who bore a striking resemblance to the young woman she had seen in stills from the true crime documentary. 'Is that her?'

'Looks like her to me.'

'How old is that photo?'

'The date on the website redesign is this year. So it's recent.'

'It could still be an old photo.'

Ellis shrugged. 'It could be. But it's worth a look, surely?'

'We should tell Minsh.' Bennett watched Minshull head over to Anderson's office and knock on the door.

'The Sarge has enough to deal with at the moment. Potential murder, a whole army of nutters ready to strike? He doesn't have time to think about Marilyn Stokes. But we do.'

'Drew, we should tell him.'

'Tomorrow. If we find something worth reporting. If we don't, nobody else needs to know. Can you imagine the grilling we'd get if they knew we went out after hours?' His smile became sincere at last, a completely disarming tactic. 'Come on, Kate, have a drink with me. Tonight. Unless you can't...'

Bennett thought of the empty rented house and the stack of legal correspondence that awaited her return. Ellis didn't know any of it, and he didn't need to. But the thought of doing something normal and fun after work instead of picking over the burned-out remains of her marriage was a wonderful one. And, technically, it was work. 'I can,' Bennett rushed, before Ellis changed his mind.

'Yeah?'

It was hard not to smile at his surprise. 'But you're buying.'

–

At seven thirty, Bennett stood nervously by the window in her rented home, wondering why on earth she'd lied to Ellis. He'd insisted upon driving, instead of meeting her there, as she had suggested. For want of a good excuse to refuse, she'd told him she was house-sitting for a friend away in New York for a week. Why had she done that? She was a creature of habit, a person who found strength in consistency and familiarity. Kate Bennett was the least likely candidate to willingly volunteer to stay alone in a house that wasn't hers. She was amazed Ellis hadn't laughed her out of the CID office.

Truth was, she still felt like a house sitter here, weeks after moving in. So maybe the Manhattan-bound friend was fictional, but the experience of being in a house that refused to become a home was all too real. Far too honest a confession than she was willing to make: even to Dave Wheeler, the only other person who knew about her divorce.

As soon as she spotted the smoke-grey car pulling up at the kerb, Bennett hurried to the front door. The last thing she wanted was to field awkward questions on the doorstep. She attempted to walk down the path as coolly as she could, a task not helped by the outfit she had chosen. What did you wear for an extended fact-finding mission with a colleague out of CID hours?

'Doesn't matter what you wear, people can tell you're a copper a mile off,' Russ used to mock, his theory being that people forgot how to dress like ordinary people the moment they became police officers. She used to think it was funny. But Russ Bennett was a lying bastard, shacked up with another woman and a whole other family he'd fathered while married to Kate, so what he thought no longer mattered.

It still felt strange, meeting Ellis in non-office clothes. Summer clothes, at that: the still high early-evening temperature demanding loose, cool clothing where she would have naturally defaulted to jeans.

Ellis got out of the car as she reached it, his T-shirt and cargo shorts as unfamiliar as the light cotton dress and short-sleeved cardigan Bennett had chosen. 'Evening all,' he grinned. 'Door's open.'

The drive out of St Just's winding streets seemed to take much longer than usual, Bennett acutely aware of every building, tree and shop they passed. Ellis fiddled with the radio controls on his steering wheel, finding an inoffensive pop music station that buzzed in and out of signal as they left the village and drove along country roads edged with open fields and hedgerows.

'So, house-sitting,' he said at last.

'Yep.'

'Nice house.'

'It's okay.'

A pause as Bennett straightened the hem of her dress and Ellis stared resolutely ahead. His car was spotlessly clean inside, a suspicious whiff of cleaning product lingering behind the scent of his aftershave. Bennett wondered if he'd cleaned it after work or if he was always this fastidious.

'This is weird, right?'

Finally, Bennett could relax. 'Totally. I mean, it shouldn't be.'

'Exactly. But it is.'

She looked at her colleague. 'I'm so glad you said that.'

An instant smile met her words. 'Me too. You look great, by the way.'

'*A-a-and* back to weird. You have a nice outfit as well?' The words were so ridiculous that it set them both laughing, the ice broken at last. Laughter was going to get them through tonight, Bennett decided. Make it as light-hearted as possible and it might not be wholly horrific.

'Can you imagine Minsh's face if he could hear this conversation?'

'We'd never live it down.'

'Nobody would believe you wore a dress.'

'Oi!' Bennett scolded him. 'I wear dresses sometimes. Okay, not that often. Anyway, we're not supposed to be on duty, are we? If I turned up wearing a trouser suit they'd suss us as police in seconds.'

'Do you think he'll read us the riot act?'

Bennett's laughter subsided a little. 'Probably.'

'Maybe this was a bad idea...'

'No, come on, Drew. Own it. You found a photo of Marilyn Stokes – that's more than the media or the Stokesy faithful have managed. For once we're ahead of the rest. Let's make the most of it while we have the advantage.'

The drive to Alderton took half an hour, their conversation settling to a comfortable exchange for the remainder of the journey. As the wide cream-painted building came into view, Bennett felt a shiver of nerves.

Ellis parked in the pub car park and killed the engine. Silence rushed into the car as they remained in their seats. Was this a mistake?

'Right, plan of attack,' Bennett began, the need for action overwhelming. It was the only way she knew to find control in unfamiliar circumstances: assess the situation, formulate a plan and move.

'We have a drink, maybe two. Alcohol-free for me, of course.'

His cheekiness was impossible. 'Come on, we need to agree this before we go in.'

'Yes, boss. Okay, put away the death stare, DC Bennett, I'm trying to lighten the mood.'

'Then help me out.'

'Let's just go in there, enjoy a drink and a chat like anyone else in The Swan on a Thursday night. We keep an eye out and, if Marilyn appears, we bide our time before we speak to her.'

'How much time?' Bennett asked. 'We don't want to lose her.'

'We won't. But we don't want to spook her and she won't be able to talk freely if she's working. So we wait until last orders and then talk to her as she's leaving.'

'I have to spend a whole evening chatting to you?' Bennett asked, feigning disgust.

'This job's tough.' Ellis opened his door. 'Didn't anyone ever tell you that?'

The pub was surprisingly busy for a Thursday evening, groups of locals chatting together over pints and pies. Nobody looked up as Bennett and Ellis entered, their progression to the bar unhampered by unwanted attention. Ellis ordered from the young barman and they took their drinks to a round table along one wall that afforded them a clear view of the bar.

'Looks like one bloke serving,' Ellis said. 'But it's still early: they're serving food till nine. Maybe she helps in the kitchen.'

'Possibly. She was definitely pulling pints in the photo.'

'Or they wanted a photo for the website and she went behind the bar to pose for them.'

'Would she do that if she didn't want to be found?'

Ellis considered this as he sipped his pint of cola. 'Unless she thought she was safe. Maybe it was during a quiet time between the anniversary messages. I can't imagine she's been on her guard every moment of the last ten years.'

'Watching *The Missing Son*, she didn't actually say too much. Her mum did most of the talking for the family.'

'They always ask the mum the most, though. Makes it more tragic, doesn't it? A mother devastated by the loss of her son.'

'I wouldn't know,' Bennett said, an unwelcome image of her soon-to-be ex-husband's other family returning to her mind. They had been incredibly easy to find online: the perfect photos of a smiling younger woman draped around Bennett's husband next to two small boys clearly fathered by Russ were a painful reward for her searching. How had he maintained a complete other family life while carrying on his seemingly normal marriage to her? Where had he found the time to sneak off and play happy families with Megan Hurst and their kids?

'Kate.'

'What?'

'I said, if she doesn't show tonight we might have to make this a regular thing.' Ellis was grinning, but Bennett didn't appreciate the joke.

'Or we admit defeat and forget it.'

'Never had you down as a quitter.'

'I'm not a quitter, thank you! Cheek. I've half a mind to...'

'Kate – *shh*! Look!'

A new member of staff had arrived behind the bar, carrying a large wire tray of washed glasses. She was older than the picture Bennett had seen but there was no doubt about her identity.

'Bloody hell, you were right,' she said beneath her breath.

'Trust me, I'm as surprised about that as you are.'

'So what do we do now?' She glanced at Ellis.

'We wait.'

For the next two hours, Bennett and Ellis observed Marilyn Stokes' movements from behind their glasses. To those seated around them, they were just a young couple enjoying a drink and each other's conversation. It was awkward at first, but Bennett soon found herself relaxing. Knowing they had achieved their initial aim of tracking down Ewan Stokes' sister helped. And Ellis was surprisingly good company. The turbulence of the last few months meant that Bennett hadn't socialised with her colleagues as much as she had previously. The pub quiz had been her first time out with anyone from work, encouraged to join the team by Wheeler who had apparently made it his mission to drag Bennett back out into the world again. It hadn't ended how any of them would have wanted, of course, but before the incident Bennett had found the experience cheering.

Ellis was a surprise in more ways than one, not least that he was managing to make what could have been a nauseatingly awkward situation enjoyable. Conversation flowed easily between them, punctuated by careful observation of their mark.

'She seems to know most of the customers,' Ellis said, his dark eyes tracking the movements of Marilyn Stokes across the room. 'Lots of chat and good-humoured banter.'

'So she must be local,' Bennett replied, making her own observation of the woman behind the bar.

'Either that or she's worked here for a while.'

'True. I wonder why none of the Stokesy lot thought to track her down? We found her easily enough: anyone else could have made the same guesses.'

'Maybe they did.' Ellis drained his pint and shuddered. 'I can't do another pint of that. My teeth will rot on the spot.'

'Who knew you could be defeated by a pint of soft drink?'

'Have you tasted it? The *sweetness*...' He pulled a face and laughed when Bennett did. 'Next time, you're driving.'

'Lucky for you there won't be a next time,' Bennett returned.

'Shot down in flames,' Ellis declared, clutching at his heart. 'And just when I was thinking you were enjoying my company.'

'It's better than a night in alone with nothing on the telly.' The moment she said it she knew she'd made a mistake.

Ellis caught it immediately. 'You're on your own while you're house-sitting?'

'Well, I... yes, I am.'

'So your other half is...?'

'Looking after our house.' Bennett's nails dug into her palms. The only 'looking after' Russ Bennett was currently doing was selling their lovely home out from under her.

She didn't want to lie to Drew Ellis. All he had done this evening was tell her the truth – about him, about his life, about everything. Bennett felt dirty by comparison. Russ had sullied everything with his lies, even encroaching on her police life – driving a wedge between her and Ellis for months because of her own hurt and anger.

Things had to change.

'Actually, Drew...'

'She's gone.'

'What?'

Ellis was rising from the bench seat, eyes scanning the room. 'She's gone.'

'Isn't she out the back? We should wait...'

'No, I saw her carrying a bag out and it took too long to register. We need to get outside. Now.'

The car park was worryingly empty when they hurried out of the pub, only a fraction of the cars they had seen earlier remaining now. Bennett checked them all for any sign of Marilyn as Ellis ran out to the road, scanning both directions.

'Shit!'

Bennett drew level with him. 'How did we lose her?'

'I should have been watching.'

'We both should have.'

'Maybe I should go back in there and ask the landlord where Marilyn lives.'

'Oh yeah, like he'll tell you dressed like that with no official ID.'

Ellis swore again, his hand clamped to his head. Bennett forced breath into her lungs to calm herself. She needed to think clearly and the sudden adrenaline rush was affecting her ability to do that.

Walking a little way from her colleague, she considered possible routes Marilyn could have taken. Only one way in and out of the pub car park then a left or right on to the road. Houses surrounded the road on both sides – it was possible she could have gone into one of them. The houses directly adjacent to the pub were all in darkness: if Marilyn had recently returned home Bennett would have expected to see at least one light on. By Ellis' reckoning Marilyn could only have left a few minutes ago. Even if she lived in one of the nearest houses, there wouldn't have been time for her to enter her home and move to the back, turning lights off as she went.

'If she's walking, she can't be far. Let's split up and check the road in both directions.'

'Okay.' Ellis nodded, sprinting off to the left.

Bennett followed suit, turning right on to the road and following it for as far as she guessed Marilyn could have walked.

Nothing. More houses in darkness, more quiet roads.

Frustrated, she retraced her steps to the car park, waiting in the centre of the gravelled drive for Ellis to return.

Why hadn't they been paying attention? All that time chatting had put them too much at ease, making them complacent. If they left with no solid evidence of Marilyn being here, having missed their opportunity to talk to her, what had been the point of tonight?

Accepting defeat, she walked slowly to the car. She'd wait for Ellis to return and then get back to St Just as quickly as possible. She needed a shower, a large glass of wine from her own fridge and bed. This whole evening had been a mistake.

A few minutes later, Ellis jogged over. 'No sign of her,' he said, catching his breath. Bennett imagined her expression mirrored his. 'It's my fault. I wasn't watching when I should've been.'

'Neither of us was. Don't beat yourself up about it.'

'Trouble was, I was enjoying myself too much.' Ellis gave her a rueful smile. 'That'll teach me to have fun.'

Bennett smiled, too. How could she be mad with him? She'd enjoyed the evening, too. It was easy to forget the pleasure of normal things when the rest of your life was in free fall.

A door at the side of the pub opened, the rustle of bin bags and thud of a wheelie bin lid sounding. Bennett followed the sound – and gripped her colleague's elbow.

'It's her!'

Marilyn Stokes leaned into the open door and called goodbye, then shouldered her handbag and began to walk across the car park towards them. Bennett didn't wait: she wasn't losing Marilyn this time.

'Marilyn,' she said, offering her brightest smile.

The woman froze, startled.

'Don't be alarmed, please. I just need to talk to you.'

'I can't... I'm not talking to press...' Marilyn rushed, trying to push past Bennett. Ellis moved across her path, maintaining a safe distance, his hands raised to show he wasn't a threat.

'We're not press,' he said. 'We're police.'

Marilyn's expression hardened. 'Then I'm *definitely* not talking to you.'

'Please,' Bennett said. 'Just one minute.'

'I don't have to talk to you. I don't have to talk to anyone. This is harassment.'

'You're right, you don't have to talk to us.' Bennett thought on her feet, the moment slipping away from them too quickly. She could see Ellis frown in her peripheral vision, but Marilyn's slight hesitation encouraged her to keep going. 'I'm Kate and this is Drew. We're detectives with South Suffolk CID. I know it's a difficult time for you with the fifteenth anniversary looming and these sightings of Ewan. I have no desire to make it worse.'

'Then why stalk me like this? I don't want anyone to know where I am. I don't want to be involved…' She broke off, eyes rising to the twilight sky.

'I can't imagine what it's been like,' Bennett continued, praying that it was enough to keep Marilyn there. 'And I won't even pretend to. But I think maybe you haven't had a say in much of what's happened. I know what that's like, for what it's worth. And I'm concerned things are getting out of hand. You may be in danger.'

Marilyn stared at her. 'Danger? What danger?'

Had Bennett overstepped the mark? 'The bollocks on the Stokesy-Fans forum. The recent hoax. The death of Ewan's football coach…' As the woman recoiled, Bennett pulled a card from her pocket. 'If you want to talk to someone – in confidence – please call me?'

Marilyn stared at the card in Bennett's outstretched hand. The spiky silence of the village at night surrounded them. Ellis let his hands fall to his side. Bennett kept her eyes on Marilyn.

At the last moment, Marilyn snatched the card and powered past them both, stuffing it into her jacket pocket as she left.

–

'What do you think she'll do?' Ellis asked when they were driving home. 'Bin it? Tell her family?'

'I don't know,' Bennett answered, still reeling from the encounter. 'But just for a moment I felt like we had her. Maybe she has been left out of the decisions. Maybe her changing her statement, agreeing to the documentary, even moving out here, was someone else's idea.'

'You mentioned Ted Patrick. Why?'

'I had to do something,' Bennett replied, still uncomfortable with her own actions. 'And she could be in danger, if someone on the forum decides she should be on the list.'

Ellis was quiet for a while. Bennett sank in the seat a little, the weight of the night heavy. The moon was rising over the fields, painting everything in strokes of pale light and shade. What had looked familiar on the drive out to Alderton was alien now, uncertain.

Even the lights of St Just, so often a balm to the weary soul, seemed muted tonight. It was home, but at great cost: the past ghosts of hurt, fear and loneliness forever changing Bennett's association with this place. She loved it but had been abandoned here; her certainty stolen, her search for home a renewed battle she thought she'd long conquered.

'You said you knew what it was like,' Ellis said eventually, navigating the streets in the centre of the darkened, shuttered village. 'What did you mean?'

Bennett closed her eyes. 'I'm not house-sitting. The house I'm in is the one I'm renting.'

Ellis said nothing, waiting for more.

It was too late to take it back. Only one way remained. Something she should have shared weeks ago. 'I'm divorcing Russ. He has another family I never knew anything about.'

'Oh Kate, no…'

The lights of her new street danced and morphed their shape as tears arrived. 'I haven't been able to… I couldn't talk about it because I was working through everything. I was waiting to make sense of it, but that won't ever happen.'

The car steered to a gentle halt outside her rented home, Ellis keeping his hands on the wheel even after the engine stopped. 'So all that weirdness – with us…'

'I should have told you.'

He shook his head. 'I should have worked it out. Who else knows?'

Bennett stared at the darkened outline of her house. 'Only Dave. He's been brilliant, helping me move in, being there when I've needed him.'

'Russ is an idiot.'

Bennett couldn't reply.

'I wish I'd known.'

'I'm sorry.' She reached for the door handle, looking back at her colleague. 'Tonight was fun. I needed that.'

'And Marilyn?'

'We wait and see. That's all we can do.'

'Should we tell Minsh?'

Bennett released a breath she'd held. 'Yes. We'll tell him first thing.'
She risked a smile. 'Hell of a night, huh?'

'Bit of an eye-opener.' He gave a soft laugh, pinching the bridge of
his nose. 'I didn't see most of it coming.'

'Me neither.' Bennett opened her door and got out, surprised when
Ellis did the same. She watched from the pavement as he moved around
the car to join her. 'What are you doing?'

Ellis nodded at the house. 'Seeing you in.'

'I think I can tackle the front path by myself.'

He groaned. 'I'm aware of that. I want you to know I'm here. If
you need me.'

For a simple statement, its impact was startling. 'Thank you.'

'I mean it.' He took a step closer. 'You don't have to do any of this
alone. Good night, Kate.'

Bennett hesitated for a moment, the ground beneath her suddenly
uncertain. 'Night, Drew.'

THE CLUB

** Message on behalf of Watcher89 **

Watcher89 sends greetings and thanks for your concern. Much has been said in Watcher89's absence, including accusations of abandoning the Inner Circle. I've been asked to reassure all Stokesy faithful that it is business as usual. Personal commitments have prevented Watcher89 from posting in recent days. Watcher89 is well, working for us all and ready for the next part of the plan. This is far from over. Stay united, stay sane. The day is close. #Stokesy15

COMMENTS

Leo51183 Gr8 to hear. Some of the shit posted on here has been unbelievable.

Wotcher7 @Leo51183 Legit tho?

Leo51183 @Wotcher7 Why question legit? Inner Circle has to step in. Rogues on site.

Wotcher7 @Leo51183 Rogues? Have a word with yourself. Maybe Inner Circle not fit for purpose. If they can't be strong when it counts, what's the point?

Stokesyy3 What's this? Press release? Watcher89 too good to post himself?

Wotcher7 @Stokesyy3 THIS ^^

Stokesyy3 @Wotcher7 Part of IC now. Too good for us plebs!

Leo51183 @Stokesyy3 @Wotcher7 READ THE POST. The plan's still on.

Br8veMim @Leo51183 @Wotcher7 More to come, boys. I heard the next show is coming soon.

Leo51183 @Br8veMim When?

Br8veMim @Leo51183 Keep watching. Stuff already happened we don't know about. Stokesy Friend in police tipped me off.

Leo51183 @Br8veMim Can't trust police.

Br8veMim @Leo51183 Can trust this one. Bent as!

Wotcher7 @Br8veMim Bit sad if police doing IC's job.

Br8veMim @Wotcher7 Trust me. Stuff's going on that's going to BLOW UP.

– Moderator has disabled comments on this post –

Thirty-Eight

CORA

No word from Minshull. No text, no call.

Cora stared at the frustratingly blank screen of her mobile. She'd expected something by now. Had he even spoken to Les Evans?

'I wouldn't like to be whoever it is you're mad with this morning,' Tris observed, placing a takeout coffee cup on her desk.

'Sorry?'

'Your face. You look like you want to throttle someone.'

'Oh. No, it's nothing like that. Thanks for the coffee.'

'My pleasure. I've killer almond croissants in my bag, too.' He nodded across at her phone as he rummaged in his rucksack. 'But they're strictly for eating, okay? Not ammunition.'

'Funny.'

'You're welcome. Seriously, if you want to talk…'

'Thanks, but I'm fine.'

'Did you see the latest on StokesyFans? About the plan continuing?'

'I did.' Cora took a bite of sweet, nutty pastry. 'There's been a lot of speculation. And the suggestion that someone in the police is tipping them off? That's worrying. Hang on, how come you're reading the forums?'

Tris shrugged, brushing a sprinkling of pastry flakes from his shirt. 'You got me thinking about them again. It's even madder than when I was researching them. Like a cult, for some of them. The rhetoric is insane. It's worrying.'

'Rob thinks the hoax is the thin end of the wedge. If they've prescribed a certain narrative for Stokesy and he doesn't play ball…'

'They might take matters into their own hands?'

Cora shrugged. 'It's possible. There's already been a sustained campaign of actual harassment aimed at Maisie Ingram.'

The mention of Maisie made her think of Minshull again. He had acknowledged the accuracy of her gift with the bloodied football shirt: so why didn't he accept her concerns over Les? And, considering how troubled he'd seen her about it yesterday, why hadn't he contacted her yet to put her mind at ease?

The nub of croissant in her colleague's hand paused between the paper bag and his lips. 'There. That face again. Talk to me.'

Should she share what she'd heard? Tris was a tireless supporter of her and her ability – of all the people she knew he would be most likely to understand. But this was what she had wrestled with for most of the night, the legacy of which stung her eyes and bruised her head this morning. She needed Minshull to hear her, to understand that the voice of Evans she'd heard from the fallen papers had been as real and as correct as that of Ewan Stokes from the defaced football shirt. That he hadn't received it with the same innate belief and surety worried her. Did Minshull only accept her ability when it suited his agenda?

She didn't want to think that. They had been through enough together for no question of trust to exist between them. But his response yesterday and radio silence so far this morning suggested otherwise.

'I heard something. In the CID office.'

'When?'

'Yesterday, after I'd confirmed Ewan Stokes had touched a football shirt left at his former football teammate's home.'

'Shit!'

'I know. That's confidential, okay?' Cora chastised herself for revealing the information about the football shirt. She shouldn't be making lapses of judgement like that. Another indicator that her mind was dangerously distracted.

'Of course. You know you have my confidence, always.'

Cora took a breath. 'I was passing DC Evans' desk and some papers fell from it.' She looked at Tris, searching his expression. 'He knows Maisie Ingram, the former girlfriend of Ewan Stokes. The poor woman who's been attacked and harassed for years by Stokesy supporters.'

'I've seen some of the things about her online. Horrible stuff. What did you hear?'

'"*If he hurts Maisie, I'll kill him. I'll kill the bastard…*" It was his voice, his threat. But I'd just heard him vehemently deny knowing her or Ewan Stokes in the team briefing. Accusing Rob and the others of not believing him. But you don't threaten to murder someone you've never met.'

'Bloody hell.'

'I know.'

'Did you tell Rob?'

Cora nodded. 'He said he'd talk to Les but I could tell he didn't believe me. And since then I've heard nothing. I expected a text at least, something to say he'd done what I asked. It's what he would have done before. He's always made an effort to keep me in the loop. I didn't expect this time to be different.' *I rely on him*, she added in her mind. The steps Minshull had made to make amends for his initial suspicion of her had meant so much. That she was officially part of the CID team now was largely down to his insistence that she was needed. Had hearing something confidential from his colleague been a step too far?

'Perhaps he hasn't had chance to ask yet. Or other developments have prevented him talking to Les.'

Cora had considered all of these reasons already, but the fear in her gut remained. 'I just have a really bad feeling about this. And I'm in an impossible situation here. I've only just become part of the team. People who didn't believe I was credible with the missing child case are accepting me now, but it's still so new. What if this explodes? What if they close ranks?'

'Hey, slow down. You're massively overthinking this. Rob might not have asked yet.'

'What happens if he asks and Les still insists he knows nothing? He's *lying*, Tris, and not just about whether he used to know someone in the investigation. He threatened murder. It wasn't an emotional turn of phrase: it was violent, visceral hate.'

Tris listened, shocked. 'Can you talk to Les? Confront him?'

'How? He's the one person in that team who could threaten everything I've worked to build. If he feels cornered, or spooked, he could cause real trouble to deflect suspicion from himself.'

'What time does his shift end?'

'Sorry?'

Tris dropped the remains of his snack and clapped crumbs from his hands. 'Could you catch him when he leaves work? Raise the concern?'

'I really don't think that would work.'

Tris was undeterred. 'Not as an accusation. As an understanding ally. If he's carrying this secret and having to defend himself at work he's probably feeling alone.'

'He won't listen to me. He might have been courteous to me since I joined the team but he thinks I'm a fraud.'

Tris gave a shrug. 'This'll prove to him you're not.'

'Oh yeah, and give him every reason to discredit me with the others.'

'Not if you offer to help him. And promise to keep his secret.'

Cora stared at Tris. 'But I told Rob.'

'And Les probably told Rob he didn't know Maisie. So as far as Rob's concerned, the matter's closed.'

Was this an option? Dare she risk retaliation from Les Evans by confronting him? 'He finishes at six p.m.' she replied, her mind ablaze with questions.

'You leave here at five,' Tris said, 'and you can be outside Police HQ about fifteen minutes later.'

'But what if Rob sees me? Or any of the rest of the team?'

'Be creative. Say you were popping into town to grab groceries before you drove home and thought you'd stop and say hello. If Rob sees you, invite him out for a drink or dinner. It's nothing you haven't already done.'

All of it was plausible, but would Minshull or the other detectives see through her clever excuses? 'I don't know. It isn't like me to be that knowingly spontaneous.'

'True. But what if you had company?' When Cora didn't reply, Tris spread his hands wide. 'Me. Then you could blame me for dragging you into the centre of Ipswich for food when all you wanted to do was go home.'

'I couldn't ask you to do that.'

'You're not. I'm offering. Come on, Cora, you can't go on tying yourself in knots over this. What if Rob doesn't call today? Or tomorrow? Are you going to endlessly play this out in your mind, losing more sleep?'

It appeared that Tris Noakes knew her better than anyone.

'What if Les comes out on his own?'

'Then I'll keep on walking and wait in a pub nearby for you to call me when it's done.' Tris had clearly thought this through. But could it work?

Thirty-Nine

MINSHULL

'You *stalked* Marilyn Stokes?'

Minshull didn't know whether to congratulate Bennett and Ellis or throw the book at them. Right now he was leaning towards the latter.

'We followed a hunch, Sarge. It proved to be right.'

'I don't care about you being right!' Minshull pinned them both to the spot with his furious stare as they stood in Anderson's empty office. Thank heaven for the long interdepartmental briefing summoning their superior out of CID for the next few hours. At least here they had some privacy, although he was certain Wheeler and Evans would be earwigging from the main office. 'You intentionally harassed a key family member of a missing person. You ignored her express wish not to speak to you both and instead insisted she call you. How, exactly, did you think any of that was acceptable practice?'

'Nobody else had been able to find her.' Ellis lifted his chin ever so slightly, the act only fuelling Minshull's anger. 'And we only have her mother's word that she doesn't want to be involved. She changed her statement. We need to know why.'

'We need to honour her wishes. And her mother's. Do you know how hard it was to get Olwyn onside? What you did could have seriously undermined this investigation.' He let his stare travel between them. 'We play by the book, or not at all. You know this. The previous investigation cut corners, ignored evidence, abandoned protocol. That is *not* how this investigation will be done. I thought I'd made that abundantly clear.'

His DCs said nothing.

263

What the hell were they thinking? And after weeks of strangeness between the pair of them, why had they chosen this blatant act of defiance to unite over? Minshull didn't need this, with a potential murder investigation now joining an already worrying set of circumstances centred around Ewan Stokes.

'I expected better of you both. Especially you, Kate.'

'It was my idea, Sarge.'

'Drew, with respect, that does not surprise me.'

'I agreed with him,' Bennett insisted. 'And he was right.'

'Bloody hell, you two. Don't you realise how serious this is? If Anderson gets wind of it, do you think he'll be any more understanding than me? He'll have your hides.'

'I think Marilyn might talk to us,' Bennett insisted, oblivious to Minshull's building rage. 'She took my card, after all. If we can find out what the real story was with her changing her testimony, we can start to unpack why Ewan Stokes went missing.'

How could they have been so stupid? 'You gave her your card?'

'Yes.' Bennett replied. 'And she took it. She could have refused, but she took it before she left.'

'She could have taken it straight to her solicitor as proof of the detective constable harassing her. Did you think of that?'

'Minsh, please.'

Incensed, he stared her down. 'Excuse me?'

Bennett shrank back. 'Sarge.'

'Right, back to your desks. And I think it's better if the two of you work on separate lines of inquiry for the rest of the day.' He saw their response and dared them to cross him. 'Kate, go through interviews with anyone identified as a friend of Stokes by the original investigation. We need to know anyone who might be helping him now.'

'Yes, Sarge.'

'Drew, chase up Traffic. See if there were any sightings of a white van in the Falkenham area on the day of Ted Patrick's crash.'

'Sarge.'

'That will be all. Go.'

Bennett obeyed, scurrying out of the office, but Ellis hung back. Did the kid have a death wish this morning?

'Something else, Drew?'

The DC flushed a little. It happened less and less these days, the boy who entered CID as one of the youngest DCs South Suffolk Police had ever appointed now definitely become a man. Today it wasn't embarrassment reddening his cheeks: it was indignation.

'It was my idea.'

'So you said.'

'I did it because nobody was asking why Marilyn changed her story. Or trying to speak to her.'

'Because her mother said she didn't want to be involved.'

'That's just her say-so, Sarge. What if Marilyn knows something that could help us solve this? We are chasing up every other person with any kind of connection to Ewan Stokes. Why aren't we asking his sister?'

He wasn't giving up, was he? Minshull should have been impressed by his initiative – on any other day he might have been. But there was too much at stake: too many questions still unanswered. Who silenced Ted Patrick? Was it Stokes himself or another acolyte attempting to assist their idol? Why had the white van continued to elude them? And who was helping Stokes, assuming he was behind all of these things?

Then there was the question of Cora's insistence that Les knew Maisie. Minshull had asked; Evans had denied it. With the sudden intrusion of Ted Patrick's potential murder, Minshull hadn't replied to Cora. But what would he say if he did?

Too many questions. Too many threads that didn't meet. Throwing Marilyn Stokes into the mix would help nobody. And if Olwyn Stokes–Norton got wind of it, any chance Minshull had of retaining her confidence would be gone.

'Look, you took initiative, which I can't fault. Your mistake was to do it without discussing your plan with me. There are protocols, expected routes of inquiry – these are to protect us as investigators and protect the public who are subject to our investigations. If we fail to follow them, we lay ourselves wide open for problems.'

'I know, I'm sorry. But Kate and I are convinced there's something going on there.'

'What did Marilyn say?' Minshull asked. Maybe humouring Ellis would calm him down. Anderson couldn't see him as he currently was. Nobody needed Joel to explode today.

'She thought we were journalists at first and said that she'd decided not to talk to the media. Then, when she discovered we were coppers, she said she'd never talk to us. But Kate was incredible. She suggested the decisions hadn't included Marilyn and that might make her feel as if her views didn't matter. *That's* what made her hesitate. Kate called it and she was right.'

Weariness bit into Minshull's shoulders. 'Okay, point made. We just have to hope Marilyn doesn't tell her mother or go to a solicitor about this. I suppose I should be glad you two are on speaking terms again. But pull another stunt like this and it won't be pretty, believe me.'

Far too late, Ellis dropped the attitude, his head bowing in agreement.

'Okay. Back to your desk now.'

'But you understand?'

Really? Minshull eyeballed him. 'Do you understand the position you put me in? And the rest of the team?'

'Sarge.'

'If Marilyn Stokes makes contact – *if* that happens – you tell me first. Understood?'

'Yes, Sarge.'

'Okay, go. Leave.' Minshull watched Ellis walk out of the office. He was thankful the exchange had happened beneath Anderson's radar. But what damage could Ellis and Bennett's rash act do if it blew up in their faces?

'Sarge, they're on their way back up.' Wheeler's friendly face beamed around the door frame.

'How do you know that?'

'I know Elsie Heath in the DCI's office.' He grinned. 'Spies in every camp, me.'

'Unbelievable, Dave.'

Wheeler's smile fell. 'Everything okay?'

Was it? After a night of no sleep and a morning of unwelcome revelations, Minshull could no longer tell. 'Any minute now I'm going to wake up and discover this was a stress dream.'

'Eh?'

Minshull shook his head as he gathered up the pile of investigation files he'd been sifting through when Ellis and Bennett had made their confession. 'Kate and Drew went on an unofficial stake-out last night.'

'Unofficial?'

Minshull met his colleague at the door, files in arms. 'They found Marilyn Stokes.'

'Where?'

'In Alderton.'

Wheeler chuckled. 'Just across the river, eh? Smart move for her.'

'Which would have been more than enough information for us to make a formal visit,' Minshull replied, keeping his voice low so nobody else would hear. 'But they approached her. Told her who they were. Kate gave her a card.'

'That's not good.'

'It's potentially catastrophic. And a complication we don't need with everything else.'

Wheeler's smile faded. 'How are you doing with this?'

'I just want time we don't have and answers that aren't there.'

'Moon on a stick, eh, Minsh?' Wheeler placed a covert hand on Minshull's arm. 'We're all here for you. We believe in you. Just one step at a time.'

'I know. I couldn't ask for a better team – even when some of them go off-piste.'

'They're doing it because they want to contribute. And because you give them the confidence to take the initiative. That's rare in this gig. Don't underestimate what's possible. Just keep following your gut.'

God bless Dave Wheeler and his gentle wisdom. Of course he was right: the only way to get answers was to work in the way he knew best. Forget the failures of the past that weren't his. Forget the ticking clock. Stick to facts and method. And pray everyone else did the same.

'Cheers, Dave.'

'Pleasure, Sarge. Now, hop to it.'

Nodding his thanks to Wheeler, Minshull slunk back to his desk. Time to ensure everyone was on his side. Checking the team were all working, he slid his mobile phone next to the far side of his computer keyboard and wrote a text message.

> Hi Cora
> Checked again with Les.
> He doesn't know anything. I'm sure of it.
> Don't worry. Call you tonight? Rob

Even as he sent it, Minshull was torn. He'd worked so hard to prove to Cora that he believed in her ability, the regret from his first encounter with her refusing to go away. He believed she deserved her place on the team. He'd fought tirelessly to convince her. And they'd become close – more than friendship but the rest not yet defined. He'd begun to consider the possibility of more. What could his refusal to believe her accusation about Evans do to all of that?

And if she believed he was wrong, would she ever fully trust him?

Stuffing his concerns into his pocket with his phone, he forced the question from his mind. He had done what she'd asked. Evans had given his answer. And Minshull had an investigation to run.

That was all that mattered.

Tabster
Where are you?

MaisieBoo
Shopping

Tabster
Where?

MaisieBoo
Felixstowe

MaisieBoo
I needed to get away from the boxes

MaisieBoo
Where are you?

Tabster
At the house

MaisieBoo
No need! I'll pack the rest tonight

Tabster
I brought some groceries over

Tabster
Wish I hadn't now

MaisieBoo
Why?

Tabster
Typing…

MaisieBoo
WHY Tabs?

Tabster
Typing…

MaisieBoo
What's going on? TELL ME

Tabster
Don't come home M

Tabster
Not yet

MaisieBoo
What's happened?

Tabster
Stay out as long as you can

Tabster
I'm calling police

MaisieBoo
Get out of there first

MaisieBoo
If you need police it's not safe

Tabster
I'm okay. They don't want me

Tabster
They might be watching for you

Tabster
Stay out as long as possible

MaisieBoo
Tabs what the hell happened?

MaisieBoo
I'm going out of my mind

Tabster
Stay out, M. I'll call when it's safe x

Forty

WHEELER

The plastic baby doll wore a sleeveless pink frilled dress fastened with three large yellow buttons at the back. A line of embroidered hearts ran around the hemline and pink ribbons were tied around the bare feet like ballet shoes. But these details weren't what sent bile rising in Wheeler's gut.

It was the plastic bag over the doll's head. And the elastic bands cinching it tight around the neck. And the blood-red streaks in the doll's golden curls.

'Bloody hell,' Wheeler breathed.

'This came with it,' Tabitha Ingram said, the photograph fluttering in her plastic-gloved hand as she passed it to Minshull.

It looked like Ewan Stokes.

He wore the same clothes the two cameras had picked up at Rai's Garage, and enough of his face was visible inside the hood of his sweatshirt to reveal a far older version of the young man who'd disappeared fifteen years ago. Even though the resemblance was striking, Wheeler didn't want to believe his first impression.

'Is that him, Sarge?' he asked.

'Definitely.'

'Of course it's him,' Tabitha snapped, instantly relenting. 'Sorry. This is all just… I wanted it to be a hoax like the other times, but that's him.'

'Where is Maisie now?' Wheeler asked.

'She's gone over to a friend's house. Someone that bastard and his sick followers don't know. I've told her to stay there.'

'That's wise,' Minshull agreed. 'When did this arrive?'

'About an hour ago. Someone rang the doorbell. I was putting stuff in the fridge and by the time I got to the front door there was nobody there. Just *that thing* and the photo. There's a message on the back.'

Minshull flipped the photograph over and read the scrawled text.

> HI BABY DOLL
> IT'S NEARLY TIME.
> ARE YOU READY FOR ME?

'*Baby doll?*' Wheeler repeated. 'Is that significant?'

'Yes,' Tabitha replied. 'That's why I called you. When Maisie was with him, he called her *baby doll*. Never in public, only once when I was in the room. But later she told me it was what he'd say when she was in trouble. A red flag.'

Minshull looked up from the photograph. 'How do you mean?'

Tabitha Ingram folded her arms tight across her body. She appeared smaller today, worry etched into her features. 'It was a warning sign. A tool of coercive control. It was how he kept her in line. If he called her *baby doll* it meant she had done something wrong. She would do anything then to avoid the inevitable punishment. So he got whatever he wanted without having to lift a finger.'

Wheeler swallowed the comment he wanted to make. *Evil bastard.* How anyone could get their kicks from terrorising a partner was beyond him. He instantly thought of his wife Sana, preparing for the start of the six-week summer holidays with their boys. He would do anything for her; lay his life on the line in a heartbeat. Even the thought of making her unhappy was anathema to him. You didn't threaten someone you loved. And if you did, how could you ever claim to love them?

'Could anyone else know Stokes used that term for your sister?'

'No. He was careful to hide it. And it wouldn't be something he'd have bragged about, either. That's where he got his power, wasn't it? Her word against his if any of his filthy shit got out.'

Minshull crouched down beside the doll, his face grave. 'Dave, get some photos of it and we'll bag it up.'

274

'Okay, Sarge.' Wheeler sent Tabitha a reassuring smile as he headed back out towards the car.

The heat of the day was rising after a morning held back by hazy cloud. It was going to be another scorcher, no doubt about that. He collected the camera and a large paper evidence bag from the boot of the car and retraced his steps up the garden path. But as he neared the open front door, he stopped. Something on the sun-scorched front lawn was catching the light, glinting in the strengthening sun.

What was it?

Wheeler picked his way across the yellow, brittle grass and bent down to look. Taking a handkerchief from his pocket he carefully picked it up.

It was a small, round disc, about the size of a five-pence piece, domed on one side and flat on the other. The flat side bore dirt-speckled traces of adhesive, the few remaining scraps of which now held fragments of straw-like grass. But it was the domed side that immediately alerted Wheeler. The silver detailing over its dark blue background formed a V and a W.

Volkswagen.

Wheeler knew immediately what it was. His brother had not long replaced a similar one on the key fob of his ageing VW Golf.

'The original badges stick for years,' Luke Wheeler had explained over a lazy post-Sunday-dinner pint a few weeks back. 'But when they come off the only thing you can get are cheap replacement ones from eBay, that stick for about five minutes unless you superglue them on.'

Heart thumping, Wheeler hurried to the house.

'Sarge. A word?' he called, leaning in through the open doorway, careful not to disturb the plastic doll on the doorstep.

Minshull turned to Tabitha. 'I'll just be a moment. Why don't you go into the living room and sit down?'

As she wordlessly complied with his request, Minshull joined Wheeler.

'What's up?'

'I found this on the grass not far from the path.' Wheeler held out his hand to reveal the VW logo badge, tiny against the folded handkerchief in the centre of his palm. 'It's from a key fob. Originally stuck on but my brother says the older the fob gets, the more likely the badge is to dislodge.'

- Minshull examined it. 'How long could it have been there?'

'No idea, Sarge. But it doesn't look like it's been in the sun long. If it'd been there for a while I reckon the top surface would have faded or cracked with the heat we've had.' He lowered his voice, despite Tabitha Ingram being a room away from them now. 'The van we've been looking for – the one only Stokes had access to – it's a 2004 Volkswagen Caddy.'

Minshull stared at Wheeler. 'Could be a coincidence.'

'Could be. But what are the chances of finding it the same day an up-to-date photo of Stokes and a doll referencing his private term for Maisie Ingram turn up here? We'd need to check dimensions to be certain – different Volkswagen keys have different-sized badges, my brother says. But I reckon it's from our elusive van.'

'Bag it. We might not get anything from it but it's too significant to ignore.'

'Would Cora be able to hear anything from it, too?'

'Possibly.' Minshull's expression was odd. Usually, he lit up at the very mention of Cora. What was going on there? 'Let's get the photos done and work out what we do next.'

He pulled a small evidence bag from his pocket and he and Wheeler carefully transferred the badge from the handkerchief into it. Sealing the bag, Minshull went back into the house as Wheeler photographed the doll. Beads of moisture had formed in the heat where the bag gathered around its neck, giving it the appearance of captured final breaths. Wheeler had seen it once before on an adult victim of death caused by asphyxiation and the memory still haunted him. He let the camera see it, averting his eyes from the screen as soon as the shot was aligned. Some things you didn't need reminding of.

When he was finished, he put the camera on the doorstep and pulled on plastic gloves before gently lifting the doll from its resting place. Its wide-eyed stare slowly disappeared as he slid it into the bag and sealed it. The relief he felt was considerable. Nobody should see a sight like that: horrific enough from its appearance alone but downright sick when linked with a term associated with control and abuse. What was wrong with some people?

As he approached the entrance to the box-filled living room, Wheeler could hear the gentle rhythm of Minshull's voice, respectfully soft and low as he spoke to Maisie Ingram's sister. Wheeler could see the burden of it all weighing on his colleague. It must have been impossibly hard for him to confront his dad at the beginning of the case; that he'd done it said a hell of a lot more about the son than it did the father. And to lead an investigation that uncovered his dad's mistakes at every turn must be worst of all.

Minshull was a great copper, worth a thousand of his old man, but Wheeler could see the shadow of the old bastard looming over the son whenever Minshull doubted himself. He knew Joel Anderson saw it, too. It was good that Anderson appeared to be looking out for the kid after spending no inconsiderable amount of time at loggerheads with him. But the DS deserved far more joy than he seemed able to afford himself. The weirdness between him and Cora wouldn't help this, either.

Wheeler entered the room, vowing to keep a closer eye on his DS for as long as this investigation ran. Minshull needed allies, especially as his greatest foe right now appeared to be himself.

'All done, Sarge,' he said, careful to match his tone to Minshull's.

'Thanks.' Minshull's smile was brief before he turned back to the woman seated on the sofa. 'Do you have somewhere you can go?'

'I'm fine. He has no issue with me.'

'All the same, until we have more information it might be wise. Could you maybe join your sister where she is?'

'She won't be staying,' Tabitha replied, her tone as hollow as her stare. 'As soon as she knows what happened she'll insist on coming back. She won't want him to think he's won.'

'I really think you need to make it clear to her that she's in danger,' Minshull returned. 'Everything points to this being Ewan Stokes, not one of his acolytes. I understand the harassment you've both endured but this is a credible threat from someone with every reason to carry it out.'

'She won't listen to me.'

'Try. Please. For your sister's sake.'

Tabitha let out a sigh, her hands rubbing along her arms as if a chill wind had broken into the house. 'I'll keep her at our friend's house for as long as I can.'

'Thank you. In the meantime I'll ask for a patrol to be stationed outside. If he comes back, he'll find us waiting.'

–

Ten minutes later, Wheeler and Minshull raised their hands in farewell as Tabitha Ingram drove away from the house. Minshull finally released a groan Wheeler had sensed him holding since they arrived.

'What the hell, Dave?'

'I know. How likely is it you'll get the patrol?'

'Slim.' Minshull drew a hand through his hair, leaving damp streaks where his palms made contact. 'I'll make the case, and if necessary ask Anderson to beg DCI Taylor.'

'He'll love you for that.' Wheeler's comment masked his concern for his sergeant.

'Reckon that'll be a permanent strike off his Christmas card list.'

The glimpse of humour was a good sign, Wheeler decided. 'I wouldn't worry. Joel's idea of a decent Christmas card isn't worth being on a list for.'

Minshull stared at the empty road Tabitha Ingram had just driven away on. 'It's him, isn't it? We can't ignore the evidence.'

Wheeler felt his spirit sink. 'I don't reckon he's doing it alone, though. Someone has to be helping him – taking that photo, for a start, but also getting him into the UK without anyone noticing, and supporting him all those years. Someone who'd just wandered off wouldn't be doing all this.'

Minshull looked back at the house. 'Why now? Why fifteen years? What's significant about that length of time?'

'Looks good in the headlines?'

'Not for the poor family, it doesn't. Olwyn said she's found it hard, all these strangers second-guessing where her son is when she just wants him home. But if they don't know where he is, who could be helping him?'

'I don't know, Minsh. What do we do with this?' He raised the sealed evidence bag in his hand.

'We get it back and let Anderson see it.'

'And Cora?' Wheeler asked carefully.

Minshull's sigh was long and heavy. 'I'll call her.'

Forty-One

CORA

First the text message dismissing her concerns, then an urgent summons for her to return to CID. What the hell did Rob Minshull want from her?

So much for her plan to apprehend Les Evans after his shift. Now Cora would be in the room with him, knowing the truth he was hiding from everyone, alongside Minshull who was convinced she was wrong. If he didn't believe what she had definitely heard from Evans, what hope was there that he would accept what she told him about the item he wanted her to assess?

It felt like she was being used. She might have expected it from someone else, but not Minshull. His sudden refusal to believe what she'd heard from Evans cast into doubt everything he'd said about her ability.

'We need you here as soon as you can,' he'd said, his tone flat and a hundred unspoken words crammed between each spoken one. She could picture him, head bowed, hating making the call, hating asking her. How had he gone from being her close ally to this?

Tris was sympathetic when the call from Minshull came, offering to be in Ipswich anyway in case she needed him. Cora declined: there was no point in their scheme now.

She swiped her card at the door from reception, retracing her steps up to the first floor. If Minshull thought this callback would cancel out his dismissal, he was wrong.

And when she was done with this, she was going to confront Les.

Pushing open the double doors at the top of the first flight of stairs, she saw Minshull waiting in the corridor. Steeling herself, she walked towards him. The distance seemed greater than before, the space between them stretching further than her steps could broach. It didn't help that she caught sight of the long sigh that raised and dropped his shoulders moments before she reached him.

'Hi. Thank you for—'

'In there, is it?' she cut across him, preparing to turn left into the CID office.

'Cora, wait.' Minshull stepped forward, close enough to halt her progress.

She stopped, staring ahead. Seeing him brought the fury and frustration she'd battled for hours rushing to the surface. It prickled her skin and constricted her throat. 'I'm here to do my job. Please let me pass.'

'No. Not until you hear me. I'm sorry, okay? I should have called you last night, told you what Les said.'

'No need. I know what he said.'

'I doubt it.'

'He denied it, made you feel dreadful for doubting him, probably brought up the slashed tyres on his car.' She glared at Minshull who shrank back a little. 'Am I close?'

She didn't need a reply to know she was.

Minshull began his defence. 'Les said…'

'It doesn't matter.' She hated herself for asking the question that would follow, but without it she wasn't certain she could continue here. 'Do you believe in what I hear?'

'Yes,' Minshull rushed, realisation following on its heels. 'In everything else, I do.'

'Will you believe me if I hear something now?'

'You know I will.'

'Do I?'

The words stung the space between them. Minshull looked up at the ceiling as if an exit route beckoned there. 'I don't know how we got here.'

Cora didn't reply.

'Look, can we talk? Not now, but later – after you've seen the new object?'

'I don't know.' She glanced at the door to CID. 'We should go in.'

'I need to know you're okay before we do.'

'I'm okay for this.'

'It's something that was delivered to Maisie Ingram.'

Cora stared at Minshull.

'We think Ewan Stokes left it on her doorstep.'

'Like the football shirt?'

Minshull nodded. 'I think it's him. And what worries me is that if the Fifteen Year Return rumours are true, does that mean the revenge story is, too?'

'So he's threatening potential names on the list?' Catching Minshull's surprise, Cora relented a little. 'I've been reading the forums. I've seen the theories.'

'Then you'll know that the football coach died in a suspected hit-and-run on Wednesday.'

'You think that was Stokes?'

'He's been mentioned as a possible revenge target on the forum. And the news of his death was accepted by some with alarming glee. We can't rule out Ewan Stokes causing it, silencing Ted Patrick before he could speak to us.'

'Les might be on that list,' Cora said.

'He said he doesn't know her.'

'He's lying. I know what I heard.'

Minshull ducked his head. 'I think because you don't know him well you can't see how his personality overshadows his true feelings sometimes.'

'He knows Maisie. And Ewan Stokes. And he wants to protect Maisie so much that he's willing to kill.'

'What?'

'Ah, Cora, you're here!' Anderson's voice reverberated down the corridor as he headed towards them. 'We need to make a start.'

'Guv.'

282

'And you'll have a patrol at Maisie Ingram's place from seven tonight,' Anderson said.

Minshull's relief was palpable. 'How long?'

'Twenty-four hours. I know, it wasn't what we wanted, but I'll apply to DCI Taylor for an extension tomorrow. It's the best of a bad job.' He opened the CID office door and stood against it for Cora and Minshull to enter first. 'Shall we?'

The detectives acknowledged Cora as she walked in. The usual rush of secret voices from their wastepaper baskets and desks washed over Cora, her muting of them now so practised that she did it automatically.

Evans didn't look up, his attention summoned by a thick evidence file before him. The voice from his discarded coffee cups and fast-food containers whispered Maisie's name in hushed urgency, the strain of concealing the powerful emotions behind them evident in every forced syllable. It was as if he knew his subconscious thoughts were under surveillance as much as his physical reactions.

Pushing away her own strong emotions, Cora steadied her mind. Whatever else was happening, she had a job to do.

To her surprise, Anderson beckoned her into his office, closing the door quietly as Minshull followed her in. On his desk was a large paper evidence bag, its surface bowing in peaks and troughs to indicate a sizeable object held within.

'I asked Joel if we could do this here,' Minshull explained. 'This case is becoming highly emotional and the whole team are feeling it.'

Highly emotional? Was that a reference to her? Cora blocked out the possibility as she'd silenced the object voices in the main CID office. 'What do you have?'

Anderson moved behind his desk, taking the sealed edge of the evidence bag in both hands. 'It's a child's toy that has been badly defaced. I warn you, it's not a pretty sight.'

Cora nodded. 'I'm ready.'

Minshull joined Anderson and they solemnly placed plastic gloves on. Cora did the same, although she didn't intend to touch whatever was about to be pulled from the evidence bag. She moved beside the desk and prepared herself.

With a nod, Anderson opened the bag and Minshull reached inside to pull out a blonde-haired plastic doll, its head encased in a clear plastic bag tied at the neck, gruesome blood-red streaks flaring out from its scalp and staining the golden curls crimson. As it left the paper evidence bag multiple versions of Ewan Stokes growled out.

Get ready, baby doll…

My baby doll…

Baby… doll…

The same hate and urgency characterised each repeating voice as the hissed threats attached to the football shirt. But this delivery was different.

Laced between the words, curling sharp, thorn-like barbs into each one, were spreading threads of deep pain. Cora felt it physically, as if rapidly constricting curls of barbed wire were surrounding her, shrinking and twisting around every limb, tearing at her skin. Cora breathed against the pain, pushing her mind's focus out beyond to the space around the words. The forward movement strengthened her as she pushed into the sound, the air around the words, seeking out places of reverberation and compression.

She had developed this over the last year, pushing her ability to the edge of possibility. As the layers of sound around and above the initial voices slowly peeled away, she caught the sense of something else.

Closing her eyes and numbing her skin to the encroaching pain, Cora pressed in.

There! A rumble of sound at a different pitch.

A radio, maybe? Or a television playing in the background?

She increased her focus. The rumble strengthened and grew, like an object shrouded in thick fog gradually taking shape as Cora reached for it.

Her head ached now, a shrill ringing of stress filling her ears. It was becoming harder to breathe, as if the air around Cora were growing stale. Soon she would have to retreat, but the competing sound drew her in.

As the edges of sound became clearer, Cora understood.

Not a competing sound: a new voice, lighter and more insistent, padding between the hissed threat of the original speaker. She caught the fresh emotion of it before words emerged: a belligerent, opposing force.

Don't do this. You'll give the game away...

...Baby doll, my baby doll... the first voice argued back.

The pressure became too great; the attacks on Cora's mind at the point of becoming unbearable. She had pushed harder, travelled deeper than she ever had before. But it was too much to sustain.

Carefully, she withdrew, the layers of sound closing off before her, until she opened her eyes back in Anderson's office.

Minshull and Anderson wore horrified expressions, the doll now lying on the evidence bag on the desk.

Cora brought her hand to her cheek and found it damp with tears. Self-consciously, she wiped them away. 'It was Ewan Stokes. And someone else.'

Anderson glanced at Minshull. 'Who?'

'An accomplice. At least, I think they're supposed to be. But there's disagreement there: violent opposition.'

'Like they changed their mind?'

'Like they were scared.'

'The doll was a step too far?' Minshull asked, concern flooding his expression.

'I think so. I tried to make out words but it was embedded too deep in the sound contours. But the strength of emotion was unmistakeable. Whoever it was, they were begging Stokesy not to deliver the doll. They said, *You'll give the game away...*'

Cora waited while Minshull and Anderson considered this. Every inch of her skin felt bruised, her head throbbing. She kept her focus on Anderson, not wanting to make eye contact with Minshull. In the corridor she had come so close to revealing exactly what she'd heard from Evans' desk; now she was glad of Anderson's interruption. Minshull was determined to defend Evans. Why offer him more information to summarily dismiss?

The atmosphere in Anderson's office had changed: become lighter for the knowing yet somehow darker, heavier, as the true scale of the situation had become clear.

'We knew he had to be working with someone,' Minshull said. 'And if the words you heard are correct it sounds like someone more invested in strategy than just logistics.'

If the words you heard are correct. Cora bristled.

'The words *are* correct. The tone sounded a shade higher than mid-range and I couldn't make out any more, but the intent behind them was crystal clear. It was someone who expected to be heard – and was furious that they weren't being listened to.'

The last part of her sentence was imbued with far too much personal association. Cora should have reined it in, but she was too angry, still in pain from the journey to retrieve the voices.

Anderson's eyes flicked between her and Minshull. 'Did you get the impression Stokes is changing an agreed plan?'

'Very much so. There was fear in the other voice, too.'

'Fear that he's taking matters into his own hands?' Minshull asked.

Cora kept her head high. 'Exactly.'

The two detectives could not hide their concern.

'So, who's helping Stokes? Who are we aware of already who had close links with him? Who might he have trusted to help him plan and carry it out?'

'Or whose agenda has he been following up to now?' Cora said, causing an unwanted stare from Minshull.

'You think this delivery wasn't part of the plan?' Anderson asked.

'It doesn't feel that way.'

'I agree,' Minshull said, his sudden support a shock. 'Maisie's sister told us that *baby doll* was the term Stokes used when he was about to punish her. It was a warning shot to drag her back into line. That and the photo...'

'There's a photo?' Cora asked.

Anderson gave an apologetic smile. 'Forgive me, I was about to mention it.' He picked up two smaller evidence bags from the desk and moved to Cora's side. 'The photo was delivered with the doll. And there's also this...' In the smallest of the evidence bags lay a round disc, domed on one side, bearing a navy-blue and silver VW logo. 'Would you mind?'

She hadn't expected three items, her mind and body still caught up in the aftermath of the first. But this was her job now: the faith Anderson had in her ability was unwavering. That was what she would keep her attention on, not the suddenly unstable support of Rob Minshull.

'Of course,' she replied. 'Which one first?'

'The photograph,' Anderson and Minshull chorused.

It should have been a moment of light relief; instead, Cora felt irritation creep across her shoulders. Anderson passed her the photograph first, still encased in plastic. The photo of the black-clad man with stubble smattering his chin and thick, pronounced shadows cast into the contours of his angular face certainly looked like Ewan Stokes. The now famous photo of him taken in 2008 – used on every missing-person poster, reprinted in countless news articles and flashed up on-screen in every news report – was strikingly similar to this. Time had not been kind to Stokesy. Or perhaps it was fifteen years of hate and anger. The image caused Cora to shiver. He looked cruel. The kind of person who would take pleasure from someone else's discomfort.

Someone like Maisie Ingram.

And Les Evans?

Did he know about the delivery yet? Had Minshull waited for Cora to see it first before briefing the team? How would it affect him? If the thought of Stokesy coming back for revenge on Maisie gave him murderous thoughts, what might actual threats do?

When she turned it over, the writing on the reverse made her blood run cold. 'This is the same as the writing on the shirt.'

'You're sure?'

'Compare the two, if you like. If it isn't identical, it's a very good impression.' Centring herself, Cora slowly pulled open the bag.

A torrent of hate coursed out into the office, unheard by all but Cora. The same hissed repetition of the words, the force behind them as real as physical shoves. Though her mind protested, Cora pressed into the sound again. There, beyond the bile and fury, the constricted opposing voice continued, its words all but drowned out by those of the repeated message. She leaned harder – and made out one word:

DON'T

The surrounding noise was too great to be able to assess the competing voice, but it *felt* the same. Taking her time, Cora eased her mind back through the layers of sound until the buzz of the strip lights and gentle hum of the fan on Anderson's PC replaced all that she'd heard.

'The same,' she said, registering the slight cracking in her voice. 'This time I could only hear the quieter voice saying: *Don't*. I couldn't make out any more.'

'That's enough. You're doing a sterling job.' Anderson sealed the bag and passed it to Minshull. Then he handed Cora the VW button. 'And this?'

Within this bag the soundscape was markedly different. Here, peripheral sound bustled in the background, while Cora experienced a rush of gentle heat – like walking through a shaft of warm sunlight in an otherwise cool space. What noise there was seemed muted, as if far away from the object. 'I can't hear a specific voice,' she said, closing her eyes to focus on the sound. 'Just a burr of noise in the background. Like a conversation is happening some distance away.'

'Can you hear anything that matches the voices from the doll and the photograph?' Minshull asked. Cora could hear the hope in his question, could sense all that was riding on her reply.

'I'm sorry, no.' She opened her eyes. 'Has it been somewhere for a while? I feel like the sound is wholly peripheral – as if it's a bystander to the action. Watching from a distance, but unconnected to any particular voice.'

In truth, it was a relief to experience the sparse sonic landscape after the intensity and pain of the previous two. It was evident, however, that Minshull and Anderson didn't share this sentiment. Anderson watched his DS as Minshull punched his hands on his hips.

'Is that all?' Cora asked, a sudden need to be out of the room rising within her. The deep exhaustion she experienced after pushing into the emotional sound was already setting in. She needed fresh air and stillness. And she needed to find a way to confront Les.

'We're just about to brief the team on this,' Anderson said, indicating the evidence bags on the desk with a wide sweep of his hand. 'You're welcome to stay.'

Minshull was watching now, his expression unclear.

'Unless you need me in there, I'll head off.'

'Of course. Thank you.' Anderson offered his hand, closing his other over Cora's when she accepted it. The warmth was soothing, the sincere gratitude even more so. 'I can't express enough how valuable your skills are to my team.'

'It's my pleasure,' she replied, meaning every word.

'I'll see you out,' Minshull offered.

'You have a briefing,' Cora said, cutting him off with as much force as she dared. 'I can find my own way out.'

Minshull's consternation bit at her back as she walked away.

Forty-Two

CORA

Sitting in her car in the busy car park of Police HQ, Cora was shocked to see Minshull and Anderson emerge from the fire escape door. She ducked low in the driver's seat, watching them, her heart beginning to race. This wasn't what she'd planned. She'd intended to wait in her car until the end of the day, hoping to intercept Evans on his way out. But the DS and the DI standing there presented a huge problem.

She couldn't drive out of the car park now without the danger of her police colleagues noticing. She'd already waited for over an hour – how would she explain her delay in leaving if they spotted her? Minshull knew her car and would surely recognise it.

Cora shifted position, wishing she hadn't chosen to park in the part of the car park that was bathed in full sunshine. At least she'd had the foresight to open the windows when she'd returned to her car, but with hardly any breeze now it was stiflingly hot inside. She checked her watch. At least another hour until Evans was due to finish his shift, and that was assuming he would leave on time. With the sudden escalation of events in the investigation into Stokesy, any new developments could keep the team in the building longer.

Looking for something to occupy her mind while she waited, Cora reached into the back seat for the battered novel her mother had lent her a few weeks ago. Sheila Lael had now added a book group to her busy schedule of social events, a fact that pleased Cora greatly. The change in her mum from grief-battered recluse to the woman now rediscovering her life had been nothing short of remarkable.

The pages thrummed with the sound of Sheila's enthusiastic comments, the presence of her voice a constant companion, so that for Cora it was as if her mum was reading the story alongside her. The experience calmed her, in the way that few of the emotional echoes she heard ever did. She made a note to tell Tris about this when she next saw him at work. Another detail of her ability for him to feast on.

I can't believe he just did that!
She's going to regret trusting him...
That woman's hilarious! I love her!
Bill would have loved this...

It was good to have allies after so many years of her ability pushing people away. Tris and Sheila's unerring support lifted Cora. She'd counted Rob among her allies until yesterday. Now, she didn't know if she still could.

Without thinking, her eyes strayed to the two figures standing at the top of the fire escape ramp. Anderson with a face like thunder, Minshull bowed by burdens Cora didn't have to see to know were there. The anger that had clung to his words in Anderson's office was shocking, even though it was directed more to the circumstances than towards her.

Her mother's voice soothed from the closed book on her lap as Cora slumped further in her seat. It was as if the past year hadn't happened, the victories and possibilities wiped out by Minshull's choice to stand by Evans. They were back to how they had been in the beginning: Cora as the kooky academic, Minshull as the professional cynic. Had it all been for nothing?

And then she saw a third person arrive at the top of the ramp. The person at the centre of all the issues.

Her straying thoughts dismissed, Cora watched Les Evans share a brief exchange with Anderson. Were they asking him again? His flushed face and stern expression suggested this might be the case. Was Cora right to confront him today? Should she wait until questions from his colleagues about Stokesy and Maisie Ingram ebbed away?

And then Evans left Minshull and Anderson, jogging down the ramp towards the car park. Towards Cora's car...

In an instant, any question of her confronting him vanished. Checking the ramp she saw Anderson clamp a sympathetic hand to

Minshull's shoulder, the two men walking back into the building. Looking back, she caught sight of Les Evans moving behind one of the Support Unit vans.

This was the moment she'd waited for.

Cora left her car and quickly headed after Evans, checking back to make sure nobody else appeared at the top of the ramp. Skirting the row of vans and patrol cars, she scanned the space beyond for the man she needed to see. Her route took her between the line of light and shadow, her eyes taking a moment to adjust as the bright sun disappeared behind the roof of the building. When her vision cleared, she saw Evans beside one of the police vans, his back to the high wall, cigarette in hand. He was red-faced and sweating, his tie knot pulled loose at the neck as if it had been strangling him.

He looked up as Cora approached, packing away his shock behind a hastily applied frown.

'I thought you'd gone.'

'I wanted to see you.'

'Oh, yeah?' Evans gave a derisory snort. 'Come to offer me a reading, have you?' The cigarette waved in a circle beside his head. 'Do your mystic shit? Bring me a message from beyond the veil?'

Cora let it wash over her like the unwanted voices she encountered every day. She wasn't going to rise to his jibes.

'I want to talk to you about Maisie Ingram.'

A flicker.

'I don't know her.'

'You're lying.'

On its way to his mouth, the cigarette stopped. 'Excuse me?'

'You told everyone in there that you've never met Ewan Stokes. That you don't know Maisie Ingram. But you were lying, DC Evans.'

'Oh, yeah? A ghost tell you that, did it?'

'No.' Cora held her ground. 'You did.'

Her words were a direct punch to his gut. He was blindsided for a moment, quickly rallying. 'You're talking shite, sweetheart.'

'Am I? *If he hurts Maisie, I'll kill him.*'

The sound of his own thoughts relayed to him rooted Evans to the spot, gripped with shock. Cora might have enjoyed it had the truth of his words not been so vital to the investigation.

'Who said – where did you hear that?'

'From the pile of papers that fell off your desk yesterday. Every one of them carried your voice. *If he hurts Maisie... I'll kill him... I'll kill the bastard.*' Each repeated thought relayed was a body blow to Evans, who backed closer to the wall, the stub of hand-rolled cigarette falling from his lips. 'You don't know what you're talking about. This is all bollocks...'

How does she know, his voice demanded from the tumbling cigarette.

'*How does she know?*' Cora repeated, the power of her gift emboldening her.

'You're a witch! Playing mind games! I'm not staying here and taking this.'

'I can help you,' Cora stated, her voice steady and calm.

'No, you can't. You just want to punish me for not believing your mumbo jumbo.' He was scrabbling for words now, terrified by Cora's accuracy.

'I don't want to punish anybody. I want to protect Maisie, Les, just like you do.'

'You don't know what you're talking about!'

'I know you care about her. I know you're scared she'll come to harm.' She lifted her hand and placed it over her heart. 'I felt it, *here*, when I heard your voice. You're terrified Stokes will hurt her.'

'Why are you doing this?' His voice had become a whine, as if she were inflicting physical pain on him.

'Because I think she's in real danger. I heard Ewan Stokes' voice all over that doll. He means her harm, Les. Whatever you think of me, if you care about Maisie like I think you do, you have to let me help you.'

Evans stared back, jaw grinding. Cora waited, not sure if she'd said enough or too much. If she'd scared him he might throw her under the bus with the team to save himself. But what could she do if he agreed to let her help him? She hadn't thought this through, only motivated by his unspoken concern for Maisie and her own fears for the woman's safety.

'You can't tell anyone,' he began, eyes locked with hers. 'They all believe what I said. And this isn't a game. There's so much more at stake than you know.'

'So tell me,' Cora urged. 'Let me help you.'

The rumble of a vehicle began, moving towards them. They would be seen as soon as it passed by. Panicked, Evans reached out and grabbed Cora's arm.

'Behind here!'

He pulled her bodily behind the police van into the small gap between the rear bumper and the wall. Cora's back grazed the bricks as he did so, the old gunshot injury at the top of her shoulder blade protesting furiously.

She gave an involuntary yelp, clamping a hand to her mouth too late to stifle it.

'Shh!' Evans hissed, flattening his back against the wall, the scent of old tobacco and sweat filling the space, turning Cora's stomach.

It took an age for the patrol car to amble past, its inhabitants too busy chatting to notice anything around them. When it was completely out of sight, Evans released his grip.

'Sorry,' he rushed, shoving his hand in his pocket as if hiding evidence.

Cora leaned gently against the wall and tried to steady her breathing. In her peripheral vision she was aware of Evans watching her.

'Are you going to tell Minsh?'

Cora closed her eyes. As if he'd listen now... 'No. But you have to tell me what you know.'

'I will. Just – not here, yeah? I'm due back in the office. I'll be missed if I'm away too long.'

Cora looked at Evans. The change in him was significant: gone were the sneer and the clever words – in their place, real fear.

'Where, then?'

'I can meet you. Somewhere we won't be seen.' He gave a shaky sigh. 'Tonight. It should be tonight.'

It had been a tough day following a night of little sleep and Cora wanted nothing more than to crawl into her own bed. But this couldn't wait: if she had a hope of discovering what Evans knew they had to talk before he had chance to reconsider.

'Okay. Where?'

Evans dared to look at her. 'There's a viewpoint for the Orwell Bridge on the B1456. Park in the lay-by. I'll meet you there at eight.'

With one last nod, he edged past Cora and hurried away.

Cora willed her thundering heartbeat to slow, dizzy with adrenaline. She imagined Evans returning to CID, flustered and smelling suspiciously of cigarettes. He would probably joke his way out of his elongated absence, admit he hadn't quit smoking as he'd told them all: a lie to cover a lie.

How does she know, the still-smouldering stub demanded at her feet. *How does she know?*

Cora raised her heel and ground it into the scuffed tarmac, the voice dying to a whisper, then silence.

THE CLUB

Watcher89 [thread moderator]

Sharing this following confirmed sighting, Langley Avenue Sports Field, Felixstowe. It's been verified by Inner Circle. Spread the word. #Stokesy15

*** NEW SIGHTING! ***

Just reported at 6.45pm by @CallMeMal. Video posted in comments on SuffolkView website, subsequently picked up by Suffolk Herald, Daily Call, Daily Signal. Langley Avenue Sports Field – where the football tournament took place the night before Stokesy vanished. Full video below. It's him. Hood off. No doubt. List confirmed, too! Tell EVERYONE. #Stokesy15

– Comments disabled –

– 18,403 likes –

Forty-Three

MINSHULL

'DS Minshull! Any comment on the video filmed here?'

'Do you know the names on Stokesy's list?'

'Are South Suffolk Police anywhere close to finding Ewan Stokes?'

'No comment,' Minshull muttered, moving through the gaggle of journalists blocking his path. Two uniformed officers either side of him did their best to clear the way, jostled and elbowed by eager hacks wanting the best view.

Reaching the simple steel gate in a run of thin wire fence that couldn't even keep a cat out, let alone a crush of media representatives, he gave the stressed PC manning the entrance a sympathetic grimace and squeezed through the gap before it was yanked shut behind him.

So much for a quiet night.

He'd planned a curry and beer, fortifying himself for what he had to do. Phone Cora. Make it right.

He couldn't change his position on Evans, but he wanted to meet Cora halfway. Find out exactly what had caused her theory and the information he'd been denied by Anderson's arrival earlier.

...*So much that he's willing to kill.*

Had he heard her right? How on earth could she reach that conclusion? Evans was often disgruntled, sometimes angry. In the aftermath of the vandalism to his car he had displayed something akin to fury. But *kill* someone? Minshull couldn't imagine the DC capable of enough commitment to consider it, let alone carry it out.

But he needed Cora. A day without her on his side had left him floundering. He had to find a way back to where they'd been before. They had come too far together to let it be destroyed now.

He followed the scuffed earth and gravel path from the gate to the small, yellow-painted metal building with a grey roof, grandly referred to as the sports pavilion. It had the appearance of a wider-than-average shipping container, the high, square windows around its sides and large single central door all fortified with criss-crossed thick bars, as if the crown jewels were stored inside. Minshull glanced back at the pathetic excuse for a fence and gave a wry smile. Someone needed to sort their priorities for security around here.

'Lovely evening for it.' PC Steph Lanehan grinned as he neared the entrance. 'Don't say we never drag you out to the best places, Sarge.'

'Wouldn't dream of it, Steph.' A friendly face was reward enough for the late call-out and what would surely lead to an abominably long shift.

'Got to say, I was a bit disappointed when I got here,' she grinned. 'Name like *the pavilion* – I was expecting a bar at least.'

'Is it even in use?' Minshull asked, taking in the flaking paint, graffiti tags and rusting sides.

'Yes, believe it or not. Eric on the gate plays Sunday league here with his mates. Says it's heaving on a weekend. Anyone else from CID coming, Sarge?'

'No. I called DC Evans but it went to voicemail.'

It had been a test, of course, the slightest niggle in his mind concerning Cora's assumption refusing to be rationalised away. Bringing Evans here, to a place well known and now forever connected to Ewan Stokes, would have been a perfect opportunity to observe his responses.

But he wasn't answering his phone. Minshull had little time to keep trying and, besides, the rest of the team had endured enough today. It made sense for him to be here, even if coming alone let Evans off the hook.

'DI Anderson offered to come if I need him, but I reckon the two of us can handle this, if you're up for it?'

Lanehan beamed. 'Always happy to help the suits in CID do their jobs. Even if they think we're liabilities. Present company excepted, of course.'

Minshull accepted her comment with a groan. He'd heard other detectives over the years despairing of Uniform, but he didn't agree. All of them had been PCs once and it was a bloody hard, thankless task – especially now, with resources scarce and police numbers slashed. Everyone in the CID team had run from Uniform as soon as they were able, and while a job as a detective was no walk in the park, it was warmer, drier and considerably safer than patrolling the streets day in and day out.

'Okay, so what do we know?' he asked, peering into the gloomy interior of the pavilion building.

'Video went up in the comments section of SuffolkView website sometime after six p.m. and was spotted by someone who sent it to that lot of gannets.' She stabbed a thumb over her shoulder, towards the crowd of journalists. 'We had a call-out at six fifteen p.m. and just about managed to set up a cordon before they all arrived.'

'Have you seen the video?'

'Thought you'd never ask,' Steph said, pulling a phone from her holster. 'Got it right here.'

She handed it to Minshull, who pressed play.

It was a portrait-shot video, its letterboxed sides created by opaque shadows of the action. The hooded figure stood by the faded metal pavilion, thrown into sharp contrast against the dirty yellow walls. He held a sign, as he had in the earlier captured images, but this time the message was different.

$$1 - 2 - 3$$
WAITING FOR ME?

The figure began to walk towards the camera, more of his features coming into view as he filled the screen. In the final moments of the video, the hooded man reached up a black-gloved hand to his hood and yanked it back. Ewan Stokes glared into camera for a second before the video cut to black. A hashtag in white flashed up at the centre:

#Stokesy15

…and the video ended.

The photo with the doll had convinced Minshull that the hooded man appearing across Felixstowe was Ewan Stokes, but this was confirmation for the masses. For the Stokesy faithful. For the media who, predictably, were willing prey. For the wider general public who were now becoming aware of the bizarre set of events unfolding in this part of the world.

'*1-2-3?*' Minshull asked. 'What's the significance of that?'

'It's the list. My Fred's hooked on that web forum now and he told me that the speculation on there has gone nuts since Ted Patrick was killed.'

'So three names remaining on the list.'

'Exactly.'

'Any idea who?'

Lanehan shrugged. 'Not a scooby, although I can guess his ex-missus is one of them, poor thing.'

'We have a patrol at her house now.'

'I know. My Sarge wanted Rilla and me to do it but we've already done two extra shifts this week.'

'So instead you come here and do another shift anyway?' Minshull grinned.

'*Que sera*, Sarge,' she replied, drily. 'Not sure I want time off anyway, not with this idiot on the loose. Dave said you think he was driving that van me and him chased by the lock-ups? The one that drove at us after the quiz, too?'

'We think so.'

'Then I'm more than happy to be here to help nail the bastard.'

The venom in her reply chimed with Minshull. They'd all joked about it in recent days, but the shock and horror of the incident was clearly still at work.

'Can we get a screenshot of his face when the hood comes off?' he asked.

'Ah, now there's one advantage of being one step behind the media,' Lanehan said, swiping the video from the screen to be replaced with a perfectly framed, pin-sharp image of the missing man. 'You get the pleasure of those bastards doing your work for you.'

There was no doubt now. And the video would ensure that everyone who saw it knew Ewan Stokes was back. As a piece of publicity it was inspired. As brand-new evidence it made Minshull's spirits sink lower than they had been all day.

'Was there anything left at the scene?' he asked. 'Or in the pavilion?'

'It was locked when we arrived, Sarge. The groundskeeper opened up for us. Not sure he should have bothered, judging by the inside. There's nothing there. Few changing benches, a toilet I wouldn't let my dog use and about forty million spiders.'

'Maybe he's amassing a spider army,' Minshull mused, the joke his only remaining weapon.

'If he is then I'm requesting a transfer.' Lanehan shuddered. 'I can cope with drunks, thieving gits and punch-ups, but I draw the line at dealing with those eight-legged gits.'

A shout from the gate saw the young PC admitting a stern-faced, splendidly bearded man in green overalls, who puffed his way across the worn grass towards them.

'Officers,' he panted, offering a damp hand. 'I'm Stuart Colman, chair of the Sports Field Friends. Sorry I'm late. Bloody journalists have completely blocked the avenue. The neighbours are fuming: nobody can get on or off their drives.'

Minshull shook the newcomer's hand, not entirely sure why Mr Colman was there. 'Nature of the job, I'm afraid,' he replied. 'How can we help you, sir?'

The man beamed. 'I'm here to help you. The Friends take responsibility for the pavilion. Anything you need to see, I can show you.'

'The groundskeeper already opened up for us, Mr Colman,' Lanehan replied, at the exact moment the Friends' chairman noticed the open door. 'But thank you for coming down.'

Colman's smile fell. 'Bloody Frank. I might've known he'd hightail it down here. That man craves publicity like most of us crave cheese.'

'We'll still take a look inside, sir,' Minshull offered the crestfallen chairman. 'Check that nothing's been moved or tampered with.'

'I would appreciate it, Detective. But that isn't why I'm here.'

'It isn't?'

'No. I know who took the video.'

Minshull stared at the unlikely carrier of this bombshell. 'Who?'

Stuart Colman looked past Minshull to the pavilion's open door.

'My son.'

Forty-Four

CORA

The Orwell Bridge was a construction Cora had never viewed up close. She'd driven over it many times on the A14 – and had been diverted around it whenever it closed – but from the banks of the River Orwell it was an impressive sight. Spanning the wide river, banked by flat grassland, an arc of sky above.

The viewing point was a simple lay-by just before a bend in the road, but the vastness of the view made it appear remote, despite it being close to the marina in Ipswich.

She was early, allowing extra time to find the location, but now as she watched the minutes passing her nerves grew. What if Evans didn't arrive? What if he'd thought better of it? In the rush to arrange their meeting there had been no time to exchange numbers, so she had no way of contacting him.

Why hadn't she considered this?

The light over the river was becoming golden, streaks of pink and pale blue stretching across the sky. The thunder of the A14 passing over the bridge was muted but ever-present, an ominous tone underscoring everything. Cora opened her car door and stepped out, the sting of freshening air so welcome after a day of oppressive heat.

It was beautiful here, in a sparse, empty way. Flat and open to the sky, the simple lines of the bridge providing a striking focus. It had the feeling of being on the edge of things, a passive bystander to the rush and grumble of the traffic speeding overhead.

This appealed to Cora. For so long she had felt on the periphery of what others called 'normal' life, kept there by her ability, watching from a distance. It had led her here, to this place. To the conversation she needed to have.

'If Les Evans arrived.

There was a narrow line of shingle alongside the river, a desire path snaking down to it from the lay-by tarmac through the grassy scrub. Cora followed it down, the gentle movement of the river calming as she neared it. From here the arcs of concrete appeared even taller, seagoing birds dipping beneath the arches and passing her close to the water. As she watched them, the ping of her mobile phone sounded.

> Hey C. Don't know if you've seen this already.
> HUGE Stokesy development. It's definitely him! Tris x

Cora clicked the attached YouTube link and waited for the patchy internet signal to connect. As soon as she saw the hooded figure, the terror of his voice flooded back. The stuttering playback froze at the moment he reached for his hood, his revealed face caught in a mocking snarl. Shuddering, she closed the video.

She didn't need confirmation that Stokesy was at work – the shock of his voice from the football shirt, the doll and the photograph was enough to convince her. But the new video was more than proof: it was a warning.

Had Les seen this? Is that why he wasn't there?

Another text arrived:

> 3 people on the list, he says. You need to warn DC Evans.
> I would lay money on Maisie Ingram being one of them. T
> x

'Thought you'd skipped out on me.'

Cora turned to see Les Evans standing up on the bank, unfamiliar in T-shirt and jeans. He appeared younger than in his work suit, more at ease. Although there was no ease in his expression. He looked terrified.

'I got here early,' Cora replied, walking towards the path to meet him.

'Stay there,' he said, hopping down from the grassy bank to the head of the path. 'I'll join you.'

Cora caught the glance he made over his shoulder before heading down to the water's edge.

'I wasn't sure you'd come,' she said.

'Yeah, neither was I.' Nerves bled from him, his feet restless on the shingle, fingers scratching at his arm. 'Mind if I smoke? I'll stand downwind.'

'Go ahead,' Cora replied.

'Cheers.'

In silence she observed him pulling a pack of papers and a tobacco pouch from his back pocket, his hands fumbling as they constructed a cigarette. Stuffing the packets away again, he turned away to light it. The crunch of the lighter wheel sounded several times before he pocketed it again. Blowing the first batch of smoke away, he turned back.

'Before I say anything, I need you to promise me none of this goes further.'

'It won't from me. But to help Maisie you need to tell Rob.'

'No. Absolutely not.'

Was he really going to argue this? Cora wondered if he was aware of the latest development, which would have her sharing it immediately if she'd been in his position.

'What are you going to do? Tackle Ewan Stokes all by yourself? You don't even know where he is.'

'Promise me, or no deal. I'll decide what I want to do.'

What choice did she have? She had come this far: to back out now would serve nobody. Even if Minshull changed his mind, what Cora knew already would make little difference. She had to know the whole truth.

'Okay. But if you care about her like I think you do, you have an obligation...'

'Let me be the judge of that.'

305

Cora conceded. 'So, tell me the truth.'

Evans took a faltering drag on his cigarette, the smoke curling out through his gritted teeth. 'I knew them both.' Watching this news sink in with Cora, he continued. 'Knew them from the village, then the pub. After that I played in the Kesgrave team with Stokes. That's where I got to know Maisie.'

'How long ago was this?'

'Two-and-a-half years before Stokes went missing.'

'Why did you lie about it?'

'Because I always have.'

Cora frowned. 'What do you mean?'

Evans sent another cloud of smoke into the sunset sky. 'I lied first time to avoid being interviewed in the initial investigation. I was still in Uniform, working my backside off for the National Investigators' Exam, and I couldn't have any suspicion surrounding me. It could have ruined my chances of making DC.' He gave a smile-less laugh. 'And yeah, I know, the picture of me working hard for anything doesn't fit what you see today. But it mattered then.'

'And now?' Cora couldn't halt the question. How did someone go from wanting something so much they'd go to any lengths to protect their chances to becoming a lazy parody of their former selves?

'It still matters. You think I take the piss in my job, and yeah, maybe I do. But I would destroy anyone who tried to take it from me.'

'Like Ewan Stokes?'

His stare fell away to the wide, flowing river. 'That's not why... I wasn't protecting myself regarding him.'

'Just your job?'

'My job could have been a casualty, but that wasn't why I kept schtum.'

The air around him had begun to compact itself. Cora sensed it, constricting, pushing in, as if to pressure the truth from the detective. It was carried in the flakes of ash falling from the cigarette in his fingers, myriad tumbling repetitions of her name.

Maisie...

Maisie...

Maisie…

'Tell me about her,' Cora invited him, as softly as she could to still be heard over the insistent sounds of traffic and water.

Evans hung his head, picked a scrap of ash from his tongue. 'I loved her.'

Cora didn't dare speak. Her breath stalled as she waited for more.

'I haven't said that out loud for fifteen years.' He shook his head. 'I didn't say it when I should have. Everything could have been different if I had… We were close. I saw her at the pub in Kesgrave where she worked evenings. It was quiet most of the time, little village pub, you know? On the edge of an estate, only locals ever bothered with it. Got demolished about eight years ago. I doubt anyone mourned it by then. When she wasn't serving she'd stand by the bar and we'd chat. It helped that I knew the deal with the football team – the gossip, the cliques, the stupid power struggles. She liked not having to explain it all, just to chat safe in the knowledge that I already knew. That's where it started.'

'Did she know how you felt about her?'

'Not at first.' He dragged long on the cigarette, the smoke leaving his mouth as he continued. 'We were just mates, having a laugh. I didn't try to hit on her and she liked that. I don't think she'd known many blokes who did that. Maybe she thought I wasn't interested. Maybe it was a relief. And I didn't know how I felt in the beginning, just that I liked her and we connected.'

The colours of the setting sun above them were beginning to glow now, streaks of golden light painting the sky and the water beneath. The constriction around Evans continued: there was more to come.

'So tell me about Ewan Stokes. Were you friends?'

'Nobody was friends with Ewan Stokes.' Evans spoke his name as if it soured his taste buds. 'Not in the way you expect. You stayed *in* with him because it was better to be on his side than not. He wasn't a buddy. I only ever went for a pint with him if the rest of the lads on the team were there, too. And I have him to thank for getting me the transfer.'

'Transfer? You went to the Felixstowe team with him?'

Evans nodded. 'Fancied myself a star defender, didn't I? Only my bloody knees begged to differ. Spent more time on the bench than the field. In the end I reckon old Ted Patrick kept me there to spare my feelings.'

'But the news report Dave Wheeler found – you weren't in that.'

'For good reason. I was injured. Out of training for eight weeks. The cameras came when I was at home.' Evans gave a cough. 'With Maisie, as it turned out.'

'Did Stokes know?'

'No fear! Do you think I'd just have had a knee injury to worry about if he had?' He dropped the small cigarette, grinding it down between the river stones with the heel of his trainer. The whispers of Maisie's name ebbed away as they were buried. 'She was studying sports massage alongside her day job at the leisure centre and offered to help me with physio. She worked so hard, wanted so much for her life. Until that bastard got his claws into her. Persuaded her to quit the course, told her not to apply for a better job she was offered at a gym. Chipped away at her confidence with every comment, every lie, so she started to believe she could only function with him there...' He broke off and gazed out at the river as if Maisie Ingram were emerging from it.

'That must have been hard for you to see. As her friend,' Cora added quickly.

'I could see it was going on before she said anything. You always can, can't you? The worst part is waiting for them to see it for themselves.'

'When did she tell you what was really happening?'

'First time he hit her.' He shoved his hands deep into his pockets, shoulders knotted in tension. 'First time she admitted it, at any rate. I don't think it was the first time.'

'I can't imagine how hard that must have been for you to hear.'

Evans glanced at her as if surprised by her words. 'Nobody ever asked me how I felt before.'

Cora risked a smile. 'Occupational hazard.'

'Yeah, I forgot you were a shrink.'

She didn't correct him. It wasn't the first time she'd been confused with a psychotherapist.

'So, she confided in you.'

Evans nodded. 'For about eighteen months. I spent all of that time telling her to leave him, telling her I would be there for her, trying to undo the damage he'd done.'

'Did you love her by then?' Cora was struck by the oddness of their conversation, the sudden change from barely a sentence shared to this riverside confessional.

'I did.'

'Did you tell her?'

Evans looked back out at the river and said nothing. Cora waited but his silence remained. She changed tack, conscious of the developments in the Stokesy investigation looming large over everything.

'She's in danger, Les. Real danger. If he found violence so easy with her when they were together, imagine what fifteen years of recrimination might make him capable of.'

Evans closed his eyes. 'I can't.'

'Why?'

'Because if they discover I lied now, they'll question why I lied then. Minsh's bastard dad asked me, days after Stokes went missing. He pulled me out of a patrol and demanded I tell him what I knew. I swore I never knew him.' His tone dropped, the invisible pressure around him almost at breaking point. 'Never knew *her*.'

'Are you in contact with her now? Tell me the truth.'

'No. I haven't spoken to her in years.'

'Why?' Pulling back a little, Cora picked her words like a surgeon selecting instruments. 'You'd been there for her all that time. She'd finally left him. Why didn't you stay with her, tell her how you felt?'

'Because she left me, okay?' The sudden rise of his voice sent a moorhen skidding across the water, shrilly voicing its panic as it flapped away.

Evans brought a hand to his balding head as if trying to swipe the memory away. Cora waited, watching him.

'I helped her leave him. I told Ted Patrick my knee was playing up so I didn't have to go to football practice. Then I went to Maisie's place and packed all Stokes' things. We shoved them into bin bags and I drove them to his lock-up. Dumped them there. I left a mate at her house changing all the locks. When I got back, I took her to a hotel in Ipswich, where he wouldn't find her.'

'But she left you?'

Evans shook his head, reaching for his tobacco pouch and papers again. 'Not then. Weeks later, we got drunk at mine and I told her how I felt. Said if she were mine she'd be cherished… Bloody one and only time I used that word with a woman. We ended up in bed. But next day, the news broke. She panicked, said it was a mistake, she wasn't thinking straight, all of that. Told me it would never happen.'

'Wait – the day after? So the night you spent together was…?'

Evans fixed her with a wide-eyed stare. 'The night of the football match. She was upset, she came back to mine, we drank too much… So I lied. Because she begged me to. She was terrified she would be in the frame if they knew she spent the night with the copper who helped her leave Stokes.'

'Bloody hell, Les.'

He shrugged it off. 'You wanted to know. Not the unrequited love story you were hoping for, I'll bet.' He clamped the newly rolled cigarette between his teeth and fumbled with the lighter.

Cora wasn't satisfied with his reply. She pressed in. 'But you still care about her. After all this time.'

'I don't want her to get hurt.'

'You said you'll kill him. That's more than worrying about someone. Do you still love her?'

The lighter drew back from the unlit cigarette. 'You have no right asking me that.'

Cora stared at him, not certain she had heard correctly. 'Excuse me? Why are we here, Les? Why all the cloak-and-dagger stuff and deep confessions if you don't care about her?'

'You wanted the history. You got it.'

'I want the truth. Not just then but now.'

'I've told you *enough*!' He stepped back, stumbled along the shingle a little way. 'You said you wouldn't tell Minsh. You promised. So now you know, drop it.'

'You have to tell him what you know about her. They'll be looking anyway, now they know it's definitely Stokesy.'

He froze. 'What did you say?'

So he didn't know. Cora found the report on her phone and held it out to him. 'There was another sighting. Just after six tonight. A video this time. And there's no doubt who it is.'

Evans turned back, staring at the phone in Cora's outstretched hand as if he suspected a trick. Then he paced back to her, snatching the device from her fingers. The sound of the video drifted up into the flaming sky, the look of horror on the DC's face painted red and orange and gold.

'I can help you,' Cora rushed, not certain how. 'There's time. But you have to tell me everything you know. Other friends who might be one of those three names. Information you withheld last time.'

'And Minsh?'

Cora held his stare, her mind as ablaze with questions as the sky above their heads. 'Leave him to me.'

Forty-Five

'I *just* did the *video*!'

The teenager was leaning forward now, after almost forty minutes spent slumped in the seat beside his father. Minshull and Lanehan watched impassively from the other side of the interview desk. Stuart Colman chewed harder on the inside of his cheek.

The decision had been made to bring Seth Colman into Police HQ for a voluntary interview, despite the late hour. Anderson had requested it over the phone and Stuart Colman had agreed to accompany his son. The poor bloke was in shock: Seth's throwaway confession of taking the video now leading to a stifling interview room with the potential for real trouble. A father's worst nightmare.

Minshull, also wishing himself not in the room, kept his voice steady. It wasn't the kid's fault his planned curry night had been scuppered. Seth was scared, the initial bravado he'd displayed at his house abandoned in the starkness of their current surroundings, far from the safety of home.

'I know you took the video. What I'm asking is why.'

'Because he asked me to.'

'The man in the hoodie?'

'Yes. I've told you already.'

'So, let's go over it again. Just so I'm one hundred per cent certain of the facts. You went to the sports field with a friend...'

'Jake T. My best friend.'

Minshull checked his notes. 'Jake Tillson?'

Seth nodded. 'We meet our mates there. Hang about, talk shit…
Sorry, Dad.'

'Make videos?'

The teen scowled. 'Sometimes. TikTok and that.'

'So you were down there with Jake, waiting for your friends and –
what? The guy just showed up?'

'Yeah. We were by the pavilion, mucking around, and he comes
up and asks me to make a video of him.'

'A random stranger asks you to video him?'

'Yes.' He glanced at his despairing father. 'What? It was just a video,
it wasn't like he was coming on to us.'

'Oh my *lord*…' Stuart Colman's head dropped into his hands.

Minshull pressed on, aware of time. 'Did he say why he wanted
you to film him?'

'He said it was a message to wind his friends up. They'd tricked him
before and he wanted his own back.' He looked between Minshull and
Lanehan. 'I mean, I got it, you know? Getting one over on someone
who thinks they beat you. He was laughing when he said it. Not like
a threat. So I did it for him.'

'On your phone?'

'Yeah.'

Minshull paused, driving home the point. 'Why not his?'

'Said he didn't have it with him.'

'That didn't strike you as odd?'

Seth gave him a look as if he'd asked if the sky was green. 'He was
old. Like you – no offence. You lot never know what to do with your
phones. I mean, Dad is useless with his.'

Minshull didn't rise to the bait. 'What did he ask you to do?'

'Just stand there and film him.'

'Did he explain what he was going to do?'

'No. He said it would make sense to them.'

Minshull added to the lines of notes on his pad. 'And when you'd
done it?'

'I said I'd send it to him but he just gave me the website address
and told me to post it direct. So I did.'

'You just posted a random video in the comments section of a local-view webcam website?'

'Yeah.'

'Like an idiot,' his father interjected. 'Did your mum and I teach you nothing about internet safety?'

Seth muttered something indecipherable and slumped back in his chair.

'Do you have the piece of paper he gave you?'

'Nah. Binned it after I'd posted the video.'

'Where?'

'Bin by the pavilion. Does it matter?'

Stuart Colman stared at his son. '*Does it matter?* This is a police investigation, we're sat in an interview room being interviewed by a detective and you ask if it matters?'

'Sir, it's okay,' Minshull replied, Lanehan's badly hidden amusement in his peripheral vision. 'Just a few more questions and we'll let you go, all right?'

The flustered father nodded.

'Okay. Seth, did you recognise the man?'

'No.'

'Did he give you his name?'

'No.'

A groan from Colman senior.

'We believe he's Ewan Stokes – known as Stokesy. He's been missing for fifteen years. Does that name mean anything to you?'

Seth was staring now. 'The bloke off the CCTV? That's who it was?'

'Yes. We're trying to find him. It's vital that we do.' He let the revelation sink in with the teenager for a moment. 'Did you see him arrive?'

'Yeah.'

'By foot? Bike?'

'Van,' Seth Colman stated. 'Old beat-up white van. The front of it was stuck on with silver gaffer tape.'

Of course. Minshull baulked at the inevitable confirmation of his fears.

'Did you see the make?' Lanehan asked, glancing at Minshull to check she was clear to speak.

'VW. An old one, though.'

Minshull felt his pulse quicken. 'This is really important, Seth: was anyone in the van with him?'

'Yeah. Couldn't see them well because they stayed in the passenger seat, but it was a woman.'

Minshull and Lanehan looked at each other.

'A woman?' he repeated. 'Are you certain?'

'Hundred per cent. She just sat there, hunched up like my sister does when she's got one on her. Couldn't tell from what she was wearing – hoodie like his and a baseball cap. But then she wound down the window as I was posting the video and shouted, "*We have to go*". Definitely a woman.'

–

'What do you think, Sarge?' Lanehan asked as one of her colleagues escorted Seth and Stuart Colman out.

Minshull stared after them, his mind in a thousand places. Cora had heard another voice behind the bile and hate of Ewan Stokes. He'd assumed, like Anderson, that the second voice had been from a male. But what if it were a woman?

'I think we need to start looking at the women active on the forum and anybody identified as a close friend of Stokes in the original files,' he replied. 'Find anyone who's been vocal in their support of him, especially in recent years.'

Lanehan frowned as she looked at him. 'You think they'll be on that forum?'

'Who knows?' Minshull replied, the daunting task ahead becoming fully real. Every step forward revealed five possible routes to pursue. They knew Stokes had help. Cora had called it: now confirmed, they had a new line of inquiry. But where they went from here was anyone's guess.

He had to think. Formulate a coherent plan.
And he needed to talk to Cora.

Forty-Six

WHEELER

Minshull looked like death warmed up.

Catching sight of his own reflection in the glass-fronted file cabinet, Wheeler chuckled. He didn't look much better.

He'd come in early this morning, enjoying the cooler air on his cycle into Ipswich before the sun was at full strength, and was surprised to find Minshull already at his desk.

'What's this, then?' he'd asked his weary colleague. 'You get a taste for early mornings after that Zoom call to Australia? Or were you hoping for more of Pete York's excellent coffee?'

'Always hoping for more of that,' Minshull had replied, his smile fading the moment he turned back to his screen.

Now, with Wheeler's decidedly less impressive coffee made and both detectives settled, he opted to broach the subject. 'Everything okay?'

The sigh Minshull hefted would have outweighed an elephant. 'I think I screwed up with Cora.'

The uncharacteristic nature of his reply threw Wheeler for a moment. 'In what way?'

'She told me her concerns and I dismissed them.'

'People survive differences of opinion all the time, mate. You should see me and Sana. Only thing we can agree on is that we love our boys and we're crazy about each other. Everything else is pistols at dawn.'

His kind words did little to lighten Minshull's mood. 'I didn't believe her. The most important thing. I don't know, Dave, I thought we were getting somewhere. But now...'

'Have you spoken to her?'

Minshull nodded. 'She called me late last night. She'd seen the sighting posted on StokesyFans and wanted to know if I'd seen it, too. I told her she'd been right about the other voice and that it was a woman. She was just really odd about it, like it was proof I was wrong to question her. Then I tried to talk to her about Les and she wouldn't discuss it.'

'He says he didn't know Ewan Stokes and Maisie Ingram, though.'

'Cora thinks he's lying. And I thought about it last night: Les has been unusually quiet with this. No jibes, no mickey-taking of Ellis, no dodgy sweepstakes. He's not been himself. And I don't know if it can all be explained away because of what happened to his car.' Minshull rubbed at his chin, a definite smattering of stubble there. 'What if Cora's right? What if he knows more than he's saying?'

'All you can do is follow your gut, Minsh. It's all any of us can do...' Wheeler broke off as Ellis and Bennett walked in, chatting. That was a sight for sore eyes. Knowing what he knew about Kate's divorce, Wheeler felt particularly protective of her. The return of fun between them was an answered prayer. Bennett deserved some lightness after everything she'd endured alone.

'Morning, Dave, Sarge.' Ellis grinned.

'Morning to you both,' Minshull replied, rallying a little. The certainties of everyday CID office chat were always good for the soul.

'I was just saying to Kate we should do a CID team night out when this is all over,' Ellis said.

'He's obsessed with finding rural pubs now,' Bennett said, giving her colleague a despairing look. 'Also having someone else drive there. You should have seen him the other night with his pint of Pepsi.'

'Aw, Drew, did they give you a special straw and everything?' Wheeler asked, enjoying the banter.

'It was *manly* cola,' Ellis returned, feigning offence.

'Oh yeah,' Bennett laughed. 'So manly it defeated you!'

'Pub quiz is a good idea,' Minshull replied. 'On two conditions – one, it isn't anywhere a vehicle can mow us down; and two, it isn't a pub in Alderton.'

Bennett and Ellis responded with sheepish smiles.

'Cora should come, too,' Ellis suggested, turning to see Evans slouching in. 'And Les.'

'*And Les* what?'

'Team night out. When this job's done.'

'Only if you're paying,' Evans replied, heading to his desk.

Wheeler and Minshull exchanged glances. Maybe the universe was being restored after all.

'Right, everyone, grab a drink and then we'll go through where we're at with everything,' Minshull said.

Ten minutes later, the CID team gathered around the whiteboard, Minshull pacing the floor as their chatter died down.

'For those of you that don't know,' he glanced at Evans, who wasn't looking, 'last night there was another sighting, at Langley Avenue Sports Field. A video this time, and it's definitely Ewan Stokes.' He stuck an enlarged still of the hoodless man in the centre of the board. When he looked at Evans again, the detective was staring back, defiant. 'He asked a young lad to film it, who happens to be the son of the chairman of the local Friends association. We brought them in at eight thirty last night on a voluntary interview and the teenager told us Stokes wasn't alone. That confirms our theory that someone was helping him. The kid also revealed that Stokes arrived in a white van with a damaged front right wing and that there was a woman with him.'

Wheeler saw the hesitation, the slight touch to the brow before Minshull continued. 'When Dr Lael inspected both the doll and the photograph delivered to Maisie Ingram, she reported hearing a second, lighter-toned voice behind that of Ewan Stokes. The sighting of Stokes' female companion last night supports this.' He nodded to himself as if affirming the news. 'Cora was right.'

'Who is she, Sarge?' Ellis asked.

'The teenager couldn't see her features well enough for a clear description, only that she too was wearing a hoodie with a black baseball cap. He said she didn't look happy about being there and was urging Stokes to leave.' He popped the top from his whiteboard pen and wrote *FEMALE ACCOMPLICE?* next to the CCTV footage of the van speeding through St Just on the night of the accident and the new image of Ewan Stokes, snarling into the camera. 'So, who is she? Which female friends were cited in the original investigation files? Who are his most vocal female supporters on *StokesyFans*? Who appears to be speaking on his behalf?'

Wheeler made notes, observing the now stony-faced detectives as he wrote.

'Kate, go through the most recent posts on the forum and check the profiles of anyone who might be helping Stokes.'

'Sarge.'

'Thanks. Drew, have a look for anyone interviewed by the press about the case, either at the beginning or after the documentary. Find any female commentators, anyone particularly outspoken in his defence.'

'No problem, Sarge.'

'Great. Dave, Les, go back to the original investigation files and see what you can find there. The video yesterday also mentioned three names on Stokes' so-called revenge list. Find anyone interviewed at the time who gave a less than favourable account of Ewan Stokes. We're looking for opposition, disputes, even rumours about them that witnesses might have relayed.'

'On it, Sarge,' Wheeler replied, not waiting for Les to respond.

'Thanks, both. I'm going to brief the Guv on these developments when he arrives and then talk to DCI Taylor about extending the protection patrol at Maisie Ingram's house.'

'You think he'll try to go there?' Wheeler asked.

Evans didn't look up from his notebook.

'I think she's top of the list. And as she's still refusing to go somewhere safer, we have a duty to protect her at her home.'

'Can't someone persuade her to leave?' Wheeler asked.

'Even her sister's had no luck. I'd rather we prepare to defend her at her house than waste time arguing the toss. Thanks, everyone.'

As the team returned to their desks, Wheeler noticed Evans pocket his phone, grab his tobacco pouch, cigarette papers and lighter and swiftly leave the office.

THE CLUB

Davep221 POSTED A POLL

Just a little light-hearted fun, folks. Three names on Stokesy's smokin' hot hit-list. Who's your money on? Vote below!

Q: Who are the names on Stokesy's list?

Maisie Ingram (ex) 34.20%

Olwyn Stokes (mother) 3.31%

Marilyn Stokes (sister) 20.16%

Glen Stiles (ex boss) 17.07%

Other 25.26%

Me54c Glen Stiles?

Grumpyg1t Builder. Stokesy allegedly working for him fortnight before he went missing. He moved to Cambridge ages ago.

Me54c What about one of the football team? The other striker? Coach?

Grumpyg1t Coach snuffed it.

Me54c When?

Grumpyg1t Few days ago. Car accident.

Me54c Bloody hell. Timing?

Grumpyg1t Bad timing for him. Wasn't Stokesy.

Me54c Why not? Coach was on some lists on here.

Grumpyg1t Not his style. He'd have told us, wouldn't he?

Me54c Guess so. Why the mum and sister?

Grumpyg1t Sick bastards on here. That family's been through enough.

Me54c Maisie Ingram, odds-on favourite. Hope she has life insurance.

– Moderator restricted comments on this thread –

Forty-Seven

ELLIS

'So, who do you reckon the woman is?' Ellis asked, leaning across in his chair towards Bennett.

Bennett groaned and resolutely stared ahead. 'Not this again.'

'Don't give me that. I know you. You have a theory – you always do.'

'Well, this time I don't.'

Ellis hid his grin. Winding Bennett up was his new favourite game. It was needed now the pressure of the investigation had become so great. Minshull's countdown on the whiteboard was scarily low. Everyone saw it whenever they looked up from their work. Ellis swore the drawn number grew in physical size every day his superior changed it, its dimensions increasing as its value diminished. Minshull and Anderson's hushed conversations were becoming more frequent, the two of them disappearing into Anderson's office whenever they suspected the team were listening. Any moment of lightness was vital to survive.

'Thirty-seven,' Bennett said, snapping Ellis out of his thoughts.

'Your age?'

'Sod off.'

'Sorry. Thirty-seven what?'

Bennett looked at him. The smile playing on her lips was the only reward he wanted. 'Thirty-seven female or female-identifying active members of StokesyFans. There may well be more, but those are the ones I've found participating in the forums.'

'Why would any woman join in with that rubbish?' Realising how that sounded, he backtracked. 'Sorry – I mean…'

'Because delusion is sadly not limited to men,' Bennett returned. 'They're in the minority on the site but they're participating more than a lot of their male counterparts. I have no idea what the attraction is for anyone. Belonging, maybe. Being part of a posse. A club. United behind a belief. It's church without the commitment. Nobody's going to demand they do anything, beyond watching and discussing.'

'Are any women sticking up for Maisie?' Ellis asked. He'd seen occasional arguments and differences of opinion on the forums, more in recent days since the revelation of the three-name list. 'Surely not everyone agrees that she's the enemy?'

'The vocal ones are pretty much toeing the party line. *It must be the woman's fault* – like it's the most obvious explanation for his disappearance. But who goes missing just because their partner leaves them? He hadn't shown any signs of depression. Anger, definitely, possibly all channelled at his football coach and Damien East because they were natural targets. But not heart-crushing grief.'

'Not everyone takes break-ups well,' Ellis said, his words cut dead by the glare his colleague sent him. 'I didn't mean – you're doing brilliantly.'

'Keep your voice down!'

Ellis held up a hand and mouthed *Sorry*. Bennett shook her head and returned to the list on her screen. 'So, which of our thirty-seven is helping their hero?'

'Maybe he has a lot of them. The Stokesy harem.'

'*Not* helpful.'

Denied his fun, Ellis groaned and looked back at his own work as Bennett's mobile buzzed on her desk.

'DC Kate Bennett, how can I help…? Wait – hang on – speak slowly…'

Ellis jumped as Bennett's hand reached out and gripped his arm.

'Okay, where are you? We'll meet you. No, stay there and we'll be with you soon. I'll text when we're close. Hang tight.' Ending the call, she shut down her computer, grabbing her notebook and jacket. 'Come on.'

'What? Where are we going?' Ellis asked, struggling to save his own work before logging off.

'Out,' Bennett murmured through gritted teeth. She skirted her desk and headed for Minshull's.

Ellis watched their hurried exchange and Minshull's glance back towards him. And then Bennett was back, grabbing a set of pool car keys as she ushered Ellis out of the office.

'Where are we going?' he repeated, jogging to keep up with her. When Kate Bennett put on a burst of speed, you'd better be ready for it. *Like a terrier after a rabbit*, Wheeler had joked once, early in Ellis' CID life, when accompanying Bennett on a shout had become a virtual race in her wake. At least his hours in the gym meant he could match her pace now. He felt her equal, after a long time of trailing behind.

Bennett pushed open the double doors at the end of the corridor, glancing back as Ellis slipped through. 'Marilyn Stokes.'

–

The pool car sped along country lanes to the remote location Marilyn had specified, Bennett's eyes bright as she focused on the road ahead. It was some sight: Kate Bennett chasing the scent of something. Ellis tried not to stare as he threw questions at her – his preferred way of processing news. He could think while he formulated his inquiries.

'Why now? What made her change her mind? I thought we'd never see her again, did you?'

'I don't know why now. She wouldn't say what changed her mind. And no, I didn't think she'd call.'

'How did she sound?'

'Scared. Worried someone would see her.'

'What do we do when we meet her?'

Bennett glanced at him from the wheel. 'Listen, Drew. First and foremost, we listen to her.'

Ellis sat back in his seat, the dappled shade of branches sending shadow patterns racing over his arm where it rested alongside the window as they passed through a corridor of wind-bent trees. The road ahead narrowed, turning sharp left, following the contours of the fields.

'Where are we meeting her?' Ellis asked.

'Burgh.'

'What the hell is she doing there?'

'It's out of the way. Far enough from Alderton to not be seen.'

'Burgh,' Ellis said, shaking his head. 'First time for everything, I guess.'

White Foot Lane was little more than a narrow track, turning off the main road by a small, well-kept green with a bench, ornamental millstone, a wooden gabled village noticeboard and red telephone box. It snaked away from the few houses it passed, under a canopy of trees and alongside a high-hedged section. Just after a national speed limit sign, a small patch of hardstanding came into view on the right. A single car was parked there, a silver Ford Fiesta, its wheels and bumper caked with long-dried mud.

Bennett parked beside the car.

'That's her.' She made to open her door, but looked back. 'Let her talk, okay? Hold back the questions and *hear* what she has to say. I get the feeling nobody's listened to her for a long time.'

Ellis took a moment to observe Bennett as she approached the silver car. Gone was the driven, speeding whirlwind; in its place, slow, methodical movements, made with the utmost care.

What did Kate Bennett know that chimed with Marilyn Stokes' life?

A glare from his colleague over the roof of Marilyn Stokes' car made Ellis hurry out to join them.

'You remember Drew?' Bennett asked, as he arrived.

'Yes.' Marilyn's eyes flicked to him, then back to Bennett.

'We can help. That's what we're here for.'

Marilyn took a shuddering breath. 'You might not want to, when you know.'

'Know what?' Ellis pulled back when Bennett raised her eyebrow. 'We're here for you. To listen.'

'None of this is what it seems,' she said, her gaze straying to the wide field beyond the car park. 'I'm supposed to play along, say nothing. But it's getting out of hand now and I can't...' She gulped at the air. 'I can't be part of it any more.'

Bennett kept her focus on Marilyn. Ellis watched them both.

'Marilyn, what do you want to do?'

'I want to tell you the truth. And I want to be safe.' She raised her head as if setting her intentions. 'Ewan isn't missing. He hasn't ever been. I know where he is and I know what he's planning. Because I've been helping him.'

Ellis fought to steady his expression. He could see Bennett facing the same battle. The woman in the car, the other voice Cora had sensed, insisting reason in the face of horror. It hadn't been one of the thirty-seven Stokesy fans Bennett had identified. It was his own sister.

'I'll tell you everything I know,' Marilyn promised. 'But I want protection. And I want you to stop him. You *have* to stop him.'

Forty-Eight

MINSHULL

Marilyn Stokes walked slowly along the corridor by the interview rooms, flanked by Bennett and Ellis. Minshull and Wheeler stood a small distance away, taking it in.

If what she had indicated to the DCs on the way here was true, Marilyn's testimony could blow the whole investigation apart. But could they trust her? The old files Anderson and Wheeler had pored over had revealed a less than flattering picture of Marilyn Stokes. She had changed her statement three times in total: the initial one given in the earliest hours of her brother's disappearance, stating that she'd watched him play alone that night and seen him arguing with Maisie Ingram as she left the sports field; the second, where she'd confirmed that her mother, Olwyn, had been there and Maisie had slapped Stokes and wished him dead; and the last, revealed at the eleventh hour when DCI John Minshull had already stated that he was shelving the investigation, where Marilyn alleged Stokes had admitted to her privately that Maisie was violent towards him.

'What d'you reckon, Sarge?' Wheeler whispered as the party entered Interview Room 2. 'The truth, or damage limitation now old Stokesy's going off-piste?'

'At this moment, I couldn't tell you. I guess we'll find out.'

Wheeler patted his back as he made to leave. 'Well, don't have too much fun, will you?'

Fun wasn't the word Minshull would have chosen.

It was crowded in the small interview room. Marilyn Stokes had requested both Bennett and Ellis to stay with her: Minshull hoped to persuade her otherwise. A duty solicitor had been called, his briefing just completed. In the height of summer, with five bodies in an airless glorified cupboard, this interview promised to be a treat.

Nevertheless, Minshull wanted to be in the room. They had worked long, thankless hours to reach this point. And while he knew Anderson would be planning a very long and uncomfortable debrief with the two DCs who'd seen fit to go chasing a potentially valuable witness unbidden, he couldn't fault the results.

Marilyn sat beside her counsel, fingers busy with the paper cup of water in front of her. Ellis had somehow folded his tall frame into a chair in the corner; Bennett sat next to Minshull, notes open.

At Minshull's signal, Bennett commenced the recording, making the verbal introductions and waiting while Marilyn confirmed her name. When the formalities were complete, Minshull offered Marilyn a swift smile. 'Thank you for contacting us, Ms Stokes. I know you've talked with DC Bennett, so she'll start. I have some questions for later.'

Bennett smiled across the interview desk. Minshull saw the effect it had on Marilyn, who returned it. 'Marilyn, we're just going to talk through the things you know and the things you've expressed a desire to share. Let's start with your reasons for contacting us.'

'My brother, Ewan Stokes, is not missing. It's been assumed he was and my family has played a large part in that. For fifteen years. And now I'm scared that the original plan is being abandoned for something… Something I can't stand by and watch.'

Minshull let the news sink in. When Bennett had called him from the pool car, she'd said Marilyn had potentially explosive information. She hadn't been exaggerating.

'You mentioned an *original plan*,' Bennett repeated. 'Can you tell me what that was?'

Marilyn took a sip of water as her counsel watched her closely. 'We sent Ewan away.'

'Who do you mean by "we"?'

'My mum and my stepdad.'

'Okay. Why was Ewan sent away?'

'He'd fallen into bad company, made some stupid decisions. There were rumours of people gunning for him, and the consequences of his actions catching up with him. My family thought it would be safer for everyone if he disappeared for a while.'

'So you faked his disappearance?'

'Yes.' She frowned. 'Actually, no. My family made up the whole going missing thing. They deliberately didn't tell me. I think they knew I'd crack before they did. I thought my brother was gone for the best part of four years. I was convinced he'd died, that police would find a body in some woods somewhere. I lived on a knife-edge that whole time, desperate for news but fearing the worst.'

'When did you discover the truth?'

'When the police officially dropped the investigation. My mother was so distraught that she sought out the true crime production company and offered them an exclusive. They told me the following year, just as it was about to air.'

Bennett made notes. Ellis did his best to hide his shock. Minshull's mind was blank. What could anyone say to a plan so blatantly designed to mislead, recounted so dispassionately? And how had the initial investigation failed to spot the discrepancies?

He didn't buy any of her *they kept me in the dark on purpose* story either. She'd seen the lay of the land before her family had and was protecting herself. No heartbreak, no Damascus Road-style revelation. Simple survival.

'Okay. So your family suggested Ewan go away for a while. Was he left to make his own arrangements or did he have help?'

'My stepdad arranged it. Billy Norton. He had some business associates in France, some distant family in Italy and his best friend lives in Spain. He got them all on board and they agreed to host Ewan if he worked for them.'

'Working doing what?'

Marilyn's expression clouded. 'Bits and bobs wherever he could. He'd worked on some building sites around here before. Cash-in-hand stuff. He was good with practical things. Especially driving.' She dabbed at her nose with a tissue. 'That's what got him in trouble.'

'The trouble he ran away to avoid?'

Marilyn nodded. 'He did a job for a friend, driving their van. It went wrong and we heard the police were looking for him. So Billy told him he couldn't stay in Suffolk. Their plan was to have him stay away for a couple of years, then come home. People would be so delighted he was back safe with us that they wouldn't question why he'd gone in the first place.'

'And when you found out the truth? Why didn't you tell the police?'

Marilyn stared back. 'Go against my family? How would I have done that? I was living at home because I couldn't afford a place of my own. Billy found me a job in one of his businesses, running accounts. Everything I had I depended on my family for. If you'd arrested Ewan in the beginning, he'd most likely have got off on a first offence, or been given a couple of years, tops. What was likely to happen to me then?'

'So what's changed?' Minshull nodded his apology to Bennett for interrupting. 'Why have you come to us now?'

'Because he isn't following the plan any more.'

'Which plan?'

'The fifteenth anniversary. The CCTV appearances. It was meant to delight his fans.'

'What was your part in that?'

'I drove him round, taking him to all the locations.'

'Which vehicle did you use?'

'His van. From the lock-up he had with Lindsay Carlton. The 2004 VW Caddy van.'

Now Bennett and Ellis were on edge. Minshull sensed the mood in the room shift, darken.

'Did you drive that van through St Just on the evening of Sunday 16th July?' Bennett asked carefully. Minshull saw her knuckles whiten as she gripped her pen.

'No. I drove to Felixstowe Pier, though. The first webcam.'

'And after that?'

'I left the van with Ewan and Billy. I was meeting friends for a late drink and didn't want to travel all the way back to the lock-up to take it back. So Billy did it with Ewan and they brought my car back with them.'

'Did you notice anything different about the van the next time you drove it?'

Marilyn's brow furrowed before light dawned. 'Oh, the accident. But how do you know about that?'

Not trusting Bennett to reply, Minshull cut in. 'Because we've been turning the county upside down searching for it. That van drove at a party of pedestrians, including me and three of my officers, with intent to cause harm.'

Marilyn was cowering now.

Minshull had no intention of letting up.

'It drove deliberately at them, narrowly missing them and hitting a bollard. *That* was no accident. So tell me, Ms Stokes, who exactly was driving that night?'

'I don't know.'

'Choice of two, Ms Stokes. Which one told you they'd had the accident – your stepfather or your brother?'

'It was Ewan. Billy said he was mucking about, driving too fast. He didn't say he'd driven at people.'

'Would it have made a difference if he had?'

'Yes! Of course!'

'And yet you took the van out again the next night, for the appearance at Rai's Garage. Why?'

'Because they told me to.' She wiped her eyes, reached for another tissue from the box on the interview desk. 'I thought I was making a fun game for the fans on the forum, a puzzle they could solve that would end with their hero coming back. But my brother is no hero, Detective. He's a monster. And you have to stop him.'

'What makes you say that?' Bennett's question was a softly spoken contradiction to Minshull's fury.

'The plan was never about him coming back to hurt anyone. All the Maisie stuff came from the forum, not the family. But it kept people talking, so... I'm not proud to say we milked it.'

'Why?'

'Because it was easier to blame Maisie for making Ewan run away than come up with a viable reason for why he left.'

'You talk like you influenced the fan forum,' Bennett said. 'But I thought it was something that began after the true crime documentary aired. Did your family have access to the forums?'

Marilyn looked down at her hands. 'We started it.'

'You started the forum? Which one?'

'Just StokesyFans. The others spread from that.'

'Tell me about that.' Thinly concealed disgust punctuated Bennett's words. It mirrored Minshull's reaction perfectly.

'Mum said it would be like a street team, ensuring Ewan remained in the public's mind. Nobody thought it would spiral like it did, or that the fans would become so – avid.'

Avid, thought Minshull. Try *rabid*.

'My stepdad knew the guy who ran the SuffolkView website. He'd set up a forum on that site and said it would be easy to do one for us. He sent viewers to it through a private link. It was invite-only for the first few months, testing the water in the wake of the documentary being aired, but then he moved it to public viewing when the take-up rate soared.'

'What's his name, please?'

Marilyn blinked. 'Rick Beech.'

Minshull, Ellis and Bennett stared back.

'Are you aware Mr Beech impersonated your brother to intimidate a former teammate?'

Marilyn's hands began to twist and writhe on the interview desk. 'I know now. That was his idea. First we heard of it was when Rick was arrested. There had been some talk of the number of forum posts dropping on StokesyFans, so he figured he'd do something to get everyone's attention. It was based on his own strange theory: he didn't agree with Ewan not wanting to punish Damien East. He made a stupid mistake.'

'But then the football shirt was left at Mr East's home. Who put it there?'

'My brother. He saw the reaction to Rick's hoax and wanted to outdo him. That was when I knew it was getting out of control. First the shirt, then the doll…' She welled up again. 'You have to believe me, I never agreed to that. Terrifying people. Having a revenge list. It stopped being fun when he did that. I tried to stop him, but he won't listen to me now. And then yesterday – after the pavilion stunt – Ewan told me he'd taken Ted Patrick out.'

'The football coach?'

She nodded, red eyes burgeoning with tears again. 'He was proud of it. Bragging, like it made him this big gangster. Said he *helped Ted off the road* because Ted was going to tell you about the gang Ewan was mixed up with when Mum sent him away. And then...' She gave a cough, her voice constricted as if hands were slowly squeezing her throat. 'He said, *that's what happens to people who know too much.*'

'He threatened you?'

Marilyn nodded, pressing a tissue to her eyes. 'That's why I called DC Bennett. I'm terrified he's going to kill someone else. He's out of control and no longer taking orders from Billy. It's like he's seen what people are saying on the forums and believing he's some kind of god.'

The duty solicitor, who had been passively observing and taking notes, raised his pen. 'I think now might be a good time to break. There's a lot of information that's been shared and I would like to discuss next steps with my client.'

'Agreed,' Minshull nodded. 'I just have one last question, Ms Stokes. Where is your brother now?'

'Billy wouldn't tell me. And Mum doesn't know, either. I just met Ewan when it was time for the next appearance. But he has to be pretty close to Felixstowe.' She leaned a little further over the desk. 'You've got to get Maisie Ingram out of her house. Please. He's coming for her. Soon.'

Forty-Nine

CORA

'Today we are doing the Romans,' Reece announced, moving the flame-haired doll up and down in front of his toys seated in rows facing her, as if she were pacing at the front of class.

Cora did her best to focus on the game, but her mind kept straying to a conversation from last night. Minshull had called around nine p.m., confirming what Cora had heard from the items left at Maisie Ingram's home: there had been a second voice present. Ewan Stokes was being assisted by a woman – witnessed by the teenager who had shot the video for Ewan Stokes. The news was delivered with an almost-apology; so vague that even now Cora couldn't work out how sincere it had been.

'You were right. I should have listened to you.'

'I know what I heard,' she'd replied, unable to conceal the sting in her tone.

'I should have believed you.'

Had he been talking about the female voice, or was it an admission that what she'd heard from Les Evans was correct, too? Cora couldn't say. The uncertainty snapped at her heels as she watched Reece moving toys around the makeshift classroom setting.

She'd encouraged Reece to play the classroom game with his toys several times since the first. His insistence on Dave Bear as 'security' interested her. It was clearly a protection the boy had established to ward off the deepest of his fears. If she could just encourage him to explain Dave Bear's role further, she was convinced he might reveal what was at the root of his fear.

Today, Dave Bear was at the back of the class: a change from his usual position by the teacher.

'Does Dave know about the Romans?' she asked, steering the conversation towards the security guard teddy.

Reece nodded. 'Dave Bear knows everything. He has to.'

'To keep everyone safe.'

'My dad says information is like a superhero power. If you know a lot of things you can do whatever you like.'

'And Dave Bear knows a lot on purpose? To help everyone?'

Reece looked up, a small frown line appearing between his eyebrows. 'To help the children.'

'To help you?' It was a gentle nudge, a test of the water.

Reece responded with a shy nod, the bitten lip making another appearance.

Over by the window, Alex Bickland looked up from her magazine. It was a tactic she and Cora had agreed: to sit and read while Cora played with Reece, so that the boy relaxed and wasn't alerted to any specific tension regarding the answers he gave. Alex wasn't reading any more than Cora was interested in the toy school's new topic: both were listening to Reece in their own way.

The boy's blue eyes were peering up at Cora now, as if waiting for more. Cora went with her gut.

'Do you feel safe when Dave Bear is in the classroom?'

Another nod.

'Is that a good feeling?'

'I like it.'

'Why's that?'

'Because he won't let the phone ring.'

Forgetting the weariness of her body, Cora focused on the boy. 'Why can't the phone ring?'

The wide-eyed stare remained on her as his head shook.

Too far. Cora retreated. 'How does Dave Bear stop the phone ringing?'

'He stares at it with his scary teddy eyes.' Reece reached for a scrap of red satin material he had chosen for a centurion's cape and began to

336

pull it around the neck of a Captain America action figure. The fabric twisted and slid across the shiny plastic body, refusing to yield to the boy's attempts at knotting it. 'Dave Bear only brings out his scary eyes for baddies.' As he spoke, the red satin slipped from his fingers, gliding to the floor.

For the man, it whispered in Reece's voice.

Cora pressed into the sound with her mind, seeking the space around it, pushing into the words. The fear contained in the repeating three words chilled her, sending a lump of taut emotion into her throat.

For the man… For the man… For the bad man…

'Cora.'

Shaken, Cora looked up to see Alex Bickland standing next to her, knuckles whitening as she gripped the magazine in her hands.

'I'm so sorry to do this – I know consistency matters – but I have to go out. I do occasional sessions at the golf club spa to cover for my friend and she's just texted me. She's unwell and has to head home. Chris is fixing something in the office – I'll get him to come up instead. Is that okay?'

It was the worst possible time for a change in guard, especially as Reece was far more communicative with Alex present than he ever was with Chris. But it was what it was.

'Of course.'

Relief flooded Alex's expression. 'Thank you. I'll go and fetch Chris.'

'Why are you going, Mum?' Reece asked, a note of panic in his question.

Alex crouched beside him. 'Auntie Noreen's not well, so I have to do some work for her at the golf club. I won't be long.'

The boy frowned. 'Can't she just have some Calpol?'

The sweetness of his question broke the tension, Cora and Alex sharing smiles as his mother stroked his hair. 'I don't think Calpol works for grown-ups, I'm afraid.'

'Well, *that's* rubbish,' her son stated. 'Can Cora stay?'

'Of course I can,' Cora replied, still reeling from what she'd heard the child's subconscious voice reveal.

The game resumed, Dave Bear keeping a watchful eye on the class. But a few minutes later, Alex returned, her expression thunderous.

'Cora, forgive this, Chris is just outside by the car and wants a word.' She shook her head. 'I've told him I have to go in five minutes.'

'No problem.'

It was a problem, just like the Bicklands' request for her to visit on a Saturday morning. Ordinarily, weekend working was reserved for the most urgent cases, but Cora had accepted in this instance it was necessary. Rightly so, as what she'd heard this morning from the boy had proved. But she felt bruised by the past few days, weary beyond words, and the sight of the anxious journalist waiting for her on the drive when she left the house made her heart sink.

He bounded over to her, a too-bright smile in place. What was going on with him? The overenthusiastic attention felt smothering.

'Thanks for popping out,' he rushed. 'I want to pick your brains before we go back in.'

'Okay, but your wife needs to leave very soon.' She made a show of looking at her watch, hoping it would dissuade him.

It didn't.

'This won't take long. I have a morning conference I should be at today. Only, as you can see, I'm here. I need to watch remotely so I can file my report as soon as possible, but the electrics in my office have an issue. I have a guy coming out to fix it but he won't get here until later this afternoon. I can lay everything out in the kitchen, set up my mic and laptop and have my tablet linked with my editor in London. The problem is, Reece might hear it. And the topic being discussed might summon his anxiety.' He gave Cora an apologetic smile. 'I mean, I think it might. I don't claim to be an expert in these things. But I've noticed he's sensitive to tension in conversation.'

'We're at a stage where any tension may cause an issue,' Cora said, her heart sinking. With Alex gone and the potential for Reece's anxiety to be triggered, continuing Reece's session may cause more harm than good. 'Maybe it's best we abandon things today and resume on Monday morning?'

'No! No, there's no need for that.' His smile had become a pulled grimace, the forced brightness of his reply little cover for his frustration. 'I need you here so that I can focus on the press conference. I'm sorry, I know how important consistency is – location, routine, repetition and everything. But this is part of the investigation I was telling you about. Other journos are circling, my editor's threatening to pull the plug if I don't get something soon...'

Now Cora was listening. The Stokesy investigation. The case Chris Bickland didn't know Cora had personal knowledge of. 'I'm sorry, did you say a press conference?'

'Yes. I can't stress enough how vital it is that I watch it. There's a private live stream and I have to be in the room, as it were, because I can't be *in the room*...'

'Press conference with who? Police?'

Bickland shot her a wry look. 'Hardly. The police monumentally dropped the ball on this case, from the first investigation to the current one which, according to my source, is faring no better. The son of the original chief investigator is even leading it, did you know? I mean, how corrupt is that? So he can wipe his hands of that poor family for a second time?'

Cora pushed away the anger rising in her gut. How dare he lump Minshull in with his father like that? Or dismiss the team working round the clock to find Ewan Stokes?

'Who called the press conference?' she asked, as steadily as she was able.

'The family! Most of them anyway. Olwyn Stokes-Norton, her other half Billy Norton, some of the cousins will be there, too. Not Marilyn, oddly enough. The official line is that she's not coping well with all the press attention and is too upset to take part. And who can blame her? It's nuts around this story and only going to get worse. This is *huge*. I can't even tell you what a coup it will be to get them all in a room. We've heard nothing from the family since the documentary. And this is on their terms: they're not being paraded out by the police to grab the sympathy vote.'

'Do the police know?'

'Can't imagine they're invited. I expect the family will have a fair few words to say about the investigation.'

Minshull had to know. Cora wondered how she could send him a message without drawing attention to herself. 'So you want me to look after your son while you work?'

'Exactly!'

'With respect, I'm not a babysitter.'

'I know – I know that. And I wouldn't ask but it's vital I work. I just need twenty minutes of quiet – forty, tops.'

'Can't you watch with headphones?'

'No. I've applied to ask a question. I need complete silence around me when I ask, or my slot will be reassigned. They've signed a big deal with ITV News for the exclusive: us press journos have been allowed in to make the conference look packed. I can't stuff this up.' He took a step towards Cora, causing her to back involuntarily towards the house. 'I know it's a big ask, but I need this. You're good with kids and Reece loves the games you play with him. Why don't you suggest a game of hide-and-seek, or something? Somewhere other than the living room? You can go anywhere you like in the house. He loves hide-and-seek.'

He'd pushed too far now. Tiredness and the strain of past days converged, fury firing through Cora. 'I am a *professional*, Chris, not a hired help. Playing games with your son is part of a structured, finely balanced approach designed to best suit his needs. *Hide-and-seek* is not part of that strategy. We should reschedule today's session…'

'No! Please… Forgive my arrogance, I meant no offence. Is there one of your planned activities that could take place elsewhere in the house?'

'I'm sorry, no.'

'On the balcony, then? I'll open the bifolds, so Reece can still see me. There's enough room between there and the kitchen to minimise any sound. Please. Just keep him there while the press conference is on?'

Cora didn't want to do any of what he'd suggested, but moving the session to the balcony meant she could send a message to Minshull without Chris noticing.

'Fine,' she said. 'But the moment you finish, we come back in for the final task.'

'Yes. Absolutely. As you wish.'

She followed Chris back inside, her head whirring with the news. Why would the family call a press conference now, when they'd avoided talking to the media since the sightings? Was it damage limitation – a chance to disprove the more violent rumours of Stokesy's intentions circulating widely in the press? Or a final opportunity to put the boot into the police investigation they claimed had failed them? Or could they be appealing to Stokesy himself?

The memory of his hate-fuelled tirade rising from the grotesque baby doll returned, together with the softer, more desperate-sounding voice far behind it, pleading with him to reconsider. If the family had been scared by the rumours of their son's intentions, might this be an eleventh-hour intervention?

Alex met them at the top of the stairs, thanking Cora as she hurried out. Cora caught the pointed stare between Alex and Chris as she left.

She wondered again if the key to Reece's issue lay in this discrepancy of boundaries between his mum and dad. She could sense it there but couldn't define it beyond an instinct.

'Why don't the two of you go and enjoy the big chairs on the balcony?' Chris asked his son. 'When I've finished my boring work I'll bring you out some lemonade lollies.'

'Deal!' Reece yelled, dragging Cora towards the bifold doors and a set of smart, square armchairs made from woven rattan set around a tempered glass coffee table with a woven base on the stone balcony. 'Come on! Mum never lets me sit on these.'

Cora cast a glance back inside the living space to see Chris connecting all of his devices, satisfied with himself.

What must it be like, she wondered, to be so privileged you couldn't even see it? To demand the world shifted for you and expect it to comply? Is that why Bickland couldn't handle the situation with his son? Had he demanded the issue to leave his household and been shocked by its failure to obey?

When they were seated and Reece was happily building a new spaceship, Cora slid her phone from her pocket. Keeping it hidden behind the line of the chair's arm, she found Minshull's last text and typed a reply.

> Stokes family press conference at 1 p.m.
> I don't know where.
> ITV has exclusive – plans to stream it live.
> Family called it. More soon. Cora x

She kept the phone between the soft linen seat cushion of the chair and the lines of basket weave forming its sides, her eyes flicking to the screen between bursts of interaction with Reece, watching out for a reply.

'This keeps everyone safe,' Reece said, indicating a long length of shiny green satin ribbon he'd wrapped around his completed spaceship.

'Like a force field?' Cora asked.

'That's right.' Reece beamed at her comment. 'But more powerful. If the bad man comes too close it *melts* him like butter on toast...' He mimed melting away, waving his arms and bending down until he was almost kneeling on the floor. Cora laughed, her eyes straying to her concealed mobile phone screen. No reply from Minshull, but the clock confirmed the time: 1:05 p.m. The conference had begun.

From within the first floor of the Bicklands' house came the furious sound of typing. It cut through the summer air with ominous foreboding, the intention firing the keys far uncertain. Cora felt her nerves tip on edge and instinctively looked at Reece to gauge his response. If he sensed the tension too it could...

Wait...

Where was he?

'Reece?' Cora called, careful to keep her voice quiet. She peered beneath the glass of the table, stood up, scanned the length of the balcony with its perfect golf course view and strengthened-glass walls.

No sign. Anywhere.

No sign of the boy.

Where was he?

For a sickening moment, Cora forced herself to look over the edge of the stone balcony, praying she wouldn't see a fallen child on the manicured grass below. Relief flooded in when she found it as empty as the balcony itself.

And then, she heard the scream…

It was high-pitched and other-worldly, a banshee war cry that tore at Cora's senses and sent her mind into overdrive. Fear stabbed at her heart: intense, primal fear that sucked the air from her lungs and suffocated her where she stood.

She wavered for a moment, blindsided by violent emotion, until her instincts fired into life and she grabbed hold of the sound with her mind. It wasn't her own fear: it was fear emanating from the tortured, terrified screaming. Using the sound as a guide rope, she leaned into it, stumbling forward as she followed its trajectory. It led her inside, through the living space, to the kitchen, just as Chris Bickland's tablet flew to the ground and shattered.

Reece was clawing at his father, superhumanly strong as panic coursed through him.

'Get away! Get away!' he screamed, fists and kicks raining across Chris, who was trying to hold him off.

'Reece,' Cora called out, lowering her tone as Tris Noakes had shown her during training, the stronger, deeper notes designed to soothe the terrified child. She raced towards him just as the picture on the laptop screen zoomed in on a smartly dressed man with a sweep of pure white hair.

'We just want Ewan to know he can stop running…' he was saying, his voice booming into the kitchen as he leaned into the microphone on the desk.

'*No! No-o-o-o!*' Reece wailed, his fist flying at the screen and narrowly missing.

'What is it, Reece?' Cora urged, reaching for him, the sound landing physical blows to her mind. 'Tell me what's scaring you.'

'He just went crazy!' Chris cried out, his arms crossed in front of his face.

'His mother just wants him home…'

'*No!* He has the bad man's voice! Daddy, get *away*!'

'It's just a man on TV,' Cora insisted, her hand finding the boy's shoulder. 'Reece, the man can't hurt you. It's just a picture...'

'*No!* He wants to hurt Daddy!'

'Your daddy's fine, sweetheart. He's safe... Chris, tell him...' Cora turned to Chris to urge him to reply, but the journalist was staring at the screen, hands braced against his son's fists. 'Tell him!'

'The *bad man*!' Reece wailed, flinging himself at his father, small hands slapping at his face as he tried to push his head away. 'Don't listen, Daddy, don't look at the bad man!'

Chris said nothing, his eyes trained past his writhing, weeping son to the laptop screen.

Cora lurched forward and took hold of the boy's arms with enough force to prevent their forward attack without causing him pain. 'Daddy's safe, Reece, he's here with us. The man isn't a bad man.'

'He's going to hurt Daddy!'

'That's not going to happen. Take a deep breath for me, like we practised, okay?'

'He's going to hurt my daddy! I know he is.'

'How do you know?'

'*His voice told me!*'

A strangled cry emanated from his father.

Shocked, Cora faced Chris, holding Reece back as best she could. 'What did the bad man tell you, Reece?'

The child shook his head violently.

Heart crashing in her mind, Cora fought to remain calm. 'I need to know so I can make it go away.'

'No...'

'Reece. What did the bad man say?' Cora insisted.

'He's going to hurt my dad. When I'm not with him. When I'm at school...' the child sobbed, his small frame slumping a little as Cora held his arms.

Lines were forming between the scraps of truth, forming solid pathways. Chris Bickland's horror, Ewan Stokes' stepfather on the screen, the journalist's investigation of the case...

Cora didn't dare let go. The answers that had evaded her were suddenly within reach. 'When did the bad man say this?'

'When I first got scared.'

'About school?'

The boy twisted to look up at her, terror-stricken eyes searching hers, his face flooded with tears. 'I was meant to watch Daddy. All the time. Or the bad man was going to kill him.'

Chris cried out and gathered his son to him.

Cora kept her hand on the boy's shoulder. 'Reece, how did the bad man say this to you?'

Soothed by his father's tight embrace, Reece Bickland's voice strengthened. 'On Dad's phone.'

'He called me here?' Chris whispered, the terrible realisation setting in.

Ignoring her own horror, Cora crouched beside the boy. 'Tell me exactly what happened and we can make this all better.'

Reece peered at her against his father's chest. 'I was getting ready for school and Mum was in the bathroom. I came in the kitchen and Daddy's phone was ringing...'

'Go on,' Cora urged.

'I thought he'd be pleased if I answered it for him. He'd showed me how to tap the screen and make the call start... So I did it and I said, hello, this is Reece Bickland, how can I help you? And the bad man said, are you Chris Bickland's boy? And I said, yes, I am. And then...' His eyes shut tight, his body shuddering.

'My boy...' Chris moaned, and stroked his son's hair.

'And then what did he say?'

'...Then he said he was going to tell me a secret. I like secrets, I said. You'll like this one, he said. And then he said Dad was a bad man. He said Daddy asked too many questions and it was my job to make sure I kept an eye on him...' Tears burgeoned again as he stared at Cora. 'He said, don't let your dad out of your sight. Because the moment you do, I'm going to kill him.'

Hearing such words from a distressed child, repeated verbatim, broke Cora's heart. Her own tears threatening, she pressed on. 'And so you didn't want to go to school?'

A shake of the head.

'Because you were supposed to be watching your dad?'

A nod.

'Reece, the bad man lied. He lied to you. He said terrible things to make you scared. But they weren't true. Your dad is safe, here, with you and me.'

Slowly, the boy closed his eyes, turning his head back into his father's chest.

Cora fixed Chris Bickland with a look. 'I'm going to call the police. You're going to call Alex and ask her to come home to be with Reece. And when the detectives get here, you are going to tell them everything you know.'

Chris nodded, mouth pressed into a tight line.

'*Everything*,' Cora repeated. 'For your son.'

Fifty

MINSHULL

It had been a day of revelation.

And it wasn't over yet.

'Sarge,' Wheeler called across the office. 'They're in.'

Minshull glanced at Cora, seated quietly beside him. 'Another thing I owe you for.'

'Where did they find him?' Cora asked.

'Kind of easy to find someone if they're in a room stuffed with cameras,' Minshull replied. 'If you hadn't told me the press conference was happening, Billy Norton may well have gone to ground.'

'And Stokesy?'

'He's on his own for now. His sister's here, his stepfather's just arrived. If he hears about the police escort his mother just had home from the press conference he won't risk contacting her for now. The family can't hide any longer, and Stokes is running out of allies.'

'But what if he panics? If he takes matters into his own hands?'

'I don't know.'

'Or if his fans decide to do his work for him?'

That was a very real possibility, one that Minshull didn't want to consider. So far the only fan to do anything in real life rather than on the forum had been Rick Beech. He was on his way to Police HQ for questioning, too, PCs Lanehan and Davis only too happy to escort him over. The word he'd had from Control was that Beech was behaving himself impeccably...

It should have been cause for a huge celebration. But the threat of Ewan Stokes still at large hung over everything.

And where was he with Cora? She'd received his lame attempt at an apology on the phone last night and welcomed him sincerely at the Bicklands' home, the shared thrill of a significant breakthrough firing between them. But when he'd mentioned Evans, she'd dismissed it. What did that mean? Had she decided to overlook Minshull's denial or was resentment still at work?

'How's Reece doing?' he asked, changing tack for his own sanity's sake.

'Shaken, but he's with his mum, so he'll be fine. And now we know the cause, we can start to rebuild his confidence. It helps that he met a real-life detective today.' She blessed him with a smile. 'You were great with him, by the way. Thank you.'

'He's a good kid. Maybe he'll make a great copper one day. *Getting all the bad men and locking them up*, apparently. Dave Bear is training him well.' He paused, wondering if he should continue. 'What you do is incredible. With kids. Uncovering their fears – discovering the root of their issues. I wouldn't even know where to start.'

She observed him for longer than felt comfortable. 'Thank you.'

'Listen, about the *other* thing…'

'Sarge, Norton's brief is done with him,' Wheeler confirmed.

Denied the chance to say what he'd considered all day, Minshull packed away his frustrations as he collected his notebook and file. 'I've got to go. Will you be here when I get back?'

'I have to give a statement about what I witnessed with Reece. So maybe.'

It wasn't a slammed door, at least.

Minshull joined Wheeler and they made their way down to the interview rooms.

'Does he know we have Marilyn?' Wheeler asked by the door to Interview Room 4.

'I don't think so. I doubt she told her family she was meeting Kate and Drew this morning.'

'So what's the plan?'

'Keep our cards close. Let him talk.'

Billy Norton was a giant of a man, blessed with an impressive quiff of pure white hair that didn't look likely to ever recede. He dwarfed his solicitor, an angular man who looked uncomfortable in his chair whichever position he chose. A thick gold chain sat around Norton's neck, nestled amid a bed of white curls visible where the wide collar of his open-necked shirt met the first button. He wore a permanent smirk, which gave the impression that he found everything cynically amusing.

Minshull introduced himself and Wheeler, shaking hands with the solicitor but notably blanked by Norton when he offered the same greeting. Wheeler started the recording, stating the names of those present, Norton confirming his name before folding his arms and eyeballing them both.

'Mr Norton, thanks for coming in.'

'Didn't have much of a choice, considering.'

The solicitor's smirk matched that of his client. Clearly it was going to be one of *those* interviews. Minshull met his mocking stare with complete detachment.

'Do you know why you're here today?'

'Not really. I'm hoping you'll enlighten me.'

'You are the partner of Olwyn Stokes-Norton, correct?'

'Husband, for my sins.' A snort. 'Love of my life, she is.'

'And how long have you been together?'

'Going on thirty years now. We married ten years ago.'

'And you are stepfather to her children?'

Norton nodded.

'Could you say that aloud, please? For the recording.'

'Yes, I am. Raised them like my own.'

'Marilyn Stokes and Ewan Stokes.'

'Yes.'

'Your stepson, Ewan Stokes, has been missing for fifteen years, is that correct?'

'Fifteen years this coming Thursday.'

Beside him, Wheeler shifted.

'Do you know where your stepson is?'

'What kind of a question is that? He's been missing for fifteen years!'

'But there have been sightings of him reported over the past week. And just this afternoon you and your wife gave a press conference saying you believed Ewan was coming home. You must have some idea of where he is.'

'If I knew that, I could finally give my wife the gift she's desired most. Don't you think I'd race to find him and bring him home if I could? Do you have any idea of how terrible it's been, living with the loss? The not knowing?'

It was a bravura performance, and had Minshull not already been in possession of Marilyn Stokes' testimony he might have been convinced.

'So you don't know where he is? Or his van, that's been spotted driving around the St Just and Felixstowe areas in recent days?'

A momentary flicker of doubt. 'No.'

'We have a witness,' Minshull returned, enjoying the shock registering opposite. 'We know you've known exactly where Ewan was for the last fifteen years. You arranged it all, didn't you?'

The solicitor stopped writing. Norton didn't move.

Minshull continued. 'What was Ewan in trouble for?'

'He – he wasn't…'

'So much trouble he needed to disappear for a while? Was it dodgy work on building sites? Getting into fights? I have another witness who claims your stepson threatened to kill him. A witness who, days ago, received a defaced football shirt with that same threat scrawled onto the back. Or was it the driving? I heard he's good at driving, too.'

'You can't… You know nothing.'

'Are you denying it?'

'I – I… no comment.'

Minshull acknowledged a point scored. 'Our witness says you had friends and associates in several European countries who let Ewan stay in exchange for work. Who were they?'

'No comment.'

'Did they owe you? It's a heck of thing to ask someone – harbouring a wanted man. Did you threaten them?'

'No comment.'

'How did Ewan live, while he was away? Sustain himself?'

'You'd have to ask him.'

'Did you send him money?'

'How would I? I didn't know where he was!'

'And whose idea was the fan forum?'

Norton's jaw dropped. 'You can't level that at me. That wasn't my idea.'

The solicitor tried a different position on his chair but found little comfort there either.

'Then help me, Mr Norton, whose idea was it?'

His eyes flicked between Minshull and Wheeler. Minshull imagined the frantic calculations being made beneath Norton's perfect white quiff. 'My wife's.'

Minshull stared back. 'Your wife, who's distraught at the prolonged loss of her son?'

Norton nodded, his hands curling into fists on the interview desk. 'She thought it would bring the community together. Galvanise support. Your lot had consigned him to be lost forever. We put him on the map. His *memory* on the map.'

'What was Ewan in trouble for, Mr Norton? What was so horrific that he had to disappear for fifteen years to escape it?'

Finally, the smirk vanished. 'It was nothing to do with me. I got him work. Decent work, on the level.'

'If I could just brief my client…' the solicitor cut in.

Norton groaned and slowly lifted a hand. 'Tony, it's okay. It's time.'

Shocked, the solicitor fell silent.

Norton turned back to Minshull and Wheeler. 'Driving job. He'd sworn to his mother it was legit, but that little shite wouldn't know legit if it bit his arse. Your lot were looking into it: thefts from warehouses, post office raids. They suspected a gang – I can't comment on whether they were right to do so. But Ewan was the driver. His mum panicked, thought the apple of her eye was about to be nicked, so – I knew some people. I made some calls and got him out of the country.'

Careful not to break Norton's flow, Minshull eased into the conversation. 'How did he travel?'

'Someone he knew gave him a fake passport. Nothing to do with me.'

'Under what name?'

'I believe it was David Kern. K-E-R-N. Someone's dead uncle.'

Hardly believing what he was hearing, Minshull made a note to check flight records. 'And the yearly messages?'

'His idea. Pandering to the pervs on that bloody forum. He started it: out for clicks and likes. *Stokesy is well and watching...* Load of bollocks. And those idiots lapped it up. Sad little bastards with sad little lives, looking to live someone else's adventure. That's what caused the trouble.'

'What trouble?'

Norton's smirk became a snarl. 'He started to believe it, all the shite written about him. The fifteenth anniversary, the revenge list – like some bloody awful action movie. He's a lunatic. And they're just egging him on. He'll kill someone, I'm certain of it.'

Minshull sensed more being hastily pulled back from the brink. 'Why are you telling us all of this now?'

Norton glanced at his solicitor. 'Honestly? Because it's gone too far. I've tried my best to keep him in line for his mum's sake, but I'm done. Kid's a loose cannon. He's got it in his head that he's invincible, so he'll do whatever he likes. And now I'm in here, not meeting him as I'd arranged, there's nobody to stop him.'

The solicitor gave up even trying to find comfort on his chair.

'So you've been protecting him?'

'Yeah, like I said. I did what was necessary. But no more.'

'Is that why you terrorised the young son of an investigative journalist?'

Norton gawped at him.

'Did Chris Bickland find out about Ewan? About the fake disappearance, the questions surrounding his criminal activity?'

'No way. No bloody way. You're not pinning that on me.'

'Oh, I don't need to. We have the direct testimony of the boy. He positively ID'd you from the press conference.'

Norton's mouth flapped.

'I think you should tell us what Ewan is planning for the fifteenth anniversary.'

Norton's shoulders fell. 'One murder. Public. Justified by his fans. He thinks he can get away with it. Because he's done it before.'

Silence claimed the interview room. Minshull knew he was staring, as Wheeler was beside him. But the bomb had dropped without warning. Even Norton's solicitor was rooted to the spot.

'How do you know?'

'I don't for certain. But my guts tell me Ted Patrick's car didn't veer off the road into that tree all by itself.'

That was what Minshull wanted: the corroboration of Marilyn's testimony. He held his nerve, sensing more.

Sure enough, it came.

Billy Norton was scared now, the fear leaking from him and the words tumbling out.

'Ewan took the van out by himself the day Ted Patrick died. I thought he was blowing off steam, kicking back against everything. But I noticed more damage to the front of the van next morning. He'd been drinking – I thought he'd pranged a bollard or something. But he'd spouted all this stuff before about Ted being a danger. Ted knew about the gang Ewan was driving for. Took his striker position off him in the team and shoved him on the subs bench for the big match to teach him a lesson. If Ted had told you lot that, you would have sussed the real reason he went missing.'

'Are you saying Ewan murdered Ted Patrick?'

Norton's brow fell. 'I believe he did. And I'm sick of protecting his hide. His mother doesn't believe me. But I *know*. He murdered Ted Patrick and he'll murder again: only this time he'll take the credit.'

Dizzy with the suddenness of it all, Minshull leaned forward. 'Who will he murder?'

Norton fixed him with a desperate stare. 'The person he's hated for fifteen years. He won't stop until he destroys them.'

Maisie Ingram. The hatred Cora had heard from the baby doll, his fury at no longer being able to control her as he had before.

'Where is your stepson, Mr Norton?'

'He's waiting for me by the van lock-up.'

Wheeler was left hastily ending the interview recording as Minshull raced from the room.

Fifty-One

CORA

'Stokes is at the lock-up!' Minshull yelled, running through the CID office. 'Drew, I want an all-units call-out to the location.'

'Sarge.'

'Is Anderson back from observing Marilyn's statement?'

'He's still in there,' Bennett replied, rising to her feet. 'Shall I get him?'

'Yes. Tell him it's urgent. And then alert the patrol at Maisie Ingram's house. If we miss Stokes at the lock-up, we know where he'll be heading.'

Bennett ran out as Ellis called Control.

Cora stood, not sure what to do. Evans, across the office from her, did the same. As she stared helplessly back, the notification tone sounded on her phone. Opening the message, her heart hit the floor.

> CHANGE OF PLAN
> The party's coming early.
> *I'm back!*
> Enjoy the show.
> #Stokesy15

'Rob!' Cora called, summoning Minshull back from Anderson's office. 'Look!'

Minshull swore loudly.

'Sarge.' Ellis rushed over, face ashen. 'The new patrol at Maisie Ingram's won't be in place until seven p.m.'

'What?'

'There was a delay in DCI Taylor approving them.'

Minshull's face grew thunderous. 'How long?'

'It's been clear for two hours.'

'What the actual… So we've left a vulnerable, high-risk woman – against whom there have been several credible threats – unprotected for *two bloody hours*? Get someone over there! *Now!*'

Instinctively, Cora looked over to Les Evans.

But his desk was empty.

'What the hell?' Anderson appeared in the doorway, red-faced from his sprint up the stairs.

'It's a mess, Guv. They left Maisie Ingram's house unguarded for two hours.'

'What?' Anderson roared.

Cora slipped past them both unseen, the horror and fury that gripped them summoning their attention. Reaching Evans' desk, she saw the list of interviewed friends and acquaintances Evans had been going through, abandoned and hanging half-off the stacks of papers.

I'LL KILL HIM, it roared in Les Evans' voice.

Without stopping to think, Cora sprinted out of the office towards the car park exit.

Fifty-Two

EVANS

Fear jabbed at every muscle as Les Evans took the stairs two at a time. He was going to land in the shit for this; his career might never recover. But suddenly it didn't matter. None of it did.

All that time spent protecting his own sorry hide, when he should have fought for her. The only thing he'd ever wanted.

How had he been so stupid?

Last night, he had told Cora Lael that he'd stopped caring for Maisie Ingram the moment she branded their night together a mistake. But that was a lie. Another lie to add to the great stinking pile Evans had surrounded himself with. So many lies that he'd lost sight of the truth. But last night, by the river bridge, it had all become clear. He loved her.

The day he'd helped Maisie move Ewan's stuff out, he'd asked a few of his uniformed buddies to keep Stokes busy. They'd pulled him over and spent two hours getting him to dismantle the trailer attached to his van, insisting they had good evidence that he was smuggling drugs. He wasn't, of course, but that was a minor detail. In the resulting two-hour delay, Evans and Maisie had cleared every last sign of Ewan Stokes from her home, an exorcism that would finally give her the right to her own life.

He hadn't told Cora, but Maisie had kissed him that day. It had been unexpected, but life-changing. He would have swept her to bed there and then had he not promised to take her to a hotel in Ipswich for her safety. It hadn't been right to act, then.

But night of the football match had been the moment they could no longer deny their attraction. He blamed the booze, but they'd hardly drunk any: in his bed before they'd had chance to eat the pizza he'd ordered in. She had been everything. And he'd never found another.

Maisie was in danger now and he had to find her. The future consequences could bring what they may; let the past be damned.

Reaching his car, he fumbled in his pocket for keys, just as a shadow crossed his path.

'If you think you're doing this alone, you can think again.'

Evans stared at Cora Lael. 'Go back. They'll miss you.'

'They didn't notice me leave. And I'm not letting you go on your own.'

'Get out of my way.'

The annoying woman stood her ground. 'I could always yell, let everyone know you're here.'

'You're insane!'

'I'm not moving until you let me in.'

What choice did he have?

'Fine. Get in. And shut up.'

His phone began ringing before they'd left Ipswich. Evans pushed the sound to the back of his mind, leaning on the accelerator and swerving over a crossroads as the traffic lights blazed red.

'Are you going to the house?' Cora asked.

'I'm going to get her out,' he snapped back. 'And I told you to be quiet.'

'I didn't agree to that.'

'Evidently.'

His phone rang again.

'You should talk to them,' Cora said, like that would somehow magically solve everything. To talk to Anderson and Minshull meant admitting he'd lied: not only to them but also to their predecessors. It would come out in time – he was resigned to that. There was no need to hurry it along now.

'They'd try to stop me. There's no time for a delay. You heard Drew – her house has been unguarded for two hours. What if he already has her? What if *the show* is him hurting her wherever he's taken her?'

'You have to try to calm down,' she insisted.

'I can't,' he hissed back, bristling at the blared horn from the car he'd just overtaken.

'For Maisie,' Cora insisted. 'What use will you be to her if you're so wound up you aren't thinking straight?'

Evans forced air into his lungs. It did nothing to ease the scream of tension in his ears or his crashing heartbeat. 'It isn't working.'

'Keep going. Eyes on the road. Focus on your breath.' She glanced at the road. 'What are you going to do when we get there?'

'Find Maisie. Get her away from the house.'

'And if she isn't there?'

Shocked, he stared at her.

'Eyes on the road!'

He swerved, narrowly avoiding the kerb. 'What the hell is that supposed to mean?'

'I'm thinking of contingencies. If she isn't there – if he already has her – where would he take her?'

'The lock-up.'

'Your colleagues are already on their way there. Where else?'

'What is this?'

'I'm hoping it won't matter,' Cora said, clinging to her seat as Evans threw the car straight over a mini-roundabout. 'But where else could she be?'

How could he think when all he wanted was to find her? 'I don't know!'

They were almost in Kesgrave now, the too-familiar roads and streets coming into view. Evans had once imagined he would stay here forever. Now it bore too many memories to ever be home.

Turning into St Ives Close, he stopped dead.

Cora saw it a split second after.

A white van, parked beside the kerb, a hooded figure already by the front door.

And, catching the light from the sun as the figure hacked at the wood, a large carving knife…

Fifty-Three

CORA

'Stokes!' Evans yelled, sprinting from his car, the driver's door left wide open. He took off across the pavement, trampling the parched plants of the neighbouring garden as he headed for Ewan Stokes.

The intruder continued to slash at the front door. Was Maisie on the other side? Was the hooded man trying to hack his way in?

Cora raced after Evans, not thinking of the knife or the danger. She was almost at his heels when Stokesy picked up a planter by the splintered front door, smashing it through the living room window, then kicking at the remaining glass trying to get inside.

'No!' Evans cried out, hurling himself at the hooded man's ankles, sending them both crashing to the ground. Ewan Stokes' head slammed against the concrete doorstep with a grating crunch as Cora grabbed the knife that fell from his hand. As she did so, she saw what had been carved into the door.

Four jagged letters in a vertical line, forming a single word:

M
I
N
E

Evans fought his way onto Stokesy's back, grabbing his elbow and jamming it upward, spitting obscenities by his ear. At that moment, the sound of sirens split the summer air, two patrol cars wailing into the street, blues and twos ablaze.

Cora tossed the knife as far away as she could, the wide, angry blade skidding and bumping across the sun-brittle grass. As feet thundered towards them, she stepped back, catching the swift grin of PC Rilla Davis as the officer dogpiled on Stokesy's back.

PC Steph Lanehan followed close behind, stopping alongside Cora. 'You okay, girl?'

'I'm fine,' Cora managed, dragging breath into her lungs. 'He had a knife. I threw it over there.'

'Good work.' Lanehan grinned, jogging across the front lawn to retrieve it.

Cora looked back to the front door, where Evans and three uniformed officers were hauling Stokes to his feet.

'Ewan Stokes, I am arresting you for the attempted murder of Maisie Ingram,' Evans panted, yanking back the hood.

A raven-haired woman Cora recognised from the press conference lifted her chin, a cruel smile spreading across her thin lips. 'You'll have to find him first,' said Olwyn Stokes-Norton. 'And Maisie...'

Fifty-Four

MINSHULL

'Sarge, Olwyn Stokes-Norton has been apprehended at Maisie Ingram's house.' Lanehan's voice trembled slightly as she spoke. 'She was dressed as her son and was carrying a long-bladed carving knife. She hacked the word "MINE" into the front door and smashed the front window attempting to gain entry.'

'And Maisie?' Minshull demanded.

'She's not here. Olwyn won't tell us where she is.'

'What about Les?'

'He legged it as soon as we realised it was Olwyn. Cora is with him.'

'What?' Minshull leaned his head against the passenger side window of the pool car, his mind racing faster than his superior was driving. 'Where have they gone?'

'I don't know, Sarge. He barked something about knowing another place. Cora went after him. I'm sorry, we tried to keep them here.'

'Just get Olwyn back and into custody. I'll try calling Cora.'

'What the hell is going on?' Anderson growled from the driver's seat.

'Olwyn Stokes-Norton was arrested at Maisie Ingram's house, dressed to look like her son. She had a knife. I don't know whether she intended Maisie harm or whether it was for show, but she did some physical damage to the house.'

'And Les?'

'He left. With Cora.'

'Cora? What on earth is she doing there?'

'She must have followed him.' Minshull could beat his head against the dashboard. Cora had been right about Evans, hadn't she? She'd heard his voice with the exact same clarity and accuracy as she'd heard the others. Why had he taken Les' word over hers?

'Call her,' Anderson yelled. 'Find out where the hell they are.'

Finding her number, Minshull dialled. It rang four times, then went to voicemail.

'Hi, this is Dr Lael. Leave your name and message and I'll get back to you...'

'Cora, it's Rob. Where are you? Call me as soon as you can.' He rang off and immediately dialled again. When the voicemail message repeated, he ended the call and dialled a third time.

Come on, he willed her. *Answer me!*

There was a click and a burr of static met his ear. 'Cora? Cora, it's Rob. Can you hear me?'

Two more crackles sounded: rhythmic, as if someone were speaking through them. Then the line went dead.

'*Shit!*'

'Keep trying,' Anderson insisted. 'At some point we'll hit signal.'

As Minshull hit send, a notification banner dropped on the top of the screen. An update on StokesyFans, posted five minutes ago:

THIS IS A MESSAGE FOR LES EVANS

You want her? Come and get her – like you did after the game.

Who wins this prize? The field is wide open...

'Take the next left!' Minshull yelled, breathless, the pieces finally falling into place. 'I know where they are!'

THE CLUB

Watcher89

URGENT MESSAGE TO ALL FORUM MEMBERS

The last two posts were not posted by me or Inner Circle. I believe Stokesy posted them. Inner Circle has gone. The plan has been abandoned. Stokesy is at large. **This is not part of the plan**.

It looks like he has Maisie Ingram and intends her harm. Whatever you think you know about her, it's wrong. You've been had. Stokesy was never missing. He was hiding out because he was in trouble. We created this site as a game, to catch your attention. We never expected your response.

If you are near Langley Avenue Sports Field in Felixstowe, please try to stop him. Call the police. Tell them this is real. Spread the word as far as you can.

I'm sorry we lied to you. Help us save Maisie.

Rick Beech aka **Watcher89**

Fifty-Five

CORA

Langley Avenue Sports Field looked different in real life. On the TV reports that followed Stokesy's video message from here, it had seemed vast and lush. Up close it was faded and failing, the grass scuffed beyond repair where goalposts had been and the dirty yellow metal building a place nobody would want to spend time in.

The field was still when Cora and Evans raced from the car. The pavilion building was padlocked, the surrounding grass empty of people.

Had they got the wrong place?

Evans looked around, his eyes frantically searching for any sign of life. 'Maisie!' he called out, met only by birdsong and the hum of a distant road. 'I'm here, Ewan. Like you wanted.' He spun around listening for any indicator of life. 'You don't want to hurt her. You loved her. You said so, many times. But she came to me, didn't she? When she had the chance. That night. She came home to *me*…'

'They're not here, Les,' Cora said, her hand in her hair as she scanned the field. 'Where else could they be?'

'Keep looking,' he hissed back. 'Come on, coward! You've waited fifteen years to have a pop at me. Well?'

'Les…'

A dull thud sounded somewhere ahead.

A metallic thud.

Cora pointed, her finger to her lips. Slowly, she and Evans edged towards the metal pavilion. As she neared the front door, Cora could see that the padlock was unconnected, hanging from the handle as if recently placed there. Evans skirted around her, reaching the door first.

The moment he took the handle, the door crashed outward, catching Evans on the chin and sending him flying backward.

'Losing your touch, *old man*,' Ewan Stokes sneered, walking towards the prone detective, a large metal bar in his hand. 'But then you always were a bit slow.'

Evans scrabbled to his knees, thrown to the ground again when the metal bar swung heavily into his ribs.

'What? Got no reply? Try this…' Stokes swung again, Evans rolling clear.

Fury coursing through her, Cora launched herself at Stokes, catching him off guard. He stumbled but regained his footing, kicking Cora to the ground.

'Who's this? Latest shag? She's shit, too.'

In pain, Cora rolled to the other side of the door, grasping its sides to steady herself.

'Where's Maisie?' Evans growled, kicking away from Stokes to roll back to his feet.

'No idea. Mum went to her house and she wasn't in.'

Evans stared back. 'Then where…?'

'It was never about that bitch. It was only ever about you. I *had* Maisie. My baby doll. But you wanted her…'

From somewhere far in the distance the air began to shift. Cora sensed it before she felt it, the crackle of static before a storm, the sudden movement of heated air.

And then came the sound.

A dull thudding, growing, magnifying.

Ewan Stokes heard it, too. He lifted his head as he bent over Les' prone body, the iron bar momentarily stilled in his hand.

The pause gave Cora the advantage she needed. With all her might she slammed the heavy steel door at Ewan Stokes, causing him to fall. Evans struggled up and flew into action, kicking and punching the hooded man with a ferocity Cora had never witnessed before.

Beyond them the heavy air began to churn and swell, and Cora was suddenly aware of voices. Layer upon layer of subconscious fury, mixing and melding with actual sound. Pounding feet, screeching tyres.

Purpose.

Cora turned as a crowd of people smashed through the gate. She caught the rush of their voices before they reached her, anger and hate falling from them like storm-ripped leaves as they raced ahead. The sheer force of sound sent her spinning back against the metal pavilion walls.

Hate.

Recrimination.

Hurt – wave upon towering wave of betrayal and injustice, a furious riptide tumbling over and over, impossible to stem.

There were too many voices to mute, each one demanding to be heard. Cora curled into a ball, her arms shielding her head as thought-audible blows rained all around.

And then, two actual voices appeared: loud and commanding over the crowd.

'Get back!' Anderson yelled over the din. Cora heard his voice rising as a challenge to the waves of thought-voices flooding the field.

'Maisie is safe!' Minshull called out. 'She's with her sister. Stokesy doesn't have her!'

Evans turned, his bloodied face radiating relief. He opened his mouth to reply…

…then crumpled to the floor.

Ewan Stokes stood over him, blood-smeared metal bar raised.

'One more step and I finish him!'

The crowd fell instantly silent, their thoughts shocked into obedience.

Against the side of the metal pavilion, Cora sagged from the sudden release of sound.

'You got the audience you wanted,' Minshull shouted. 'Here they are, Ewan: the Stokesy faithful. Show them what a hero you truly are, eh? Let Les go.'

'They wanted a show,' Stokesy snarled back. 'They expect revenge. So enjoy, everyone. Watch how an enemy dies...'

Cora screamed, covering her eyes as the bar came down.

But beyond the darkness of her vision, a thunderous onslaught of sound arose.

Voices.

Pounding feet.

And the muffled, terrified cries of a fallen man.

'Back! Get back!' Anderson yelled. 'Police! Get back!'

Cora opened her eyes as the furious crowd of followers surged past her colleagues, overwhelming Ewan Stokes and dragging him under, his struggling body quickly submerged in a tumbling, punching, kicking torrent of pure hate.

The last sounds Cora heard from Ewan Stokes were his visceral, agonised screams ebbing away beneath the weight of bodies and thoughts...

Fifty-Six

MINSHULL

Outside the door of Interview Room 1, Minshull paused. The nausea that had assaulted him since he'd learned the truth about the woman waiting inside refused to leave. He could feel bile burning the back of his throat, his stomach cramping.

His father had been right.

Not about the rest, but about this.

And it was Minshull's determination to dismiss every word from John Minshull that had led them here. Ted Patrick dead. Les Evans beaten senseless and now in a hospital bed. Ewan Stokes lying in intensive care.

And the worst of it was, on his very first meeting with Olwyn Stokes-Norton, he'd had the exact same gut reaction about her as John Minshull had. He'd *known*, but he'd kicked it away to spite his father. To be better than the revered DCI Minshull. To win, where he never had before.

This was his mistake. His hurt stealing the judgement he relied upon.

It could never happen again.

'Rob.'

Minshull closed his eyes for a moment before looking round. 'Guv.'

'Do *not* blame yourself.'

'I should have seen it.'

Anderson raised an eyebrow. 'And how could you have done that, eh? We were all fooled. Largely because Olwyn Stokes-Norton knew we wouldn't suspect her. The tragic mother, the stoic defender of her son for fifteen long years. The wronged woman by mistakes in the past you had no say over.'

'But Dad called it. He was right.'

'No, Rob. John Minshull got lucky once in the tide of his own failures.'

'But if I'd listened...' The words came despite every fibre of Minshull's being wanting them to remain within. But Anderson wasn't going anywhere – Minshull strongly suspected he never would as long as they worked together. Like it or not, they were bound by this, as they had been since Minshull's first case as SIO.

'So listen now. You're leading the interview.'

Minshull stared at his superior. 'No, Guv. You should.'

Joel Anderson stood his ground. 'Your gig, not mine. Let's go.'

There was no point fighting Anderson's resolve. This had to be done: it was his job to see it through. Forcing down his fury, Minshull opened the door.

Inside the interview room, Olwyn Stokes-Norton was imperious beside her solicitor. While her brief fiddled with his notes, his brow glistening with sweat, Olwyn observed Minshull and Anderson with statuesque disdain.

And that was the touchpaper Minshull needed.

He began the recording, giving the introductions, Olwyn speaking only to confirm her name. Then Minshull rested his hands on his notes and faced her.

The moment he did, her solicitor jumped in. 'My client has instructed me to make a statement on her behalf, beyond which she will answer no further questions.'

Minshull held himself in check, he and Anderson betraying none of the frustration they felt. It was part of the game, expected. But after all that had happened – all that had been broken and destroyed, misled and threatened – maintaining control was an act of sheer will.

'"I was aware from the outset where my son was. I believed him to be in danger from people who wished him harm. I asked my then partner, now husband, Billy Norton, to find a safe place for Ewan, using his contacts in Europe. I acted in good faith to protect my son.

However, I accept that my decision to claim my son was missing was wrong. I thought he would be away for a few months and then return safely. I am sincerely sorry for my actions that caused distress to friends and family and wish to apologise to the police for misrepresenting my situation.'"

Passing the prepared statement to Minshull and Anderson, the solicitor sat back, satisfied.

He had no idea of what awaited them.

Minshull allowed himself a breath. 'You acted in good faith.'

Olwyn smiled.

'Did you act in good faith when you created the StokesyFans forum?'

The solicitor's smile was suddenly absent. 'My client won't answer additional questions...'

'Did you act in good faith when you planted the theory of the Fifteen Year Return a few months before you contacted the film-makers from Quaesitor Co., the production company responsible for the true crime documentary *The Missing Son*?'

'I really don't think this is relevant to...'

'Did you leave it there for the film's researchers to find? To make them believe people were holding Ewan in such high regard that they would form a cult around him?'

Anderson didn't move to stop Minshull. He remained still beside him, eyes trained on Olwyn Stokes–Norton. She returned the stare.

'Did you act in good faith when you pointed the finger at Maisie Ingram? When you engineered discussions on StokesyFans to discredit her, to blame her for your son's alleged disappearance?'

'My client had nothing to do with the discussions! Ask the people you brought into custody from the sports field about that,' the solicitor warned, leaning across the table now. 'I believe there were several.'

'Fifteen,' Minshull confirmed, turning his attention to Olwyn. 'Is that correct, Olwyn? Have I made a mistake?'

Olwyn didn't reply, a slow smile spreading across her lips.

'What part of this amuses you, Mrs Stokes–Norton?' Anderson growled. 'The discussions on the forums or the people who just sent your son into intensive care?'

Olwyn's face fell. 'What?'

'You don't have to say anything...' the solicitor began, but Olwyn batted away his concern like a bothersome fly.

'Ewan's hurt?'

'He's lucky. If we hadn't intercepted his followers when we did he'd be dead.'

'I don't understand...'

'Rick Beech told us the truth, finally.' There was no small amount of satisfaction for Minshull in seeing the effect his words had on the woman opposite. 'But before that, he posted a confession on Stokesy-Fans. Told everyone it was a hoax, that they'd been had. And he put out a plea for forum members to head to Langley Avenue Sports Field where Ewan was attempting to murder my colleague, to stop your son achieving his goal. And like good little acolytes, they did as they were told.'

'No. You're lying.'

Rick Beech had handed himself in, two hours ago. He'd claimed he owed Olwyn's partner a large sum of money and Billy Norton had offered not to bankrupt Beech if he moved the StokesyFans forum on to his server. They had made him part of the inner circle: Billy, Olwyn and Beech, with Beech effectively running everything, posting as @Watcher89.

His self-planned hoax had been an attempt to boost discussions on the forum when interest had begun to dip in the supposedly returning Stokesy. His eleventh-hour decision to do the right thing might well have saved Stokesy's life – even if right now the prognosis for the object of the forums' affections was shaky.

'I need time to go over this with my client,' the solicitor stated, his expression blank. 'I request a recess in order to do so.'

Anderson glanced at Minshull. 'Agreed. Interview suspended at 18:15.' Ending the recording, he and Minshull collected their files and made to leave.

'I want to see my son,' Olwyn rushed.

'I'm afraid that isn't possible right now.'

'But he's hurt. He needs me.'

'The doctors are doing all they can. When we receive an update on his condition, we'll inform you.'

'But I need to find him!' she wailed, all vestiges of pride and control gone. What remained was a terrified woman, her dark-rimmed eyes wide with fear, her hands like grasping claws at the cuffs of the black hoodie that swamped her. She looked now as she'd always claimed to be: a desperate, terrified mother, facing the horrific reality of losing her precious son. 'I did all of this to protect Ewan. How can I protect him when I'm here?'

In the interview room doorway, Minshull turned back. 'You can't.'

Fifty-Seven

ANDERSON

The hospital ward was low-lit, the deep hush creating a sense of quiet calm. Days passed into nights and back, here – glimpses afforded occasionally when curtains were pulled back from around the rows of beds revealing the narrow windows. It was dark beyond them now, or as dark as the wards ever allowed.

Anderson's dislike of hospitals had only grown as he had spent more time passing through them, forever attempting to silence the incessant squelch that his rubber-soled shoes made against the pale green floors. Difficult for a man of his height and frame. The endless corridors and wards of the hospital had clearly not been designed with striding Scots in mind.

'Stop pouting,' his wife whispered beside him.

'I'm not,' he hissed back, knowing she was probably right. Ros Anderson knew him better than he knew his own skin – mostly a blessing, but not on occasions like this.

'It's bad enough coming here on duty, let alone a day off,' he grumbled, the volume of his voice dropping low as a tired-looking nurse powered past them. Incredulous, he watched her walk away. 'Her shoes were identical to mine. How come she doesn't make the squelch?'

'Joel. Shush.' Ros gave him a sharp elbow to his ribs, just about on the right side of playful. 'We're here to support your friend.'

Anderson wasn't sure he would use that exact term to describe the man in the bed at the end of the ward, but the sight of him warmed his heart more than he'd prepared for.

'Ugh, not more visitors,' Les Evans scoffed as Anderson and Ros pulled up plastic chairs beside his bed. 'Can't move for them in this place.'

His head was heavily bandaged, thick lines of it around his chest, too. His face was currently a rainbow palette of bruises, one wrist in a blue cast.

But he was alive. Having seen the state he'd been left in when the mob dragged Ewan Stokes off him, Anderson had feared the worst.

'I was worried your annoyance levels weren't being properly catered for,' Anderson replied, his relieved smile leaving Evans in no doubt of his true response.

'Appreciate you tipping the balance, Guv.' Evans winced as he laughed. 'Although bringing this one cancels out the desired effect.'

Ros smiled and reached across the bed to rest her hand lightly on his. 'How are you doing, Les?'

'I've felt better.'

'Looked better, too.'

Evans rolled his eyes. 'Cheers for that, Joel. And there was me thinking rainbow bruises were my colour.'

Anderson spread his hands wide. 'Always a pleasure. You know that.'

Evans pressed his lips together, tension flicking in his jaw. 'I'm sorry, Guv.'

'Ah now, hush your noise. There'll be time for that.'

'Noted.' Evans' eyes reddened, despite his smirk. 'On cakes for a month, right?'

'A month? Try six.' Anderson chuckled. 'Get yourself well and we'll discuss it later.'

Evans offered a pained smile – which instantly vanished.

Anderson tensed, fearing tears from the man in the bed. He'd never known how to deal with them from friends: when it came to work colleagues, he was a floundering mess and of no use to anybody. But Evans was no longer looking at him, his eyes focused over Anderson's head. Anderson turned at the same moment Ros did.

Another visitor.

She was standing at the foot of the hospital bed, half obscured from view by the sweep of pale blue curtain that hadn't been fully drawn back. Maisie Ingram looked drawn, her cheekbones hollowed in shadow, her blonde hair pulled back into a high ponytail. Restless fingers played with the red leather strap of the bag she wore across her body, her gaze fixed on Evans.

The covers over Evans' chest began to noticeably rise and fall.

Anderson, not wanting to stare, looked back and forth between the two.

Ros was the first to speak, half rising from the grey plastic visitor's chair. 'Hi, would you like to sit?'

Maisie glanced to the next bed. 'There's a chair here. I can bring it over.'

'Allow me,' Anderson hurried, pushing his chair back with an irritating scrape and instantly feeling like a fool.

'Actually, we were heading off,' Ros countered, shooting a pointed look at her husband. 'Have mine. It's closer.'

Anderson saw her wince at her own words.

Maisie gave a nervous laugh and jigged an awkward do-si-do with Ros to reach the chair. As she sat down, Anderson felt the familiar tug of his wife's fingers at his elbow.

'We'll be off, then,' he announced, completely unnecessarily as neither Evans nor his latest visitor were listening. 'Take care, Les.'

Retreating from the ward bay, Anderson couldn't help looking back. Les and Maisie hadn't moved – him with his arms over the bed sheets, her clutching her bag strap.

'Come on, leave them alone,' Ros said, resting her cheek gently against Anderson's bicep as she coaxed him away.

'They haven't moved. Maybe we should stay…'

'Joel, they are more than capable of looking after themselves. Leave them be.'

Reluctantly, Anderson let her lead him from the ward.

'I'm not bringing you next time,' he muttered as they made their way down the long corridor towards the stairs. 'You're no fun.'

The sound of his wife's laugh echoing around the walls was a multitudinous joy, impossible to hear without smiling. 'I'm the best fun you'll get and you know it. Stop worrying, they'll be fine.'

Anderson rolled his eyes, loving the game. 'Okay, boss.'

'Besides,' Ros continued, pushing open the door to the stairs. 'If it's fun you're after, there's a certain pub quiz team in St Just awaiting your genius…'

Fifty-Eight

CORA

He was *definitely* cheating.

Cora eyed Minshull as they huddled around the too-small dark-wood pub table.

At least he was cheating for their team this time.

She sent Tris Noakes an overblown eye-roll as he stifled his laughter. But it was good – all of it: the cheating and the random answers, the suggestive team name they'd chosen for the quiz and the filthy jokes passing between them.

Calm. After so much noise.

Minshull grinned back, not completely forgiven yet. He'd apologised and she'd accepted. But the disbelief had caused a wound that might take time to heal.

'I give up,' Minshull announced, throwing down his pen. 'Let's drink instead.'

'Excellent plan,' Bennett replied. 'Pint of cola, is it, Drew?'

'Never again,' Ellis shuddered. 'Next time we're getting a taxi.'

Lanehan's eyes narrowed. 'Next time for what?'

Ignoring them, Minshull raised his pint. 'To Les.'

A solemn air passed between them as the toast was made. The update Joel and Ros Anderson had brought from the hospital was promising, but it was clear Les had a long road to recovery ahead of him.

Minshull waited until the others were deep in conversation, the quiz sheet abandoned in a pool of spilt beer, before nudging Cora. 'Fancy some fresh air?'

'Sure.'

They edged out of the crowded space and on to the darkened street beyond. Minshull shoved his hands deep into his pockets. 'I hope Les is okay.'

'Physically he'll heal in time. Emotionally might take a lot longer. You're all going to have to watch out for him when he finally comes back to work.'

'We're ready to.' He shook his head. 'Never thought we'd all be grateful for Les Evans being on the team. And yet, here we are.'

'Life can be weird sometimes,' Cora replied, her attention drifting to the darkened newsagent's shop further along the street where Ewan Stokes had attempted to drive into them. It felt like a lifetime ago, not a fortnight. 'Did Ewan Stokes drive the van at us because he knew you were police?'

Minshull stopped walking, his eyes straying to the same spot. 'Maybe. Maybe he thought Les would be there. Or maybe it was to cause a stir. Until he regains consciousness we won't know.'

'Do you think Stokesy will recover?'

'If he does he'll be charged with murder.'

'And Olwyn?'

'Conspiracy and fraud. Obstruction. Not to mention intimidation and assault. It isn't looking good for her or her husband.'

What had it all been for, if Ewan Stokes died or all three of them ended up in prison? What had all of their carefully constructed plans brought them? Cora doubted she would ever understand it. 'Will Les carry on in CID after this, do you think?'

'Of course he will,' Minshull assured her. 'He's too bloody-minded not to. It'll just take time.'

The clouds had cleared overhead, the first glimpses of stars above the ancient roofs of St Just. Cora breathed in the stillness, the familiarity.

'And what about us?'

Minshull's eyes were intent on her when she looked back.

How was she supposed to answer his question? There were many things she could say: many things she *should* say. But tonight wasn't the moment.

Reaching out, her fingers found the warmth of his forearm. 'That's going to take time, too.'

A cheer from inside the pub shattered the moment, causing her hand to fall back.

'Sounds like they need us.' Minshull grinned. 'Shall we?'

Book Soundtrack Playlist

For every novel I write I compile a soundtrack playlist that captures the emotion and atmosphere of the story I want to create. For *Leave No Trace* these are the songs and pieces of music that characterised the story. Enjoy!

MAIN THEME: MOONWAKE – Elephant Sessions – *For the Night*

INTO THE WOODS – Second Light – *Into the Woods (Single)*

THROW ME A LINE – HAEVN – *Holy Ground EP*

TO THE SHORE – John Smith – *The Fray*

LUST – RURA – *In Praise of Home*

I WAS GONE – Finnegan Bell – *I Was Gone*

REBIRTH – Elephant Sessions – *For the Night*

Acknowledgements

Writing Cora's third case has been a challenge in many ways, but a puzzle I've loved solving. I've been so fortunate to have the help, wisdom and insight of a stellar team of superstars without whom *Leave No Trace* wouldn't be here.

Huge thanks to my editor, Keshini Naidoo, whose unflinching belief in Cora and the CID team and enthusiasm for the stories I want to tell have been a major driving force for this series. Thanks to my wonderful agent, Hannah Ferguson, for her support and constant cheerleading. Thank you to the amazing team at Hera and Canelo – Thanhmai Bui-Van, Iain Millar, Francesca Riccardi and Elinor Fewster. Thanks also to Ross Dickinson for insightful copy edits and brilliant comments, and to Jenny Page for proofreading.

My sincere thanks to the brilliant PC Steve Franklin for his expert advice and insight into police life and Dilwyn Roberts for advising me on CID procedure. Any mistakes in police procedure are mine alone.

Thanks to fab author chums for their constant support and championing of the Cora Lael series – A. G. Smith, Craig Hallam, Cally Taylor, Rob Parker, Steve Cavanagh, Luca Veste, Rob Parker, Chris Callaghan, Joanna Cannon, Adam Simcox, Ian Wilfred and Mick Arnold.

My wonderful viewers of my weekly Facebook Live show, Fab Night In Chatty Thing, are brilliant and continue to champion Cora and the South Suffolk CID team. I hope you love their latest adventure! Thanks also to Katy and William from *Tea Leaves and Reads* and my followers on Instagram, Twitter and Facebook for all their support.

Love as ever to my mum Liz and fab in-laws, Phil and Jo. Thanks for your support and avid cheerleading!

Big thanks to my lovely Flo, for choosing and naming all of Reece Bickland's toys, lending Dave Bear to the story and advising me on aspects of Reece's school life. And, as always, all my love to my husband Bob, for endless plot chats, meals and perfectly timed cuppas! I love you both to the moon and back and twice around the stars xx

And to you, dear Reader, for choosing this book. I hope you enjoy it!

Miranda x